DARKNESS UNLEASHED

(SKY BROOKS SERIES BOOK 6)

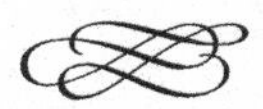

MCKENZIE HUNTER

This is a work of fiction. Names, characters, businesses, places, events, and incidents are either the products of the author's imagination or used in a fictitious manner. Any resemblance to actual persons, living or dead, or actual events is purely coincidental.

McKenzie Hunter

Darkness Unleashed

McKenzieHunter@McKenzieHunter.com

ISBN: 978-1-946457-86-8

ACKNOWLEDGMENTS

With each book I write, I'm increasingly humbled and thankful for my friends and family who continue to support me unconditionally. I have to offer a special thanks to: Vanessa Rodrigues for her Portuguese translation and John and Kari Underwood, Esq. for taking time out of their busy schedules to offer their experience and expertise about the legal system. Not only was it extremely helpful, it was exciting to learn. It was a pleasure working with you two and I can't thank you enough. I'd like to offer thanks to Agata Krakowiak for giving me "Skyven". It's a very fitting quip for Winter.

I'd also like to thank Oriana for the beautiful cover, and Stacy McCright and Luann Reed who work so diligently to help me tell the best story I can.

Last, but never least, I want to thank my readers for following Sky throughout her journey and allowing me to entertain you. Her story is coming to an end (one more book in the Sky Brooks series) and I hope that you've enjoyed reading it as much as I've enjoyed writing it.

CHAPTER 1

Ethan kept his eyes on the computer screen, occasionally looking up from it, anticipating another question. I'd been questioning him since the night before, when I'd watched Steven get arrested. Ethan returned his attention to the laptop. He was calm, which should have soothed me. It didn't—he was too calm. My irritation flared. Fourteen hours had passed since Steven's arrest. Every time I thought about it, I remembered the look of desperation and fear on his face. The haunted look in his olive-green eyes, the vulnerable and trapped way he'd looked when they'd placed him in handcuffs. And now he was probably locked in a cell, a cage, waiting to be formally charged.

I clenched my hands so tightly my nails dug into my palms. "When do you plan on going to get Steven out?" My voice was strained, irritated.

"The answer hasn't changed since you asked me thirty minutes ago. They have to process him. Once he is, I will be there to post bail," he responded in a low, even tone, biting back his annoyance.

I considered sitting next to him and watching the evidence against Steven: a video clip, no longer than four minutes, showing him killing three men. It had gone viral right after his arrest, and anyone could view it on YouTube or any social media site. To most, it depicted a calm Steven approaching three men and their dog. What others thought was an incipient argument that became inexplicably explosive was actually an altercation between were-animals over territory. Most viewers didn't know that when the men tensed up, it was an act of aggression. When they stiffened and moved back as if they were cowering in fear, they were actually giving themselves room to shift to their animal forms. And the so-called dog Steven killed was in fact a shifted canidae, but at a glance, which was all the video allowed, I couldn't tell which type. The clip ended before the canidae could revert to human form, as shifters did in death.

When I finally tired of pacing the floor, I took a seat next to Ethan. "You really need to get some sleep. Once his bail is set, I promise I can go get him. He won't be there a minute longer."

"This isn't the first pack arrest I've dealt with," he said.

"Who else has been arrested?"

"Sebastian, Gavin, and—" He paused. "Me."

He must have thought his being arrested would shock me—it didn't. I would have been more surprised if he hadn't landed on the list at least once.

"And every time, the charges were dropped," he said confidently.

"Were they murder charges? Was there a video of the murders?" I spouted back, my voice coarser than I would have liked. Anger and frustration were making it more difficult to control. "Did they have a jerk with extensive resources?"

"It will be okay," Ethan said, his hands covering mine, but his words didn't possess the same confidence that they had earlier. Perhaps he'd realized the magnitude of the situation. It was Dexter who had become a pain in our ass. Not only had the mage aligned himself with the witches to create a formula that would nullify were-animals' immunity to magic, but he had also orchestrated Steven being filmed because we'd dared to stop his plans. Thinking about it piqued my anger.

Winter's head snapped back when my fist connected with her jaw, and she retreated a couple of steps and then grinned—a prideful display that had an undercurrent of sadism and the same adoration and lust for violence that was innate in most were-animals. That was where our differences were most notable. I didn't revel in the barbarity of fighting but they did. Something about fighting, exerting dominance, defending themselves against any threat spoke to them on a primal level where the beast dwelled. I just didn't want to die. That was my sole purpose in learning to fight. Feeling weak and preyed upon was something I never wanted to experience again.

It wasn't about protection today; I wanted a distraction, and defending myself against Winter's violent onslaught was just the thing. I couldn't think about Steven and his predicament. Nothing seemed to keep Dexter out of my head, and the rage he inspired fueled my assault on Winter. She was a special type of strange—she seemed happy that a roundhouse kick had landed her on her back several feet away. I glanced at the window in the door of the room where we always sparred when we weren't at the pack's house. I preferred being at the pack's house, where people rarely watched us; if they did, it certainly wasn't with the wide-eyed, morbid intrigue or ardent disgust our aggressiveness drew in this place.

It was one of the few gyms that had the type of room we needed. Upstairs contained the latest and newest equipment, areas for CrossFit, classes, and plenty of endorphin-junkie members and people just attempting to lose those last ten pounds or so. Winter and I didn't have any interest in the beautiful equipment and always went straight for the door at the far corner of the gym that led to the basement, which was rightfully referred to as the dungeon. It was dark and dingy, and it was obvious minimal work was put into its upkeep. Dull white walls had large patches of exposed drywall—the owner had given up on trying to repair the damage. A boxing ring took up part of the room, and in the corners were heavy punching bags. Free weights cluttered the floor; no one really followed the rules of returning the equipment. Upstairs, hints of sweat, cleansers, soaps, and body sprays wafted out of the locker rooms. The smells of sweat, blood, and aggression dominated the dungeon. People used it to spar, practice martial arts, and fight. Some members joked that it was where gladiators were made.

Winter was great at teaching me how to survive. If I could walk out of a session with her on my own two feet, I was more than likely going to hold my own with someone else.

"We have an audience again," I said, positioning myself into a ready stance. I was always on the defensive with Winter and prepared for anything.

"Don't we always? We're the women who have 'something really wrong with them.'" She grinned, using the back of her hand to wipe the blood from her lips from a strike I'd delivered just moments before the kick.

I forced a chuckle, but there wasn't enough levity in me to make it convincing. I moved toward her and threw a jab; she blocked and countered with a hammer strike, which I subverted. I dropped to the ground and swept her leg. She hit the ground, and I moved back before she could retaliate. I'd learned the hard way to never let her get me to the ground. She was fast. She whipped into her holds so quickly she made me think that somewhere in the process she'd shifted to her animal—a snake. It wasn't vampire speed, but it was faster than any were-animal I'd seen.

The movement back cost me precious time, and she recovered, stood, and attacked with a series of kicks that caused me to retreat and go on the defensive. The room became nothing more than the sound of aggressive parries, strikes, kicks, and loud thuds from our falls and tosses to the ground. I landed a hip toss, hard, and before she could get back on her feet, I was over her, delivering several strikes. She blocked most of them but finally said something that struck me harder than any blow she could have delivered.

"I submit." She pushed the words through clenched teeth. It was barely a whisper, but I heard it. I'd just defeated Winter for the first time ever—and I had that pain in the ass Dexter to thank for it.

Once she was on her feet, she grabbed a towel and patted her forehead dry. If I looked anything like she did, I needed to prepare for the stares and abhorrent looks we would get when we left. On the bright side, these looks stopped most of the people in the gym from wanting to spar with us. We were usually smeared in blood and covered with bruises when we were finished, but onlookers weren't aware that in a couple of days, there'd be no evidence we'd been in a fight. Which was why we alternated session times, hoping we wouldn't run into the same person during any one week. Sometimes we did, and we were met with expectant, inquiring gazes. I often wondered if they thought we knew secret makeup tricks.

"You might want to close your mouth," she suggested, strolling toward me.

I snapped it shut as I repeated her words—*I submit*—over and over again. I memorized the tone and the lilt of them. I committed it all to memory with the assumption that it was the first and last time I would ever hear those words from Winter. I was pretty sure I'd be considered a bad winner if I did my happy dance and maybe even broke into song.

"You have a lot of aggression in you. You're kind of hot. I totally get Ethan now."

I frowned. "What's wrong with you? That isn't something you should find sexy in a person. Ever!" I said with an exasperated huff.

She shrugged. "A woman who can possibly kick my ass is sexy."

"Why are you all so disturbed?" I took a drink from the bottle of water I'd grabbed out of my bag. "We have a pack therapist. He's there for a reason. You should consider a daily visit. He's there for us, you know."

Her lips lifted in a sly grin. "I don't think I need it."

"Trust me, you do. Because a woman punching you in the face is considered assault by most people's standards, not the prelude to a romantic liaison."

"Different strokes," she said dismissively leaning against the wall, a smirk playing on her lips.

"No, it's not. Let's play a game. Let's say two women want to show they are interested in you: one person punches you and the other person buys you a drink. Can you tell me which one is a chargeable offense and which one is a nice social gesture?"

She shrugged. "It really depends on the spirit in which each is delivered."

I exhaled a breath of defeat as I realized that was who she was. I added another page to my "something is wrong with you" mental profile of Winter.

Laughing, she asked, "What's got you in a mood?"

I assumed she knew the difference, but it was a lesson I fully intended to address later. "I'm worried about Steven."

She studied me for a long time. "Don't be. This isn't the first time one of us has been arrested."

I slanted my eyes in her direction. "How many times for you?"

The fact she needed time to count indicated it wasn't a small number. "Arrested about ten times, actually charged four. But they were dismissed each time."

"How many of them were for first-degree murder or manslaughter?"

"How do you know what he's been charged with?"

Warmth brushed my cheeks and the bridge of my nose. "I've been on Google and Wikipedia researching the charges he could get based on the video."

Her face relaxed into a sympathetic smile, and when she spoke, her tone matched. "They have an altered video and, thanks to Josh, no evidence that Steven was even at the crime scene. If that's not enough, Ethan is an outstanding attorney. Believe me, I don't have any charges and I probably deserved at least two of them. And the last one I was *so* guilty, I'm really surprised the charges were dismissed."

She hit me lightly with her towel, and her smile widened. "It's only a matter of time before you and Steven are hugged up, giving each other little kisses and spouting your love for each other. And the annoying duo of Skyven can continue once again." She rolled her eyes and mumbled, "So annoying." She grabbed her bag and started out the door of the dungeon.

"Don't pretend you don't miss him!" I yelled after her.

She stopped and considered my response. "I do. I bet not nearly as much as you, though."

When I reached the pack's house, I parked behind Ethan's car, the gray Hennessy Venom GT, which awed most people. Each time I saw it, I stared, trying to figure out what I was missing. I stood to the side of it, brows furrowed, looking over the sleek lines of the body, custom paint, large tires, and soft, buttery leather seats.

"It's just a car," I muttered, tilting my head to study it again.

"You'll never get it," Ethan said behind me.

I turned to find him at the entrance of the house, nearly twenty feet away, leaning against the doorframe, a smirk lifting the corners of his lips.

Freak.

The smile faded as I approached, and his gaze traveled over the patches of raspberry and muddled blue marks on my face and arms. His fingers lightly traced along a fading bruise on my cheek.

"You and Winter play too rough."

"We do, but guess who got Winter to submit," I said.

He leaned in, his breath warm against my lips as his tongue slipped out to taste them before he spoke. "Really?" he asked. Heat radiated from him. His hands slid around my waist, and he pulled me closer. I could feel him, all of him, as he responded to violence the way weres often did—with an odd attraction.

"You know that psychologist is here for us. Maybe you and Winter can go back to back so he can block out his morning for the same type of crazy," I suggested.

He stepped in again; I sidestepped and slipped past him into the house. Grabbing hold of the back of my pants, he tugged me back against him, wrapped his arms around me, and kissed my hair. "Congratulations, Sky."

I was happy about it—he seemed ecstatic, a little too enthusiastic. I could feel his "enthusiasm" against me. I pulled away, narrowed my eyes at him, and tried not to be disturbed by how much my winning fights excited him. It was weird. Ethan liked self-reliance, formidability, and strong fighting and self-defense skills. He'd never made a secret of it, but there was more to it than that. "You know I'm never going to challenge anyone, right?"

He gave me a solemn look. "Sky, why would you? You're a Beta now."

"What? Beta—what are you talking about?"

His solemn look melted into a frown of incredulity. "How did you pass orientation?"

"I took the test and made a passing grade like everyone else." I shrugged, returning his incredulous look. "And if you all ever consider making changes in the pack, you should start with that two-hundred-question final exam. It's really unnecessary."

"Well, if you'd listened instead of watching animals performing tricks, stupid human stunts, and a lion cub trying to roar for the first time, and *yes, we all heard about it*"—he gave me the same disparaging look he'd given me so often it had lost its effectiveness—"you would know when someone is mated, they assume the same rank. Which is why a lot of were-animals vie for the affections of an Alpha."

I knew that, but since Ethan and Sebastian were so effective at toeing the line between questionable and ethical behavior, guarding the pack's secrets like a troll at a bridge, using the tactic of "getting people to see the reality they want them to see"—in layman's terms, *lying*—and keeping the pack safe, I couldn't imagine them delegating those responsibilities to anyone else.

The idea of not being expected to challenge anyone was a relief. I didn't have it in me to do it, and I really didn't want to be a ranked pack member. But coincidentally, now I was.

"You know, I didn't mate with you for your position."

He chuckled. "Believe me, I know that." He strode past me and started down the hall.

I wished I was above doing something as petty as sticking my tongue out when he turned his back but I wasn't.

"Real mature, Sky," he said, his back still to me. When he turned, his lips were kinked into a condescending smirk. "As I've said many times before, you occasionally surprise me, but most times, you are quite predictable."

He continued down the hall with a slight limp from when the East Coast Alpha had crushed his ankle during a challenge a couple of days ago. It was almost healed and probably would've healed faster if he'd actually adhered to Dr. Jeremy's protocol. But if Ethan was nothing else, he was stubborn to a fault. He was headed to the new addition to the house. Or rather, the converted room that was now the new headquarters of the pack formerly known as Worgen. The Worgen pack had been absorbed into ours when Sebastian decided he would no longer allow fringe packs in his territory after one had attacked and almost fatally wounded me. Of the people who'd joined our pack, the Worgen had proven to be our greatest asset. In the past, we'd used them if we needed anything IT-related done. Gavin and Steven called them the geeks. I'd thought it was a term of endearment, but after walking into the room one too many times when they were playing their games or speaking Klingon, I'd learned it was more than apropos. They were a different type of were-animal. I wondered what information they were getting for Ethan now as I followed him down the hall to their new office. Sebastian called my name before I could get there.

I turned and went to the open door of his office. He extended his hand to a chair, inviting me to sit. Once I did, he relaxed back in his oversized leather chair. Although he overwhelmed his office as he did most rooms, the vast area suited him. A large executive desk of dark wood with carved designs along the front anchored the space, and matching bookcases lined the back wall. Wildlife paintings, something seen throughout the house, covered the walls. All of Sebastian's paintings were of wolves baring their teeth in attack poses. Most people had pictures that relaxed them in their offices—it was unsettling that these comforted him.

His appearance never belied his feral alertness. He was handsome, no doubt about it, but the wolf was always front and center. It wasn't something he could turn on and off because it was entwined into his being, his very essence. Even with the knowledge that the bottom row of his bookshelf housed first editions of John Keats and Robert Frost and the poetry of Allen Ginsberg and Nikki Giovanni, which I had discovered while snooping in his office, I was very aware that I was facing a predator.

After appraising me for a long time, he finally settled upon a wisp of a smile that tugged at the corners of his lips. When he spoke, his voice was soft and earnest. "A pack can be complicated, and the nuances of its functions and the members' effects on it can be hard to understand and describe." He shifted forward, his gaze holding mine with an astute intensity. "The emotional state of it is more fragile than we often care to admit, and some members have more of an influence on it than others. Most often, it's the one we least expect. You have never ceased being an enigma, possessing a strength that is always underestimated. Your anxiety is palpable, and your high distress is noticeable. It reeks and feels uncomfortable."

I blinked several times, trying to grasp what he was saying. "Are you saying I'm stressing everyone out?" I asked, incredulously.

"I felt it even before you walked into the house." His eyes went to the floor, and I tried not to gawk at him, but it was the first time Sebastian's unwavering strength had folded for a moment. He was concerned for me, or rather perplexed by the situation. Or maybe it was a confluence of both.

"I can't help how I feel—I can't control it."

He rested his elbows on the table and then steepled his fingers in front of him. His tone remained soft and low as if he were trying to soothe an agitated animal. "Steven isn't going to prison. I give you my word."

I didn't have any doubt that Steven wasn't going to prison. It was how this goal would be achieved that bothered me. Sebastian couldn't guarantee that Steven would be acquitted of the charges. I was sure Ethan and Sebastian had a nuclear option already in place, but how radical would it be? Would Steven have to leave the country? Would we have to resort to dark tactics to free him? There were so many *ifs* about the situation.

Sebastian screwed his eyes together and winced.

"Sorry," I said. I wasn't sure what a surge of anxiety felt like, but from the look of him, it was like bile creeping up into his throat. "But you can't promise me he'll be acquitted, can you?"

After several moments of deliberation, he nodded. "Yes. I can guarantee he will be acquitted."

Wow, I guess Sebastian is a wizard.

Despite Sebastian's confidence and bravado, I was still concerned about consequences if Steven was found guilty. The only other option would be for them to send him away. He'd be a fugitive and couldn't come back to the States.

Before I could question his assertion and ask if sending Steven away was their backup plan, there was a knock at the door, and I saw unruly chestnut waves of hair before Quinn, a former member of the Worgen pack who went by the moniker Casper, stepped in. I'd assumed the name was a reference to the friendly ghost; however, when I'd asked, he'd given me some long, convoluted answer that had eventually caused me to lose interest. Apparently, he got the name because he was capable of getting into any system without leaving a cyber fingerprint behind. No one ever knew he'd been there. He might now go by Casper, but I was pretty sure if he kept hacking, he would eventually go by the name inmate-number-whatever.

Quinn seemed to be the Worgen's Alpha. He possessed a quiet, coiled strength that was quite noticeable. Even when he was relaxed, he appeared restrained and tense, as if he struggled with control. Maybe that was it; he was struggling to control his animal half. Most of our pack had a symbiotic relationship with their animal half, so much so that it was often difficult to decipher the line between person and beast.

My curiosity got the better of me as I speculated about him. I watched him with intensity, and he gave me a forced half-smile as he entered the room. Oddly, he looked more comfortable with Sebastian than with me. Was I really putting off emotions that heavily? Did he view me as having a toxic aura? When his nose flared and he noticeably smelled the air, I inhaled, too, but I didn't smell anything except for hints of cedar with an undercurrent of cinnamon. I gathered Quinn smelled something different. Was anxiety as easy to detect as fear, which had a strong, undeniable scent?

"They still haven't processed Steven." It felt like Quinn was offering me the information instead of Sebastian.

"You can see that information?" I asked.

"Yes. I cloned their system. I can see everything they do, and once Steven is processed, I'll let you know so bail can be issued," he said in a flat tone. Maybe it was just me, but when you admitted to doing something that blatantly illegal, you should at least have a tinge of shame in your voice.

Sebastian nodded. "What about Dexter? Have you found him?"

He shook his head. "I'm monitoring all his financials. He hasn't used his passport, and there aren't any records of him flying, so I assume he's still in the country. I can prohibit him from accessing any money; I think it will force him to surface faster," Quinn offered.

Wow, that doesn't sound remotely legal.

Sebastian considered his suggestion for an extended period of time. I made myself believe that he was debating the morality and legality of doing it and battling his conscience. I was eternally optimistic.

"Don't do anything to Dexter's account," Sebastian finally instructed.

"I can do it without triggering suspicion," Quinn said with confidence and a look that said he'd been waiting for the okay to meet the challenge.

"But if you don't, we are not in a position for you to fail. I suspect, if Dexter is as cunning as he's proven to be, it will be a trap. You do it and it'll trigger something."

"They've never caught me before." And then he listed all the websites and agencies and banks he'd hacked in the past. I wished I hadn't heard that. I really wanted plausible deniability. My attention bounced between the two of them.

Sebastian's eyes stayed steady on him, but not with apprehension like mine, but with consideration. Sebastian possessed power, resources, aggression, and an overwhelming presence that commanded subjugation; Quinn and his crew were just as dangerous in their own right. When it came to hacking and cyberattacks, they had us beat. It was never easy to guess what went through Sebastian's mind. I could only speculate because he was always playing the long game, putting the pack at an advantage in the worst-case scenario. He did it with ease, and it wasn't until he had shown his hand that a person realized they'd been out of their depth the whole time.

He finally shook his head, dismissing Quinn along with his proposal. "No, I don't trust Dexter not to be setting a trap. Let's be more careful."

Once Quinn left, closing the door behind him, I gave Sebastian the same shaming look I'd given him when he'd failed to adequately address my discovery of how the pack was financed. Our pack was large, and each member gave it a percentage of their personal income, which was invested in several holdings and businesses owned by the pack. A stipend was issued to each member based on money invested in the pack. The Worgen pack took a different approach. When Sebastian had had his "welcome to the pack, I'm sorry I had to disband yours" meeting, I'd expected him to at least vehemently denounce their past ways of doing things, especially how they financed their pack—by funneling money out of bank accounts.

They used the polite and willfully wrong word *funneling* as opposed to *stealing*, the accurate word. And instead of telling them that all stealing was wrong and wouldn't be tolerated in his pack, Sebastian had told them they would have to stop stealing money out of bank accounts. In response, they'd astutely pointed out that they didn't steal; they simply funneled a dollar from every account holder in the bank. The problem was that for most major banks, a dollar out of each account could easily hit high six to seven figures.

I'd developed muscle fatigue from scowling, my mouth dropping in morbid disbelief, and glaring at Sebastian over his handling of the situation. The new additions to our group had seemed obviously out of their depth, used to a different way of life, and had now been absorbed into a pack with strange politics, rules, and fealty expectations.

I'd questioned whether they would assimilate well. And I'd seen the same concern in Sebastian's eyes as he'd looked upon his new members, dressed in their t-shirts with weird slogans—very different from Ethan's brother, Josh, who wore his ironically. And a couple of them had worn rings on their fingers, their homage to the *Lord of the Rings*. I'd realized assimilation wasn't possible. At best, we should expect them to adapt. And during that meeting, they hadn't gotten the chastising I'd expected; instead, Sebastian had said he was very aware of what they were capable of, what they had done in the past, and how most of them had acquired their nicknames.

Instead of condemning their deeds, Sebastian had pointed out that the more they did things like that, the bigger the risk was of them being caught, and how important it was to minimize risk. And as I'd stood with my mouth gaping open, giving him my full-on look of judgment, he'd smiled and shrugged. "I told them to stop."

I guess being the pack's moral compass is my job. "Really, because I've heard you tell people to stop things. It usually involves the weird eye thing, growling, and occasionally your hand wrapping around someone's throat. That, Mr. Alpha, was the most pitiful berating I've ever seen you give. It's fine if you're scolding a kid for taking goodies from a store, but their 'funneling' is a federal crime."

"And they said they wouldn't do it."

"When exactly did they say that?" I'd asked. "I didn't hear that one time. Did they breathe it in Morse code or something?"

Sebastian had looked over his shoulders at the guys, his tone deep, firm, and casually dismissive as he had asked, "You all won't do that again, will you?"

Almost in unison, with mischief in their eyes and half-smirks on their lips, they'd said, "Of course not."

"You heard them. 'Of course not.'" And he'd left me behind.

As I sat across from Sebastian, reliving that day with the nearly acquired Worgen pack, I felt like I was experiencing déjà vu. Just as with the conversation before, a charming smile had settled over Sebastian's features, and it was quite easy to be disarmed by it. It held a beguiling allure, intentionally generated to make a person forget they were dealing with an apex predator with human intellect. Being aware that he was doing it didn't make it easier to ignore; I was just cognizant that I was falling for it.

I settled back in my chair and relaxed the scowl and the squint in my narrowed eyes. "Okay, it's all fun and games until SWAT teams and the FBI get involved," I said coolly.

"Sky, you're being dramatic."

Sebastian," I said firmly, standing my ground.

"I do believe we've had this conversation quite often. Let me ask you, Sky, has it changed anything?"

"What conversation?" Ethan asked, only knocking to notify us of his entrance.

Sebastian grinned. "Apparently, I've failed to adhere to Sky's strict code of black-and-white ethics and have delved too deep in shades of gray for her liking. It seems I am, once again, on the receiving end of her scathing looks of judgment and disapproval. Perhaps, at this point, I should be quivering under her harsh displeasure."

Oh great, he thinks he's funny, too. The mocking half-grin confirmed it.

Behind the smile remained unwavering imperiousness, a constant reminder of the Alpha that lingered. "Did you need something else, Sky, or do you wish to continue to provide an assessment of my dereliction of duties as the Alpha? Or have you forgotten I *am* the Alpha?"

I smiled, genteel and demure, and spoke in an overly cloying tone. "Mr. Alpha, I could never forget that. And if by chance I do, you'll just do that weird eye thing and growl to give me a friendly reminder." This time, I exposed my teeth when I gave him a sugary smile.

He leaned back in his chair, studying me. "Really. It hasn't seemed to work on you lately. Perhaps I need to change my tactics."

Sebastian didn't bring out my fight-or-flight response the way he once had, but I was never unaware that he was a very dangerous were-animal. "But you are different. Always have been." He wasn't evaluating me as the same oddity, the magical abnormality he had in his pack or the woman who he worked so diligently to hide their secrets from. And I wasn't under any illusions that some of those secrets were still there. I held his gaze for longer than I'd intended to.

"Very different," he acknowledged quietly. His look of unsettled curiosity remained as he directed his attention to Ethan.

"Are you sure he will get bail?"

Ethan nodded. "He was arrested for a triple homicide and animal cruelty, so it will be really high."

"He didn't kill an animal!" I snapped, not at Ethan but the situation. "They were about to shift and attack him. If they'd had their way, he would be the one dead. And the other one had already shifted. It was justified." I was fuming, and some of that anger was directed at Sebastian. He was the one who'd sent Steven out to confront that pack. And I had to shoulder some of that guilt as well because I was the reason Sebastian no longer allowed fringe packs in his territory.

"We know that, Sky," Ethan said softly. I tried to shrug off my anxiety and frustration because based on the tension in Ethan's shoulders, he was feeling it as if it were his own.

"I can see what happens at the bail hearing. Between that and the arraignment, I suspect the charges will be downgraded. They have no evidence except an altered video, which probably won't be admissible."

I was used to Ethan being overly confident and borderline

arrogant about everything, but now it was distilled. Not totally gone, but not nearly as flagrant. I wondered if at any point he'd considered that dealing with misdemeanors, corporate law, and pack business hadn't adequately prepared him for defending an accused murderer. A murder trial was different from one for assault; in the latter, he could probably handle most of it before the trial and strike a deal.

Ethan moved closer to me, and my gaze locked with his, making that connection that was intimate and solely ours. I forgot others were in the room. It was just us. Pressing his hand against my cheek, he said my name, his tone honeyed, low, and velvety smooth. He spoke almost in supplication. "I need you to trust me. Okay? Steven will be fine."

The heaviness seemed to lift, and I couldn't explain it. Ethan seemed to be sharing my burden, and I willingly gave it. I wasn't sure if it was real, but it was definitely something I needed.

CHAPTER 2

Ethan made a face as I picked up his phone and checked it for the fourth time. "Sky, I told you they aren't likely to release him on a Sunday, and I can assure you they won't do it at eleven o'clock at night. Tomorrow. We will have him out by tomorrow." His tone was easy and gentle, but I'd heard the light tinge of irritation. Blindly following him or Sebastian and accepting that "they would handle it" was difficult. I wanted to be proactive.

"Sebastian shouldn't have sent Steven," I finally said. Ethan placed his hand over mine and gave it a squeeze.

"Sky, we aren't having this conversation again because it won't change anything." His voice tightened, and the change in his mood was apparent. I couldn't see my injuries from the attack by the small pack, but I could still feel them, and they'd been bad. Dr. Jeremy had thought I was going to lose an eye, I'd had multiple breaks, and I'd been in so much pain and so afraid that I couldn't shift. The tense muscles in Ethan's neck were a reminder that he was remembering that day, too. He hadn't responded well to it.

"I understand why we don't allow lone packs; I don't understand why Steven has to deal with them the most often."

"He has the best temperament—he's less threatening and often chooses diplomacy when most wouldn't." Ethan failed to add that Steven's gentle demeanor and cherubic appearance caused people to underestimate him to their peril, which was what had happened the night he'd been arrested.

"Did you enjoy yourself?" Ethan asked, using the rearview mirror to look at the canvases placed against the backseat. The attempt at a smile was the same one he'd worn throughout the wine and canvas event we'd used to pass the time. I looked over at his canvas, the nice lines, the strokes that didn't look like the work of an amateur, and the complementing colors that had drawn several people to our area to look at it. Ethan had played the part; although his emotions were never easy to hide, I felt them. He hadn't enjoyed it, but he'd done it for me. The day had been his attempt to distract me, and for the most part, he had. Between dinner, going to visit Claudia at her gallery, and wine and canvas, I'd only checked his phone or asked him to check it a few times.

"It was fun. Did you have fun?" I asked.

"Of course. In my final days I will remember the day I painted 'Love' on a canvas while drinking cheap, overpriced wine. Yes, the memory will stay with me forever."

"Your sarcasm is neither warranted nor appreciated," I shot back, grinning, and playfully jabbed him with my elbow.

He ran his tongue over his lips. "You liked it, that's what matters." He paused for a moment. "We can store them in my garage"—he looked back at the canvases—"which is a better fate than they deserve. Once we have all your things in my house, we'll find a place for them. I'm assuming there won't be too many of them."

"What?" I spluttered. "'Once we have all my things'?"

Ethan continued to speed down the road, but his eyes drifted in my direction and his brow furrowed. "Yes. I assumed you would move into my house. It's bigger. The forest behind it is larger—more space for us to shift and roam."

He kept speaking, and I really wanted him to stop. I hadn't thought about our living arrangements and wasn't ready to discuss them. Ethan brought the conversation to an abrupt stop as he pulled into my driveway. "Your vampire is here." His voice had become rigid and cool, a contrast from his playful tone.

Quell walked out from the shadows, his face expressionless and his eyes hollow. When I got out of the car, he tentatively advanced in my direction. Ethan had eased to my side and taken hold of my hand. Quell didn't need to breathe, but he sucked in a breath anyway as his eyes trailed from my face and down my arm to Ethan's fingers interlinked with mine.

I gave Ethan's hand a squeeze. "Will you give us a minute?" I asked him softly.

Ethan hesitated, giving Quell a hard look, before barely nodding in agreement. Quell and I watched as he disappeared into the house.

"Will you walk with me?" Quell requested quietly. He didn't wait for an answer—he strolled into the woods, into the thick bosky area, until the many trees that surrounded my home obscured us. When he stopped, I left several feet between us. For several minutes, his midnight-colored, sorrow-drenched eyes remained fixed on me.

They were so hard to hold. Even thinking fondly of when they'd once been an odd vibrant green didn't make it any easier. And the long, weighted silence that existed between us was becoming increasingly difficult to bear. Closing the distance I had put between us, I gently touched his hand, hoping it would urge him to speak.

The silence continued, cold, uncomfortable, and onerous.

Closing the distance, he swallowed up any space I'd left between us, his movement nothing more than a blur. Leisurely, his finger trailed down my arm until it met the bare skin of my fingers, which he stroked absently for several moments. Then he stopped all movement and stared past me, the heaviness of his mood displayed solemnly on his face.

"Michaela's dead," he finally said. The air carried his soft words and they continued to echo.

I was angry with myself for feeling guilty about killing Michaela. There should never have been any guilt because her death had been deserved. For years, she had terrorized me and my pack for the sheer pleasure of it. She was undeserving of my remorse, and if it weren't for Quell standing in front of me, I doubted I would've had any of those feelings. But I wasn't remorseful that she was dead. I felt bad because I knew it had hurt him, and that was the last thing I'd wanted to do.

Quell and I shared a tragic existence, one that couldn't be easily dismissed. He turned from me and walked away. I followed him through the crowded, lush forest on a path that had been made by Steven and me constantly taking the same way whenever we went into the woods. Most of the time, it was my paws that trampled down the coarse grass. Quell walked slowly, his hands by his side, his long fingers periodically stroking mine nonchalantly. I was aware of the coolness that pressed against my skin every time he touched me.

We'd been walking in silence for several minutes when the mood changed. It wasn't heavy, but an acceptable resolve that seemed fitting as we stood in the deep verdant area, surrounded by trees, in a somnolent quiet—an easy silence that existed between us.

When he turned to face me, his eyes still looked sorrowful and withdrawn. I remembered the time I'd forced him to feed from me because I hadn't been able to let him die. I glanced over at the large leaves that extended from the poplars, reminded of how vibrant and green his eyes used to be. That color was evocative of the plant the Hidacus, which he'd fed from instead of humans. He'd abjectly refused blood from humans, whom he'd considered unworthy of the humanity they possessed.

"I miss you," he admitted softly, his voice carried lightly in the wind.

"I miss you, too," I said it, and I meant it. I felt a pang of guilt and betrayal about missing another man when I had Ethan. But the relationship I had with Quell was so different from what I had with anyone else. It transcended romance and friendship. It was odd, unexplainable, and something I treasured. Its nebulous existence was difficult for most people to understand.

"Ethan said you have a donor now. How is that going?" I asked, aware of the way his gaze trailed along my features and down the curve of my jaw to the lines of my neck, where it stayed. I saw the thirst, something he'd denied himself. It was inexplicably who he was, no matter how much he denied his urges. At the end of the day, he was a vampire, and he had bloodlust. He required blood to survive. Although he approached it with a detachment that seemed clinical at best, he enjoyed taking human blood.

"Had. I *had* a donor," he murmured and then turned to walk away. I grabbed his arm, stopping him. I turned him to face me.

"What do you mean, *had*?" I asked with repressed fear and agitation. I remembered the time he'd gone through bloodlust and killed several people. Not just people. Women who'd looked strangely like me.

He continued to move. "I sent her away."

"How long ago?"

"About a week and a half ago."

"Why?" I asked, rooted in place, allowing him to increase the distance between us. But there was more than just space between us. I knew he'd figured out I was responsible for Michaela's death. Confession felt better than accusation, so I blurted out, "I killed Michaela."

"I know." His shoulders sagged into the sigh. "That's why I'm here," he admitted.

"For what, retribution? Revenge?"

Quell's eyes widened, then he frowned. "Of course not," he

said. And in a blink, he was in front of me, with a stake in hand. He studied me for a few minutes before placing it in my hands and grasping them between his. He lifted the stake to his chest. "I'm ready for you to do the same to me."

Wincing at his request, I let his words replay in my head in a loop as if they'd somehow change, hopeful I'd missed something or he'd misspoken. "What?"

"I'm ready for you to do the same to me," he repeated.

I knew what he was talking about, but I needed him to say it. I needed him to vocalize that he was asking me to take his life. Perhaps if he heard how ridiculous it sounded, he'd recant.

Without missing a beat, or even reconsidering his words, he said them again; voice flat. "You've taken the life of my creator, and now I am asking you to do the same for me."

Anger rose out of my confusion. I gawked at him, disgusted. "What is wrong with you?"

He shook his head and looked stunned by my anger, as if he'd thought I would have willingly accepted taking his life for no other reason than he'd requested it. As if it were some odd circle I needed to complete or some peculiar task I had been committed to by killing Michaela.

"Why does everything have to be so dramatic with you!" I shouted. I spun around, the stake still clenched in my hand, and walked so fast back toward the house I was nearly jogging.

"Sky?" he said my name again, entreating me with a gentle timbre as he requested understanding. "This is inevitable. It's been a long time coming."

I hadn't realized how much progress I'd made toward the house and was just several feet away when I sensed Ethan's presence in the darkness. Cloaked by it, he stayed out of sight. Once again, the gentle lilt of my name crossed Quell's lips. It didn't sound nearly as ominous or cruel as his request. It implored forgiveness, though I wasn't willing to give it. I was so angry I couldn't tamp it down. And as much as I wanted to ignore that little tug of guilt that lingered, it emerged as well. I did what most people did in a situation like this—I lashed out. I spun around and pulled my lips back, exposing my teeth. "What do you want me to say? That I'm sorry?"

"No, I want you to honor my request."

"I will not be a performer in your fucking production of angst and self-deprecation." I closed my eyes and inhaled the air, hoping it would cleanse the memories and soothe my fiery anger. It didn't. Rage blazed in me and rode me hard, along with the guilt. I forgot all the cruel things Michaela had done, all the havoc she'd wreaked, and only remembered that I'd killed the one person who linked Quell to the vampires. His creator, the person he'd loved unconditionally. I searched my emotions. Everything had melded together, and I couldn't sort them out. Anger. Frustration. Sorrow. Confusion. For several moments, we stood in silence. His flat, despondent eyes seized my emotions in a manner I couldn't understand. I stared at him.

"She was cruel, and so are you. If you want to end your life, there are several ways you could do it. Instead, you came here and made me a participant in your self-loathing pity party. Don't bring me into this. Don't ask me to understand the screwed-up relationship you had with Michaela. And don't you fucking dare ask me to assist you in ending a life you don't feel worthy of living now that she's gone. I thought you were better than this. You want to die—I'm sure there's a line of people willing to do it."

"What you perceive as cruelty is nothing more than my final request for kindness."

I didn't want his soft, gentle explanation. I wanted him to be angry and emotionally uncontrolled the way I was so it would be easier for me to deal with everything. I'd lost this battle because this was exactly what Michaela had wanted. If she couldn't have him, no one else could, either, even as a friend. She'd wanted him in a perpetual state of sorrow, and she'd accomplished that. I looked at his grief-stricken eyes and felt lost. Helpless. I didn't know what to do.

"If only I could get the same kindness you request from me from you," I growled back. Ethan had emerged from the darkness and was just inches from me. I spiked the stake into the ground, embedding it in the soil near Ethan's feet.

He looked at it, then at me, and allowed his gaze to travel in Quell's direction before he knelt to pick it up.

I growled and bared my teeth. They were clenched so tightly my jaw ached. "Don't you dare pick that up." I was fully aware that what I was reluctant and unable to do, Ethan was fully capable of. My scowl relaxed as he looked at me with defiance. I knew it was hard for him to deny a challenge, and I'd just challenged him. That beastly part of him that denied subjugation was defiant. The predator flashed, but he reined it in as he stood and took several steps away from the stake.

I slowly backed away and Quell moved in my direction. I heard a hard thump, and I assumed it was Ethan's palm hitting Quell's chest to stop him because I heard Ethan say, "Let her go."

I was glad Ethan had stopped him. I was in a bad place where I couldn't talk to him and be civil or kind. The cool air breezing across my skin wasn't enough; I still felt like I was suffocating. *Damn you, Quell.*

Once I started walking, there wasn't any doubt where I would end up. I strode past the long stretch of forest, a vast area that gave me the space I needed to keep the necessary distance from my neighbor. I enjoyed my privacy, but this was one of the times when I wished David lived closer. Next door would be great. The sun had long set, and the moonlight lit the path up to his darkened home. *Please be up,* I thought as I knocked on his door.

David answered the door with a nearly full wineglass in hand. He assessed my appearance, and his smile faded. His lips turned down into a frown. "Aw, what is it, pumpkin spice?" he said, stepping aside to let me in.

Really. But it was better than being called kitten or a cream-filled pastry, so I dealt with it.

I walked in. Trent, his partner, was sitting on the sofa. As usual, I was underdressed in my V-neck t-shirt and dark blue jeans. They both had on slacks and pristine, crisp button-down shirts. And as usual, they had bowl-sized wineglasses in hand.

"What's the matter, sweetie?" David asked.

"I don't want to talk about it," I mumbled, walking into his outstretched arms. He wrapped them around me and held me tight. Relaxed, I appreciated the warmth of his hug and rested my head against his chest. Then I felt the heavy heat and weight of another body. Trent's arms encircled me, his face pressed against my back.

"Did I make it weird? This is weird. I think I just made it weird," he mumbled into my shirt.

"So. Very. Weird," I agreed, my words muffled as I pressed my face deeper into David's shirt.

"You want me to move?" he asked.

"No."

We stayed in the bizarre three-person hug for several minutes before untangling from it.

I made my way to the sofa, and minutes after I had made myself comfortable, David handed me a large glass of wine and placed a tray of cupcakes in front of me.

"You definitely know how to make a day better," I said and took a long drink. I wished it really would've made me feel better, but it didn't. The cloud of despair hung heavily around me. Quell wanted me to kill him. For so many years, I'd underestimated his connection with Michaela. And I would probably die never really knowing or understanding the attachment he had to her solely because she was the one who'd created him. He was the very person who had given up on humanity, which made it hard to understand how he could cling to someone who'd brazenly chosen to do everything possible to be inhumane.

I gave David and Trent a faint smile, aware they were looking at me, waiting for me to talk. I just couldn't gather the right words to say that someone had just asked me to kill them. To assist them in their own suicide.

"Can we talk about it later?" I asked.

They weren't subtle about hiding their relief. They had been plunged into the otherworld and were privy to information others didn't have. They had been introduced to a realm of darkness, violence, supernatural politics, and posturing. I didn't blame them for wanting to distance themselves from it, to be blissfully ignorant of the many things I had to deal with, to hold on to that innocent part of them. I relaxed back in the sofa, wine in hand, shooting them derisive looks as they became engrossed in a show with surgically enhanced bodies, extensions flinging through the air, and long manicured fingers pointing at other women as they made their mean remarks.

"Oh, sweetie, you turn into a wolf once a month. Don't judge us," Trent said as he took a sip from his glass and gave me a playful grin.

I wrinkled my nose. "I'm judging. And you can't stop me."

He shrugged and made a dramatic gesture as though he were flinging long hair back as well. "And you can't make me care."

I laughed because he knew I was a closeted lover of these things. And watching them with David and Trent made them even more entertaining. I let the shows enthrall me and the wine make me hazy enough to let the image of Quell's face slip away. Being tipsy from wine and a chocolate rush had put me in a better mood, a calmer frame of mind.

"I've decided I'm going to stay here forever," I informed them as I placed my glass on the table in front of me. I knew David would eventually refill it again. We both made faces at the five empty bottles sitting on the table.

"Like you can stay away from him," David teased. I wasn't sure who he was more enamored with, Ethan or Steven.

"Eh, I'll visit him periodically."

He and Trent gave each other a look and then directed said look at me. "I'm sure you will," David said with a miscreant grin. "And I don't blame you."

"Not for that! I actually enjoy talking to him and being around him—you know that, right?"

"Among other things, I'm sure."

I ignored them and tried to focus on the TV, but in my peripheral vision, I could see the looks they kept giving me. And just when another spat started on the TV, with heads rolling so hard their extensions smacked them in their faces, manicured fingers being pushed in another woman's face, and enough scathing names being spat to garner our attention again, someone knocked on the door. It wasn't someone; we all knew who it was. Ethan.

They hesitated before answering, waiting for me to give them the okay. I nodded once. David opened the door, and before Ethan could ask, he said, "She's here."

"I know," Ethan said.

That ability was something I'd always been curious about. When I'd first met him, he'd seemed to have the gift of always being able to find me, and I'd attributed it to were-animals being good hunters. But I'd had no idea why I could always find him, even before we were mated. Something had happened after we'd performed that spell together to remove his dark elf magic. Somehow, we'd become linked. Ever since then, I could feel a magical nudge in his direction. A magical connection that always led me to him. The more I found out about Ethan, the more complicated I realized our connection might be. Best-case scenario, we were linked by that spell. Worst-case—by the Faerie spirit shades we each hosted. Just thinking about it filled me with a sense of dread; not because he was a host as well, but because of the person he hosted. I'd nearly forgotten about it—not really forgotten, but stored it away with all the other things that were too difficult to think about. Ethan hosted a spirit shade that was so horrid and despicable that his own kind had forced him to live life as a shade. I wondered why they hadn't killed him. What did he possess—what type of magic did they want to preserve or what information did he have that made him an asset they refused to kill?

Ethan stayed at the door; the silence swelled and became uncomfortable. That was David and Trent's cue to exit—or they took it as one. They seemed more than happy to leave and remain unaware of the drama that was about to unfold.

Ethan took a seat next to me, glanced up at the TV, furrowed his brow at me mockingly, grabbed the remote, and turned the TV off. He clasped my hand in his, brought it to his lips, and kissed it.

"I'm not going to do it," I whispered.

He nodded slowly. "Okay. I didn't come here to talk you into it."

"Then why are you here?" I asked, unable to keep the irritation out of my voice. Displacing my irritation with the situation on Ethan. A problem I didn't know how to fix, that seemed so cold and unreal. *Who asks someone to kill them?*

With a faint smile, Ethan brushed the hair away from my face and sighed. "Quell is the type of person who asks something like that."

I didn't ponder how Ethan knew what I was thinking, I'm sure it was expressed on my face. Closing my eyes for a second, I took a deep breath and slowly released it. "It's not fair that he did."

"You're right. It was a horrible thing to ask you. But it's his last wish, and it's selfish to deny him that." He dropped his eyes to the floor, and I didn't know if it was the look on my face that was too hard to bear or if he was about to say something and didn't want to look at me after he'd said it. "Sky, it's okay to be selfish. I won't ever judge you for that. But I want to know why you're being selfish. Why do you need Quell in your life?"

"I don't *need* him in my life. I just don't want to have his death on my hands."

"Even if it's what he wants?"

"I don't give a damn what he wants because what he wants is absolutely absurd." There was a long, uncomfortable silence between us. I searched for the right words but came up empty. Ethan's thumb ran along the side of mine as he kept a firm grasp on my hand.

He assessed me in silence, gunmetal eyes fixed on me. He leaned forward, gently trailing his fingers along my cheek. His tone was the polar opposite of his sharp gaze.

"I've asked you whether you loved Quell, so I won't ask you again. But I need to know what this hold is that he has on you."

"It's not a hold." I dropped my eyes to my hands, unable to bear his gaze. "I feel—"

"Look at me, Sky."

I lifted my eyes to meet his and continued, "I feel like ..." But the words faded. I didn't have an answer that would make sense to anyone because it didn't make sense to me.

Ethan's tone was still level, soft, emotionless. "You feel as though you know more than him." His gentle, condoling touches were replaced by feather-light kisses. "He's close to eighty years old. You don't know more than he does. Have you ever been to a movie that was terrible? Some people stay, hoping it will get better, and others walk out immediately. Some stay close to the end, and when they realize nothing good will happen, they finally leave, but they've already stayed way too long."

"Life isn't a movie, Ethan."

"In many ways it is. At least with a movie, you can leave and just live your life. You can even catch another show. But this is his only show. He's lost his creator, the person he once liked enough to form a special bond with. She's gone, and he doesn't have a Seethe that wants him. You can't be the only reason for him to stay alive. You can't make that decision. He has the right."

"I have the right to say I don't want to be the one who does it," I snapped back. Ethan didn't take offense.

"Fine. But you are wrong." He ended the conversation. He'd said his piece, voiced his opinion, and it was out there for me to act on.

As far as I was concerned, he was wrong, too, and defiance caused me to just stare at the hand he extended to me once he'd stood.

"Sky?"

After several moments, I took it. "I won't change my mind."

"Okay," he acknowledged in a flat, mild tone. I felt like a petulant child, and I was pretty much behaving like one. Once again, I found myself out of my depth, floundering in a world I thought I'd learned to navigate.

As I walked next to Ethan, I tried to find comfort in the things he'd said. *It's okay to be selfish. Own it.* I repeated it several times in my head, but by the time I got to the house, I hadn't convinced myself of it. I wasn't selfish—not intentionally. But I knew for sure I wasn't Quell's guardian. I was his friend.

Instead of following Ethan to the front door, I moved around to the back and slowly approached the wooded area behind my house. I knew Quell would be there. I picked up the stake, which was in the same spot where I'd stabbed it and continued toward him.

I clenched it tighter, aware that my pace had slowed and I was barely moving. The same anger flooded back, and it was hard to master. I stopped just a few feet from Quell, who stood still, with the same vacuous look I'd become familiar with and oddly found comfort in. It was anything but comforting now. It didn't offer any succor. Instead, it was the face of heartache, of pain, of a person who had given up. All the emotions I had blended together; I couldn't distinguish them. I knew I felt a sordid version of hate for Quell for asking me to do such a thing and forcing me to make this decision. I despised him for causing me to regret killing Michaela.

I clung to those feelings because I needed them to do this. It wasn't possible for me to consider this an act of love or mercy, so I had to make it something else. Anger and hate were all I had.

They just weren't enough. My feet were rooted to the ground. Seconds later, Quell had cleared the distance between us. In silence, his hands covered mine and moved it over his heart. He squeezed my hand and kept his dark gaze on mine. It seemed like a lifetime had passed since they were green. My eyes drifted to the ground, and when I finally lifted them, I found him looking at me, expressionless. Desperately, I wanted to see an inkling of apprehension, fear, or anything that would give me a reason not to do it. Nothing.

"Why me? You could have had anyone do this," I whispered.

"No, I couldn't have, because you're the last person I needed to see."

The tears I'd been fighting spilled and blurred my vision so I couldn't see what I was about to do. My hand shook, and I fought to keep it steady enough to complete the task. I'd staked vampires before. I drew back, my mouth as dry as the Sahara.

"Do it," he urged.

I nodded, drew back even farther, and held, for just a second, before driving the stake forward. It was an inch or so from his chest when Ethan took hold of my arm, slid his hands down until they reached mine, and took the stake from me. His thumbs swept over my face several times, removing tears. He kissed me.

"We need to talk," he growled through clenched teeth and grabbed Quell roughly, yanking him back. Quell jerked out of his hold, moved back several feet, and bared his fangs. Ethan automatically assumed a defensive position, snarling. He shifted his gaze from his target, Quell, to me, and with great effort, he forced himself to relax. He tossed the stake aside.

"We need to talk. Now." He glared at Quell, and after a few moments of consideration, Quell shook his head.

"It wasn't a request," Ethan growled, ire putting a sharp edge to his voice. "You will do it. The manner in which you do is up to you."

After several moments of hostile silence and sharp glares, Quell nodded and followed Ethan deeper into the woods.

I didn't bother to listen. I knew they would be too far away for me to hear. And honestly, I didn't want to. I wanted to be anywhere but there.

I went into the house, showered, and went to bed. I lay there in the darkness, waiting for Ethan. It took nearly an hour before he returned, and he went straight to the shower. The smell of Quell on him probably bothered him.

Naked, Ethan slid into bed next to me. For a long moment, there was a pregnant silence between the two of us. And then he rolled over on his knees and hands and straddled me, his face just inches from mine. He leaned in closer and kissed me lightly, his tongue laving my bottom lip as he pulled away, tasting it. He kissed me again on my cheek and ran gentle trails down my neck until he came to my breast and delivered the same treatment to each one. He was gentle and warm, but a controlled primal lust was there, ready to be unleashed. He nestled between my legs. His teeth nipped at the tender skin around my neck, my shoulders, and my stomach, and then he moved lower. His tongue left moist trails down my legs before he settled in, tasting me. Just before I went over the edge, he stopped and sheathed himself in me. Our bodies moved in a slow, serene rhythm as he savored the moment. His eyes fixed on me, warm, intense, wanton. I wrapped my legs around him as he curled his hands around me, pulling me closer to him, moving in a rush as we found our pleasure. His body collapsed against mine, and heat radiated around me, warming me. I stroked his hair and listened to the gentle rhythm of our hearts, connected, moving as one. He placed warm, tender, kisses on my shoulder.

He pulled away to look at me, his eyes gentle and entreating. "Skylar," he started softly. "How long are we going to pretend that Quell isn't in love with you?"

"Quell isn't—"

"Sky, don't."

"I'm not pretending. Quell's and my relationship is anything but typical. And you knew this." I pressed my hand against his cheek to relax the tension in his face as his jaw clenched. He rolled to the side, and we lay back, looking at the ceiling.

"It's something I just don't understand. I get the relationship you have with Steven. It's weird, but I understand it. And I understand the affinity you have for my brother. But this thing with Quell—I don't get it," he admitted, the moonlight that streamed through the window showing the strained lines on his face.

"Ethan, I don't get it, either. I remember he was okay with dying and I forced him not to because I couldn't bear it. He's here because of me."

"He wants you to end the situation." Ethan's voice was cold, even cruel, but I had to give him credit. I knew he was willing to rectify that situation but only resisted the temptation to do so because of me.

"I'm never going to be cavalier about life. I wish I could be. It would make life so much easier. But I know him. I've spent late nights having conversations with him." I ignored the growl that reverberated in Ethan's chest and continued, "He's my friend. And I don't think it's as simple as Michaela missing in his life—"

"Michaela isn't missing in his life. You took her away. You killed her. And there are consequences anytime things like this happen. There are *always* consequences, Skylar. Sometimes, they are negligible, but oftentimes, they aren't."

Ethan was right. That heavy burden of guilt rested over me like an old blanket pulled too tight, making breathing more difficult. Everything we did had consequences, most of them unforeseeable. Dexter was the consequence of an action we'd taken. It had been justified and the right thing to do, but now we were dealing with the consequences.

"I don't know if Quell loves me in a platonic or romantic way. I only know how I feel about him. And I care about him. I don't love him, not in the sense you think."

"I don't think anything. I just need to understand."

Ethan had made a good point—I was selfish. I wanted Quell to live because he reminded me of my humanity, something I saw slipping away with each passing moment. I had a tenuous grasp on it, and at times, it seemed invisible, as if I'd shrugged it off like a cumbersome jacket. He represented the expectations of humanity, goodwill, and altruism. Letting him die was letting part of me do the same. I knew it was silly, but I couldn't stop feeling that way.

"Just let me fix this, please."

"Okay." Ethan rolled away from me, and I felt more than physical distance between us. I leaned forward and kissed his shoulder, then he turned to face me.

His scowl wouldn't relax. He watched me for a long time and was careful with his words when he finally spoke. He seemed to have shifted from my lover, my mate, to the Beta. I knew I wasn't going to like the way this conversation went. "Sky, I want you to fix this. I want it not to be a problem for us or the pack. Quell in your life means we have to deal with the Northern Seethe and Demetrius. This is bigger than my mate having an odd relationship with another man. He's a problem and always has been. So fix it if you think you can, but if you don't, I will."

I nodded, accepting the responsibility, knowing that inevitably, someone would intervene if I didn't resolve this.

I fell into an uncomfortable, restless sleep.

CHAPTER 3

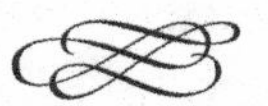

When I woke up, I realized it hadn't even been two hours since I'd attempted to sleep. I knew I wasn't going to sleep. Every time I closed my eyes, I saw Quell's face. The sorrow. The anguish. The tortured existence. I rolled out of bed and quickly pulled on underwear, a bra, jeans, and a t-shirt and started out the bedroom door.

"Tell Demetrius if he touches you, what I will do to him will be used as a cautionary tale for years to come. And some people will have to skip the more gruesome parts."

"Should I tell him that before I greet him or afterward? If I tell him before, I doubt he'll let me in. And if I tell him after my greeting, it will make me sound insincere," I said lightheartedly.

Poking the bear. That's exactly what I was doing. I shouldn't have. Ethan was being uncharacteristically calm, and I knew he was doing it on my behalf. Because I needed this. "I'll be safe, I promise."

Before I left the house, I stood in front of the umbrella stand where I kept my sword and debated whether to take it. Showing up with a weapon didn't exactly facilitate open and amicable dialogue. But, I was dealing with Demetrius—I doubted I was going to get gentle banter. I decided against the sword and moved toward the front door when I heard Ethan say, "You really should take it with you."

I considered ignoring him, but he was right. Demetrius had fangs; I needed something, too. I grabbed the sword, the knife I kept stashed in the coffee table drawer, and my handy nine iron, which I kept by the door. I used the sword more often because all I had to do was swing and cut. It served its purpose, and I wasn't treated to the same derisive looks I received when I pulled out the golf club. I stood firmly by my belief that it was an acceptable weapon. It wouldn't lop off a body part, but it was far from harmless. Those who doubted and mocked it didn't feel the same way after I'd wacked them with it.

I spent twenty minutes outside the house trying to come up with other viable options besides talking to him. I went over my decision as I drove to Demetrius's. He was the Master of the North, and his power and control were undeniable. Given his long history as the Master, he had to have dealt with a situation similar to Quell's.

I sighed loudly. This was definitely among the top ten bad choices I'd made over the years. Sawdust filled my mouth at the idea that I needed Demetrius. He wouldn't make this easy—benevolence wasn't in his nature. Indifference was his usual. He cared little about anything except power and Chris, former Hunter and recently made vampire. His hatred for Ethan was another exception. Was it caused by Ethan's past relationship with Chris, or Demetrius's primal desire to subjugate another dominant person? It was hard to know if that need was instinctive—a desire to feel safe—or his ego, which was enormous.

I waited in my car for a few minutes, staring at his house, which was peculiarly inviting but extravagant like most vampires'. Their homes often leaned toward the ostentatious. Grand structures surrounded by intricate and lavishly designed pillars, with wrought iron gates separating them from a community that knew little of their existence. Some people came to visit and never returned home; others were used as toys, even food, and compelled to meet an innumerable number of the vampire's needs.

I left the sword and the nine iron in the car and shoved the knife into the back of my pants once I was out of the car. The blade was long and sharp. I couldn't cut off a vampire's head with it, but I could cause a lot of damage if one attacked me. I got a glimpse of that mark on my wrist. The small interlocking black rings were a reminder that I no longer had access to magic. That I had performed—or attempted to perform—a very powerful spell that came with the penalty of death. I was torn between how I felt about the consequences of doing the spell. I didn't have access to magic, which I'd gotten used to, but I wouldn't have it if Demetrius misbehaved—which was likely. I ambled toward the large Mediterranean-style stone home that was so uniquely misplaced among the other nondescript suburban homes. As I made my way up the winding path, I passed a familiar SUV. Winter. When I stopped at the window, she gave me a little wave and flashed a small grin.

I tapped on the window, and she rolled it down. "Let me guess. Ethan told you to come here."

She shrugged. "All I know is that he promised I could kill vampires. I'm just here for the vampire killing. Whatever bizarre vampire business you have going is none of my concern."

I peeked into her car. She was there for more than just an altercation; she'd brought an arsenal of weapons. I made a face. She dismissed me with a wave of her hand.

"Like I said, I'm just here for the vampires. If you have a problem with this, I suggest you call Ethan."

"I guess I will," I said in the stern voice.

She grinned, a devilish look, and took out her phone and handed it to me. "Fine, I'll wait. Go ahead. Call him and tell him you want to go into the vampire's lair with no backup a few days after you killed his Mistress. In your self-righteous indignation, tell him you want to meet with a man who took a chunk out of your neck with just the security of a knife hidden in your pants. This might be the most entertaining thing I'll see all week." She rested back in her leather seat, firmly wrapped in smug derision.

Humility had a chalky aftertaste.

I ignored the phone and fixed her with a hard glare. "Fine. You stay out here. Don't you dare go in there unless you're absolutely sure I'm being attacked," I commanded.

"Ethan instructed me to give you ten minutes, and that's exactly what I'm going to do. Whatever you need to do, you need to do it fast."

"And I am instructing you to give me time. Ten minutes isn't enough. Unless you hear something break, like glass shattering, don't come in. I'll be fine." I saw the conflict on her face. As Ethan's mate, I held his status, but he'd commanded her first. My life with Ethan was just a myriad of complications, rules, and acts of propriety, and it wasn't getting any easier. I glanced inside her car again and made a face. "Who carries a flamethrower, you freak?"

"It's called being prepared. The foundation of being prepared is *not* hanging out with vampires, and it's definitely not going into their homes in the middle of the night. That's just asking for trouble. But you march to your own drummer—he's tone-deaf and possibly on drugs. Go in there. Try to save the world and hope Demetrius finds it as annoying as everyone else does." She grabbed the large blade next to her and ran her finger along its edge.

I opened my mouth to defend myself but decided against it. Nothing I said would justify this in her book. She was like many other were-animals when it came to vampires; they thought the only time to talk to a vampire was to explain why they were staking or beheading them.

I stood planted in front of her.

She shooed me away. "Go prattle on about whatever you plan to do and hope he has the poor sense to actually touch you. A touch is all he has to do for me to kick his ass."

I didn't point out that the last time she and Demetrius had fought, when I'd first met the pack, he'd kicked *her* ass. She didn't need the reminder—something like that would likely leave her with a grudge, which explained the cache of weapons she had with her. Eventually, Demetrius would pay.

I backed away from her, dismissing her statement with a flick of my eyes. When I was two feet from Demetrius's front door, I heard a rumble; glowing eyes peeked out from the woods that surrounded his home. As moonlight hit the shimmering black coat, the stately animal moved forward to make his presence known.

"Hi, Kitty. I guess you're here to rip somebody apart, too."

Baring his teeth, he made a low roaring sound. He wasn't nearly as happy to be on my security detail and possibly a vampire slayer as Winter was. The two of them were the pack members who could get to Demetrius the fastest. I should have known I'd have guards. Ethan had been too passive about me going to meet with Demetrius. No wonder he hadn't been waiting for me at my car as I'd expected. I'd been prepared to tell him that if he showed up, Demetrius wouldn't be as helpful and would probably be a total jerk just to piss Ethan off.

I hadn't attempted to be quiet as I made my way to Demetrius's door, and he must have heard me because the door was slightly ajar, and he was watching me as I approached. Arrogance shrouded Demetrius's expectant appearance and he smiled as he opened his front door wider, giving me room to enter. His smirk didn't falter as he took several steps back. "To what do I owe this late-night visit?" he asked, his tone low and sultry. My eye roll came automatically. He could make the word *butterfly* sound salacious and dirty. "I hope it is to inform me of the day on which you plan to return Chris to me."

"Quell is back," I blurted, ignoring his question about Chris.

"I'm aware," he offered nonchalantly.

A cold, hard silence overtook the room as he fixed me with a look of indifference. He broke it by saying, "Elisabeth," with a gentle, satiny rhythm as if he were reciting an ode.

Moments later, a slender woman with hair as dark as coal and dewy, honey-colored skin approached him. She was definitely human and walked with the grace of a trained dancer. Rose and currant wafted through the air upon her arrival. Describing her as beautiful wasn't adequate. She was striking and exquisite. Her light brown eyes weren't hollow, however, but soft and delicate. Trying to understand vampires was an exercise in futility, but I'd pegged them as overindulgent children only interested in things they perceived as beautiful. They were self-professed collectors of beauty.

As I looked around his home at the exquisite art that decorated the walls, tables, and stands, I wondered what they found so unpleasant about life that they needed to always surround themselves with eye candy. Case in point: Elisabeth. Once she was within reach, Demetrius curled his arms around her waist and pulled her to him. His fingers caressed the satin dress draped over her frame. She wore nothing under it—the thin material left nothing to the imagination. Without Demetrius asking, she tilted her head, exposing her long, slender neck to him.

He smiled, baring his fangs before his tongue slowly slid over her neck. Then he sank his fangs into her. His long, languid fingers roved over her body intimately as he fed on her. I wasn't sure which was more disgusting, her purrs of pleasure or the lascivious way he was touching her. Demetrius was putting on a show to make me feel uncomfortable. He kept his eyes on me as he took long draws from her. I refused to give him the satisfaction of my discomfort. I watched. After several minutes that felt like hours, he pulled away. He didn't bother laving the bite to cover it.

Elisabeth's eyes were hazy, and her face was relaxed in a euphoric, erotic state.

"Would you like to join me?" he asked, offering her to me. He licked her neck leisurely as his hands moved over her, cupping her breast and touching her suggestively with his fingers.

"Not even a little."

"Your eyes show otherwise; are you sure?"

I assumed my *terait* was showing. "My eyes are deceiving. I'm so sure it can be written on my tombstone. There will never be a time in my life when I will eat anything you've had, licked, or even looked at too long. I don't want blood or anything else you're offering."

His brows rose, his tongue moving languidly over his lips without removing the trail of blood that ran along the side of his mouth.

"Elisabeth, you can leave." She looked dejected, as if my rejection of Demetrius's offering were a slight. Turning to face him, she licked the rivulet of blood with her tongue before covering his mouth with hers. Another uncomfortable moment that stretched far too long as they locked lips in a sensual kiss. He released her, and as requested, like a submissive servant, she left us. I could no longer hide my disgust.

"I see you're still mourning Michaela's death," I said.

His dark chuckle filled the large room. "I don't think I need to go over the fact that we don't recognize the emotional standards and limits you all put on pleasure and joy. I am indeed still mourning Michaela. I just don't mourn based on your beliefs. I've lost before. When you've lived as long as I have, experiencing great loss is inevitable." He closed the distance between us.

The deep rumble of his voice held a hint of warning. "Unless you are ready to give me Chris, there is no reason for you to be here."

"Quell isn't well."

"So? That is of little interest to me. He was Michaela's pet, not mine." He moved to the window, where he had to see Winter and Gavin. "You left your home in the middle of the night, leaving Ethan, to do what? Ask me to help Quell?" He chortled, a loud, jovial sound that seemed too light for the Master of Darkness and Death.

In a flash of movement, he returned to his position in front of me. Close—too close. His breath was cool against my cheek as he spoke. "You left your mate to beg me to assist another man." Before I could push him away, he laughed again and moved back several feet. "Ethan can't be enjoying this. Delectable. This is absolutely delectable. My vampire has that type of hold over you. A hold not even Ethan has. How did he look when you told him you were going into the lion's den to ask for help for another? I do believe I'd pay a handsome fee to see the look on his face when you told him."

I swallowed hard, searching for a defense and something as scathing as his words. He was right. I'd given little thought to how Ethan felt about me leaving in the middle of the night to speak with Demetrius to help Quell. My mouth dried, and my stomach curled at the thought of being so selfish and inconsiderate, but I refused to let Demetrius get the upper hand.

"Ethan's confident in our relationship and understands that Quell and I have is a friendship."

He chuckled again. "*Friendship*," he spat with disgust. His gaze remained on me, evaluating me with a peculiar interest.

"Yes, and if you knew how to have a real one with Chris, perhaps she wouldn't have left you."

He dismissed my comment with a quick jerk of his wrist. "Chris is having a little fit and making a statement."

"Yes, and the statement is she hates you. And it's loud and clear. She's never been one for subtlety."

He flinched and looked as if he'd been slapped. For a brief moment, the arrogance, confidence, and hubris faltered. He appeared wounded. He was a man who had a distorted view of love, relationships, and friendships. He'd never been denied and couldn't deal with rejection. I forced myself to remember his arrogance and cruelty. The indomitable vampire who felt the world and the people in it existed only to please him didn't deserve any emotions that were anything close to sympathy. Then I focused on Elisabeth, whose life he'd probably turned upside down. She probably hoped he would turn her one day, but instead, she existed only to feed him and satisfy his other cravings. I couldn't be cruel and revel in his moment of unhappiness, but I wouldn't give him any form of compassion, either.

"She hates you, and it isn't without reason. Have you ever considered treating her as anything other than 'a wild one you'd like to break' or a possession?" I said, tossing back the very things he'd said about her in the past.

"I created her. She is mine to do with as I please."

Welcome back, jackass.

"Which is the very reason she isn't here. She *isn't* your property, and you don't get to do with her as you please. You saved her life because it meant something to you. Don't twist it into something it isn't and make it seem as though she owes you blind loyalty." From his fixed look of entitlement, it was clear I wasn't getting through to him. I backed up toward the door. "You're cruel without cause and unnecessarily selfish. You don't think of anyone but yourself. You rule by fear and totalitarianism, but eventually, that won't be enough. Maybe you can descend from your fucking high horse and show you are capable of selflessness and actual acts of kindness. Then people might follow you for more reasons than obligation and the obscure bond that exists because you created them. As you can see with what happened with Chris, that bond eventually won't be enough."

The hard lines of his lips stayed stiff. "She doesn't hate me," he whispered.

"Who are you trying to convince, me or you?"

I backed out the door, watching his eyes go blank and the

expression slip from his face. I didn't know if he was considering what I'd said or working on another way to get Chris back.

"She doesn't hate me," he repeated, even lower.

"You haven't given her reason to do anything but. You said you enjoyed breaking the wild ones—I think she does, too. Right now, you seem to be the broken one." I gave him another long, assessing look. He wasn't broken, but distraught. Was it from genuine loss and emptiness over Chris's absence or a blow to his inflated and fragile ego? He was so used to doing as he pleased with impunity. With Chris, his actions had consequences.

I left Demetrius's not totally convinced that Chris hated him. Their relationship, much like his relationship with Michaela, was something I would never understand. Maybe he was right and she was making a point. Nevertheless, she'd left him. Part of me knew that if she truly hated him, she would've killed him when she'd held a knife to his throat. She'd let him live. Perhaps there was some truth to the bond between creator and created, sired and master. I didn't understand it, and it would probably take me a lifetime to ever do so.

Ethan was up when I returned home, sitting in the living room with his laptop open. When I opened the door, his eyes lifted from the screen in my direction. His voice was just as emotionless as his face when he spoke. "Did you resolve your issue?"

I shook my head, moving over to the sofa and sitting next to him. He rested his hand on my leg and squeezed.

"I'm sorry," I said.

"About what, Sky?" His tone betrayed no emotions; there might have been some legitimacy to what Demetrius had said. My life was a combination of odd relationships I couldn't quite understand, and my relationship with Quell was the epitome of them.

"Quell. I don't know why I care so much about him and feel

connected to him. But I am, and I feel like I should do whatever I can to help him. Part of me feels like it's wrong to care about him the way I do. Explaining it is impossible."

He closed his laptop, put in on the table, and turned to face me. After a long moment of deliberation, he frowned, and looked away. Eventually, he returned his attention to me. "I don't understand you and Quell," he admitted. "You would move heaven and earth for him. *For him.* And do questionable and even dangerous things for *him*. You even built that greenhouse for him, knowing it made you the target of Michaela's wrath. You have a connection with him, different from those you have with Josh and Steven. It may be platonic for you, but it's not for him. There's something else to it. It's like I'm sharing you, because no matter what happens, if Quell shows up, there's a wedge between us."

Words moved around in my head and I tried so hard to find the right ones to defend my actions, to say the justifiable thing, the appropriate thing to fix this, but I doubted there was anything I could say that could explain it or disprove that he was sharing me. "You aren't sharing me with anyone," I murmured.

He leaned in and kissed me lightly on the lips. It lacked his typical passion and sensuality. It was pensive and disconnected, similar to his voice moments earlier. He kept his lips pressed against mine. It was as if he couldn't detach himself from me. "I won't share you, Sky."

Pressing my hand flat against his cheek, I kissed him. It was warm, gentle, and emotional. "I broke him and forced him into a life he didn't want," I whispered. "That's the only thing I can say. I'm not sure if you can understand it. He was content to die—ready for it."

Ethan's eyes shone with interest and a desire to understand. I wasn't sure if it was for me or because he couldn't function in the unknown. He had to know, even if the reason was twisted or incongruous with the norms of behavior. All facets of a situation needed to be revealed to him. It was his personality, who he was, and it supported his role in the pack. He needed to know and understand, but there wasn't anything more ambiguous than my relationship with Quell. Patiently, he waited for me to gather my words.

"He was ready to die, and I made him feed on me. I made him taste blood, *my* blood. A bond was formed. It was my blood and my decision to save his life that left a disconnect between his old life and his new one. He's seen so much. Functioning in this new life is hard for him. I think he sees himself as a monster—"

"He is a monster," Ethan interjected.

I shook my head. "No, he's a person who was forced to do things he found reprehensible to save other people. He's the furthest thing from a monster, and the fact he still mourns the deaths he caused is a testament to it. He's more than a monster, more than human. He can't forgive himself, but he deserves to." I sighed. "I just want him to stay around until he can do it, so he can at least live a life where he's not burdened by it."

"And if that day never comes?"

"Then, I will let him go."

Ethan nodded, his thumb gently stroking my cheek in silence. I didn't see the understanding I wanted in his eyes. There was still intrigue, concern, and a regretful acceptance, and I wasn't sure exactly what to make of them.

He rose to his feet and started for the bedroom. "He asked you to take his life—I think he's asking you to let go. You're not willing to." And with that, he disappeared into the bedroom.

I showered because I didn't like Demetrius's scent on me any more than Ethan did.

Easing into the bed, I reflected on Ethan's words. Quell was asking for it. I just couldn't. I wished I could. I tried to attribute the disdain I held for most vampires to him, but I couldn't do it because he wasn't just some vampire.

CHAPTER 4

Ethan left early that morning to post bail for Steven. As I waited for him to return, I finally understood what Sebastian was talking about. I was a tightly wound ball of emotions, and everything felt overwhelming. I checked my e-mail, but no one had responded to the number of job applications I'd completed over the week. The pack stipend paid my bills, but once I could no longer pay my membership fees, that money would dwindle. That was just another thing added to my mountain of worries. I tried to focus on Steven, but the situation with Quell constantly entered my mind. Would he give up on me and find someone else to take his life, or would he do it himself?

For several hours, I busied myself working on resumes and sending them out. When Steven stepped into the house behind Ethan, I felt palpable relief. It had only been two days, but it felt much longer. The fact that Steven seemed undisturbed lifted the heavy weight I'd been carrying. I wasn't sure if he was playing it cool for my benefit or if, in fact, it wasn't a big deal.

"Are you staying here today?" I asked hopefully.

Steven grinned. "Yeah." He pulled away from my tight hug. "Today only. My mom will be here tomorrow." His eyes darted in

Ethan's direction, and I knew there was something they weren't telling me.

"What's wrong?" I asked.

"Nothing," Ethan said in a tight voice.

I gave him a look, searching for the truth behind his words, but his stoic appearance made reading him impossible. Standing taller, expressionless, his fingers hooked casually in the pockets of his pants, he didn't look like a man hiding anything, which meant he was hiding a lot.

Steven inhaled. "I need a shower."

He did. But I had a feeling he was using it as an excuse to leave and not be part of the conversation or at least the cover-up Ethan had started.

Steven eased away from me and went to the guest room, which was formerly his room. Once I heard the shower running, I said, "Ethan, there can't be secrets between us."

"There aren't any. I'm trying to figure things out. The bail was set exceptionally high, even for his charges, and they added two charges I didn't expect." He paced the floor and then rubbed his hands over his face. "I'm meeting with Quinn today. He has new information and seems a little nervous about it." He stopped, his gaze focused outside. "*And* there's a lot of activity in this neighborhood."

"What does that have to do with anything?"

He shrugged. "Maybe it's nothing. There's more traffic in this subdivision. Unfamiliar cars are in the neighborhood more often. They don't seem to have a destination. They're just driving through and watching. I'm not sure if it's us they're watching or what."

I had a healthy amount of skepticism. Ethan hadn't always been upfront with me, and he seemed to be holding something back. "And?"

His attention was still outside. "Something is off, magic-wise. Josh feels it, too. But you don't."

I shook my head. Things had been different since the Creed had blocked my magic. I didn't feel Ethan's magic the same way I used to. I felt the difference between him and other were-animals, but I wasn't sure if it was because we were mated or the mark had changed how I interacted with magic. Perhaps I was just feeling its purity now that mine didn't distort it.

I ran my finger over the mark.

"Does it hurt?"

"No, but it burns and tingles sometimes. It's not painful; it just feels odd." I hadn't thought anything of it. An occasional uncomfortable prickle on my skin was far down on the list of things that occupied my attention.

It wasn't until Ethan dropped his stoic mask to display his concern that I considered them more than just peculiar but harmless sensations.

Sebastian and Quinn were already waiting for Ethan, Steven, and me when we arrived at the pack's house. There were stacks of paper and an iPad on Sebastian's desk, and Quinn sat in a chair in the corner, his large laptop open as he scrolled through web pages.

The pensive look on Sebastian's face gave me pause. Ethan stood next to me, eyeing the stacks of paper.

"What's wrong?" Steven finally asked.

Sebastian sucked in a sharp breath and then sorted through the papers on his desk, some highlighted with notes on them. His mask of confidence never broke, but it was overshadowed by the anger he was having trouble containing.

He pushed the papers in Ethan's direction. Ethan's mood changed quickly as he looked over the pages and then handed them to me. I saw highlighted names, and then there were notes indicating *DA, officer, judge, reporter*.

"What does this mean?"

"It means we might be screwed," Quinn said, rising to his feet. He walked over and turned his computer to face us. "People always suspected that supernaturals existed. They range from the true believers to those with a healthy dose of cynicism who are open to their existence but aren't going to dedicate their lives to finding out. And we can't forget the fanboys and fangirls, who are harmless. Then there's a group that calls themselves the Red Blood. They're far from the typical nut jobs chasing down the elusive werewolf or vampire. Their main goal seems to be to expose the otherworld.

"Their group is on the dark web, and it took a lot to find it. They're serious. This is the problem: they now have someone in the otherworld feeding them reliable information."

"And you suspect that person is Dexter?" I ground out. He'd become even more of a pain in the ass. Was he insinuating himself into the group, betraying us just because we'd pissed him off?

"I've been at this for hours, trying to match usernames with their real-life identities." Quinn directed his attention to Ethan. "I know they have the burden of proving it was Steven and you don't think they have enough evidence to do that, but they only have to validate the video and prove it wasn't altered. Your case hinges on the fact it isn't Steven in the video. The people in this group are connected—three are judges—and I'm sure they won't have a problem finding someone to verify that it is unaltered. Image recognition software can then confirm it's Steven."

He pulled up comments and even a thread dedicated to getting Steven convicted.

"Why are they going after Steven—after us? Why not vampires, elves, and witches?"

Sebastian blew out a ragged breath in an effort to calm himself. It didn't work. "We are the easiest to prove. Few of us can control our change when we are called. And we definitely can't hold off answering the call of the moon for months. I can't even do it. If he goes to prison, he will eventually change while in there and prove we exist. It's just a matter of time before the others are exposed."

That made sense. If they outed us, people who changed to animals, then people who wielded magic, or who were immortal, or who used magic to control the weather or create hybrid animals weren't that big of a stretch.

"And they are so dedicated to the cause they're willing to perjure themselves to get the conviction." Quinn presented another group of papers, e-mails from the DA and ADA. He'd crossed a line, but I didn't question how he'd obtained the information and didn't really care. I instinctually wanted to protect my pack.

Ethan looked at the information, and his lips pulled into a tight line. "We need to prepare for damage control."

Steven and Quinn got the hint and quickly left the room. I took the seat where Quinn had sat just moments before with every intention of staying. Sebastian and Ethan stared at me; I stared back.

"Sky," Ethan said quietly and jerked his head at the door. I got up and closed the door to give us privacy.

"With you on the other side of it," Sebastian said coolly. It was every bit a command from my Alpha. I wanted to pull my Beta card but had no idea how it worked. Begrudgingly, I left, seething.

I was torn between following Quinn to his office and staying near Sebastian's with the unlikely hope of hearing through the door.

Instead, I went to the library. Although there wasn't anything in it that could help, it would give me something to do. Make me feel like I was being proactive and give me some sense of control in a situation that was slowly spiraling out of any semblance of it.

Josh barely looked up from the notes he was slumped over when I walked in. There were several open spell books laid out on the table. I greeted him. He regarded me for a short time, then gave his typical wayward smile. His cerulean eyes were as bright as the barbell of a new piercing in his upper ear. I looked at it and him for a while, debating whether I should suggest that he talk to Claudia about the promise he'd made not to get more tattoos. He appeared to be having difficulty keeping it. A tapestry of symbols, signs, and other indelible markings ran up and down his arms, torso, and back. At the rate he was adding them, his body would soon be covered. I suspected piercings might be his loophole in his promise to his godmother.

"Research?" I moved to the table and looked at the paper in front of him, covered with his writing, and the dry-erase board next to him that had more scribbled spells. He was merging spells again.

"Yep" was his terse, evasive response. Josh had recently been inducted as one of the pack's secrets keepers, a responsibility he didn't take lightly. It went against his personality, though. He preferred to be open since he'd been on the other side of the secrets, most of them between him and Ethan. He considered the position nothing more than a pack obligation he was bound to uphold.

I watched him in intrigued silence. He looked up, his gaze traveling down the length of my arm to the binding mark on my wrist.

"You're trying to figure out a way to remove it?"

He nodded. More perceptive than most, he seemed to know what I was thinking. He gave me a faint smile. "It's just in case of emergencies," he said.

"Sebastian asked you to do this?"

He nodded and slid a piece of paper toward me. "I think this might work."

"They said it would take as many witches and as much magic as it did to perform the spell."

"Just the same amount of magic." He sighed heavily enough to rumble his lips. "We boosted your magic with the use of a spell in the Clostra and the Gem of Levage; I assume it can be done again."

"You don't know for sure?"

"The only way to know is to try it." He didn't seem confident.

Again, the mark started to burn, and I wondered if Josh was trying a spell on it.

"Have you tried to remove it yet?"

Focusing on my wrist, which I kept rubbing, he asked, "No, why?"

I explained to him the prickling and burning I'd been experiencing over the past couple of days, and he got the same concerned look on his face as Ethan had.

"What?" I asked.

He shrugged; it could be nothing. But when his fingers came to his mouth and he started to chew on his nail beds, I knew it wasn't nothing.

Pulled deeper into his thoughts, he relaxed back in his chair, studying me. Now that my magic was muted, I felt the variations of his and how heavily it coated the air and inundated my senses. It was a reminder of why Marcia, the former leader of the Creed, had hated him. Not as well-trained as other witches, not even his friend London, he possessed magic in droves. And when he unleashed it violently, he was a resolute force.

"I'm going to remove it." But since we were trying to maintain an alliance with the new leaders of the Creed, removing a magical block they'd seen fit to administer because I'd broken the rules of magic wasn't a good idea. "I'll make sure I can reverse it as well. I think that maintaining our relationship with the Creed is important," he admitted softly. There was a hint of hopefulness in his voice. It was obvious he wanted more than what he'd had before with the witch community and its leaders, the Creed.

Josh's blood alliance with the pack had broken the fragile link he'd once had and solidified his position as an outsider in the witch community. Often, his loyalty was in question, rightfully so, because he wouldn't choose anyone over Ethan. The pack required unyielding fealty, and I assumed the Creed did, too. He couldn't manage both.

I plopped down in another chair at the table, looking over the spell, as amazed as I was the first time he'd found one to undo the curse that had been inflicted on the pack.

"You'd be dangerous if you actually finished magic school," I teased.

He winked. "I like to think I'm dangerous now."

"You do okay. Sometimes you can be impressive, but I don't want it to go to your head." I winked back, flashing him a grin.

"Granted, I can't do the things my brother does. And maybe I won't ever reach his level. Like you, Ethan has access to very unique magic. You two are quite the anomalies."

I swallowed the sigh and attempted to do the same with the guilt that came along with keeping secrets. I hated them, and while Ethan didn't have a problem with the many secrets that surrounded his very existence, and to an extent, Josh's, I did.

"Or maybe if you'd paid more attention to Mom's teachings, I wouldn't seem like such an anomaly for being able to perform and recall simple spells," Ethan said at the door. I slid over to a bookshelf and pretended to look for a book because my look of incredulity was going to give things away. Ethan could detect a lie with ease by listening to physiological changes, even minor ones like changes in respiration and speech cadence. Feeling his weighted gaze on me, I looked at him, keeping my back to Josh. *Tell him*, I mouthed.

Giving me a stern stare, Ethan barely moved into his answer. *No*.

Now, I mouthed again.

He continued to look at me, his obstinate appearance unchanged. I moved to him, just inches away, and then I leaned in, my lips pressed against the edge of his jaw. It looked like I was kissing him, but instead, I said, "Tell him or I will." My voice was so low only Ethan could hear me. One of the benefits of being a were-animal.

His dark chuckle drifted through the room. Josh squinted, and his attention bounced between the two of us, but we only held his interest for a few seconds before he returned to his notes. "There are plenty of rooms in this house. Pick one," he suggested, exasperated. "Between you two and Kelly and Gavin, I've had more than an eyeful of the mating habits of were-animals. At least I haven't caught you all in the act in *my* library."

I doubted he was the only one who'd seen Kelly, the pack's nurse, and Gavin. They might not have mated, but since he'd changed her a couple of weeks ago, their peculiar friendship had become more intimate, and neither one was shy about displaying it.

I leaned in closer to Ethan and whispered, "Either you tell him, or I will."

With a taunting half-smile, he grazed his lips against my cheek as he spoke. "No, you won't. You made a promise, and you would never break a promise." It was the same thing he'd reminded me of months before.

His self-assured taunt grated at my defiance. *He's a smug bastard.*

"You're an ass," I said low enough for our ears only.

Baring his teeth, he said, "I know." He took a perverse pride in the title.

I wanted to tell Josh everything. Pulling my hand away from Ethan's, I was reluctant to let him lead me out of the library. A battle of wills plagued our relationship; I'd acquiesced earlier, and it was difficult to do it again.

"Sky," he coaxed, quietly, extending his hand to me. After several moments of consideration, I took it and let his fingers link with mine as he led me from the room.

"I can't tell him the truth," he said, his voice heavy with apprehension. He'd dropped the arrogance and was genuinely concerned.

"Ethan, I understand. You think he will be hurt. Whatever he's speculating about you and your magical ability is probably a lot worse than what it is. You saved his life. Right now, with everything that's going on, do you think keeping him in the dark is the best thing?"

"My mother chose him over me." His tone dropped, low and sorrowful. A dark shadow cast over his face, and I knew he was thinking of the awful decision his mother had had to make by choosing which son she would allow to be cursed with death on their eighteenth birthday as a penalty for her performing a forbidden spell. Her decision to choose Josh, to give them time to nullify the curse, was a hard burden to bear, but it wasn't Ethan's fault. He had nothing to atone for. It was the most logical decision to pick the youngest child. Guilt and logic never seemed to run in the same circles. I saw it a lot in Sebastian and Ethan. They were the fixers. They kept the pack and its members safe, and it came with a responsibility I couldn't understand.

When it came to the pack and how to handle its affairs, Ethan was a strategist and could be cruelly objective. When it came to Josh, he was an emotional mess, and it was difficult for him to see things clearly. I needed to be his eyes, the clarity in his clouded judgment.

"It wasn't because she loved him less, Ethan. It was so you could have time to find a way to block the curse. And you did. You saved his life. That's not something you need to hide." It had taken him hosting a Faerie, who could provide him with enough power to use the Vitae, a protected object, to circumvent it.

"Tell him," I urged. "Life will be a lot simpler without you spending so much time trying to shield him from the truth and pain. You can't anymore."

I took the extended time he took to think about it as a good sign. The many times he ran his fingers through his hair was an even better one. His hair was mussed and his eyes were a clearer blue, the steely gray of his wolf absent. It was one of the few times he appeared solely man. A vulnerable man. "I have a feeling if I don't, this topic will dominate most of our conversations."

"See how well you know me?" I said with a smirk.

He had barely moved into the nod when he took my hand and started for the front door—the opposite direction from where his brother was. I dug my heels in. "Wrong way, Ethan."

"Not now."

He knew me well, and I knew him, too. My many interactions with him were at the root of my cynicism.

"Then when? When will you do it?" He'd agreed to do it but hadn't given a time—his defense for the next time I broached the topic.

He shrugged, his eyes darkening with a glint of gray, a clear sign he wanted the subject dropped. "When it's a good time," he said, casting me a defiant look.

The weight of our collective stubbornness thickened the air.

"Okay." I raised my voice to call out, "Josh!"

He didn't answer immediately. Eventually, he poked his head out of the library. "What do you need?" he asked.

I kept a steady eye on Ethan, whose eyes were now drowned in deep gray, without a hint of blue. That wasn't going to deter me. This was important. We didn't have time for secrets, especially not this one. His secret about being a dark elf had placed a wall between him and his brother. This could destroy their relationship.

"Ethan wants to know if he can have brunch with you tomorrow. He really needs to talk to you." I looked over my shoulder to find Josh's brow furrowed in curiosity.

"About what?"

I wasn't sure who he'd directed his question to, but Ethan couldn't answer because his lips were pulled into a rigid line. He couldn't do anything other than growl, and a deep rumble emanated from his chest.

"Ethan," I whispered. He closed his eyes and pulled in a slow breath, and when he opened them, he cut a sharp look in my direction.

Leaning in, I said, "That look doesn't really work on me."

Again, Ethan and I found ourselves in the awkward position of balancing our relationship with his position in the pack. Out of principle, he didn't like being told what to do and coercion made him more resistant. I stood my ground on this and wouldn't waver. I'd compromised a lot in our relationship, but this was something I couldn't give in on. I hated the secrets between them. I hated secrets in general.

Ethan ran his hands along his face as if he were rubbing a beard, but his face was clean-shaven. "You seem to have a lot of questions about the things that have occurred over the past few months, and I want to clear them up for you. Especially the ones you have about me being able to perform spells you can't and how I can break protective fields."

Josh's curiosity was piqued. His lips kinked into a little grin. "Why wait until tomorrow? I'm free now and I'm pretty hungry. We can have a late lunch."

I was looking up at the face of a Faerie-hosting, very upset wolf. I returned his snarl with a cloying smile. I could hear Ethan's heart beating faster than it ever had, and mine responded with a slight uptick. Anxiety. I didn't think *he* was capable of it.

I said his name softly and slipped my hands over his. In a low voice, for his ears only, I asked, "Are you okay?"

The tension relaxed some, but he was noticeably uncomfortable. Ethan lived in the shadows and was ruled by secrets. They were so entwined in what and who he was that he had to feel raw and exposed. This was chipping away at what he had become to protect the pack and his brother. It took a few moments before his fingers laced through mine.

His voice was as soft as mine and barely audible to anyone not immediately next to us. "I'm fine." Sighing heavily, he looked at Josh. "Now is fine."

Josh swiftly moved toward the front door and waited for Ethan to join him.

Reading over Josh's notes reminded me just how talented a witch he was. I was reduced to relying heavily on Google to translate the Latin. It appeared he was close to a solution or rather had narrowed down the many spells he'd come up with. It wasn't surprising that he'd left the one Clostra out. It was pretty harmless since we didn't have the other two. We'd had to give them to the witches as a condition of their helping us with a curse. First, we'd had to retrieve the Clostra from the indomitable Samuel, who was dedicated to ridding the world of magic. In the end, the Clostra had simply switched from his possession to theirs. I frowned when I opened the volume in front of me and discovered the pages were blank. The spells weren't revealing themselves to me—I couldn't read it anymore.

"You can't read them, can you?" Steven asked, sitting on the table and looking down at the blank pages.

I shook my head; that bothered me more than anything. My ability to use them had been an advantage for the pack so many times.

He chewed on his lips and moved his attention to the books on the shelves and stacked on the table. "This is a mess, isn't it?" he said in a constricted voice. He was talking about more than just my inability to read the Clostra. He had the same tone I'd heard various members use when they'd carried the burden of something that had harmed the pack or one of its protected.

"Didn't you do what you were instructed to do?" I asked.

"I should have waited until they changed or maybe approached them at their homes." He'd had time to compose several alternative scenarios. His emerald eyes were dull, and he wore a rigid frown. Worry had achieved something he'd been struggling to do for years: it had aged him. Despair hung on every note of his words.

"I doubt any of those alternatives would have ended with a different result. Let's put the blame where it belongs. They had the option to be lone wolves or join us. They weren't even working on their own—they were working for Dexter. Make no mistake, he knows what he's doing," I assured him.

"Do you think we're giving him too much credit? Is he really diabolical and Machiavellian or just a guy stumbling into some success and becoming a pain in our ass?"

"Don't underestimate him." I frowned as I remembered the state of the basement where he'd been experimenting on people and were-animals for a way to nullify our immunity to magic. "Doing so will be to our detriment."

He considered it. "My mother isn't dealing with this well. It's causing problems between her and Sebastian. They rarely disagree, and she never challenges him. They are on the phone now and ..."

"It's expected, Steven. She's as protective of you as you are of her. I'm sure Sebastian realizes it's not the Southern Alpha challenging him, but a mother."

"I know. I just don't want to be the reason there's a strain on their relationship." Sebastian and Joan's interactions were peculiar. He was far more lenient with her than the other Alphas, and she was afforded courtesies the others weren't.

"What's the deal with Joan and Sebastian?" I asked. "They seem closer than other Alphas are."

He shrugged. "I'm not sure. You should ask them." He'd given me the same stock response that Josh, Ethan, and Winter had. It wasn't as if the pack was above petty gossip—there was plenty swarming around—but when it came to talking about Sebastian and Joan, I was referred to them, as if I would get an answer from either one. Joan gave information far more freely than Sebastian, but she also didn't mind pulling from the Alpha playbook, responding with a look of cool examination and a breath of incredulity. It didn't encourage more questioning when they simply responded with, "Is there a reason that information is important to you?"

"Because I'm nosy as hell" wasn't an answer that would get a reply.

I looked at my phone again, frowning. Not just at the fact that Ethan hadn't returned any of my text messages, but also because my mark had started to prickle, a light burning that flared and disappeared.

"What's wrong?" Steven asked.

"Nothing."

"Should I point out which one changed: your heart rate, the cadence of voice, or the number of times you've blinked your eyes?"

"Sure, and I can point out what a freak that makes you. You all can continue with your party tricks, but it doesn't make it any less weird," I said pointedly.

He laughed. "You do it, too, but for some odd reason you lower your head and blink, keeping count with each beat. Now that's weird."

I'd never get used to how observant they were. Predators to the core, they often noticed things that others didn't. Everyone else was reduced to nothing more than prey and studied and watched as such.

"Are you going to tell me what's wrong?" he asked softly, taking a book off the table and absently thumbing through it, occasionally looking down at the pages.

I shook my head. "I don't want to talk about it right now."

With a great deal of reluctance, he nodded. There were few secrets between us, and I didn't want this to be one, but I needed time.

~

Ethan and Josh had been together for nearly four hours. Ethan had a lot of secrets, but no matter what circuitous route he'd taken to explain them to Josh, it shouldn't have consumed that much time.

Ignoring the rising uneasiness was getting more difficult. Maybe I was wrong. Ethan knew Josh better than I did. There was probably a reason for him not telling his brother, and I'd missed it. I'd pulled at the threads of the relationship and might have damaged it. I frowned.

"I think I screwed up," I whispered, looking up from the page I'd been looking at for over an hour, unable to concentrate because I was focused on Ethan and Josh.

Steven pushed his book forward and relaxed back in his chair as he clasped his hands in front of his stomach, giving me his undivided attention.

"There are things about Ethan I felt he needed to share with Josh, and I pushed him to do it. I think that was a mistake."

"Does it have anything to do with killing Ethos?"

My eyes widened. "You saw that, too?"

Steven gave me an incredulous look. His eyes flickered with bemused disbelief. "Sky, we all saw it. We tend to be observant. No one knows the specifics, but there's something different about Ethan. It's one of those things we all notice but don't talk about. I figure he has a reason for not telling us. Maybe keeping us in the dark is his way of protecting us."

It was hard to accept the idea that sometimes darkness was the safest place. It didn't matter that many in the pack believed it; I thought the darkness made us vulnerable. I found comfort in the fact that Steven was okay with being in the dark, so I didn't elaborate on the topic of Ethan and Josh's conversation.

He leaned forward and patted my hand gently. When he left it there, I felt the comfort I desperately needed. "I've seen Ethan punch Josh in the face, not once but twice. Josh has used magic to throw Ethan through a wall. Take a look at the wall in the den near the door. You have to look hard, but you can see where it was repaired. Then there was the time Josh pinned Ethan to the wall for nearly an hour, which led to Ethan punching him in the face a second time. If their relationship can survive that, I'm sure it can survive a few secrets."

Steven's confidence eased my anxiety.

I covered his hand with my free hand and gave it a little squeeze. He always made things better. I smiled when he didn't try to move it. We were still in the same position when Ethan walked into the library.

"Are you ready to go home?" he asked. His voice and expression were level, and his uncharacteristically mild demeanor caused Steven to sit up straighter and watch him with a prey's unease. His eyes tracked Ethan as he moved closer.

"How was lunch?" I asked.

He responded tersely—"Fine"—then repeated his question, "Are you ready to go home?"

I nodded and straightened everything on the table, putting it back the way I'd found it. It ended up a lot neater than it had been originally.

We were heading out the door when Ethan stopped and looked over his shoulder at Steven, who hadn't moved. "Are you coming?"

"No, I need to talk to Sebastian. I'll get a ride. I'll catch you all later." It was doubtful he had anything pressing to talk to Sebastian about, but it was never difficult to detect Ethan's emotions—unless he worked to hide them. Ethan was working so hard that Steven knew something was up.

Most of the drive home was spent in silence. I wondered why Josh had gone straight home instead of coming back to the library. Was that a good or bad sign?

Ethan's indiscernible look gave me no feedback. A four-hour

lunch where Ethan had disclosed secrets he'd kept from his brother for years. The world as Josh knew it had changed; Ethan had admitted that he'd colluded with Sebastian, and even Claudia, to keep secrets from him. How would anyone respond to that? After several furtive glances at him, my curiosity had sharpened to a blade and suppressing it was impossible.

"How did it go?"

"I'm going to give you the same answer I gave you twenty minutes ago. It hasn't changed. Lunch was fine."

"Just *fine*. That's not an answer, Ethan."

His laughter filled the space as he enjoyed my unsated curiosity. Ethan was having just as difficult a time dealing with his role as my Beta as he was with being my mate. As a member of his pack, I should have been more biddable. He was used to, and expected, compliance from his pack members. But anyone who'd dated Chris couldn't have become accustomed to acquiescence from a lover. Their tumultuous relationship had been nothing but challenging. It had been dysfunctional to the core, and they seemed to have found an odd comfort in it. Our relationship was different—or I thought it was—but being part of the pack and dating Ethan were incompatible. Seeing his fading smile, the attention he paid to the road as he drove—something he never did—and the times he clenched his lips between his teeth in thought eased my nagging concerns. He had them, too; we were bonded by our mutual struggle and that offered me some comfort. But that wasn't an excuse for him acting like a Betahole.

"That is an answer, even if it's not the one you want. Am I correct?" he offered. His jaw was set. His lips quirked into a smile, but he refused to commit.

"Ethan, how did it go? I want specifics."

"More specifically, it was fine. I talked, he listened, and we had lunch."

My cheeks burned with anger; this was a less than subtle act of defiance, censure for my having coerced the situation into my timeframe and not his.

"Ethan!"

He laughed, amusement coursing over the planes of his face. He took his eyes off the road to look at me. He obviously found a great deal of pleasure in my frustration. More than what I'd found earlier when I'd gotten him to commit to telling his brother. Ethan had a patent on being a stubborn wolf, and at the moment, it was on display.

"It went fine, Sky. He was upset and rightfully so. But"—his smile broadened—"he took it well. He'll be okay. We are fine." There was palpable relief in his voice. He patted me on the thigh and kept his hand there, where he continued to caress it. After several moments, he gave in to his relief.

"I told you so" people were annoying, and I prided myself on never having been one—until now. If there had been enough room in the car, I might have done an "I told you so" dance. I settled for fixing him with a smirk.

"So," I started off slowly, "I was right, and this is a good thing."

He shrugged. "I'm not sure. I was planning on doing it anyway."

Did he really say that with a straight face?

"What? When were you planning to tell him? On your deathbed?"

Another shrug as he bit back his own smirk. "Now we will never know because you intervened. Quite unfortunate, isn't it?"

My mouth hung open for several long moments before I snapped it shut. Ethan was enjoying the situation too much, and I was obstinate enough not to give him the satisfaction.

CHAPTER 5

Ethan was still wearing his smug look from the night before as he prepared breakfast. Steven hadn't returned to the house, texting that he'd be back that night. I assumed he wanted to give us time to discuss things without an audience.

Under Ethan's watchful gaze, I ate my stack of pancakes, stopping occasionally to take a bite of my steak or snag a few pieces of fruit from the salad. Ethan liked to cook, which worked out well because I hated it. I took the meal as his show of appreciation for my intervening with him and Josh. Contrary to what he believed, I thought he was grateful for my unsolicited intervention.

He picked up a chunk of mango and chewed it thoughtfully before asking, "What do you have going on today besides peppering me with questions about the trial?"

"Well, I figure that will probably take up a great deal of my time." I grinned, but flashes of the numbers in my bank account reminded me of more pressing things. "I guess I need to spend the day sending out more resumes. I haven't heard back from anyone."

I tried to shrug off the heaviness of my concerns. I needed a job. My last employer had had every right to fire me because I'd let pack business interfere with my job. It was the best job I'd ever had, and I'd considered emailing my ex-employer to ask if she would reconsider. But after considering my performance over the past year, I'd realized if I were in her position I would never rehire an employee like me. The four basic form letter rejections I'd received just compounded my feeling of bleakness.

A smile curled Ethan's lips. "Josh is looking for an assistant. You can work for him."

"I would love to work for Josh if I actually knew what he did for a living. I haven't seen him do anything but flirt with pretty women, dance with pretty women, drink with pretty people, and host salacious events for pretty people. Does he really need help doing that?"

"You know he does more than that," Ethan asserted.

"How would I know? I haven't seen him do anything *but* that."

"Give it a try. If you don't like it, quit."

Working with Josh would likely be fun. Probably more fun than I could handle, and everything else in my life revolved around the pack. I wanted a little slice of it to be different and just my own. If I took a job with Josh, in a pack-owned business, 100 percent of my life would revolve around them. I was embarrassed that I always had that knot in my chest, that apprehension that I was just one event away from leaving. It was silly, and I was past that—or at least I thought I was. But the feeling resurfaced more often than I liked to admit, that overwhelming claustrophobic feeling of having been dropped into a world I was inept at navigating. I'd been thrust into a clandestine land that was constantly unraveling, each event more unsettling and portentous than the last. Among those things was my mate hosting a spirit shade who was a dangerous and powerful Faerie.

"Your expenses can't be that much. I can cover them. Once you move in with me, your only expense will be your car."

I didn't respond. Rendered silent by his comment, my mind went into hyperdrive.

Expenses? Live with you? What?

When he brought it up before, I knew we would have to address it at some point; but I didn't think it would be soon. My eyes widened, and it took me a while to realize my mouth had dropped open and I'd lost the words I wanted to say. "W-what?" I stammered.

He looked around my house, which could fit inside his house with room to spare. "I don't think it's a good idea for me to move in here. Your neighbors find me inconvenient."

"They aren't finding *you* inconvenient. It's your clothing-optional take on life that bothers them. We put on clothes before we go to our car to unload groceries. We are clothes-type people —like the rest of society—while you believe they are optional." I gave his boxers-only attire a disparaging look. If I thought he planned on dressing, it wouldn't have bothered me as much, but I knew from experience he was perfectly fine going for a run around the neighborhood that way.

"I don't think they all mind." I rolled my eyes. Humility, along with modesty, were things Ethan lacked.

I forced myself to smile. It was stiff and mirthless as I tried to wrap my head around the idea of living with him. I moved my attention to the window behind him, focusing on the scenery: the trees I wouldn't see anymore, David's house, nosy Mrs. Rykes, who, for an elderly woman, hadn't lost interest in the male form as evidenced by the attention she paid to Steven and now Ethan. This was my home.

He seemed quietly concerned and asked, "What exactly did you think would happen after we mated, Sky?"

I clearly hadn't thought that far ahead and bit back my answer. *Sex, dating, and occasionally spending the night together.* I decided on a half-truth. "I hadn't thought about it much."

His brow furrowed, and I tried not to buckle under the weight of his gaze. "That's not the truth," he said in a sobering, low voice. "I want the truth, Sky."

"That *is* the truth. Or at least part of it. I really haven't thought about it. Part of me felt like things would just stay the same."

"But things aren't the same. They're different. Very different." He leaned in closer and lightly trailed a finger along my arm. He looked concerned. "If you don't tell me the problem, I can't fix it."

"The problem is me, and I don't need fixing. Ethan, this is a lot. *You* are a lot." I sucked in a ragged breath, trying to keep my composure; it didn't work. "Ethan, I love you, but—"

His expression changed, and his gaze intensified.

"What's wrong?" I asked. Something had changed, and I couldn't put my finger on it. He seemed muted and perplexed, unsure. Nothing like the Ethan I'd grown accustomed to.

"This is the first time you've said you love me."

Immediately, my thoughts went to the first time he'd said it to me. I'd been so thrown by it, shocked by his reluctant admission, that I'd never thought to say it back. I'd assumed he knew. I never considered that he'd actually want to hear it. I thought by becoming his mate it was implied. Now I imagined how he felt about things. There was Quell, and now I was resisting moving in with him. I wished conceding to the idea was easier.

"I do, and you have to know that. But you also have to know this is all new to me, and Ethan, you are ..." I paused, searching for the right word to describe Ethan, his very existence, his being. To convey that he was primal, sexy, and overwhelming; that the symbiotic relationship he had with his wolf always radiated an implied danger; that a person needed to proceed with caution around him. I couldn't silence my instincts to do just that—proceed with caution. He was mine, but that didn't make what and who he was any less intense. I finally continued with the only description that seemed apropos. "Intense. Ethan, you are intense, and it's fine when I get you in small doses. But to live with you and be around you all the time would be hard. We're still figuring out our relationship within the pack and your role as Beta. You don't realize that your position as Beta shouldn't extend to our relationship."

It wasn't Ethan's position as Beta that was suffocating me; it was Ethan. He was used to taking command in his relationships. He was arrant, powerfully alluring, and dominant.

He looked away from me and asked, "Do you think you've made a mistake?"

The conversation was going in a direction I hadn't expected. Less than twenty minutes ago, we'd been discussing my employment prospects and enjoying the breakfast he'd prepared. Now we were discussing me moving in with him.

"I'll move in with you."

"That's not the question I asked you, Sky. Do you think you made a mistake?" he asked, flat and even as if he were negotiating a business deal.

I shook my head but couldn't answer.

He swallowed loud enough for me to hear. Or perhaps it wasn't any louder than usual but just seemed that way because everything had reached a higher level. The connection between us had been pulled and tugged until it felt fragile and delicate—a tendril threatening to break. We were in a liminal state, and the wrong word or comment could break us apart. I hated everything about it.

"I've never heard of it before, but I'm sure our situation isn't that abnormal. I'm sure the bond can be broken," he suggested quietly as if he didn't want me to hear him. I searched his face, waiting for him to look at me, but he didn't.

"I don't want that."

"Are you sure?" he asked doubtfully, as if he'd heard the change in my voice, a hesitation, or maybe even detected my lack of confidence.

"Of course," I said firmly.

He nodded, but his expression didn't change. He forced out,

"Okay. You stay here as long as you feel comfortable and then move in when you're ready."

He rose and started to clear away the dishes. Heavy silence remained even after he'd left under the pretense of needing to speak with Quinn and Sebastian. I wasn't foolish or naïve enough to believe that was the case.

~

I sat next to Steven on the sofa, and we slipped into our comfortable routine. He crunched on hot-sauce-covered dill pickle chips while I crinkled my nose at the smell and frowned each time he offered me his concoction. With the growing changes in my life, Steven was the constant I needed.

"This is awful," he said, lowering the volume on the television before facing me. "Are we going to talk about it, or am I going to have to ignore your pounding heartbeat for the rest of the movie? If it's the latter, I need to turn the volume up because it's distracting."

It was approaching ten in the evening. Ethan had called earlier to tell me he was going to be late. It had sounded like talking to me was obligatory, a remnant of our uncomfortable conversation. As I sat next to Steven, I attempted to push it aside, to focus on the movie and allow it to be a much-needed distraction.

"I miss this," I said because it was simpler to talk about than what had transpired that morning.

Steven's brows arched, and his lips twisted in thought. "So, your breathing is ragged, you're distracted, and you look like you just witnessed a puppy being abused because you miss watching bad movies with me?" he asked in disbelief.

I nodded. "I miss the simplicity of us. Our relationship isn't complicated."

"What? We are the most complicated thing in this pack. Do you know how many meetings and 'counsels'"—he put air quotes on "counsels"—"I've endured because of us? Ethan wasn't particularly happy with me moving in here in the first place, and this was before you two were mated or romantically involved. No one really understood it. It might have been easy for us, but for the pack, Ethan, and Sebastian, it was anything but simple."

"Why am I just hearing about this?"

He shrugged. "It wouldn't have changed anything. I wanted to be here, and you didn't mind it."

"Is it terrible that I still want you here?"

"I wouldn't say it's terrible, but it's pretty damn weird. What's the problem? What are you running from?"

"Nothing. Ethan wants me to move in with him."

He made a face and shook his head. His voice barely masked his incredulity when he demanded, "What did you expect would happen once you and Ethan mated? You'd live separately, have date nights, have the occasional conjugal visit, and resume your lives as if you were just buddies?"

I met his mocking gaze. His eyes widened and flashed with amusement. *Well, when you put it that way, it sounds stupid.* I opened my mouth to say that, only to let out a bloodcurdling scream. My arm was on fire; it felt like someone was stripping the flesh off it. Pain caused tears to well in my eyes. I fell to the floor, grabbing my aching arm and trying to soothe it. The pain intensified and concentrated in the mark the witches had placed there to restrict the Faerie magic—to stop Maya, the spirit shade I hosted.

"Sky!" Steven shouted, but my howls of pain nearly drowned him out. "Change!" he instructed.

I rolled onto my hands and knees, willing my body to accept its wolf form, but I couldn't do it. Steven pressed his hands against me. He was trying to help me to change. My phone buzzed and then Steven's. Reluctant to answer it, he craned his neck to see the number and then quickly grabbed it.

"Ethan. Something—"

I clenched my teeth together, biting back another scream, the burning and ripping feeling persisting.

"I can't change her. How close are you? Okay. Hurry."

An aura of magic added to the pain. It coated my tongue and weighed on me like a shawl Then coolness wrapped around me, and the pain subsided. Fatigued, I felt like I'd engaged in a battle and lost. Before I gave in to the darkness that came over me, I glanced at my arm. It no longer bore the witches' mark. I slipped into my wolf form, finding comfort in it. I felt Maya's presence but not the magic.

I closed my eyes and drifted to sleep.

I awoke with Ethan sitting next to me, his hands gently gliding across my fur. Feeling exhausted, I considered staying in my wolf form.

"Sky, can you change?" he asked in a steady voice. There was a hint of something else there: worry.

It took longer than usual, but I shifted and sat up. He handed me a blanket. I wrapped it around me as I looked around at the people in the room: Ariel, Josh, Sebastian, and Steven. Everyone looked concerned except for Ariel, whose eyes remained fixed on the place on my arm where the mark had been. I inhaled magic-drenched air—Ariel's, Josh's, and mine. Ariel continued to scrutinize me, and the look she gave me was filled with tightly woven cynicism and distrust. I understood where it was coming from. Unexplained things happened in this pack, and this had been added to the list.

Ariel's demeanor and dress reminded me of Claudia's. She had a preference for white; I suspected she liked the dramatic appeal since the other members of the Creed were often uniformed in black. Now she had on all black. A simple, fitted black shirt, black slacks, and black heeled boots. The only jewelry she wore was a ring that looked like the oddly shaped medallion Josh had tossed at Marcia's feet when he'd denounced her and her followers. Her dark brown hair was tucked behind her ears, giving a full view of her sharp, assessing brown eyes. The slight glow of her tawny skin dulled the intensity of her resting scowl. When she finally spoke, her voice was heavy with skepticism and wariness. She moved toward me and examined my wrist. "Can you do magic?"

I gave a little magical push and erected a protective field around me, which I quickly dropped. She studied me for a moment and then shifted her gaze to Josh. "To answer your question from earlier, no, we had nothing to do with this."

She moved back. Her subsequent silence revealed her apprehension about the pack, and about me, although she seemed to make a great effort to mask it. I suspected she'd operated under the belief that the rumors about the Midwest Pack were exaggerated tales. We were cloaked in secrecy and often the center of unusual things. The pragmatist in her wanted to maintain the alliance with us, it shone in her eyes, but an intrinsic need to run from danger made it difficult for her.

"I appreciate you calling me about this." The former gentle cadence and soft lilt of her voice were gone, replaced by something flat and professionally breezy. She turned to face Sebastian, easing the scowl off her face and replacing it with a gentle smile. "I guess this is just another one of those unique things that seem to happen to your pack and your pack only." She reluctantly accepted that Sebastian probably wouldn't elaborate.

Sebastian was stolid before giving a small smile that matched hers. "We have our share of oddities. Rest assured, if one affects the witches, you will be the first to know."

Their smiles couldn't have been any faker if they'd been on mannequins. "Of course," she said quietly and then leaned into him, her voice dropping even lower but not enough to be inaudible. "Unless it will affect your pack. Then it will go into the vault of secrets like most things."

She didn't bother to wait for a refutation because anyone who knew Sebastian or anything about him knew he wouldn't give one. There was truth to her statement. Sebastian's eyes displayed a combination of amusement and interest as they followed her to the door.

"Ariel, I am committed to this alliance. I will protect my pack, but I will also make sure no harm befalls the witches," he offered.

She nodded but didn't respond because she knew the former was the most important. She gave Sebastian another look over her shoulder before leaving.

"Josh?" Ethan focused on his brother but stayed at my side. He was having difficulty hiding his uneasiness, and Josh didn't put any effort into masking his. Gnawing at his nail bed, something he did when he was nervous, Josh paced.

"Did you feel anything?" he asked me.

"Besides the excruciating pain?" I shivered, remembering it. "No." But I felt something at that moment. Magic, lots of it, rampaging through my body as if days' worth of it were stored in me and needed a release. I extended my fingers and nudged the chair over, then easily lifted it and let it hover in midair. Then I eased it back down. A simple parlor trick that relieved the heaviness in me. I couldn't deny what was happening: Maya had awakened and needed to feel her magic. It felt encumbered, fettered to her, and I was again forced to keep her at bay.

"You need to find out what happened and who did this to me."

"I know." Josh's latent worry reflected how I felt. And despite their being better at hiding it, it was obvious Ethan and Sebastian were concerned as well. Who wanted Maya unrestricted and why? And the most pressing question: who had the type of magic to remove the mark from a distance?

Several hours had passed since the mark was removed, and I found myself under Ethan's and Steven's heavy stares. I was the freak at the table again. The anomaly. The wolf they couldn't figure out.

Steven and I had long since stopped trying to watch our movie because Ethan's excessive questioning kept interrupting it. On my third trip to the kitchen under their constant surveillance, I stopped and spun on my heel.

"What?"

"How do you feel?" Ethan asked.

"Hungry. The same way I felt when you asked me a half an hour ago." I was more than hungry; I was famished. I'd always had a healthy appetite, but now I had a hunger I couldn't satisfy.

He nodded. I wouldn't get much out of him. As usual, his answers were terse and he provided information sparingly. Pulling it out of him was a task I didn't want to deal with. I directed my attention to Steven. When our eyes met, I entreated, "What's wrong?"

Silence swelled, and Steven seemed reluctant to answer. I wasn't sure if he'd been sworn to secrecy or didn't feel it was his place to disclose whatever was going on, but his clenched jaw relaxed as he said, "No one could change you back to human. No one." He might have been trying to look relaxed, but his voice was laden with concern as he evaluated me. He ushered the scowl off his face and replaced it with a placid smile.

Included in "no one" were Sebastian and Ethan. I brushed it off with a shrug. "If it's any consolation, I couldn't change myself back, either."

My pettiness reared its head as Ethan leaned in, waiting for me to continue. I wanted so desperately to be miserly with my information and make him work for every morsel of it. It just wasn't in me to keep it up—it was more exhausting to tap-dance around information and phrase things so they were nothing more than lies of omission. "I struggled to turn back." *Struggle* didn't seem like the appropriate word. An internal battle had raged in me. Maya had desperately wanted to claim my body, and my wolf had fought to protect me and retain its form, where Maya had the least control. Just thinking about it made me want to slip into my wolf to give myself a reprieve from the magic pulsing through me. I considered performing magic, but fear lingered. She'd used me, my words, against my pack; I wouldn't let her have an opportunity to do it again.

"What do you mean 'struggle'?" Ethan pried.

"My wolf was trying to protect me and keep me in that form," I admitted. "Now I feel like I have too much magic." Sucking in a breath, I said, "I'm afraid to do strong magic because of what happened before with Maya and the curse."

Ethan frowned. "Are you losing control?"

I blinked back tears and pushed the words through my teeth. "Yes."

Silence loomed for several minutes, and I found calm in Ethan's steady heartbeat, his unwavering strength, his serene voice.

"It will get easier. You have to master her. You're her host, not the other way around. Continue to treat her as such—a spirit shade, a source of magic to be used when *you* need her. Tap into your wolf's strength—it will help you." I'd noticed that he used magic sparingly; he'd clearly figured out the problem early on. He fully gave in to his wolf so he'd have the resolve to control his spirit shade. I'd somehow known that would be my only choice. I'd kept my wolf at bay for so long I didn't know how to be one with her—but I had to.

"We can have the witches replace the mark, but I have a feeling it will be removed again. We need to find out who wants it gone and why."

"I don't want it replaced," I said with a lot more confidence than I felt. I closed my eyes, took a deep breath, and reconciled myself to what needed to be done for me to survive. "I've got this."

CHAPTER 6

Three days later, Josh wasn't any closer to finding an answer, and he wore the failure poorly. I'd spent many hours watching him as he moved between his notes, the books on the table, and his laptop like a caffeine-addled rabbit. I considered suggesting he take a break, but I knew it would fall on deaf ears. At the rate he was going, by the time I returned to the pack's house, he would probably have crashed and fallen asleep on the desk. If not, Dr. Jeremy was keeping a cautious eye on him and wasn't above taking matters into his hands and sedating him.

Josh's words of caution to be careful stayed with me as I walked into the courthouse alongside Steven. They'd carried a note of worry and fear, and he'd given me a haunted look as if he'd discovered something troubling. Or maybe uneasiness plagued him about the level of magic it took to remove a spell cast by eight powerful witches.

I looked down at my unmarked arm again, just as cameras flashed. My hand shot up to hide my face. Ethan managed to look intimidating in his dark suit; the platinum-colored silk tie matched the cool gunmetal glare he shot anyone who walked alongside us attempting to film Steven. I thought people would have lost interest in the "angel face" killer, but apparently, they were waiting for the actual trial to start. The video continued to be available on the Web despite our efforts to scrub it. It was still being sensationalized, likely the handiwork of Dexter. Clips had played on the news just the day before.

Steven kept his hair longer, which made him look even more cherubic. He didn't look like he could perform an act of malice of any kind, let alone a murder. His three-piece brown suit complemented his ruddy cheeks, which flushed even more as people shouted questions at him. His large green eyes tracked the people standing outside the courtroom, taking pictures, videotaping him, and peppering him with questions. He remained silent and allowed Ethan to respond confidently that Steven was innocent. Even the reporters seemed unconvinced that Steven was guilty of the charges.

I'd settled for dark blue slacks and a long-sleeved pearl-colored shirt, and I'd wrangled my curly tresses into a sleek bun. When I'd looked in the mirror, I'd appeared older, and the frigid frown I wore couldn't be helping. Nor could the pallor of my face, which even blush couldn't counter. The case worried me as much as Josh's dire warning. Although Ethan was sure the judge wouldn't accept his motion to dismiss, I hoped he would, based on the lack of evidence. The prosecutor had no prints or evidence that Steven had been at the site of the murders, leaving them with a leaked video that had been modified and an anonymous eyewitness to the crimes. Ethan suspected, however, that they would present testimony from members of the Red Blood, who were willing to do anything to expose us, including committing perjury. Even Ethan's unwavering confidence wasn't enough to keep my fear that this could end badly for Steven at bay.

In the courtroom, I focused intently on the pretrial motions. I listened to the evidence the DA produced; he was as confident as Ethan had been with the reporters outside. The DA was a short man dressed in a suit that didn't flatter his stocky build. His face was round and his hazel eyes gentle, making him seem candidly sincere—an advocate for truth and justice. His words rang with truthfulness and earnestness. He pleaded for the opportunity to rid the world of criminals and monsters—like Steven. And when he looked over the faces of the people sitting in the courtroom, my eyes followed, and we fixed on the same person: Dexter. DA Price allowed a smile to settle on his lips before returning his attention to the judge. I couldn't remember if his name was on the list of professionals who were part of the Red Blood.

Dexter was flanked by two broadly built men, definitely shifters. Dressed in a crisp blue shirt and dark blue pants, he personified self-entitlement and smugness. He caught my eye, grinned, and tugged at the sleeves of his shirt. Was he saying he had something under his sleeves? Mage magic wafted off him, an easy, ineffectual breeze. The fact he possessed so little was proof of the existence of universal balance. He would've been menacing if he'd possessed even a modicum of witch magic. Anger boiled in me as he flashed a cruel, taunting smile. He was the reason we were in this mess, and he didn't try to hide his contempt for us. Before Price finished his argument, he glanced over his shoulder at Dexter, making eye contact again. Ethan turned as well. His eyes homed in on the mage, who responded to the sharp look with a cynical grin. Ethan wouldn't give Dexter the satisfaction of any more of his time. He rolled back his shoulders, stood up, and gave the judge a charismatic and gentle look.

"Unfortunately, this case is riddled with circumstantial evidence and built on a foundation of anonymous tip-offs that are by no means true. As you look at the evidence I've provided, you'll see that the software used to identify my client is only seventy-eight percent accurate. The software we use did not bring my client up as a match, and it is ninety-four percent accurate. And finally, my client has no connection to the victims. Why would he do that? A person without a criminal record decides to go on a rampage and kill three strangers and a dog?"

Attorney Price rebutted. "His alibi is thin at best. Phone records show him being on the phone at the time of the crime. Those records could prove that the murders were premeditated." He slid a look of derision in Ethan's direction, earning him a wolfish smile.

"I can assure you that anything the state has is thin," Ethan shot back dismissively. He went to work, even though he was sure his motion to dismiss would fail. He compiled all the information, noting there was no physical evidence connecting Steven to the crimes and pointing out holes in the DA's logic and in the editing of the video. If the case went to trial, Steven's defense would be that he'd been wrongfully accused. Ethan had said this was the best option because the burden would fall on the state to prove otherwise. If Steven had claimed self-defense, his attorney—Ethan—would have had the burden of proving it was. Ethan was convinced that would be a very difficult case to prove. Each time I looked at the video and saw the three men about to attack Steven, self-defense seemed easier to prove than him not being there. I hadn't gone to law school, though.

The judge did what I assumed most of the jury would do during a trial: he glanced over at Steven raking his fingers through his thick waves of hair and giving a full view of his ethereal appearance. His soft round eyes made him look innocuous. It wasn't the face of a killer. And when he spoke, his gentle Southern lilt could round off the edges of the worst curmudgeon.

The video was the crux of the case, and Ethan was hammering home what he and the pack wanted the world to see. "The time stamp on that video is an hour and a half before my client was arrested. You saw the video, you saw the fight, you saw the brutality of it. And yet my client didn't have a mark on him. He wasn't photographed with a black eye, or blood on his clothes, or injuries to his knuckles. You can try this case, and I'll bring expert after expert to prove there was no way he was there."

"That means nothing. Maybe he didn't injure himself," Price countered.

"And maybe my client's a superhero with supernatural abilities. I don't care how skilled you are as a fighter—there is absolutely no way a person could be involved in a fight with three other men without sustaining an injury."

"If it's not him, then who is it?" the DA snapped in frustration.

Ethan flashed him a smile. "That's not my job. The city has several unsolved murders, and unfortunately, this may go down as another. I'm sorry and I regret this, but the right person should be held accountable for this, not just anyone."

I turned to see Dexter's reaction. The muscles in his neck bulged as his teeth clenched. My first thought was he was disgusted with the DA, but then I noticed Sebastian, who had just slipped into a chair in the back row.

Dexter glided out of his seat, his shifter bodyguards moving in unison with him. Sebastian rose and followed them out of the courtroom. I leaped up and trailed Sebastian, oblivious to the court proceedings. Dexter turned and gave Sebastian a sweeping, dismissive look before closing the distance between them. He held Sebastian's gaze as long as he could; it was difficult for him and his eyes wavered several times.

"Your pack destroyed my things and cost me a lot of fucking money, and for what, one woman? She wasn't even part of your pack. I was going to return her when I was done."

It took a great deal of restraint not to react, and each moment that passed pulled at my control. I was ready to snap. I wanted to punch Dexter. That was being generous. I wanted to beat the hell out of him. Pummel him until he was nothing more than a bloody mess on the ground and couldn't curve his lips to form one of his haughty, taunting smiles because they would be too swollen to function.

"She was our responsibility. If you think what you did was merely insulting, imagine what I will do if you keep fucking with us," Sebastian said. He leaned in and his voice dropped, laced with threats of unbearable pain and retribution. "You *really* don't want to screw with me."

"I don't want to just screw with you. I want to destroy you all, and I will." Dexter's arrogance had to be backed by more than the two shifters standing next to him.

He's armed with something else.

Sebastian was as stiff as a board, unable to move, seized by the anger he was struggling to control. Amber-drenched eyes stared down at Dexter. I felt the primal virulence from my position ten feet away. The people around us might not feel the tension the way I did, but they could see it. Sebastian's fists were clenched at his sides, his eyes fastened on the prey in front of him, his stance easily enabling a strike.

"Sebastian," I whispered.

It drew Dexter's attention. A deviant smile kinked the corners of his mouth. "You should listen to her. Or you could attack me here." He scanned the people standing in the hallway. One looked like a reporter; the others were ready to be smartphone journalists. "Do you think Attorney Charleston can get you out of it? You're welcome to test how truly talented he is."

Dexter took a step back, but Sebastian could have easily cleared the space between them. "I guess then the Red Blood wouldn't have to work much harder at exposing you, would they?" The mage's eyes slowly roved over me. It made me feel like I needed a shower. He ignored Sebastian and directed his comment to me. "You know why they call themselves the Red Blood?" He rolled his eyes. "Because humans bleed red—as if our blood is another color. Foolish people with rigid ideologies are easy to incite. They have their sights on supernaturals, specifically the were-animals. It's relatively easy to prove the existence of people who turn to animals when called by the moon." He turned on his heel, his detail close to him, and started toward the exit. "All they need is a little nudge, and I'm in the mood to do just that.

Hmm, if Steven is convicted, how long will it take for the world to pull you out of the closet?"

The thin thread of control snapped hard—not mine, but Sebastian's. I stepped in front of him just in time, but I wasn't totally confident he wouldn't plow through me to get to Dexter. And as Dexter walked away, his laugh lingering in the air like an ominous threat, it became harder to stand between the two. If we were going to be outed, I'd like it to start with Dexter being ripped apart by a wolf. No one was more deserving of such an ending.

When we returned to the courtroom, Price and Ethan were at their desks, calendars open as they scheduled Steven's trial. Ethan sought my face out among the crowd, his eyes gentle and placid, attempting to offer comfort. There wouldn't be any. We were going to trial, and there was a chance Steven would be convicted.

After the hearing, Ethan left with Price to work out a deal. I followed Sebastian back to the house. He retreated to his office and closed the door. I went to the IT room and took up a place at the door, next to Gavin, who acknowledged me with a flick of his midnight eyes in my direction.

"They aren't even trying to fit in," he complained, a frown forming as he carefully regarded them. The Worgen were distracted by their computers. One of them had his legs crossed and was staring at rows of information scrolling over his large screen.

The third largest room in the house had been converted into a workspace for them. It now had white walls, something atypical in the pack's house. Were-animals preferred color—it hid bloodstains—and faux finishes, which concealed the multiple times the walls had been damaged in a fight or by an ill-controlled temper. Most of our wrecked walls had been the result of spats between Ethan and Josh. They weren't known for playing well with each other or resolving their conflicts with words. Or rather, they played fine together and had discussions, but their language was punches, childish insults, Josh's magic, and Ethan's brute force.

Life-size cutouts of superheroes and video game posters decorated the walls here. Gavin was right; the guys in here were geeks and wore that badge with honor. Although they'd put minimal effort into assimilating, they'd proven to be an asset to the pack and that was all that mattered. They could probably march around in Storm Trooper armor and Spock ears and get away with it.

But they were hard at work, firing away codes and monitoring scrolling screens. Quinn circulated among them, helping them. I didn't want to be here—I needed plausible deniability when things went wrong—and the looks they gave me over their shoulders made it clear they didn't want me here, either.

Quinn finally turned and crossed his arms over his chest. "Did you need something, Skylar?" He always dealt with me with an unusual level of reverence, and I wasn't sure if it came from my status as Ethan's mate or as the pack's overbearing moral guardian. Usually, whenever I entered, there would be a flurry of activity as they exited windows on their computers.

The various screens displayed personal information on people and an impressive mapping of the Red Blood's relationships to companies and social organization. A printer spewed out an endless list of names.

"What is this?" I asked.

Quinn's face tinted an odd rose color before he bit his lip. "It's all the people who were summoned for jury duty in the past three months." He looked down at the list. "We are checking the list against the one on the screen. More than likely, they will be in the jury pool when Steven's case comes to trial."

"Is that public information?" I asked.

"It can be found on the Web," he offered evasively.

I scrutinized the monitors for a few minutes while I weighed the value of the information against the questionable legality of the ways we'd acquired it. I backed out of the room, giving Quinn a quick wave, and relief spread over his face. Ignorance was my best course of action. Gavin was heading down the hall. No doubt he'd grown bored; he'd given his usual signal, which was to leave without saying a word.

Kelly came around the corner, caught him by the arm, and then slid her hand down until her fingers met and entwined with his. Their features and personalities paradoxically contrasted with and complemented each other. Her brown hair was thick and curly; his was jet-black, straight, and so long that if he bent forward, it formed a curtain over his face. His eyes were just as dark as his hair and glinted with barely suppressed menace. Kelly's were light brown, bright, and lively. She always wore a smile; Gavin wore a perpetual scowl. Built for stealth and speed, he was tall and lean with cords of muscle along his exposed arms. Her shorter frame was toned from years of dancing, yet she still managed to have curves. Her skin was a warm sepia, his cool and tawny.

"How was the hearing?" she asked, keeping a firm grasp on Gavin, who looked like a caged animal just waiting for an opportunity to escape. She turned into him and wrapped her arms around his waist.

"Don't ask her questions like that. She'll just blather on," he commented in a stage whisper. Even a human would have heard him.

"Gavin," Kelly said softly. "Rude."

"How is the truth rude?"

She sighed heavily. Apparently, it was a conversation she didn't want to have again.

"Go on, Sky," she urged.

I kept my eyes on Kelly, allowing them to slip in Gavin's direction as I set the scene. He seemed feral, desperate to walk away, and he would have if it weren't for Kelly. Right before I got to the part with Dexter, I stopped, uneasy because Dexter was the reason she was a were-animal. I didn't want to be the person responsible for forcing her to relive being abducted and used as a test subject.

"What's wrong? Your heart's beating too fast," Kelly asked, concerned.

I shook my head. "Nothing," I lied. "After the arguments, the judge felt there was enough information to proceed to trial."

She nodded apprehensively. I felt terrible keeping the rest of the information from her. "That's it for now." I looked at my phone. "I have to go. I told Ethan I'd meet him for drinks." I felt better at least ending our conversation on something that was true.

I'd made it to my car when Kelly called my name. I contemplated pretending I hadn't heard her and leaving.

"You're doing to me what they did to you," she said in a low, gentle voice as she approached, searching my face for the answers I hadn't given her before. Concern and curiosity cast darkness over her face. She growled out, "Don't do that to me." The animal peeked through her eyes as hunter green rolled over them. Taken aback by it, she gasped an apology and took several steps back.

Guilt wound around me; I wanted to protect Kelly, but she didn't want me to. She was right— the pack had deliberately left me in the dark before. That was a pack tactic and something I'd rejected. It might have been strategic and even considered protective at times, but it was also cruel.

"You're right. I'm the one who should be sorry." I blew out a slow breath and then told her what had happened in the hallway of the courthouse between Dexter and Sebastian. I didn't leave out any details.

She grappled with her emotions and wore that struggle on her face as they hardened her delicate features. "Emotions are harder now. Everything feels so intense." She ran her tongue over her teeth, and it reminded me of the way vampires looked when they felt the need to feed. It wasn't a vampire instinct; it was a predator's instinct. She wanted to retaliate, strike, be the hunter rather than the hunted. Lifting her nose to the air, she frowned.

"She's here, too."

Before I could ask who, I saw the round, angelic face of the young woman who'd been turned vampire before fully experiencing life. But there hadn't been much for Sable to experience after she'd been sentenced to life in prison for several counts of murder. Her supple lips curved into a gentle bow, and her wide, dark eyes were mesmerizing. Even though I knew she was a killer with psychopathic tendencies, it was hard not to find some empathy for the peculiar vampire. Her face was vacuous as she glided effortlessly toward us. Like her maker, Gabriella, she was eccentric—a dangerous quality in a psychopath.

Her hair, which was usually straight with various colored extensions, was now a halo of curls similar to Kelly's. Her head bobbed rhythmically as if she were listening to music.

Her eyes registered intrigue as she closed in on us, not with vampire speed but with slow, measured steps. Kelly was calm and stood still as Sable moved around her like a viper ready to strike. She ran her tongue over her teeth again, and once she'd made a full circle around us, she stood face-to-face with Kelly, studying her with interest.

"The human pet—or rather, the formerly human pet," she whispered. She reached out to touch Kelly.

"Don't touch her," Gavin growled from several feet away.

She pulled her attention from Kelly for a mere moment. Then she struck in a flash and had Kelly by the neck, hoisted up, her feet dangling. "If you come closer, I will kill her."

"If you kill her—"

"What?" she said in a hushed voice. "You won't see me anymore? You'll stop talking to me? You've done that already. You left me for her."

I glared at Gavin, knowing his past relationship with Sable, no matter how fleeting and casual he'd claimed it had been, now held dangerous consequences.

I inched closer, and the vampire snapped her head in my direction. "You, too," she warned. "I'll snap her pretty little neck." Again, her attention moved to Kelly. One hand held her by the throat, the other lightly stroked her cheek.

"She's soft," Sable said with a delicate note of appreciation, but not for the texture or the suppleness of her skin. Kelly attempted not to show fear; she'd been around predators enough to know that was the most intoxicating thing to them. A whiff of it triggered a desire to feel more of it. She blinked back the tears that welled in her eyes.

"What do you want?" Kelly asked in a strained voice, looking down at the cherubic, innocent-looking young woman who was anything but innocuous.

Ignoring Kelly's question, Sable continued, "He's beautiful, isn't he?" I didn't understand Sable's obsession with Gavin. The first time she'd seen him, she'd been drawn by a beauty that had eluded us all. He was handsome, but his beauty encompassed something more than just physical attributes. It was intangible, and its nuances were hard to grasp.

"Look at him!" Sable demanded.

Kelly dragged her eyes to Gavin. His eyes had spastic waves of green rolling over them. His rigid scowl, the hint of ruddy coloring that streaked the bridge of his nose, and the sharp lines of his jaw conveyed wrath and vengeance, not beauty. His body language promised unparalleled violence. Finally, a tear rolled down Kelly's cheek, and Gavin bared his teeth. He shifted his weight.

"Don't," Sable warned. Again, her attention was on Kelly. "Would it make you sad if I killed her?"

"Yes," he admitted. His voice low and pained.

Again, her head snapped in my direction and she snarled, "Stop it!" She was talking about my panicking. I could hear my heartbeat, so I knew she could, too. Magic pricked my fingers and roiled inside me as the desire to use it rose. But could I be fast enough with my magic to use it against Sable without jeopardizing Kelly's life.

"I suppose you would do anything to protect her?"

Gavin glared at her, his teeth clenched so tightly he was unable to speak. When he didn't answer, Sable squeezed harder, and Kelly made choking sounds. Still unable to speak, Gavin growled; his eyes eclipsed to green as he drew his lips back, exposing his teeth.

Sable chortled and bared her fangs. "Yours are only for show. If you don't answer me, I'll be forced to use mine."

"I would do anything to protect her," he confessed.

Sable simpered. Again, her head bobbed to a sound pitched only for disturbed vampires to hear. My patience was growing thin, and she'd depleted any empathy I'd had for her. I watched with intensity for the moment to strike, gain the advantage, and get Kelly.

Sable tilted her head, examining her captive. Her gaze lazily roamed over every inch of her face. With ease, she brought Kelly closer to her, kissed her lightly on the cheeks. She kept Kelly midair with a strong hold around her neck as she stroked her arm just as delicately as she'd kissed her. Nothing in my life had prepared me for this level of crazy. I didn't want to feel sympathy for her, but a morsel of it nudged its way in.

The tension-filled silence stretched for several moments. "You won't be able to protect her. Not from the others. They are organizing an army and hiring hunters. She is one of you—she'll die with you all."

"Who's organizing an army?" I asked.

"Liam," she whispered in a low, hollow voice. "You broke the rules. Were-animals always break the rules. You lack discipline."

It wasn't necessary to point out the kettle/pot situation. Ruled by their self-indulgence and id, vampires were unable—or rather were unwilling to deny their desires.

"How did we break the rules?"

"Your coyote was caught. It's only a matter of time before people know what you are, and then they will believe others like us must exist. You broke the rules, and now Liam is making a case to contain the situation."

I hated the word *contain*. It was a misnomer more palatable than *genocide*. They were planning to commit mass murder of a group of people.

"Liam is forming an army to kill us?" I asked.

She nodded and returned her attention to Kelly once more before releasing her so roughly, she lost her footing and started to tumble. Sable was gone by the time Kelly had dropped to the ground. Even if they lacked the ability to *travel*, essentially teleporting, vampires were so fast it seemed as though they could take flight. Kelly stared wide-eyed at Gavin. When he approached her and attempted to touch her, she moved out of his reach.

"You're all toxic," she mused in a low, raspy voice. She put her hand gently around her neck. Barely able to look at either me or Gavin, she rested her gaze on the ground. "I know it's not your intention." She looked back, her features bleak to the point of despondency. "You irreparably change the lives of everyone you go near. Sable's, Steven's, mine. I thought"—she looked at Gavin—"I could deal with it, but I can't. I don't want to feel like my life is in peril all the time. I can't have vampires trying to choke me and people forming armies to kill me. I just can't be a victim." She blinked back tears.

Gavin didn't move. "Then don't be a victim. That is in your control," he responded in a steely voice.

Kelly's eyes widened at his tone and response. Then she glowered at him.

In a few steps, he cleared the distance between them. "I will *not* be ashamed of my past. It is who I am. I changed you to save your life—the alternative would have been to let you die. Would you have liked that?"

Her lips quivered, but she didn't answer. Instead, she blinked back more tears, holding on to her look of pure shock. He got even closer to her. I vowed to set up recurring appointments with the pack's therapist and buy a stack of books on social norms for the pack. I planned to stand over them with a blunt object until they finished reading every one of them. He touched her chin lightly and tilted her face up to look at him. "I'll accept your anger and rage. I will *not* accept defeat. You have claws, fangs, speed, and the ability to change into an animal. You will *never* be a victim or be at the mercy of a vampire or anyone else again. Do you understand?"

She finally allowed the tears to course down her face. He wiped them away with his thumb. Leaning down, he kissed along the path of the removed tears.

"Winter can help her," I offered.

He shook his head and said in a low, gentle voice, "No, I'll help her." He allowed me only a fraction of his attention before he returned it to Kelly. "Okay?"

She nodded.

"Good," he breathed out. He hesitated before he lightly pressed his lips against hers. When she responded, his hands moved up to the nape of her neck, pulling her closer to him as they caressed. She slipped her hands under his shirt and curled her fingers into his skin. Their interaction became ravenous. I was a voyeur privy to something that was becoming more intimate with each passing moment. They were about to make up in a very "delicious" way—Kelly's words, not mine—and it was obvious it was going to happen whether or not I was there. The world consisted of just them. I was an intruder.

CHAPTER 7

I took another sip from the martini glass. It was the only real one I had taken since I'd ordered it while waiting in the pack's bar for Ethan. I'd known he would be late as soon as I'd told Sebastian about Liam's plans. Sebastian's fingers had drummed against his desk in a steady beat, his lips had pulled into a tight, thin line, and fiery rage had been etched over his features. Warmth had radiated from his effort to control the anger. I was sure Sebastian wanted to meet with Ethan to discuss how to handle the situation effectively. Liam probably didn't care much about us being outed—he and the elven-elite Makellos could just continue to segregate themselves in Elysian as they had before. Our exposure wouldn't affect them in any way. Liam was taking advantage of the situation to do what he'd wanted to do for years —get rid of the were-animals.

I understood why Sebastian had colluded with Abigail to initiate a civil war between the elves to get Liam under Gideon, the new ruler of the elves and a pack ally. I was awed by Sebastian's stratagem and how he was always steps ahead of a situation to protect the pack. But I also often found his behavior duplicitous and his alliances and collusions unsavory. I stood by my belief that I never wanted to be in his position. Then reality hit me: I inadvertently had his position to a lesser extent because he and Ethan functioned as co-Alphas and I was Ethan's mate. Ethan took on far more responsibility than a Beta in any other pack was expected to shoulder. In any other pack, he would be the Alpha. Sebastian was aware of that, and the strength and resilience of the Midwest Pack rested on the fact we essentially had two Alphas. Even being an ordinary Beta came with a great deal of accountability in protecting the pack. I didn't want the burden of that responsibility. The next time I took a drink, I emptied the glass.

I asked the bartender for another. A man who'd been watching me since I'd taken a seat one away from him moved closer. It gave me a chance to get a better look at him without being obvious. I recognized him from the courthouse. Besides the attorneys, he'd been one of the few people in a suit. He'd had a recorder and had been taking notes, so I'd assumed he was a reporter.

His attention was easy to ignore. He wasn't intrusive, just casting casual looks my way that he held a little too long. Once the bartender brought my drink, he slid money across the bar to pay for it.

Grabbing the money before the bartender could, I slid it back to the man. "Thank you, but I have a tab." I quickly pretended to be distracted by the exceptional number of people who were in the bar.

The man kept his place on the stool next to me. For several more minutes, he nursed a drink he clearly didn't want. Then he dropped all pretenses and stared right at me. He had to recognize me as well.

"Should I say it, or will you?" he asked with a half-grin.

"Say what?"

"The whole 'don't I know you from somewhere' spiel." A pleasant smile settled on his lips.

"Reporter?" I asked.

He shook his head. "No, just an observer. It's a very interesting case." Especially since he was lying through his teeth.

But I returned the same cordial smile and asked, "What exactly are you observing?"

"The defendant, of course. It's for a project I'm working on," he responded cryptically, giving me another brief assessment. It was going to be like pulling teeth to get a tangible response.

"And that project is?" I asked and casually took another sip from my glass.

"I'm interested in the paranormal." He leaned toward me and grinned. I wasn't sure if he was joking or trying to make his confession sound more pleasant.

"So, you're one of those people who go around looking for ghosts that haunt homes to prove the existence of creatures that go bump in the night." I was grateful I was dealing with a human; he couldn't have heard my heart skip a beat when he'd said "paranormal." I took slow, steady breaths and scrutinized him.

I needed to know if he was part of the Red Blood. "How did you get interested in that?" I asked nonchalantly, feigning far less interest than I had.

His smile widened as he gave me another sweeping look. "If we're going to get to know each other better, shouldn't I know who I'm sharing my tales with?"

"Skylar."

He extended his hand, and I gave it a firm shake. "I'm Andrew, but you can call me Drew. All my friends do."

"It's nice to meet you, *Andrew*." We weren't friends and we might end up as enemies depending on how the conversation went.

"With everything going on, don't you ever think about paranormal and supernatural creatures?"

I shrugged and took a drink before responding with disinterest. "If they existed, someone would've discovered them by now.

With technology and everything we have, it would be virtually impossible not to know about them."

"Not necessarily. You know that look you're giving me right now? Mocking judgment and that slight panic in your eyes as if you're looking for the perfect excuse to escape from a delusional person? No one wants to get that look from anyone, let alone a very beautiful woman. People know things but keep it to themselves, afraid no one will believe them. I have reliable sources who say they exist. Vampires, werewolves, and witches live among us."

"And if you ever watched an episode of *Buffy the Vampire Slayer,* you'd know there are demons as well. I hope you own a stake, a cross, and a lot of holy water. That stuff is real, right?" I mocked.

He tossed his head back in boisterous laughter. "I'm here to find out." Deep in thought, he traced a finger along the rim of his glass, "I can't help but believe they all exist. Probably types of supernaturals even I can't imagine, and I have a very good imagination."

He turned toward me and gave me a lingering once over. His intrigued brown eyes drifted along my face, arm, and fingers as if he expected to see something there—claws, maybe? I saw awareness and certainty in his eyes then. There wasn't a question in his mind about our existence; he was just searching for evidence.

"How do you know the defendant?" he asked.

"How do you know I know him?" He'd been in the courtroom before we'd arrived, but we'd entered with several people, so it hadn't been exactly obvious that I was there for Steven.

"Hmm, do you often attend pretrial motions and nervously fidget the entire time? Or is that just a nervous twitch you get whenever you're in a courtroom?" he countered with a smirk.

"This case is interesting. I don't think he's guilty," I offered. If he wanted to find out the connection between me and Steven, he'd have to do the legwork himself.

"Really? The only way I would consider him innocent is if he'd been at my house the day of the crime. But I guess it's easy to be taken in by those big green eyes and dimples. That face—seriously, who could believe he's a murderer?"

"He's not a murderer!" I snapped. Anger had gotten to me so badly I had to put down my glass for fear that I would crush it. Once again, I was faced with the undeniable seriousness of the situation. Steven was on trial for murder. He could go to prison. Cotton coated my tongue, and I finished the contents of my glass to get rid of it. Now my mouth felt like Chambord and pineapple-flavored cotton.

"And you say you don't know the defendant?" His tone made it clear he didn't believe me.

"She knows his attorney," Ethan stated in a low, crisp voice from behind Andrew as he nudged his way between us.

Andrew didn't seem too concerned with the intrusion. "Ah, but that doesn't explain the nervousness. After all, if you lose, it's Steven who goes to prison. You, Mr. Charleston, can go back to corporate law, which, based on my research, you've been practicing for the past five years."

Ethan's jaw clenched. He enjoyed arriving on the scene with all the information and didn't like when the tables were turned. "I don't like to lose, and Sky understands that."

Andrew smiled mischievously. "Well, for what it's worth, I don't think your client is technically guilty. I don't think he could help himself. His kind tends to get violent closer to the full moon."

"His kind?" Ethan asked, amusement clinging to his words.

"I believe he thinks Steven is a supernatural creature." I kept my tone light and mocking, hoping my ridicule would send Andrew in another direction.

"Vampires can't walk in the day. Witches aren't known to be violent—but werewolves are." The sheer confidence in his statement made me leery.

"Did you learn that from *True Blood*?" Ethan asked, maintaining his cool composure as he gave Andrew a derisive look.

"No. My research shows that lycanthropes are strong and fast. You saw the video. His strength and preternatural movement can't be described as anything other than supernatural. There's no other way to explain it."

"First, that wasn't my client and I will prove that. Second, what I saw was a young man skilled in martial arts and perhaps hand-to-hand combat. Third, the video has been edited. You can't be sure what you're seeing," Ethan asserted, covering the very things he'd addressed with the DA.

Andrew's eyes gleamed with cynicism and determination. "I'm a black belt in Tae Kwon Do, and I don't move like that."

"The man in the video is at least twenty-five years younger than you are. Do you expect to move like someone twenty-five years younger than you are? And anyone who moves faster and better is labeled a supernatural creature?" Ethan asked with a smirk.

Drew glowered at Ethan's slight. The broad build and well-defined muscles visible through Andrew's suit were the results of dedicated gym work and athletics. There was no gray in his hair but based on the fine lines along his lips and a few on his forehead, he should have had some. I suspected he colored his hair to stave off the signs of aging. Pointing out that he looked more than twenty-five years older than Steven didn't go over well. He smiled decorously at Ethan but slid his gaze back to me. He tossed back the contents of his glass.

He gave me a quick nod. "It was nice talking to you. I'm sure I'll see you around." His pleasant words warred with the dark look he gave us.

Ethan frowned, his eyes following the man as he walked out. "That's concerning." He looked over the growing crowd of people in the bar. Were-animals mingled with humans, who often frequented the pack's bar and contributed to its success. The magnetism that most were-animals possessed was hard to understand. It was innate, primal, and undeniably alluring, and the desire to be around it was difficult to resist for most. As a were-animal, I wasn't immune to its draw; I couldn't imagine others denying it easily.

"He knows more than he's letting on," Ethan continued in a low voice, his gaze still moving over the room as if he were gathering intel on everyone who wasn't part of the pack. They were no longer patrons but potential enemies, and he was watching them with a level of suspicion.

Josh walked in looking more relaxed than he had earlier. He'd changed from the Darth Vader t-shirt and well-worn jeans to a long-sleeved shirt and slightly darker jeans. The contrast between the brothers was stark. Josh's shirtsleeves were rolled up, exposing many of his tattoos. Ethan was a sartorial model in a dark suit. He'd discarded the tie and opened the first button of his shirt, but he still wouldn't have looked out of place in an office. Josh's earlier black mood had lifted, and the plaintive wayward smile had returned. As he made his way through the crowd of people, we saw why. London was following him. The quarter-length sleeves of her shirt revealed some of her tattoos. A distinctive tribal tat was so similar to one on Josh that there was no way it was coincidental. Its location on her forearm wasn't by chance, either.

"I know. Do you think he's a Red Blood?"

Ethan shrugged. "I don't know, but he definitely suspects you're a supernatural."

"You got all that just from talking to him for three minutes."

"I got all that from studying his body language. He was simultaneously intrigued and put off by you."

"I don't care about the curiosity. I'm concerned about what he plans to do with it. If he's just one of those people drawn to the idea that we exist, he's probably harmless. If he's a Red Blood, he could be trouble, especially if he's a reporter."

"Did he give you a name?"

I nodded. "Andrew."

"Last name?"

"He didn't give me that."

"I have a feeling this won't be the last time you hear from him."

Ethan ordered a drink and sat next to me while I did what I did best in the bar—I people-watched.

I allowed the music to distract me from all thoughts of trials, Red Blood, and the removal of my mark. Or rather, I pretended to let it distract me. It was hard to let it go, especially the missing mark.

"Your brother's working himself to the bone. He needs to slow down, or he'll give himself a heart attack from working so hard," I said, grinning and pointing at Josh on the dance floor, drink in hand, dancing with London. Every so often, he leaned down to give her a kiss, his lips brushing lightly against her cheek while the other hand remained casually around her waist.

Ethan chuckled and took a drink from the glass the bartender had just placed in front of him. "He's working. He's just working on the public relations part."

"Hmm, last month I saw him doing shots with a couple of NHL players. I'm sure that was part of some sort of marketing endeavor. It seemed like he was promoting vodka from what I saw. A couple of weeks before that, he took one for the team and shared one of his special cigarettes with the band. I couldn't help but be impressed by his work ethic." I couldn't suppress a laugh.

Ethan shrugged dismissively. "Say what you will, after Josh started managing our clubs, they tripled what they'd taken in before."

Once Josh had finally taken a seat, Ethan stood and headed toward him to do what he did best with his brother: be a killjoy. Josh rolled his eyes at his approach. Ethan leaned down, said something, and moments later, they left together. It had to be about Andrew; by the end of the night, Ethan would have Andrew's last name and know everything about him.

London appeared content to stay on the other side of the

room after Josh had left. Ethan's seat didn't stay empty long. A fair man with blond hair and eyelashes just as light sat next to me. His odd green eyes reminded me of Quell, but any similarity ended at his wiry build. I looked at him too long, because he smiled, leaned into me, and asked if I'd been at the bar before.

I sighed into my drink at his lack of originality before taking another drink and debating whether I should go find Ethan and Josh.

"I come here often," I said in a low voice, knowing he couldn't hear me over the music, deterring conversation.

"This is my first time. I'm new in town." He was lying, but at least that was more creative than the first line. He leaned in closer. "I'm Brett."

"Nice to meet you." I'd increased my volume a bit once I'd realized he was using his inability to hear me as an excuse to put his hand on my back to steady himself as he leaned in.

He glanced at my glass, which was nearly full. Based on the banality of his other lines, he was going to ask if he could buy me a drink. "What are you drinking?"

Damn, he changed course.

"French martini. She always drinks them here." Ethan's coarse voice startled Brett. Ethan moved in silence, even when it was quiet and footsteps were easily detected. With all the noise in the bar, it had been impossible to hear him, but I'd felt his presence, adding to the long list of changes I'd noticed in our connection.

Brett faked a smile. It looked tight and uncomfortable, and Ethan didn't do anything to ease it. Steely gunmetal eyes bored into Brett, and Ethan's lips lifted into a scowl. *No, more like a snarl.*

Brett broadened his smile and extended his hand. "I'm Brett."

Ethan didn't give the hand a second look. "I don't care."

Brett's eyes widened at Ethan's incivility. I wished I were as surprised by the response. A befuddled look settled on Brett's face as if he were debating how to react.

After Ethan settled in on the other side of me, it didn't take long for Brett to find someplace else he'd rather be.

I took out my phone and scrolled through it, and moments later, Ethan's phone rang. He made a face as he assessed the e-mail I'd sent him. "You sent me a book?" he asked incredulously.

"Yep, it's about social skills and norms. Perhaps you should read it tonight."

His tongue moved over his lips before he gave me a wolfish grin and made a show of deleting the e-mail. He leaned down and kissed me, his teeth nipping gently at my bottom lip before he brushed featherlight kisses along my cheek to my ear. "You knew what you were getting," he whispered. Easing himself back into his seat next to me, he maintained his smug grin.

Yep, I have myself a Betahole.

CHAPTER 8

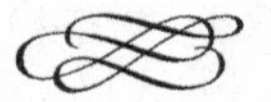

What is this? I turned the opened black ring box I'd found on the bed while making it up. I tried to make sense of it while I brushed my teeth and washed my face.

When I joined Ethan in the kitchen, I brought it to him and said, "Would you care to tell me what this is?" From his position at the stove, he glanced from the skillet on a burner to the ring box. "Sky, it's a ring." His brow furrowed. Flashing me a grin, he continued in a deadpan voice, "This is a skillet." He placed the spatula on the counter and reached to the right to grab a piece of fruit from a bowl. "This is a mango."

He put bacon on a plate and turned around to face me, still wearing the smirk. "Are there other things you need a refresher on? I have all day."

Don't kick the Betahole. I said that mantra in my head as I moved closer to him.

"I know what it is. Besides using the light that reflects off it to direct planes, what is it for?"

He chuckled. "It's for you to wear."

"I'm familiar with what to do with a ring. I just don't know why you're giving it to me," I said, looking at the box again.

After several moments of silence, he said, "I want you to wear it." He lifted his hand, revealing a silver-looking band around his ring finger. Since he couldn't wear silver, it had to be white gold or platinum.

"I'm supposed to get you that!" I shot back.

"But you didn't," he pointed out.

"So," I started slowly, "is it an engagement ring, or what?"

"It can be anything you want it to be. A *whatever* ring."

I was perplexed. Why did we need rings? It seemed like everyone in any given room knew we were mated before I even entered, as if there were a magical flashing banner that marked my status as his mate. Even Demetrius knew, and from the way Quell had looked at us the other night, he did as well.

I scrutinized him and then the ring. "I've heard of a friendship ring, a promise ring, and an engagement ring, but I haven't heard of a 'whatever ring.' You want to tell me about it?" With effort, I controlled the smile that was fighting to emerge.

It was a poorly veiled attempt to let those who didn't have the ability to detect I was mated know I wasn't available. I wasn't sure why it was so hard for Ethan to admit it.

His mouth moved, chewing on the words but unable to let them out.

I looked at the large princess cut ring again. It glinted in the overhead light. I would have preferred to wear the oversized sign designating me as Ethan's property that Josh had playfully made when he'd accused Ethan of passionately kissing me in public as a sign of our bond.

"Fine, it's an engagement ring," he blew out in exasperation.

I leaned forward and gave him a peck on the cheek before handing him the ring back."Well, don't you think you should ask me properly?"

Exhaling a sigh or maybe a growl, he started to kneel.

I stopped him. "Wait! What are you doing? I don't want to be proposed to while I'm in my kitchen and dressed in Hello Kitty pajamas."

His gaze traveled over my heart-patterned fluffy white socks, black boxers with the famed cat on them, and tank top. Clearly, my attire earned his disapproval. "About that?"

"You knew what you were getting," I retorted with a playful sneer, throwing his infamous words back at him. Tugging at my shirt and giving him a full view of Kitty's face, I pushed past him and made my way to the food.

With both a hint of humor and curiosity, he asked, "What? Do you need to be swept away to some exotic location? A fancy dinner where a violinist plays you a selection while I ask? A romantic coach ride? Sky, what exactly do you want?"

For someone who claimed I was predictable, he seemed quite flummoxed at that moment. It dawned on me that Ethan might be as lost as I was in this situation. He'd gone from one shallow relationship to the next—if they could even be considered relationships. They'd been one-night stands that had lasted too long. His most serious attachment had been with Chris. It had survived and strangely thrived by being dysfunctional. It had been further complicated by the secrets that had existed between them. They had known the superficiality and weaknesses of their relationship and hadn't cared to do anything to change it. Ethan and I didn't have secrets anymore, but our complications existed in droves.

I shook my head. "I'm simple. I just don't want to be in my pajamas." I grabbed a handful of bacon and started back toward the bedroom to shower and dress.

During breakfast, I waited for him to present the ring to me; instead, I was met with his miscreant smirk. I sat at the kitchen table, long after he'd cleared it, waiting for a proposal that never came.

When I stood, he moved closer to me. His fingers curled around my waist. Warm breath breezed against my lips when he spoke. "Is something wrong, Sky?" The subtle challenge and the smug, haughty grin ensured I would never bring the ring up again.

"No. Nothing at all."

A rumbling chuckle reverberated in his chest. "Good. It seemed like you were looking for something. Were you?"

"No, I was just wondering about Steven. Where is he?"

"Home." Before I could ask, he added, "It was his decision. Joan will be in town today with the other Alphas. I assumed he went to prepare the house for her visit. Or at least to try to make it less of a mess."

Ethan had told me that the Alphas were meeting. I figured it was to discuss Steven's situation and to address the worst-case scenarios and options if things didn't go as planned with the trial. Ethan and Sebastian always had a preemptive strategy; I was sure they'd want to address the option of us coming out if necessary to protect Steven. I hoped the other Alphas would be briefed on the Red Blood and their affiliation with Dexter and his role as the instigator of this mess.

Seeing Joan in conflict with anyone was strange, but it was completely unsettling to watch her be at odds with Sebastian. It meant the situation might be worse than we'd all anticipated. I was thoroughly uncomfortable when I walked through his half-open door to find them just inches away from each other. The tension was thick, the anger heavy, and the contention between them palpable. The scowl on Joan's face pulled so tight it sharpened her delicate, genteel features. She was every bit the jaguar that shared her body—an apex hunter, a predator.

She had an advantage over Sebastian—she was a predator trying to protect her young. That made her extremely vicious. Usually, Joan was amicable, and between the two of them, she was definitely the one more likely to compromise. From her body language, she was unable to let go of the very thing Sebastian needed her to—her feelings—and operate on reason. I heard her say she didn't think they needed to discuss anything with the other Alphas and whatever needed to be done to protect Steven was the only option.

Sebastian ran his tongue over his lips before he spoke, I assumed to temper his words and probably buy time to find the patience to deal with the situation. There had always been a subtle bond between them because of Steven. He'd spent his summers with Sebastian before joining the pack. Joan and Sebastian respected each other, but I suspected they'd been romantically involved at some point. He was always too gentle with her, uncharacteristically nurturing and tender. Even as she stood before him seething, nearly challenging him, he looked as if he wanted to touch her and comfort her.

Instead, he caressed her with his words. "Joan," he said softly, "you know I would never do anything to hurt Steven. As his Alpha, I have a responsibility to protect him as much as you do. Your maternal instinct to protect him, albeit understandable, doesn't override anything I choose to do. We've had this discussion twice, and we won't have it again. When you walk out this door, you will leave whatever you're dealing with behind. I will not continue to ignore your challenges to my authority."

Joan's jaw was clenched. She held her arms at her side, hands balled into tight fists. She looked pained, searching for words that wouldn't come. Sebastian stepped close to her and gently touched her shoulder. His fingers stroked her with a slow, easy rhythm. He leaned down and pressed his lips to her forehead. It wasn't romantic, but I was intruding on a moment, witnessing the display of a bond they shared.

Joan had found Steven near death, after he'd killed a vampire. She'd changed him so he could survive the injuries and raised him as her own child. A huge responsibility for a person who'd been in her late teens when she'd taken him as her own. I knew Steven and Joan's story. But I never knew Sebastian and Joan's. Curiosity overtook any improprieties I felt about asking about it. When I had a chance, I would ask Sebastian. It only took a moment, though, to change my mind and decide to ask Joan, who would be more likely to offer an answer. Sebastian would answer my question by asking why I wanted to know.

"This is a big decision," Sebastian said. "Although I have the authority to decide on our behalf, it will take all of us to make it successful. If we are going to come out, we all need to be on board, especially with the way things are."

Joan didn't say anything; she simply nodded.

Tension was high as everyone spilled into the large living room. The Alphas and the Betas were present, along with a few of the other ranked members from the four packs. I stood next to Ethan, watching as the room slowly filled. Were-animals' enigmatic power shrank any space they occupied. Being surrounded by outsiders reminded me of my difference. I'd accepted that it existed within my pack.

I knew the Alphas and some of those from the Southern Pack, whom I'd met when they came to the Midwest after Ethos's creatures had attacked them. I spotted Sara, a sensual, curvy blonde who'd garnered a great deal of Ethan's interest when we'd gone to New York to talk to fae friends about Josh. I suspected they'd spent the night together, but he'd told me she'd wanted information about transferring to an extension pack near us. She must have gotten the transfer because she was standing next to another woman, who seemed to be the liaison for Indianapolis, where Sara had wanted to relocate. My curiosity about her was piqued; it had only been a couple of months since her transfer request. Why had Sebastian invited her to the meeting? I'd only been invited because of my position as the Beta's mate. Was she mated with the liaison for the extension pack? I didn't feel a bond, and there didn't appear to be any interest between them.

Sara wore jeans that molded to her curves, and the buttons on her shirt were open enough to give anyone who looked her way a view of her breasts. She'd pulled back her strawberry blonde hair into a high ponytail, emphasizing her striking features. Lithe, sinewy movements quickly gave her away as a feline shifter. Her sharp eyes moved over the room until they found Ethan's. She smiled, and I automatically stiffened next to him and was unable to relax as she made her way across the room to greet him. She waved and stopped just a few feet away, giving him a long, lingering look. Then her eyes danced over to me and traveled languidly over me. A smile strained her lips as she looked at me.

"Ethan," she greeted in a tepid voice. I again was treated to a long look, and it was more than apparent she wasn't impressed with what she saw. "And your mate ..." Her brows rose in inquiry as she waited for an answer.

"Skylar," I offered. She nodded and quickly lost interest, refocusing her attention on Ethan.

"Thank you for assisting with the transfer."

He nodded slightly. "I see you've been busy moving up the ranks." Extension pack members were ranked, but their order was invalid within the parent pack. Sara had worked her way up to Beta or ranked member, but among the larger packs, she was just another member of the extension pack.

"Yes, but it's not the same as being part of the Midwest Pack, is it?" Sara admitted.

I couldn't escape her hard look, so this time, I returned it. A smile kinked her lips.

"It's nice seeing you again." She started to touch Ethan, probably to give him a pat on his shoulder. I growled.

I can't believe I fucking growled.

She stopped abruptly, jerking her hand back as if she'd touched flames. Her eyes widening. Her smile faded, and she backed away as if she'd been confronted by a rabid animal. The heat of my embarrassment rose along the bridge of my nose and my cheeks. *I growled.*

Ethan snorted, and I fixed him with a sharp look. I didn't want to be that person, growling and posturing the moment the opposite sex approached him.

He leaned down and whispered in my ear, "That's normal, Sky."

I didn't want it to be *my* normal. If my sudden departure from the room would have gone unnoticed, I'd have bolted out. Instead, I continued to stand at Ethan's side, working hard to keep from tracking Sara's whereabouts. When my willpower gave out, I spotted her near Sebastian, hanging on his every word. I'd had more than my share of conversations with him—he wasn't that interesting or particularly funny. No one would have known that from the attention she was giving him and her throaty laughter. I remembered Ethan saying how some pursued the Alpha to acquire their position through a relationship with them. Was that where her interest lay? Despite his less than hospitable personality, succinct ways, and dislike of banalities like small talk, he *was* strangely alluring.

This was more than a meeting; it was a conclave where the fate of the were-animals would be explored and debated. It was easy to shelve my embarrassment about growling at Sara, although part of me wanted to take it further and bite her when I caught her furtively glancing at Ethan. I shrugged off the emotions as a result of being surrounded by so many powerful were-animals. It brought out something primal in me. Well, that was the story I planned to stick with. I settled for appreciating being privy to the meeting. If I wasn't Ethan's mate, they probably wouldn't have told me about it for fear I'd crash it. There was no doubt in my mind I would have tried, but being an invited guest felt better.

When Ethan tensed, I didn't have to look at the door to know who it was. Cole. The Alpha didn't look like someone who had lost a challenge, nor did he display the humility that he should have after losing. The moment he walked into the room, he lifted his nose in the air, inhaled, and scanned the room. His gray eyes landed on me. My eyes trailed elsewhere, but I could still feel him looking at me. I felt Ethan's tension and anger. He was sneering, and his steely, cool eyes were homed in on Cole.

Cole flashed him a half-grin before he looked back at me. His smile broadened. *No humility there.* Perhaps Alpha arrogance kept him from feeling it. Or maybe he considered Ethan a worthy adversary to have lost to.

Ethan was taking slow, deep breaths to ease himself into a calm state, something Cole noticed and reveled in. He was making Ethan uncomfortable, and if nothing else, he found victory in that.

There was slight chatter throughout the room, making it difficult for me to distinguish what people were talking about. Most of the snippets I heard in passing were the same—what the meeting was about. Were we about to out ourselves to save one person? The consensus was an undeniable no. Anger and frustration rose again. I ran my hand over my cheek and felt the heat of magic on my fingers. Apparently, I was more emotional about it than I'd thought.

There was a reason Steven wasn't there, and I was starting to think it was a bad idea for me to be there as well. Joan's eyes narrowed as she studied each person in the room. I knew she was listening to almost everyone, trying to find out who was okay with sacrificing her son to keep our anonymity. Like me, she was wearing her emotions on her sleeve, and profound anger overtook her face.

Sebastian walked to the center of the room and silence fell. He gave it one sweeping look before his gaze landed on Joan. He approached her slowly, but she refused to make eye contact with him. He stopped in front of her, just a few feet away.

His face was professionally stoic. We weren't dealing with the

Midwest Pack's Alpha, but the Elite Alpha. His job was to be responsible for everyone, and he took it seriously. He remained in front of Joan until she eventually lifted her eyes to meet his. I strained to hear what he was saying to her, but his lips were pressed against her ear, speaking words meant for her alone. A practiced tactic for speaking in a room with people who had enhanced auditory senses without being heard. Rigid muscles stood out along Joan's neck as she clenched her teeth.

Sebastian tilted his head and assessed her for a few minutes. Then he whispered something else; she glared. She drew back her lips. The fury that radiated from her was so heightened I felt it from across the room. Sebastian just gave her another look, and she turned and left the room.

He did another assessment of the room, and his eyes focused on me. For a few seconds, I had his undivided attention. Holding his gaze was hard, especially when he regarded me with such intensity. After a while, he nodded at me, giving me permission to stay. I questioned his judgment. Could I be objective and unemotional as they debated Steven's fate?

The final person to undergo his scrutiny was Winter, who was doing a great imitation of Gavin, having faded into the background and molded to the wall, almost unnoticeable. Sebastian kept his distance, but his eyes were so intense that he might as well have been standing within inches of her. He let out a breath.

"Based on everything I've heard, I don't think I have to go over why we are all here, do I?" he asked in a level voice.

The debate over whether we should come out was a lot more amicable than I'd imagined it would be. At times, it got heated, especially for those who wanted to cling to anonymity under any condition.

It was Cole's decision that surprised me the most. I wasn't sure what I'd expected from him—probably to vote against Ethan out of spite—but with the same confidence he'd had before the challenge, that special Alpha nuance, he walked around the room, giving a skilled oration. He argued for coming out and highlighted the pros of doing it. Although his eyes bounced around the room, catching every person's eye, he spent the most time holding mine. I gripped Ethan's hand tighter, not for closeness, but to get a hold of him. I felt his heartbeat and his rage like heat from a bonfire.

"There is a benefit to us being out, although it's hard to see now. The effort we put into keeping hidden can be used for other things," Cole said.

"Yes, but then we will be under a magnifying glass. The humans will scrutinize everything we do." It was easy to determine that the West Coast Alpha had the same disdain for humans as vampires and fae did.

"True," Cole said, "but as Ethan pointed out, that interest will wear off like any novelty. We police ourselves, and I believe the government will be happy with that. We have the ability to police others. They will see the things we can offer that no one else can. Our heightened senses. We have the instincts of animals, but the higher thought process of man. It will open doors for us."

The West Coast Alpha offered, "But we are in various places: hospitals, police departments, governmental agencies, and Fortune 500 companies. Our anonymity gives us an advantage. Don't you think they'll be more careful knowing we can sense a lie and catch their scent and track them, and that we are faster and stronger than they could ever hope to be? Even if they are okay with us being around them, don't you think that will give them reason for pause, fear? I don't know about you, but I just don't have the tolerance to coddle the humans. Nor do I care to be their fascination or the interest of the moment, whether it's for three weeks or three years." He fixed Cole with a hard glare.

Cole inclined his head, acknowledging his point. "Those are valid and compelling points and things we should very well be concerned with. But keep in mind, if we can't keep Steven out of prison"—he shot Ethan a cold, hard look—"which I'm sure we will not be able to do, he will change in there. Is it fair for him to be the only one out? Don't you think we have the opportunity to show our solidarity? There are benefits and power to anonymity, but I assure you there are benefits to being open and letting our existence be known, too."

Sebastian just listened as the debate went on for several hours. Finally, he interrupted. "I've heard your arguments, and soon, we will vote. But it would be unfair for me not to give you the full picture of what we are up against." He told them of the Red Blood and their mission to out us and how some of them were connected to Steven's case.

Ethan added, "Based on our intel, they have members willing to perjure themselves to ensure a conviction." His eyes floated in Cole's direction, and his voice chilled as he continued, "Although I have no doubt I can win the case, we are dealing with extenuating circumstances. The DA is a member of the Red Blood and has made several appeals to revoke Steven's bail."

"Why?" the West Coast Alpha asked, his voice gentler than before. He might not have changed his stance, but Steven's circumstances concerned him. I hated him less.

"The full moon will be here soon; he wants Steven in jail when it happens to expose him."

A heavy silence fell over the room. It was difficult to read most of the faces, but everyone had to know that if someone was on a mission to expose our existence, it could be any one of us in prison instead of Steven.

There were more questions but most were focused on the Red Blood. Everyone wanted a list of the members in their area. Sebastian promised they would have it before they left and would receive updates afterward.

Although the vote was in favor of coming out as needed, immense hesitation hung in the air. I had a feeling Sebastian felt that way as well.

. . .

The privileges of being the Beta's mate seemed to be up to Ethan and Sebastian's discretion, which I pointed out in protest when they went into the office with the West Coast Alpha and shut me out. I suspected he kept his vote against coming out and they wanted to make sure he understood that the majority vote stood and he'd be expected to comply and behave accordingly. Once Quinn had provided everyone else with lists of Red Blood members, everyone else quickly departed—except Cole, who lingered under the pretense that he needed to speak with Sebastian.

Cole had no inhibitions when it came to the Midwest Pack's home. He took the invitation to visit as an offer to treat it as his own, which is how he found me watching the former Worgen pack in their hub. They were quite interesting to watch. Most of the things they did I didn't understand; I probably didn't want to given the questionable nature of much of their work. They had diagrams and mappings projected on the wall, and I stood in awe as they filled them out, making connections and exposing associations. I toed that fine line between being wary of them and impressed. If this was what was needed to help Steven and the pack, I would shelve my disapproval. We needed this information.

At Cole's approach, I started to leave. "Sky, should I expect you to make a mad dash whenever I come within a few feet of you?" he asked, his lips quirked into his genteel smile that could weaken the strongest walls of apprehension. "Do I make you uncomfortable?"

"No," I lied.

His smile widened. "This pack has been cloaked in secrecy for so long and lies have become such a big part of it that honesty is met with trepidation. It shouldn't be that way."

I remained silent, hoping it would end the conversation. I had the options to turn from him and take the exit leading out the back or walk past him toward the front exit and Ethan.

His eyes kept searching for mine, waiting for me to look up.

When I did, he smiled. "You chose to mate with Ethan?" he asked softly.

I nodded as I debated how rude it would be to pull a Gavin and walk away when I was done listening, which I was. Good manners kept me rooted in front of Cole, waiting for a good time to make a quick and polite exit.

"Your speech was very moving," I said, trying to change the subject from my relationship with Ethan.

Giving me a half-smile, he said, "It wasn't meant to be. Contrary to what you want to believe of me, the well-being of *all* the packs is my priority."

I bit down on my lip, holding back the words threatening to come out. He felt that challenging Ethan was the best thing for all the packs. I disagreed. Behind his gentle brown eyes, self-assurance, and congenial ways lurked something nefarious. It made me uneasy, especially since I couldn't quite put my finger on it. It seemed like a predator and prey situation, and I had somehow become the latter. As the predator, he'd subdued himself enough to give me a sense of false security, a feeling that no harm would come to me, when I'd be devoured minutes later. I didn't like feeling that way.

"Nevertheless, I appreciate it. I think it changed some people's minds." I slipped past him.

"Bye, Sky. I'm sure we'll see each other again?"

I stopped midstep and turned to look at him, doing a poor job of hiding my disappointment. "You're staying."

"Of course. It seems reasonable to do so. As you said, I was able to change people's minds. I believe that might be of some use while we handle this situation, don't you?"

No, not at all. I want you gone. I had every intention of letting Sebastian and Ethan know about my uneasy feeling.

CHAPTER 9

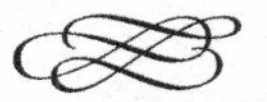

The thought of Cole staying in the city irritated me, and there was no hiding it from Steven when I showed up at his door. He assumed I was upset because of the meeting today.

"I guess the meeting didn't go well," he said, stepping aside to give me room to enter.

"No, it went fine." Walking past him, I picked up a discarded shirt, folded it, and placed it on the kitchen counter. Then I closed the milk carton and put it in the refrigerator, and I closed a box of cereal and stowed it back in the cabinet.

He blushed. "I was going to get that."

"Of course, because you would *never* leave milk or a box of cereal out." I wiped peanut butter off a knife on the counter and put it in the sink. Raising a brow, I then wiped down the counter. After that, I took a seat next to him on the sofa. Another shirt lay near my feet on the floor. *He is a pig.* I refused to pick it up and threw my look of disdain between him and the shirt until he snatched it up and tossed it on a chair. It was obviously too much work for him to fold it.

"Cole made several impassioned speeches, and I think he was responsible for changing many minds," I admitted reluctantly. I might have had my suspicions about him, but his role in shifting opinions was undeniable. Credit needed to be given.

Steven made a sour face at the mention of Cole—one that perfectly expressed how I felt.

"Yeah, that guy. He's an asshole," he said and ran his fingers through his hair, disheveling the copper waves.

I gawked at his description of Cole. Steven, like his mother, tended to describe people—except for vampires—favorably. Even when he was insulting them, his deep Southern lilt, somnolent eyes, and affable appearance rounded the edges of the sharpest words. But he was curt and harsh in describing Cole.

"What has jail done to you?" I teased.

His brief chuckle was an attempt at levity, but the weight of the situation made it difficult to succeed. "Well, he is."

"Why do you say that?"

He sat back in the chair, crossed his arms over his chest, and considered the question for a long time. I prepared myself for a laundry list of things.

"Those who really know him see him for the snake he is. He presents himself as a nice guy trying to help, and he provides enough assistance that it seems like he's on your side, but I always feel like he puts obstacles in the way that tip things in his favor to make himself look good." His face twisted into something between a scowl and a frown. "I can't prove it, but he isn't above doing that. From the moment he met you, he's made no secret of his interest, even knowing you're involved with Ethan. For most people that means you are off-limits; for him, it's like a minor obstacle. He *might* be a good guy, but I'm rarely wrong about things like this."

I considered that actionable and an easy reason to dislike him, but I was surprised Steven resented him so much for the same reasons.

He was still frowning when he asked, "Remember when Sebastian was shot?"

I nodded. It had been a hard time for me because Ethan had had to decide whether to challenge Sebastian if he felt he could no longer lead the pack. I'd urged him to forget the rules. But if nothing else, Sebastian and Ethan adhered to pack rules. I'd been convinced Sebastian would never step down, and they both believed that challenges were to the death. Ethan had since changed his stance because I'd requested it. Sebastian hadn't.

"Sebastian was not up to par when Ethan decided not to challenge him."

"That's because Sebastian was healed; he was better."

"Healed, yes. But he definitely wasn't up to beating Ethan. In that situation, I'm confident Cole would have challenged him. He's done it before, in his own pack, which is why he's moved up the ranks so fast. We're allowed to challenge if a person is too weak to maintain his position, but most people wait until the person is fully healed, even if the time needed goes past the pack's standard seven days."

We healed fast. A member could be challenged seven days after a major injury under the belief we should be fully healed by then. If it took longer, it was generally accepted that the person wouldn't get much better, which left them with the decision to step down or be challenged for their position.

"Do you think Sebastian trusts him?" I asked.

"I think Sebastian sees him for what he is but also understands his value. He's an asshole, but he is as good of a strategist as Sebastian, if not better. As you've seen, he's got interpersonal skills that are better than Sebastian's. Their approaches are different, but they both get results."

I spent several minutes looking around his new rented home. A large window gave a perfect view of the forest behind the house, which he had to use often. The open space allowed him the freedom to roam in his animal form, something he enjoyed doing. And in the short time he'd lived there, his neighbors had developed an affection for him. But most people did.

"You like living here, don't you?" I asked. I hoped he'd say he didn't, because I was going to extend him an invitation to move back in with me, even knowing he would refuse.

He shot me a broad smile. "I really do."

"Did you move out of my house because of Ethan?"

"Mostly because of Ethan."

I nodded. "Everything is just different, but I don't want you to feel like you don't have a place in my life because of him."

"I don't. But you think things will be business as usual and they won't."

That was inevitable. It wasn't Ethan and Sky anymore; it was *us* and *them*. I looked down at my ring finger, knowing a ring belonged there. I conceded, "You're right."

He beamed. "I am most of the time."

"And also the epitome of humility," I shot back with a smile just as wide as his. I gave the room another sweeping look. Crumbs were on the coffee table and there was a hint of vanilla, cinnamon, fudge, and lemon. "They feed you, don't they?" I asked.

He laughed. "Do they ever. My next-door neighbor, Mrs. Clave, has brought me dinner almost every day since I moved in."

"She's probably hitting on you," I teased.

He shrugged. "She's in her seventies, but she's pretty hot and she cooks. It could work out." There was a sparkle in his eyes, and the levity he always possessed had returned. His mellow personality made most of us forget he was a were-animal, too.

His eyes fixed on my wrist where the mark once was. I occasionally rubbed it, used to feeling it tingling.

"Josh still hasn't figured anything out?"

I shook my head. He was just as concerned as I was. Something was brewing. Someone wanted Maya unleashed, which was the reason I refused to use magic. I refused to give her an opportunity to use it to her advantage.

It was odd how drastically the mood in the room had shifted, and we both withdrew into our thoughts. Mine were divided between the removal of my mark, Cole, the Red Blood, and the army Liam was forming. And I worried about Steven's fate. I tended to push the latter aside because it was harder to bring myself back from the brink of frustration, fear, and sadness over it.

Steven chewed on his lip and then finally spoke. "Mom's going to ask Sebastian to transfer me to the South."

I kept my voice even, despite it not feeling level at all. "Do you want to go?"

"I want my mother not to worry about me and to be happy."

"You didn't answer my question. Do you want to go?"

He wouldn't give me an answer because his mother's happiness was his priority. "Moms worry—that's what they do, Steven. Whether you are here, in the South, or even under her roof, every time you go out she'll worry," I said, broaching the topic cautiously.

"But she'll worry less."

It was my turn to be the voice of reason. "True. But she'll worry nonetheless. If you want to go because that's what you want to do, then do it. But don't do it because you think it will stop Joan from worrying because you'd be deceiving yourself." *Dammit.* I was giving him the same speech Ethan had given me about him right after the arrest when I'd demanded that Steven stay with me so I could watch him. For hours, I'd rambled and Ethan had quietly listened, and in the end, he'd tried to reason with me. As with Joan, unfortunately, reason hadn't been in my grasp. I'd been reactive, and it hadn't been a good place to be. Now I was trying to do the opposite.

The words felt better as I continued, "You have to do what's best for you and this pack. And we need you." Then I looked around his home. "As far as making her happy," I said with a grin, "I bet she'd be flabbergasted if she actually walked into your home and it didn't look like a pigsty."

"Did she put you up to this? Because she said something like that this morning when she called."

"No, but doesn't it say a lot about your housekeeping skills that she knows it looks like this"—I waved my hand over the room —"even before getting here?"

"She's sending someone to clean." He looked at his watch. "They should be here in half an hour."

I snorted. "You really should be more ashamed of that."

He shot me a wolfish grin—he was undeniably part of the canidae family. "I should be, shouldn't I?"

I stayed until the crew came, and it was, indeed, a crew. Maybe Joan had suspected Steven would need an army or the service had sent more cleaners because of time limitations. I shot Steven a look of derision as I left.

He shrugged, lacking the shame one should have in this situation.

Driving home, I decided to talk to Joan the moment I had an opportunity to get her alone. She wasn't unreasonable. She was being ruled by her emotions. Her instinct to protect overrode logic and pack dynamics, but maybe once she considered her reaction, she would change her plan to return him to the South.

Consumed with thoughts about protective instincts, I hadn't noticed I'd changed directions and was heading to Quell's house. Or rather the home where he'd lived before Michaela had forced him to leave.

I might be able to convince Joan to change course, but I wasn't sure I could say anything to change Quell's mind. Or whether I should try. Ethan was right: my desire to help him had gone past altruism and into pure selfishness. I couldn't let him die, even though the only reason he still existed was because of me. I couldn't give him the death he wanted.

I had the nagging feeling there was more to this than him feeling he was ready to let his life go. Was it just something that vampires went through once they reached a certain age? Michaela's words kept echoing in my mind—vampires who reached a certain age began to long for their humanity. For years, Quell was a misanthropic vampire who despised the human race for the inhumane acts it perpetrated. He'd held himself to the same standards, revolted by the atrocities he'd committed while human during wartime. He'd tried to commit suicide but Michaela had saved him. *She'd* saved him, and he hadn't cared that it had been a selfish act. She'd considered him beautiful and another lovely body to add to her collection. He'd translated it as her loving him and exhibiting some form of humanity that no longer existed in the human world. He'd clung to that belief despite how cruel she'd been to him and to others.

Pulling into his driveway triggered memories of the time we'd spent together. Regardless of whether his feelings went beyond friendship, he was my friend. I parked behind a pearl black sedan, the same one I'd seen Demetrius drive, and quickly got out of my car.

Demetrius met me on the walkway to the house's front door. His dark eyes held a look of quiet contempt. He was no doubt still seething from me telling him Chris hated him. I wasn't sorry.

He blocked me from advancing. "He will be fine."

I attempted to go around him, and he blocked me again.

"Stay away from him. You want this to be better? You want him to accept his lot in life? Stay away from him. You aren't the cure—you're the disease."

I had been called many things, but *disease* by far felt like the worst. I considered the source, Demetrius. The things most people considered virtues he deemed weaknesses. Perhaps he thought he could indoctrinate Quell.

"You won't change who he is," I said.

"But I will try."

"Changing him will not make him better off. It won't make him happy."

"But it will save him. You asked me to help him, so let me," he said gently.

I sucked in a ragged breath, unsure what to think. Sincerity and kindness rang true in his voice, and I was taken aback. Was Demetrius capable of being concerned about anyone other than himself? Was he more than a self-indulgent, petulant man-child?

I nodded and started back to my car.

"Chris should know about this," he said.

I turned to him and rolled my eyes. He *was* incapable of selfless acts. As I moved toward my car, I caught a flash of movement. He was in front of the driver's side door. His abysmal eyes had a dangerous cast. Standing taller, I refused to let him intimidate me.

"If I do anything to you, I'd spend my days having to deal with Ethan and your pack. I'm not foolish or arrogant enough *not* to understand that. Quell means nothing to everyone but you. I saw the concern on your face when you came to visit me. His life is as important to you as Michaela's was to me." He moved away slowly, but I kept my eyes on him. "You owe me a life. I want Chris, and you have two weeks to deliver her. If not, Quell's life will be taken as payment. Make no mistake, he will be the first, but not the last. Bring her back to me!"

It wasn't the first time he'd threatened others in my life. I knew he was talking about David and Trent.

CHAPTER 10

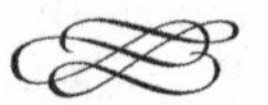

The next morning, I had dressed for the day before breakfast so I wouldn't be receiving a proposal in my pajamas. When I saw Ethan dressed in a suit and tie, I figured he'd had the same thing in mind. We ate breakfast, discussing the meeting the day before and Joan's request for Steven to return to the South. All the while, I looked around the kitchen, even searching for the bulge of the black jewelry box in his clothing. I'd peered into my glass of apple juice before drinking it, in case he'd reenacted a romantic-comedy cliché. Nothing. He watched me with a furrowed brow, a tilt of his head, and a mystified look.

"Are you looking for something?" he asked breezily, straining to fight a smirk.

I glared at him and chewed on my bottom lip, debating whether I should say something. I decided against it. "No," I said in an overly chipper voice. I used the moment to ask, "Why didn't you tell me about the DA making a motion to revoke Steven's bail?"

He shrugged dismissively. "It wasn't important. It wasn't going to happen. He was grasping at straws. He has nothing, and he's clinging to whatever ploy he can throw out there. I suppose next month he'll make another motion and will continue making them until the trial is over."

"Whether you felt it was relevant or not, I needed to know. We can't have any secrets between us."

He flashed me a grin that reminded me of the look of a cat cornering a mouse and getting ready to play with it. "Good." He leaned over the table, scrutinizing me. "You want to tell me about your visit with Quell yesterday?"

My mouth dropped open, and I quickly snapped it closed. "Are you tracking me?"

He exhaled a sharp breath. "Sky, you are unique in many ways, but it doesn't stop you from being predictable. You smelled like Demetrius, and the only way you'd see Demetrius is if it involved Quell. How did your visit with Quell go?"

I culled through the various ways to broach the topic. I opened my mouth to speak, and Ethan stopped me. "Truth, Sky. I don't want an altered version. I want the unedited story."

That's exactly what he received. I told him about the visit, the fact I wasn't permitted to see Quell, and Demetrius's threat against Quell and possibly David and Trent. Ethan sat silently, taking it all in. Concern registered on his face and quickly faltered. He stood to get another cup of coffee and then leaned against the counter. After taking a long sip, he gave me a cool, appraising look. Things had shifted; his manner had slipped into professional stoicism. Ethan the Beta. I didn't really care for that guy and didn't want to discuss Quell with him.

"You killed Michaela. You didn't think there wouldn't be consequences, did you?"

"He won't retaliate against me."

"Sky, someone will pay for her death, and it may very well be you. I agree, he probably would never consider killing you. *But* understand the only thing standing between you and a painful, torturous death at the hands of Gabriella and Chase is him. We can retaliate, but it won't change the fact you will be dead."

I tried to speak again and was silenced by a squelching look. "Let me finish. I've tried to understand what's going on with you and Quell, but, it really doesn't matter if I do. Quell is a problem and has been for some time. I won't allow him to continue to be one. This has nothing to do with us; it's for the safety of our pack member—you."

"Don't you touch him," I said sternly, putting enough steel in it to cause him to raise a brow. It was the same demand I'd made of Steven when he'd issued the same threat against Quell.

Ethan responded the way Steven had. "If he's no longer a problem, I won't. If he becomes one, I will. I'll deal with your anger—I'm sure you'll have a great deal of it. My decision won't be contingent on your feelings but on whatever is right for the pack and its members."

Neither one of us said anything for a long time. "I'm just trying to fix it."

"I know. Problem is, some things and people are broken beyond repair. That's Quell. You've forced him to stay alive when he doesn't want to. Just let him go."

A noncommittal nod was all I could give.

When Demetrius, Chase, and Gabriella entered the pack's home later that afternoon, I became aware of just how perilous the situation I'd put myself in when I'd killed Michaela. Dressed in midnight-colored slacks and a shirt, Demetrius shot me a cool look of disinterest. Oddly, his clothing made his dark eyes stand out even more. He was a pool of darkness as he glided across the floor, the reaper, death in its most beautiful form. His confidence couldn't be denied, nor could his arrogance. Sebastian and Ethan watched his approach. The room filled with strained hostility, as it did each time Sebastian and Demetrius met. They both respected and resented each other's position. Each encounter was an opportunity for a subtle display of dominance in an even more subtle attempt to subjugate the other. They barely acknowledged each other before Demetrius turned and found a position against the wall. He surveyed the room and briefly allowed his attention to land on me. Although he didn't speak, his eyes spoke volumes as he changed his posture, standing taller, rolling his shoulders back, and honing his gaze. It was a warning, a reminder that I hadn't met the obligation he thought I had to him—Chris. It all came back to Chris, and if I didn't comply, my friends would pay with their lives.

The terrible duo were dressed in pale hues of blue and tan. Gabriella was in a slim-fitting single-button pantsuit. I could see the outline of the weapons she hadn't bothered to conceal. Chase didn't look as eccentric as he typically did with his hair dyed dark brown instead of its typical wild colors. He still sported piercings in his ears, brows, and now his tongue; he kept exposing and fiddling with the latter. But the conservative light blue shirt and slacks didn't make him look as ominous as the dagger-like gaze he settled immovably on me. The bravery I tried to display wavered by the moment under their heavy scrutiny. They wanted revenge, and there was no doubt about it.

I understood why Sebastian had called this meeting. It was his subtle way of getting leaders of the otherworld together to see where they stood and if they had any intentions of joining Liam's army.

The vampires looked like classically sculpted statues and stood off to the side, without making any effort to seem less vampirey. They didn't breathe and needed to move minimally, which was off-putting. Their abysmal midnight eyes moved periodically over the room, and I was always the last place they looked. Gabriella was having the hardest time hiding her contempt.

"Do you want to step out until everyone has arrived?" Ethan asked me.

I shook my head. I'd killed Michaela; it wasn't a secret, and I couldn't hide from the truth. I distracted myself with thoughts of the recent changes in the house. Some books had been removed from the library. The dining room had been cleared out. There were several bedrooms that were now empty. The pack had several retreats, homes that were rather secret where we could go. Each pack was required to have several. This had once been one, but we'd begun to use it as a sort of community center. With more people frequenting it, we could no longer consider it a safe house or a place of refuge. Sebastian was preparing for a mass exodus.

Within a half hour, others arrived. The second arrivals were Abigail and Gideon. Gideon ruled the elves with his sister at his side. Due to antiquated and misogynistic rules, she was forbidden from ever holding the superior position, but she wasn't going to let a little thing like that get in her way. She'd colluded, manipulated, and even orchestrated an assassination attempt on her brother so she could be the power behind the throne. Gideon had said on more than one occasion that she was to be treated with the same authority and respect he received. Her decisions were his decisions. He'd essentially handed over the reins to her.

Her arm was wrapped around his as he escorted her into the room. They didn't look like fraternal twins at all, and the similarities between them were unsettling. Their platinum-colored hair and brilliant, expressive violet eyes gave them a wintry appearance. They had narrow faces, high cheekbones, and delicate mouths. They were handsomely pretty, prettily handsome, or simply androgynous.

Once hailed as the master of mischief, Gideon had settled into his more serious role quite well. With Abigail, he'd orchestrated a takeover of the Makellos, the self-proclaimed elite of the elves, without inciting a civil war. Although the Makellos were powerful, they were few in number, which had made it possible for

Gideon to bring all elves under one rule. He allowed the Makellos to maintain Elysian, their residence separate from the other elves. Their ruler, Liam, had stepped down and been given a lesser role as a delegate.

The twins promptly went to Sebastian and greeted him with a nod of respect before making their way across the room to a sofa. Sebastian and Abigail always shared a look, a hidden understanding that their collusion had given her brother his position. Abigail was to provoke a war to weaken the Makellos so Sebastian's debt to them could be forgiven when Gideon won, which Sebastian was sure of. Even if he was unsuccessful in the war, it would cause a split among the elves and render Liam insufficient as an ally. Marcia would never have aligned herself with a fractured and weak organization, which was something Sebastian wanted. Their alliance had proven to be problematic.

At that moment, I recognized the depth of Sebastian's stratagem. While everyone else was playing checkers, Sebastian was playing three-dimensional chess. Before anyone realized it, he'd won the game and knocked over the board.

Claudia, representing the fae, came in shortly after the elves. Ariel and three other members of the Creed were the last to arrive. Ariel gave Sebastian a quick nod as she surveyed the room, paying close attention to Abigail and Claudia. Finally, her attention went to Demetrius.

"It seems everyone is here. Shall we get started?" Gavin asked.

"Not everyone." Sebastian kept looking at the door, and within minutes, a tallish man, his haughty face twisted into a scowl, appeared. Liam. Sebastian's eyes were cold as he looked at him, pinning him in place. Liam didn't have the good sense to be bothered—he stared at Sebastian defiantly.

"Sebastian," he simply said as if more words were beneath him.

Sebastian greeted him in the same manner and quickly dismissed him with a bitter smile before addressing the room. "As you all may know, we have a situation."

"That situation being that Steven was charged with the murder of other were-animals, and the act was caught on video and is now circulating among the humans," Demetrius interjected.

Sebastian fixed the vampire with a hard look. "I think we're all aware. It's been discussed extensively with you all in private." He went back to business without pause. "We are not reckless and will handle this situation appropriately. Our priority is the secrecy of the supernaturals and the existence of the otherworld, and we will make every effort to maintain it," he said with unwavering confidence.

"'Every effort,'" Abigail said pointedly. "I'm sorry, Sebastian, but 'every effort' isn't enough. I'm sure you made 'every effort' not to be exposed, and yet here we are, on the cusp of it. So please accept my sincerest apologies if your 'every effort' means nothing to us."

Sebastian didn't show any surprise at her reaction and instead gave her a small smile of acknowledgment.

"Abigail, that is enough," Gideon said his voice crisp with authority that caught his sister by surprise. She looked shocked and affronted by the stern look he'd cast her way. In her mind, she was operating a puppet government and pulling the strings. Gideon was making a rare show of authority, and Abigail didn't like it. Their eyes locked in contention.

Sebastian's face clearly showed he was working hard to tame his words. "Abigail, I've been in this position for nearly twenty years, having taken it over when I was barely out of my teens, and as you know, my efforts tend to work. I am being forthright with everyone because I don't want anyone to be blindsided by anything—"

"Or you're being upfront because we already know?" Liam interrupted in a dark, frosty voice. "You have behaved like savages for so long it was bound to catch up with you. Packs, fights for dominance, restrictions on smaller packs that don't want to join your savage gang." He lifted an eyebrow scornfully. "Oh, you didn't know I was aware of that. We all are." His hand swept dramatically over the room. "As I said before, you are all savages—animals we failed to appropriately domesticate."

Several beats of silence passed as everyone waited for Sebastian's response. His eyes narrowed ever so slightly, and he ushered a congenial smile onto his face. "You're right. I have restricted who can live in this area. I didn't do it for our protection, but for yours. We started to get an influx of were-animals who couldn't be trusted and presented a threat to those I consider allies. Let me remind you that in animal form, we are immune to your magic. It takes me and many in my pack less than ten seconds to change. Enough time for me to run at you, change, and rip your throat out." He pulled back his lips, baring his teeth in what should have been a smile. Since he looked more wolf than man as amber flooded into his eyes, there wasn't any pleasantness on his face. He looked hard and vicious.

While everyone else was focused on the exchange between Liam and Sebastian, I was navigating my way through Sebastian's spin on things. The "no unaffiliated packs" rule had been instituted after a group of rogue were-animals had attacked me. *Talk about getting people to see the reality in which you want them to believe.*

Shrugging off his wolf, Sebastian presented them with one of his disarming smiles. If they hadn't seen the predator peek through the man, it probably would have worked better. He was the Alpha, and that was all they would see. "Understand if I can do that, there are others who can as well. My packs have protected you even without your knowledge. I have an alliance with Gideon; I consider him a friend." Sebastian was taking liberties with the word *friend*. He didn't hate Gideon but hadn't completely forgiven the former Master of Mischief. "Which means I do what I can to ensure no harm comes to him and those he protects. If I'm not mistaken, you fall under his protection, which is why I was shocked to discover you've been gathering an army, consulting Hunters, and have even enlisted humans to 'contain' the situation."

Gideon's eyes widened, and he gave Liam an incensed look. Abigail didn't look shocked at all; she was most likely aware of Liam's machinations. Abigail's loyalties shifted based on who could serve her agenda. I was curious about what it was this time.

"If we are indeed contained, it seems Gideon would be without allies and vulnerable. And that army of assassins and Hunters you're building might serve more purposes than just dealing with the were-animal situation. I hope I'm quite wrong in my speculations." Sebastian was good—he'd planted the seed of betrayal. Gideon wouldn't have any other option but to address it and do something about the small army Liam was assembling. For good measure, Sebastian had made it seem as though his decision to limit were-animals who weren't part of our pack was for the good of all magic wielders. He'd just finished his game of chess, but it wasn't clear whose board he was about to knock over.

"Abigail, I appreciate you informing me of this and giving me the list of recruits so I could address it. Gideon is quite fortunate to have your counsel. It's fortuitous that the rules have changed regarding women leading the elves; I believe you will make a great successor once your brother no longer wants the role for himself." Sebastian's grin widened, and Abigail returned a tight smile. Liam's face was ruddy with anger at the thought that she'd betrayed him. Whatever her plans were, Sebastian had essentially ruined them.

Look at that. There's the board he was looking to knock over.

I was shocked that in less than two days, he'd been able to do this with just the information Sable had given us. Instead of attributing it to her, which wouldn't serve any purpose, he'd made it look as though Abigail had betrayed Liam. He'd never trust her enough to consider working with her again. Ethan had the same look of innocence on his face as Sebastian had, and there wasn't any doubt in my mind he'd known this would happen.

"I am asking you to trust me on this. Know that I don't want us exposed any more than you do. But for the safety of my pack, I may have to." He went on to tell them about the Red Blood.

"Humans thinking we exist isn't anything new," Demetrius drawled from his position against the wall on the opposite end of the room.

"True, but they are different. We aren't talking about overzealous ghost hunters. Some of the people involved are respected leaders in the community. That makes the situation more difficult. We don't intend to expose ourselves, but things are getting complicated, and we're covering all avenues so it won't be a surprise to anyone if we have to."

Abigail, still seething from Sebastian blindsiding her, responded, "Then you can't really expect us to believe you can protect our anonymity. What was the purpose of this meeting, to remind us of what we already know—you have violated the implied agreement and expect no consequences?" She'd abandoned any attempts of diplomacy. She wanted immediate vengeance.

Her brother shot her a sharp, warning look that she ignored.

"If you cannot ensure with one hundred percent certainty that you can keep us a secret, then that implied agreement that you and your pack won't suffer some form of penalty for violating our anonymity is void," Demetrius said, pushing off the wall. His eyes challenged Sebastian, whose patience was noticeably on the brink of snapping.

Void? What did that mean? Would they collectively agree to kill us off, leaving any who survived nothing more than an anomaly, freaks with no indication that more existed? The thought brought images of us being hunted by the underworld to the forefront of my mind. We couldn't guarantee with 100 percent certainty that the others in the otherworld wouldn't be discovered —we could only do our best.

"I must agree with Demetrius," Abigail said. "If you cannot keep our anonymity, then we have to forbid you from coming out and"—her gaze shot in Steven's direction—"he must deal with the consequences of his abhorrent actions alone."

Ethan's hand quickly grabbed mine, working through the clench it was in. Once his fingers were linked with mine, his grip tightened, and he gave me a sideways glance. His thumb stroked my skin soothingly. Apparently, I hadn't responded well to Abigail's response because Sebastian had moved slightly, preparing to intervene. I never liked Abigail, and her attacking Steven wasn't helping the situation.

Regardless of whether she'd deliberately provoked Sebastian or held delusions of grandeur about the role the elves had in the packs' decisions, she'd ignited his rage. Amber blanketed his eyes, and he exposed his teeth like fangs. His tongue slid over his bottom lip as if he were about to devour his prey. Abigail wasn't easily intimidated; she was just as dangerous as Sebastian, far crueler, and quite skilled at his game of three-dimensional chess.

Sebastian turned to Ariel. "Do you have anything you'd like to say?"

She shrugged. "We can protect ourselves, and I hope you use discretion and do everything possible to keep us hidden. However"—she sent a stern look around the room—"if I were presented with the difficult decision of saving my own and outing the witches, I wouldn't even give you all the courtesy of this meeting. And I see this as just that—a courtesy. As leaders, we have an obligation to protect one another, but first and foremost, we must protect our own. If outing us as witches would save one of mine, I would do it in a heartbeat. I realize I'm new, but Sebastian's reputation speaks for itself. I have no worries, and if any of you are even considering me joining you in remedying the situation without giving him a chance to fix it—don't. I will not have any part of it, and to be honest, I would consider it a slight against me and mine because I would do the same in his situation." She shrugged and added, "And if I were you, I wouldn't want me as an enemy." She looked at Abigail, then Liam, and finally at Demetrius. Her obvious disdain for the vampire seemed to provoke him. His dark eyes languidly fell on her as a smile settled on his face.

Abigail fixed Ariel with a death stare, eyes so sharp they stabbed into the witch, who seemed unmoved by it. Ariel held her glare for far longer than most people could. Her lips curled ever so slightly as a wave of magic permeated the air, a less than subtle display of power. Abigail seemed unimpressed, and thunder sounded in loud, boisterous crackles that preceded a torrential rain.

Nice, a magical street fight. That's exactly what we needed to add to the tension. The stormy weather didn't stop until Gideon had placed a hand on his sister and given her an imperious look. Her face relaxed, her intensity fading to something more amicable.

Abigail started to speak, but Gideon intervened. "My apologies for this display. Sebastian, you and I understand each other. Although I'm not happy with the situation, I realize this isn't a decision you've come to lightly. As long as you give your best effort, know the elves are here to do our part to help." He glared at Liam and added, "All of us."

Sebastian nodded in appreciation.

"And I believe I can speak for the fae and offer our assistance to do what we can to maintain the secrecy of our world. Without reluctance, we would aid in ensuring that exposure isn't even an option for you. Do not hesitate to ask for our assistance as needed," Claudia added as if anyone questioned where her loyalty lay.

I didn't see Claudia as a fae at all. She was a Messor, more like the dark elves who could kill with a simple touch. She was the reaper or some distorted variation. Once I'd found out what she was, I'd tried to research it behind Josh's and Ethan's backs. Anytime I brought up what she was, they simply told me she had magic strongly associated with death. I didn't think calling someone a purveyor of death should be done so casually. But they had known her all their lives. She wasn't a reaper, a death wielder —she was their godmother.

The fae's assistance was something that could work to our advantage, but I wasn't sure how. They had the ability to manipulate minds, but could they do it on a grand scale, like to a jury? I felt that dark, suffocating feeling that I'd devolved. But I wanted to protect our pack and, more importantly, Steven.

"Well, it seems as though there is no need for us to discuss this further," Demetrius concluded with reproof. He looked at Sebastian, at me, and then back at Sebastian. "As usual, you do not feel as though you are held to the same covenant as the rest of us. You are so accustomed to behaving like animals, reduced to nothing more than your primal urges and wants, that you are capricious with your promises and deny your obligations."

It felt odd to be chastised by someone like Demetrius, who was a slave to his own primal urges and desires and felt that very few rules, norms, and expectations of civility didn't apply to him and the other vampires. They were narcissistic and self-indulgent beyond belief. Sebastian's stolid expression faltered, showing incredulity at Demetrius's hypocrisy.

Demetrius started for the door, dismissing us all with a wave of displeasure. "This is your mess. I expect you to clean it up without mine having to deal with the consequences of your negligence and foolishness." He slipped out, leaving Sebastian speechless. I could see the fight in him as he restrained himself from following the vampire. He weathered the storm and dealt with the insult.

"You all know where I stand. And contrary to what Demetrius said, I will do my best to make sure this is handled with minimal, if any, exposure for you all. We will bear the burden of this."

No one lingered to chat. Cole watched with interest as Gideon and Abigail departed, but then again, he did the same to everyone in the room.

Winter, who'd been observing everything quietly from a corner of the room, finally spoke. "He has every right to be upset. It's more than just coming out, Sebastian. We have to deal with the aftermath of being discovered." I hadn't seen so much worry on her face since Sebastian had nearly died from a gunshot wound. She continued, voice laden with apprehension, "It's easy to believe that humans will be intrigued by us—and curious. But it's not curiosity I worry about, but whether it will lead to fear. People respond poorly to fear and to anomalies." Winter was speaking from experience. Being a were-snake, she was an anomaly even among the supernaturals. They seemed to be okay with people changing to wolves, lions, jaguars, coyotes, and all variations of mammals, but changing to a cold-blooded reptile was where they drew the line. After Winter's first pack had failed to rid her of what they'd perceived to be a curse, they'd decided the only alternative was to kill her. Her mother had notified Sebastian, who'd gone to Egypt to retrieve her. He'd had to challenge the entire pack, leaving several dead bodies in his wake. Winter was bound to Sebastian and blindly loyal to him. He'd saved her life.

Sebastian studied her for a while. "I will never let anything like that happen. You understand that, right?"

"I understand you'll do everything in your power to keep it from happening. But that can't guarantee it won't," she whispered in a strained voice.

Sebastian simply nodded before turning and excusing himself to his office. Steven wasn't too far behind. After a few more moments, Winter left as well. Ethan went after Winter. I still didn't understand why those two had a way with each other, but they did. I was left alone with Cole.

Slowly he moved closer to me. "This is quite the situation, isn't it?"

I shrugged my response. I wasn't sure what to say, and there was still a part of me that didn't want to discuss things with Cole. He espoused that he had the packs' best interest at heart, but I had a feeling he reveled in the strife more than he'd ever admit.

"Winter's upset, but she'll follow him anywhere."

Unsettling discontent wafted off Cole like a stench. Was it Sebastian's power or Ethan's position that he wanted? Or was it just an ingrained desire to take what others had?

"I think we have things handled here. I don't see any reason for you to stay." I was having a hard time concealing my contempt for him.

"Does my presence bother you that much?"

"Cole, I don't trust you."

His tongue slipped over his lips, moistening them. After giving me a long, hard look, he stepped even closer—close enough that all he had to do was lean down for his lips to brush against my ear. "I don't think you mistrust me. You don't trust how you feel when you're around me. Deep down, you know fidelity has never been something Ethan has committed to, and there must be a part of you that believes being mated still won't change that. He mated with you because you're sweet and inexperienced. I don't think you're nearly as naïve as he believes you are. I think you feel it. You made a mistake. The small imperfections you tolerate will soon tire you. I suspect I'm a reminder of all the things you won't get from Ethan—honesty being one of them." With that jab, he turned and walked away before I could respond. He looked over his shoulder before he exited. "I'm sure he hasn't told you that the mating bond can be severed for reasons of infidelity. It happens so infrequently most people forget. After all, what type of person would cheat on their mate? With Ethan, it might be something *you* remember."

The urge to walk into Sebastian's office and ask that he send Cole away was so strong I had to force myself to stay planted in that spot until my anger and umbrage resolved. It took longer than I'd expected. Cole was very gifted in the art of manipulation, or perhaps he wasn't and I was constantly feeling the weight of my insecurities about our relationship. Ethan's past was something I often thought about, and I hated that Cole could easily make me worry about something I'd worked so hard to get past.

CHAPTER 11

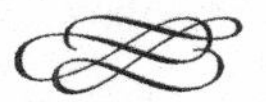

After my run-in with Cole earlier that day, I really wanted to be alone and was working on a way to ask Ethan to stay at his house when Josh knocked on my front door. I didn't want to see Ethan, and I wasn't thrilled about seeing his brother, either. I urged a smile onto my face and opened the door.

He stopped at the threshold and assessed me. "What's wrong?"

"Nothing."

His lips twisted into a scowl of disbelief, and he angled his head. "Really, because I don't believe you at all."

"Cole," I breathed. "He has a way of getting under my skin."

"About Ethan, right?"

I stammered, trying to find the right words while ignoring how awkward it was to discuss my relationship with my mate's brother.

His face was still twisted into a scowl. When he finally spoke, his voice was serene and earnest. "I've tried to get my brother to stop doing challenges to the death. I hate them and still consider it a barbaric practice. I get that few people challenge him or Sebastian because of it, but it's still hard to deal with. He stopped doing it for you. The thought of hurting you bothers him. He's never cared enough about any woman to worry about it."

He swept his hand over the room. "He stays here all the time. Do you know how much he hates your house? It's a tenth the size of his, you don't have the same privacy he likes, and you have neighbors who drop by all the time. I'm convinced he only likes a handful of people, and on most days, I'm not sure I can be counted among them."

I made a face. "Yeah, you really do irritate him."

I was treated to one of his wayward grins. They seemed to share a peculiar sibling pride from irritating each other. It was a dynamic I didn't understand. Sometimes, their interaction was reduced to puerile extremes in attempts to out-annoy each other. He moved closer and clamped his hands on each side of my face as he brought me close to him. After planting a chaste kiss on my forehead, he continued, "Do you know the level of overprotective crazy my brother has? Now I have someone to share it with, and it's still too much."

"Speaking of overprotective crazy, why are you here?"

"Magic. You need to do it."

There was a familiar pounding on the door as if a magical spell had summoned them. I wasn't surprised to find Trent and David at the door, grinning, holding my full moon basket. They handed it to me the moment I opened the door and pushed past me in their typical fashion. As usual, they were bright-eyed when they saw Josh. Initially, they, too, were charmed by the charismatic guy with the tattoos, disheveled hair, and sleek, lean physique. His looks had held their attention the first time, and maybe even the second time, until they'd seen him perform magic, and then that became his sole appeal. I imagined they'd been on their way home when they'd spotted his motorcycle. The basket was an excuse for them to visit.

Seated on the sofa across from Josh, their eyes glinted with expectation.

"You know I change into a wolf, right? Does that impress you at all?" I asked, sorting through the bag of caramel and chocolate-covered popcorn, glazed nuts, and chocolate-dipped fruit. Even though I appreciated the actual call of the moon, I looked forward to the basket more.

Trent looked at me with little interest. "Yeah, yeah. Your hot boyfriend is a wolf, the sexy mean one is a wolf, the gorgeous Southern boy is a coyote, and tall, dark, and broody is a panther. And Dark Swan with the resting bitch face is a snake. Yeah, impressive. You're all great. All animals I can see at the zoo. Good for you—a menagerie. I'm sure there's a cookie in that basket. Why don't you treat yourself to one?" My sneer made him laugh, but I only garnered a fraction of his time. His attention was back on Josh, who displayed amusement at my neighbors' interest. He might have been faking it; they didn't care.

An hour later, Josh had done his version of *Fantasia*, with books, pillows, and various knickknacks moving in a chaotic dance. He treated them to several more tricks, including moving an object from one of their hands to another, and after several moments of pleading, he traveled with Trent, moving him to the backyard and back into the livingroom in a matter of minutes. Magic never bored them, so Josh had to end the visit by telling them he had to work with me. Only then did they seem mildly interested in me. I urged them to leave because I wasn't sure what to expect from my restricted magic. I was nervous doing it even with Josh; I didn't want to risk their safety.

Josh smirked once the door closed. "Uninvited guests," he teased. "I'm sure my brother loves that."

I shrugged. "He likes them."

"I'm sure he does.... You've met him, right?"

I laughed. "He doesn't play well with others."

Josh was still smiling warmly as he stood in front of me and grabbed my arm, examining the spot where the mark had been. Concern overshadowed his face, placing a wary frown on it. He released my arm and ran his fingers through his hair several times.

"Do something easy, like a protective field," he instructed softly. Stepping back, he observed me avidly.

Tightly bundled magic packed away for storage, never to be used again, felt heavier—ready to be used and exert its energy. I relaxed into it, allowing it to release, unfurl, and course through me. As soon as I gave it free rein, it flooded through me, renewed and strong. Too strong. It was different from what Josh and I had worked with before, and he sensed that, too. He watched with caution, his hands positioned to use his magic easily if necessary. A golden diaphanous sphere formed around me, and I was surrounded by the strong magic that was neither natural nor dark. The connection felt foreign, as if it were being controlled by something else. The overwhelming feeling was similar to what I'd felt when Maya had used me to curse the pack. Pressing my lips tightly together, I refused to allow any words to come through me. I closed my eyes to concentrate, and images of people appeared. Intense eyes enchanted in magic. Their lips moved in unison, and I tried to make out what they were saying or reciting. An invocation—no, a spell. I snapped my eyes open.

Magic pulsed off the sphere so hard it pushed Josh back. A magical sandstorm whirled through the room, pinning him against the wall. He struggled, and strong magic blasted from him; his eyes went black as coal as he called on more powerful magic. A dense mass of magic formed in the bubble, suffocating me as it pulled at my breath and coursed through my body. A slow death. I pushed back; she pushed harder, working to control my words and actions. Maya wasn't fighting me, but Josh. He wore the struggle on his face.

I wasn't going to win the magical battle with her, but I refused to concede. I forced a change as she'd done when the Creed had been about to restrict her magic. She made me pay dearly for the decision as she fought the transition. I felt my bones break and screamed from the pain. The pull of my ligaments was torture as they moved to accommodate my new form. I felt the pressure of my clothes tightening around me before they ripped from my body. Hair stabbed through my skin. Fur matted to my body, but I was no longer ensorcelled. My panting was drowned out by Josh's. He rested against the wall, his face pasty and glistening with sweat. I rested for a long time, sprawled in the middle of the floor and trying to gather enough energy and pain tolerance to go through the change again. Transitioning back to human form was comparably easy and less painful; I was holding on to the excruciating pain I'd just endured.

Half an hour later, I was in human form, wrapped in the throw from the sofa and sitting across from a wide-eyed Josh.

"What the hell was that?" he finally breathed out.

"I don't know. It's not the same magic. It's not even dark magic. She's using Faerie magic." I was guessing—Faerie magic was its own distinctive brand.

"I think she's looking for a new host," he said as he rested his head back against the wall. "Me."

She was probably tired of me restricting her and was looking for someone who possessed a great deal of magic. Together, the two would be unstoppable.

"She was in my head, trying to lure me into accepting her." Fae were weaker descendants of Faeries and had the ability to compel people into artificial emotions to do their bidding. I imagined Faeries had that ability on a larger scale. From the look on Josh's face, it had been hard to resist.

Before I could question him further, his phone rang. He grabbed it off the arm of the sofa, looked at it, and made a face. "She's fine," was the first thing he said. "And if you care, I'm fine, too." He didn't have the energy to lace his words with the typical acerbic sarcasm he reserved for Ethan.

Josh answered Ethan's questions tersely until he reached the end of his patience. "I know you're on your way here. Why don't you save the questioning?" He ended the call.

"Do you really wonder why you're not often among the handful of people he likes?" I joked.

He flashed me a half-grin, which took a lot of effort. "Not at all. I take pride in him randomly taking me on and off the list."

Ethan didn't show up alone. When I came out of the bedroom, dressed in different clothes since my other clothing was torn beyond repair, I found Ethan, Sebastian, Dr. Jeremy, and Kelly in the living room. Behind them, trying to peek around, were David and Trent.

My brow furrowed in inquiry as I tried to make sense of the odd grouping. I understood my pack being there, but I had no idea why they'd invited David and Trent. I quickly realized they hadn't.

"Hi, guys, what brings you by?"

David pushed through the small crowd. "Well, my little cotton blossom," he started while I wondered how he'd come up with that one and when I would tell him to take it back wherever he'd found it. "We were at home about to have a nice dinner when our electricity went out. Everyone's except yours was out for nearly fifteen minutes."

"Mine didn't go out."

"Exactly. And I'm not the only one who noticed." He gave me a look similar to what Sebastian and Ethan gave me when they thought I'd been careless with magic. "Your secret club is having a big problem with the 'secret' part."

"Sorry. Things got a little out of hand."

David shrugged. "I understand. Just be careful. Please." There was more to his request. I knew he worried about me more than he wanted to admit. His introduction to the otherworld had been grim. He'd never admit it, but I could tell he wished he could be in blissful ignorance where vampires, fae, mages, witches, and were-animals were just tales.

With a strained smile, he looked over at Josh and me, then around the room, summing up the situation as best he could with the limited information he had. He didn't even look curious, just wary of what it all meant. Waving, he and Trent let themselves out.

"How are you?" Dr. Jeremy asked, moving toward me, penlight in one hand, emergency bag in the other.

"I'm fine. No bruises, no injuries, just a slight headache." *The latter a result of trying to figure out what the hell just happened.*

"Maya's looking for a new host," Josh informed them, disconcerted.

Ethan's face blanched, and Sebastian inhaled a ragged breath. They both knew that without Maya, I couldn't live.

"We need to find another shade," Ethan speculated after a few minutes.

"Spirit shades can't just enter someone, right? The host has to request it," I said.

"Exactly. But every time Sky uses magic, Maya takes it as an opportunity to lure someone into asking. She got in my head, and I'm not sure how." Josh started to pace, biting at his nail beds. "It was like a siren call. I had a hard time resisting it. If Sky hadn't shifted, I'm not sure I could have held out very long."

"Sky, don't do magic," Sebastian instructed. He didn't have to tell me—doing it made me feel like Maya was suffocating me. She'd offered her life to me. Was killing me the only way she could free herself? Or was she hurting me just enough to distract me and prevent me from silencing her? I'd been too busy trying to breathe to notice her attempt to beguile Josh, which added to my fears. She didn't need to cast a spell to find a host.

"You don't have to worry about that. She won't find another host she considers worthy, human or were-animal. Shifting to your were-animal prevents her from performing magic, and humans with their lack of magical ability will weaken her," Josh said.

"The biggest question is why. The removal of Sky's restrictions and Maya trying to find another host are somehow linked. This can't be a coincidence," Sebastian mused. I knew it was more than just the connection he was worried about. He wanted to know how it would affect the pack, who was behind it, and why. *Why* was the biggest question. Once we found out the why, the who would be easier.

Ethan regarded his brother. "Josh?"

"I don't know, but I plan to find out."

~

It was hard not to be offended by Josh departing as fast as he could, doing everything short of scaling the walls to keep his distance from me. I wasn't the problem; the shade occupying my body was. I couldn't imagine what it felt like to be coaxed by her, to feel the rapture of her magical seduction. Josh was highly susceptible to different and more powerful magic. It was his Achilles' heel, and he knew it. That magical nudge from Maya had been all he'd needed.

I looked around the empty house, still feeling the magic that wisped through the air. Ethan had gone with Josh to figure things out. It was only a matter of time before they realized they couldn't work together. Good intentions were one thing, but execution was another. They always intended to get the job done, only to be faced with the reality that their personalities didn't work well together. Eventually, one of them would relegate the other to another room in the most impolite way possible. Brothers.

The lingering magic felt odd. Images of the people I'd seen during the magical sandstorm resurfaced. And there was the enigmatic pull of the Aufero, which I hadn't felt in a while. I tried to shrug it off, but denying it was hard. I opened the closet where I stored it. A foggy gray coloring drowned out its orange glow as it pulsed to life. I slammed the door closed and locked it—as if that would change anything.

I couldn't just sit around; I needed to do something. With a notepad and a spell book next to me, I sat on the couch and wrote out the words I thought the people had been saying. I wrote just one word per line, afraid that if I put them all together, I would unwittingly unleash something again. I had no idea what language the people were using, so I spelled the words phonetically. I scanned the spell book for something similar. Google Translate was a bust, as did a global search.

I was doing another search, using slightly different spellings of the words, when there was a light knock on the door. A familiar knock—Quell's. I disabled the ward and opened the door wide enough for him to enter, but he stayed planted at the threshold, staring at me. The smell of blood came off him in waves; he'd either just fed or was feeding too much. Vampires always had a faint odor of blood, but it now overpowered Quell's scent.

"Do you want to come in?" I asked with hesitation. He seemed different, and I wondered what Demetrius's programming had done to him.

"Yes." He didn't move, displaying the same hesitation I'd had with the invite.

After several long moments, he stepped over the threshold and went into the living room. True to his nature, he stood unmoving in that unsettling, unmistakably vampire way.

The silence was getting to me. Had he come here to stare at me and occasionally breathe? The latter always unnerved me, because he did it at five-minute intervals.

"Are things going well with Demetrius?" I asked, ending the uncomfortable quiet.

He nodded, his appearance solemn. "He's not Michaela."

I bit my tongue to keep from telling him that was a good thing. If nothing else, it was a lateral move.

"I don't like him," he muttered. I commiserated with his dislike of Demetrius. Then he moved and added, "Ethan, I don't like him at all."

He came nearer, leaving little space between us. He reached out to touch my hand but decided against it, dropping his arm to his side as his eyes drifted from mine as if it was painful to look at me.

For several minutes, I debated bringing up Ethan's assertion that Quell was in love with me. It seemed so arrogant and the very height of hubris to assume someone had fallen in love with you. Ethan was a good judge of people and situations, though.

"Quell," I started in a whisper, aware he would be able to hear me. He lifted his eyes to meet mine. His blank expression made it more difficult to approach the subject. "Are you in love with me?"

"Yes," he responded before the last words fell from my lips.

I was speechless for once.

"I know you are with him," he mused quietly. "I would never do anything to hurt you." He was giving me the same unwavering commitment he'd given Michaela. I hated it. Devotion to his maker wasn't rooted in any form of logic, and I couldn't understand. "I love you," he said once, and then again as if committing the moment to memory, the way I looked when he said it. I knew it was how he truly felt. It made me feel worse about the situation because I didn't know how to fix it. I was okay with him loving me—I loved him. But I couldn't have him *in* love with me.

"Quell."

He silenced me by lifting his hand. "You love me, too, but in a different way, don't you?"

I nodded.

"Demetrius is right. You shouldn't visit me anymore." He paused, pouring his emotions into his words. "Or call me. I should do the same. This should be it. Nothing good can come from us trying to maintain a friendship since it can be neither what I want nor what you expect." He professed his love again. I tried not to wince; I knew he meant it, and it was unrequited.

Tears brimmed at the edges of my eyes, threatening to spill. I was losing my friend and the eccentricity that accompanied him. Another thing had changed in my life. I knew it was for the best, but that didn't lessen the pain. I simply nodded; there were no words that could change or fix things. I closed my eyes as he pressed his cold lips to my forehead. He was gone before I opened my eyes.

I couldn't fight the tears anymore. I wasn't sure if they were for Quell or me giving myself permission to let all the turmoil wash over me. Steven, the removal of the mark, everything that had occurred today, murdering Michaela, Quell's exit from my life.

Exhaling a deep, ragged breath, I allowed myself to feel all of it, because I had to move on tomorrow.

I spent the next hour doing that before I returned to deciphering the invocation of the voices I'd heard.

CHAPTER 12

"Say the words again," Ethan instructed as he pulled out of my driveway. I should have been saying them to Josh in the library, where I should have been helping him figure out what was going on. I grudgingly repeated the words, or what I thought they were. It didn't seem like the right time for Ethan and me to be enjoying a night out. He hadn't left room for me to decline when he'd informed me of the reservation. Perhaps it was him celebrating Quell no longer being in my life. His face had been blank when we'd discussed the details of the visit. He'd inclined his head into a slight nod when I'd confirmed he'd been right about Quell's feelings toward me. He hadn't gloated; if I hadn't known better, I'd have thought he seemed sad. Perhaps he'd felt sorry for me for not recognizing it in the first place. He'd given his sympathy with great effort, and I hadn't expected it. He'd kissed me lightly and whispered, *"Lamento que estejas magoada por isso." I'm sorry you are hurt by this.* His words had been sincere. Ethan was sorry that I was hurt, but not about Quell's absence from my life. I understood.

"I don't think you're saying the words correctly," he said, changing the subject.

I didn't have an eidetic memory, but I could recall things with great accuracy. I mimicked the melodious timbre of their voices while repeating words so unfamiliar I couldn't compare them to anything.

"What did the people look like?"

"They all looked alike. They reminded me of Gideon and Abigail. Fair hair and skin with an ethereal pearly glow. I remember their amethyst-colored eyes were luminous and hauntingly eerie. I opened my eyes too fast to get anything else."

Ethan's mood had changed, and I felt the heaviness of it.

"Is it that bad?"

He didn't answer immediately, and I knew why he hesitated. He was used to keeping secrets and providing information sparingly, especially to me.

"I don't want to worry you needlessly," he said.

"Ethan," I urged, "you can't protect me from everything."

"But I'll try."

"I don't function well in the dark," I reminded him firmly.

"Although you aren't pronouncing any words I'm familiar with, it sounds like Faerie. The lilt of the words is similar. The speakers' appearance is how one of my books describes it." His words were filled with frustration.

Faeries. Maya had become a spirit shade as a child; what I'd seen couldn't be her memories, but she'd shown me the past before with just a spell—images of were-animals before they'd evolved into what we were. She had access to unimaginable magic. I wondered about her: how old she was, who she'd inhabited before my mother had hosted her. What had she learned? What diablerie had she practiced? What gave her such a thirst for power—the same innate thing that had driven Ethos to behave the way he had, or a relentless desire to control the otherworld?

I was still thinking about Maya and her motives when we got out of the car. Taking my hand in his, Ethan gave it a squeeze. "Not tonight. We'll deal with it tomorrow."

I smiled. It was forced but pleasant. We really needed a night out where we weren't discussing Steven's case, the humans determined to expose us, or Maya. He kept hold of my hand as we walked into the restaurant. It had been on my list to try for years, but no matter how many times people raved about it, I couldn't justify paying for one meal what I'd usually spend on two weeks of groceries. Ethan wore a dark gray suit, and I had on a black, slinky midi dress that hugged my curves, with hints of silver that gleamed in the light. The chandeliers were white and polished silver starbursts. The entire restaurant was decorated in white, silver, and shades of muted gray. White and silver tablecloths were topped with blown glass vases of swirling silver and white in coiled embraces. Hints of colors came from exotic flowers in the center. One side of the restaurant had floor-to-ceiling windows that provided an unobstructed view of the city, iridescent in gold, orange, and pale yellow. Beautiful. Ambient music played. Regardless of whether the food was good, people were paying for the experience.

The host escorted us to the back of the room, where Ethan always chose to sit. It was an exquisite setting, and the inevitable was going to happen. I'd been hinting at the ring, searching for it in my meals, waiting for it to reappear in my bathroom or even next to me when Ethan got out of bed. Nothing. And now I was caught in a rom-com. Suspiciously, I looked for the source of the music, hoping that mid-meal someone wouldn't come to our table to serenade me. I slid into the seat and eyed Ethan; his features betrayed none of his intentions. He ordered white wine instead of his usual red.

"White wine?" I inquired after the server had left.

"I wanted something crisp. The fish here is fantastic. We should order it." Then he grinned. "But first, we should order dessert."

He relaxed into his chair as much as he could. He wanted me to leave everything that had happened over the past few days at the door, a task even he was having trouble doing. Eventually, the conversation centered on just us.

"Have you thought about our living arrangements?" After watching me for several moments, his lips kinked into a half-smile. "I guess the uptick in your heart rate means no."

"Stop doing that. It's so invasive!"

He gave me a look of amused incredulity. "Your heart rate is secret?"

"Yes."

He was still laughing at me when he excused himself. He claimed he was going to the restroom, but I didn't think it was a coincidence when the server returned immediately thereafter with wine and white chocolate mousse garnished with dark chocolate. "I was asked to bring this to you before the entrée." The server beamed as he placed it in front of me.

Moments later, Ethan returned from the "restroom."

Responding to my eye roll, he leaned in. "Are you still pretending you aren't a dessert first type of woman?" he teased.

Ethan, you are better than this.

I examined the wine, and when I found it ring-free, I took a sip.

"Do you like it?" There was a hint of amusement in his voice.

"It's delicious." It was. I enjoyed the light, crisp taste of peach and the trace of cinnamon that lingered on my palate. Ethan's brows drew together as he watched me cautiously skim through the mousse, anticipating the click of my spoon against the metal band of the ring. I didn't want a cliché moment, but I would have preferred that over me mining through my dessert, inspecting my wine like a paranoid conspiracist, and constantly scanning the area for someone coming our way with a violin. All that seemed okay compared to him knowing I wanted the ring and withholding it because he was a total ass.

After the second course, Ethan took a sip from his glass and leaned back in his chair, assessing me. "Is something wrong?"

"No," I said brusquely.

"Hmmm. Are you expecting something?"

I shook my head. He flashed me a cross between a smirk and a grin. "Are you sure? You seem frustrated." He took another sip from his glass while keeping an inquisitive eye on me.

I am frustrated, you Betahole.

People moved throughout the restaurant, a band played off to the right, the server came to our table numerous times to refill our glasses, and not one of them was an introduction to getting the ring. I was ablaze with anger by the time we settled the bill and we were ready to leave.

"You're an ass," I asserted as he stood, extending his hand to help me out of my seat. I refused to take it, glaring at it.

He maintained a solemn look as I worked on keeping my voice down to avoid making a scene—but one was begging to be made. "You are absolutely ridiculous. Everything has to be your way and when you want it. If anyone manages to not do things the *Ethan way*, you have to make a statement about it. News alert: you can't get your way every time. That's what it's like to be an adult. Things don't happen at a simple snap of your fingers. So what, I didn't take the damn ring when you offered it. I was in my pajamas. Is it too much for you to compromise sometimes? Do you have to be an ass every time you are forced to remember the world doesn't bow to your every whim? I'm letting you know, I won't have it!"

His lips pulled into a fine line, but he remained silent as if waiting for the rest of my outburst. "I guess you're finished. Are you ready to go?"

I nodded and stood. As we walked out, I kept in step with him but maintained enough distance that he couldn't take my hand or touch me.

We drove in uncomfortable silence, and I made a sound of displeasure when he pulled into the driveway of the pack's house. The last thing I wanted to do was pretend we were a happy couple in front of people, and I damn sure didn't want to run into Cole, who'd made deleterious remarks about our relationship. I didn't have the ability to ignore them or offer a rebuttal.

Instead of going to the house, he headed to the back, closer to the forest, and stood in a spot a few feet from the house.

"Tonight is the anniversary of your first solo change. This is the very spot where you did it. You didn't want to, but when I urged you to do it, you did—by yourself. That's when I knew there was more to you. You had an untapped strength and perseverance. You weren't just obstinate." He gave me a small smile. "It is also where you were when I realized I love you. You ran out of the house and looked so hurt that I was keeping secrets from you. It was the first time I had a problem with it as well because I didn't want to be the person who caused you pain. It wasn't because of guilt—it was because I cared that much about you." He took in a deep breath. "I should have told you I loved you then instead of telling you the way I did, but I didn't feel it was the right time." He made a face, and for the first time, he seemed embarrassed and sheepish. He shrugged. "And I definitely shouldn't have done it in a small room in the pack's house." He took out the ring. "You were right about the proposal. I shouldn't have made it so casual. It should be special—something we'll always remember. I wanted it to be now, on the anniversary of your first solo change, in the same place I realized I love you."

Taking my hand, he slipped the ring on my finger. Then he brought my hand to his lips and kissed it. "It's not because I need the world to know you are with me. I want you to have it as a reminder of how I feel about you."

Humble pie and remorse tasted like dirt with a strange tang to it. I looked at the ring and at him. I kissed him, long and deeply.

Pulling me close, he chuckled softly and asked, "You really thought I'd put a ring in your dessert? I've seen you eat. Unless I wanted it swallowed, there was no way I was doing that."

"I'm not that bad," I responded with exaggerated offense.

"You always attack food like you're taking down an animal three times your size."

I kissed him again, harder, pulling him to me and guiding him to a tree a few feet away. I buried my face in his neck, taking in his scent of musk and cardamom and expensive cologne. My lips ran languidly over the pulse there. Darkness shrouded us, with just a wafer of moonlight breaking through, offering pearls of light. I pulled his jacket off and tossed it aside, then went to work on the buttons of his shirt.

He grabbed my hand and secured it against his chest. I could feel his heartbeat. "If anyone's here, you know they'll be able to see us," he reminded me in a deep, raspy voice.

"So?"

He grinned, releasing my hand, and I returned to quickly undoing his buttons. He shrugged off the shirt and tossed it near his jacket. He shuddered under my touch as I ran my fingers over the sculpted muscles of his chest and down his stomach. I reached his pants and unfastened them. His hands skated gently over my shoulders, slipping the straps of my dress off and placing kisses there. Then his hands slipped around my back and pulled down the zipper. When the dress pooled at my feet, I kicked it out of the way. I was in just my bra and panties, and he pulled away to take me in smiling. He leaned in and kissed me harder, pressing me into the tree. One tug and he'd pulled away my panties.

"I liked those," I teased.

"Me, too." My bra received a gentler treatment; he deftly unhooked it, and it fell to the ground. The cool breeze brushed against my nipples, hardening them. Then they were warmed by Ethan's tongue laving them before he took one into his mouth. Slowly and gently, he delivered the same treatment to the other. He lowered his head and roved over my body, planting soft, warm kisses until he met the delicate spot between my legs. Warmth coursed through me as his tongue eased over me. Entwining my fingers in his hair, I panted as a wave of pleasure moved through me.

He came to his feet in one swift movement. Weaving his fingers through my hair, he pressed his lips to mine before sliding his hands down to my legs and securing them around him as he sheathed himself in me. He moved against me in slow, controlled, rhythmic movements. The pace quickly escalated as he thrust harder. My heavy breathing wisped against his lips, my fingers dug into his back, and I met his movements with the same voraciousness, with a need that only Ethan could extinguish. Soon, pleasure enveloped us, sating our need. Still joined, we sank back into the tree, allowing it to bear our weight. He held me for several moments before slipping out of me. He cradled my face in his hands and kissed me again.

He whispered, "I love you," with what seemed like apprehension and confusion before he moved away and redressed.

"You seemed confused by it. Do you wish you didn't?" The first time he'd said it, he'd admitted he hadn't wanted to.

"Of course not," he said gently. He looked away for several beats and had a hard time coming back to me. Expressive gunmetal eyes with whispers of blue held mine. "I'm just surprised by the depth of it."

I wasn't sure why he felt this way—Ethan rarely did anything half-assed. Even his affection for his brother reached a depth I could only call "Ethan's type of love."

Hand in hand, we walked out of the woods and were met by a massive light gray wolf. Cole. His eyes raked over us. First, he took in our entwined fingers, then the full length of Ethan, and then me. He regarded my hair, which I knew was a disheveled mess, and my dress, which I'd quickly donned without straightening the straps properly. One had slid off my shoulders, revealing more of my cleavage than I was comfortable Cole seeing. I repositioned.

"Did you need something, Cole?" Ethan said with a tone that

was undeniably hostile. The wolf backed away, and moments later, we were in front of a naked Cole, who didn't even cover his private area and just stood with his hands at his sides.

"I didn't expect to see you two here." Cole kept his attention on me. I ran my fingers through my hair, attempting to make it more presentable, feeling uncomfortable under his scrutiny.

"I can say the same thing," Ethan shot back, the sharp edge remaining in his voice.

Cole seemed to enjoy his disdain. Once again, I drew his attention, and he leered at me for no other reason than to provoke Ethan, which he successfully did. Ethan was on him, face-to-face. Cole met his primal rage with a relaxed smile.

"Ethan, you seem insecure. If she's with you, my looking at her really shouldn't bother you. After all, she's yours. All I can do is look, right?"

I hated the "yours" and "mine" they used so flippantly. It made me feel like property, not a person. But that was the least of my worries. Ethan's anger had escalated and I didn't see it ending well. The last thing we needed was infighting while trying to deal with everything else we were facing. Slipping between them, I placed my hands on Ethan's waist and steered him back a few feet. He would have to get past me to get to Cole.

"Go home, Cole. Your pack would be better served with you there, not here," I said, keeping my focus on Ethan.

Cole's lips parted, but the words were lost. *Does he think I enjoy his presence?*

After several moments, he finally spoke. "My pack will be best served knowing they won't be exposed soon. I'm here to make sure it doesn't happen." He backed away, unconcerned with modesty. "The Red Blood has been aggressively following several members of the Midwest Pack. Instead of romantic evenings, perhaps you should be using that time ensuring we stay hidden. Do your job, Ethan." And with that, Cole returned to the house.

With a great deal of effort and a lot of coaxing from me, Ethan returned to his car instead of going after him. I wanted this to be over and Cole gone.

"Let's do the full moon at my house, not with the pack," Ethan suggested as we drove away. I enjoyed the camaraderie of sharing the full moon with the pack—it promoted a connection I appreciated—but if Cole was there, I'd prefer to share it with just Ethan.

CHAPTER 13

If anyone had told me I'd feel an affinity for the full moon, I wouldn't have believed them. Now it was different—it called, and I didn't have a problem answering. The moon wouldn't be full for hours, but I felt its presence as I drove to Ethan's house with several boxes of my belongings stashed in my car. I was really moving in with him. Hours of debate last night had ended in a stalemate, with me agreeing to split my time between his home and mine. He would give me the key to his elusive office. The promise of having access to years of his research might have been the reason for my anticipation. I felt like the clear winner, even after agreeing to accept a job with Josh on a temporary basis.

I had every intention of working for a day, enough to keep my end of the bargain, and then finding a different job. One brother at my house—or me at his—and the other at my job wasn't a great idea.

Glancing at the office key connected to my keychain, I grinned, thoroughly distracted by the prospect of the information I'd find. More about the Faeries and maybe even information about the Mouras, who were tasked with guarding the protective objects. I nearly crashed into the cars stopped in front of me. People were working on what looked like the battery. There was just enough space for me to get around them. I began to maneuver past but was immediately pinned in by another car. Andrew from the bar was driving it—this wasn't a coincidence. I looked forward, preparing to ram my way through, only to find the barrel of a shotgun pointed at me.

"Get out of the car!" the man holding the shotgun demanded, his voice as gruff and coarse as the rust-colored beard that covered his face. Stout, he was solid but not muscular and didn't move like someone trained in combat or self-defense. He did, however, appear confident in his ability to use his weapon. "Get out of the car!" he barked again. When I didn't move, he repositioned the gun to my head.

His heart was too steady. He was calm, probably more than ready to use the shotgun. A man beside him held what looked like a tranquilizer gun. It was unsteady in his hand. His lack of confidence was likely due to his young age or inexperience. His snarled face didn't match his warm, brown eyes that watched me with immense curiosity. His erratic heartbeat was distracting, and he was holding each breath for too long as if he warding off a panic attack. Determining who was more dangerous was difficult: the man who definitely knew how to use his gun or the young ash-blond guy whose nervousness might get me shot by accident.

Debating whether my car could plow through to freedom in either direction, I looked in my rearview mirror. Andrew got out of the car, knife in hand, and took that decision away from me by stabbing the blade first into my rear left tire then into the right. He moved closer to the door. "Get out." The man with the shotgun moved to the side, keeping the gun trained on me.

I quickly thrust the door open, shoving it into Andrew and throwing him off-balance. I lunged at him and wrenched the knife out of his hand. My left hand caught him by the throat and the right held the blade under his chin. I pressed hard enough to draw blood, a warning that I wasn't playing. "Drop the gun and the tranq," I demanded.

The scruffy man with the gun choked out a laugh. "I don't care what you do to him. That guy's too fuckin' bossy in the first place. He's the reason you're alive, missy. When I see a wild animal, I kill it. And from my understanding, I got a wild animal in front of me." He pulled back his lips in a cruel smile. "We're about to prove that supernatural creatures exist. Our source says you're a wolf, and dammit, seeing you move the way you do, I know something isn't right with you."

"I'm not sure what delusion you're under, but it's going to get you arrested or killed." I narrowed my eyes, tamping down my emotions as much as I could. The last thing I needed was for my wolf eyes to show.

"I have a gun, you have a knife. Who do you think is likely to die?" he challenged, his finger steady on the trigger.

"I'm not sure what delusional BS you've been fed, but you're mistaken. Whatever you're looking for, I can assure you, I'm not it." My voice was steady as I pleaded my case. I couldn't quite figure him out and didn't know what approach to take. Denial was my best bet. "What do you know about your source?" I pressed the knife a little harder; Andrew lifted his head to avoid it going too deep.

"I met him once and knew right away he wasn't all there. You had to have sensed it, too," I guessed.

Mr. Shotgun kept an unwavering eye on me and the look of derision and revulsion didn't falter either. What evidence had he seen that was so convincing? Was Dexter that persuasive? He *was* quite the provocateur; he'd convinced the previous Creed and others to help him with his assault against us, which had led to many of their deaths.

"He's many things, but he's not crazy. I've heard rumors for years. I've seen a man run into the woods and a wolf come out. People thought I was crazy, seeing things, on drugs. I know what I saw. I can guarantee I'm seeing one now. We will prove it to everyone. People will know that animals are walking around pretending to be human." The look he gave me made it clear he believed I was just an animal masquerading as a human, and he wanted to treat me as such.

"You're making a mistake you'll live to regret," I warned.

The young man with the tranq gun was moving, trying to get a better shot. I kept stepping out of his line of sight, bringing Andrew with me as a shield.

Mr. Shotgun cursed and groused, "I have to do everything."

My eyes went from the kid back to him. He dropped the shotgun, snatched a concealed tranq gun from his belt, and shot. The dart stabbed me in the arm. Another one in the leg. The medicine coursed through my body, numbing but not enough to take me down. We didn't respond to medicine the way others did, but I couldn't let him see that. He retrieved the shotgun, trigger-happy and looking for an excuse to kill. As I fell, Andrew turned out of my hold. He immediately knelt beside me and checked my pulse. "She's alive.

"You know I don't really care."

"I can't believe she turns into an animal. She doesn't look like it." A new voice, probably the younger man. I smelled various scents. I lay as still as possible, using my other senses to get an idea of where everyone was. I needed the man who'd shot me closer. He was the most dangerous one. The rest I could handle.

"Remember what he said. They are deceptive-looking, like the man on trial. He doesn't look like a killer, either," Mr. Shotgun said from afar, voice eased. "Get her in the truck. You'll see what she is in a few hours when the moon is full. Everyone will."

I couldn't let them take me. But if I reacted they'd know the tranquilizer was ineffective, and they likely had more, enough to disable me. If I fought Andrew and the young man, I'd still have Mr. Shotgun to contend with. They just wanted to see me change, but I wasn't about to let them. That's the only thing that would work—proving them wrong. I hoped not changing would convince them were-animals didn't exist.

My arms and legs were secured with both zip ties and cuffs. They didn't handle me all too gently, either, complaining I was heavier than I looked as they eased me into the car. After what I thought was twenty minutes of driving, they carried me down a flight of stairs. Eventually, I was resting on my back on a hard floor. The ties were cut off and the cuffs removed. I heard several voices. There were at least four people. Then a very familiar voice spoke—one that made it difficult not to jump up from my position and snap his neck.

"I can't believe you pulled it off," Dexter said.

"This one is a wolf," said another strange voice close to me. His breath smelled like smoke and coffee, and I didn't like the way he hovered over me. He brushed my hair away from my face. "She's pretty. Very pretty." When his hands brushed across my breast the first time, I thought it was an accident; the second time was definitely on purpose.

"Yeah, but she's a dog. Are you attracted to dogs?" asked Mr. Shotgun.

"Right now, she's a woman, Barry," he said, tugging at my shirt inappropriately. As soon as he was close enough, I thrust my forehead into his nose. He yelped in pain. My next strike was to his throat, making it even harder for him to breathe. Tear-filled eyes distorted his vision, and he easily tumbled to the ground when I swept his leg from under him. I rolled to my feet, placed my foot on his upper arm, and twisted his forearm until I heard a crack.

"Don't touch me," I gasped, moving away from the body when I heard the cocking of a gun.

I was surprised to find Andrew was the person aiming it at me. "Thomas, get out of there."

Thomas whimpered, his arm secured against his body as he stumbled out of the cage they had put me in.

"I told you they were strong and prepared to defend themselves. Whatever injuries you acquired, I'd say you deserved them," Dexter taunted as Thomas stumbled away and lumbered up the stairs.

Someone followed him, leaving six people in the room as far as I could tell. Everything still had a hazy filter on it, and I wondered what they'd injected me with. I had a feeling Dexter had something to do with it and its potency. I blinked several times to clear my vision.

What would Thomas tell the nurses and doctors at the hospital? There was no way he'd tell them his arm had been broken by a woman he'd groped when he'd thought she'd been unconscious.

My vision had cleared a great deal, but there was still a light fuzziness layered over everything. It could have been the drugs or my body's response to fighting the moon. After a few more minutes, I got a better view of Andrew, who had moved away and was seated in a chair to my left. A surly-looking woman with dirty blonde hair whose scornful look pulled her lips into a thin line was perched on a stool next to him. She wasn't unattractive, but the twisted look on her face made her appear harsh and bitter.

"You think she's a werewolf?" she asked skeptically. Her dark blue eyes bored into me, summing me up and quickly dismissing the idea that I was a predator.

"Don't let her appearance fool you," Andrew asserted in a low voice. His lips lifted into a faint smile. "Your eyes. At the bar, they did the same thing as Steven's did in the video."

He moved from the chair, taking a detour to a camera pointed at me before coming toward me. "And in an hour, no one will dare mock me when I bring up werewolves," he said through tightly clenched teeth.

"They'll be visiting you in prison," I shot back, walking around the small cage. "You drugged me, kidnapped me, and locked me in a cage. How exactly do you plan to get out of this?" Then I looked at Dexter. His smug look made me want to grab him and smash his face against the bars.

"Do you think people will even consider arresting me once they find out what you are? After tonight, people will pay us bounties to capture more of you."

"Drew," the woman said in a cool, commanding voice. "You need to calm down. Five years you've been at this without success. I really hope you're right this time."

"Without success! We had a chance for success but you let him go."

"The full moon came and went and nothing happened. I believe you, but I won't go to prison for you. We were lucky nothing came of it." His friend was a reluctant supporter. She'd probably known him so long that it was hard for her to believe he was crazy enough to think that people turned into animals when the moon was full. Maybe they'd captured a were-animal, but a Felidae who wasn't forced to change until Mercury rose.

Andrew moved even closer to the cage, but he stayed out of arm's reach. He walked around it, assessing me like the animal he thought I was. "Do it again," he said. "Do it again!"

A smile tugged at my lips. "Do what?" I inquired docilely.

"Does it hurt?" he asked.

"What, being locked in a cage?" I shook my head. "But I guess you'll find out soon enough, won't you?"

"Not the cage. When you change into a wolf. Does it hurt? Is it true you heal faster? Are your senses heightened?" He knelt and pulled a knife from an ankle sheath. "If I cut you, how long will it take to heal?"

I moved away from the bars, feigning intense fear.

"Don't you dare," the woman commanded. Andrew looked over his shoulder at her, calmly, and reclaimed his seat next to her.

The situation was out of control, and I had Dexter to blame for it. I started to count backward from a hundred and thought of anything that would help me control my anger. My thirst for revenge was sweeping through me like a tsunami, and I couldn't give in to it.

Dexter could obviously sense my rage and it amused him. A deviant smile curled his lips. I glared at the person responsible for my imprisonment.

I surveyed the room. Andrew had four co-conspirators. Barry, Mr. Shotgun, was a believer; I couldn't sway him. The two leaning against a wall seemed on the edge between hope and skepticism. And the blonde woman would have to see me turn into a wolf to believe. I would make sure she didn't. She struck me as the type who could convince the others it was all fantasy.

"I will admit, Dexter, you have a way of convincing people to do things that will ultimately get them jailed or worse." I moved my attention to the others. "Did Dexter tell you how he knows me?" I asked and stepped back, easing into an unassuming manner and giving them a full view of me. The woman looked more unconvinced that I was a vicious predator, and for the first time, I appreciated how innocuous and meek I looked to others. Chris often said it was my wide doe eyes, so I widened them as much as I could. I probably looked like a Blythe doll. "He's convinced you that werewolves exist. Did he tell you how he knows me?"

I had their full attention and hoped any doubt they possessed had intensified. "He was convinced he could *make* were-animals, and he tried." That wasn't exactly the truth, but he'd have to convince them otherwise. He knew me, and there was no doubt about that. "My friend was one of his victims. We rescued her, but we couldn't rescue the other people he'd experimented on. She'll never be the same." There was some truth to that. Kelly would never be the same—she was a were-animal now.

Dexter attempted to maintain his composure, but he appeared to find it increasingly difficult under the weight of his accomplices' anger and intense scrutiny.

Throwing fuel on the fire, I added, "The people he recruited for his past project didn't fare well—only he did. This time, he'll probably walk away unscathed. His money will protect him. What about you?" I looked around the room. They likely weren't thinking about me being a wolf anymore, but about how they might have gotten in over their heads.

Barry, eyes ablaze, snarled, "You better hope she changes."

I hadn't thought it was possible, but he had doubts. His stance promised a violent response if he was wrong. Dexter's self-assurance faltered for a mere moment. He glowered at me and pulled back his lips in a snarl that could rival any were-animal's.

Any further response was cut off by the thunderous sound of wood breaking and heavy footsteps pounding upstairs. It sounded like the entire pack had come. I was grateful for the rescue, but I hoped they were able to control their eyes. The last thing I needed were humans with feral animal eyes glaring at people I was trying to convince that were-animals didn't exist.

Barry ran up the stairs, gun in hand. More crashing. Plaster drifted down from the ceiling. Barry tumbled down the stairs and landed at the foot of them on his back, his body twisted in an odd position. He was breathing and looked broken, but not enough to keep himself from using his elbow and right foot to scoot away from the people descending the stairs.

"I'm fine," I said in a calm, soothing voice, hoping Ethan would understand we needed to be that way. Sebastian, Ethan, and Gavin came down with the graceful agility of trained fighters and not necessarily of predators. Ethan was calmer than I'd expected him to be when he saw me in the cage.

Andrew's friend reached for the shotgun next to her and cocked it, aiming it at Ethan and Sebastian. I'd seen them move unnaturally fast. If she hit one, she would definitely miss the other, no matter how sharp of a shooter she was. Andrew pulled his gun again and aimed it at me. Ethan stopped advancing. I could feel his anger, the increase in his heart rate, his readiness to strike.

"What the fuck!" he growled.

I remained calm, which settled him some but not enough. I smiled. "They're waiting for the full moon. Dexter convinced them I'm going to change into a wolf then."

The room filled with Sebastian's, Gavin's, and Ethan's laughter. The deep, rumbling sound mocked every person in the room. "Did he?" Ethan asked.

Ethan's gaze met mine. He might not have figured out my whole ploy, but Andrew's presence gave him a good outline.

I nodded. Ethan glanced at his watch and so did Andrew. Dexter let his eyes slip to his wrist just for a second to see how close the full moon was. His haughtiness hadn't returned since his follower's trust in him had waned.

"And then what happens when she turns into a *wolf?*" Ethan asked. His cool incredulity made the situation seem like a worse farce than Dexter's dupes probably thought.

They were wavering.

Sweat formed on Andrew's brow, and his face flushed. It was the first time that night he actually looked as though he doubted werewolves existed. Hope drained from his face, leaving him pallid and pensive.

Frustration coursed over Dexter's features as his gaze raked over the people who were easing into a place of disbelief.

"Don't let them fool you," Dexter said, calmer than he looked. "She's a wolf and so are they." Then he pointed at Sebastian and Gavin.

Amusement feathered across Sebastian's and Gavin's faces, making Dexter's assertion appear more foolish.

"So, you're a wolf, love? You should have told me. That's something I would have liked to know before the engagement," Ethan said with humor. Dexter's frustration climbed, and Andrew looked as if he was going to be ill. Ethan kept a steady gaze on me. His grin widened, and then he turned to Dexter, fixing him with a terse look that incensed him. "Your howl, can I hear it?" Ethan was having too much fun with this. He was in his element, getting people to see the reality he wanted them to believe. They were starting to believe they'd been tricked by a man who had enough money and resources to walk away and leave them on the hook for a kidnapping.

I made a weak attempt. "Aroooh."

Ethan and Sebastian laughed again.

I was surprised when Gavin spoke. "Yes, she sounds like a dangerous werewolf. I suspect she'd rip my throat out if she wasn't locked in that cage. Thank you all for protecting us from the likes of her."

Andrew's friend shared in the frustration—she had to be wondering how they'd gotten themselves into this. The look on her face indicated this was the last time she would give him the benefit of the doubt.

Sebastian gave her a bemused grin that fed her ever-growing cynicism.

"She's a werewolf. I give you my word. Trust me," Dexter entreated.

Andrew barely moved his head in a nod of acceptance, but his face was full of doubt and regret. He chewed on his bottom lip.

Ethan's eyes fixed on mine, and he hesitated before approaching me. I could feel my body's desire for the relief that changing would offer. It longed to be distorted and manipulated into its desired form. A wolf. I resisted, keeping a placid smile on my face and my eyes on Ethan. I felt the calmness that I knew he was forcing himself into for my benefit.

I can do this. I won't change. I could hear Andrew's heartbeat pounding in his chest, his respiration increasing as his agitation rose. It was just minutes before the full moon.

"Let her go," Ethan demanded. He moved closer, and the blonde woman's eyes narrowed. Her stance became protective as she prepared to shoot.

"It's fine. They want to see what happens to me on a full moon. I'll show them, but I doubt they'll be impressed," I said.

I attempted another feeble howl as Ethan stepped closer, canting his head to the side, assessing me and the situation.

"You are one, too, aren't you?" accused one of the men who'd remained against the wall. He appraised Ethan with hostile curiosity.

"I'm what?" Ethan asked coolly.

"A dangerous monster."

Ire and the promise of a painful death slithered along the planes of Ethan's face. "I *am* dangerous, I assure you of that, but I'm not what Dexter has convinced you I am. You have my fiancée locked in a cage like an animal. Believe me, I am the most dangerous person you will ever encounter. You can't even imagine what I want to do to you," he said in a strained voice. He was working hard to keep his bridled emotions from taking over.

Time ticked by, and everyone looked at their watches nervously. Some of the conspirators glanced at the camera that might be a live feed of their failure.

I curled my fingers around the cage's cool bars as I felt the rise of the full moon. My bones ached, and my ligaments cried for relief as my body prepared to be stretched taut and distorted to give way to my wolf. My skin prickled, anticipating fur puncturing through and sheathing it. Denying my body something that it gave in to monthly was unbearable. I swallowed the torturous pain, keeping my eyes fixed on Ethan's, drowning myself in them. The minutes crept by, and I held his gaze to distract myself from what was going on.

I finally spoke. "The full moon is out. Based on mythology—"

Heavy footsteps rushed toward us. The police announced their arrival. Things became chaotic as the people in the room moved around. Andrew's face lost all color, and his mouth dropped open in disbelief. Policemen descended the stairs, ordering everyone to freeze. Before Dexter could plead his case, shots were fired. He stumbled back against a wall. His eyes widened as blood seeped from his chest. Andrew's hands were shaking as he held the gun.

He fired off another round into Dexter before the police shot him. He collapsed to the ground, still.

Every shot made me flinch. Blood pooled around Andrew, tears welled in his friend's eyes, and the others looked on in shock. I doubted this was the ending any of them had imagined.

"Put the weapons down!" an officer commanded sharply, slipping his gaze toward me. The remaining conspirators dropped their guns and raised their hands above their heads in surrender. Even Ethan, Sebastian, and Gavin displayed their hands. Anger burned on the officers' faces upon seeing a woman locked in a cage with one of the assailants holding a gun on her. The video camera pointed at me didn't bode well, either.

A policeman cursed under his breath. "Open it!" he snapped.

The youngest man, the one who'd helped abduct me, was shaking, focused on the gun pointed at him. He fumbled, pulled keys out of his pocket, and dropped them on the floor. "Leave them," the officer barked. One of Dexter's followers groaned as another officer moved toward him with handcuffs. Soon, there were even more police in the basement. Ethan provided his ID and spoke with the captain, who was sorting out the mess. All the scents in the room were merging, but the smells of blood, fear, and anxiety were overpowering. Sebastian and Gavin spoke to the police as well, and since they'd been unarmed during the raid, they weren't cuffed with the rest. As officers listened to what had happened, they periodically looked over at the cage and frowned.

Once the cage was unlocked, Ethan moved closer to me, and I rushed to him, throwing my arms around him and burying my face in his shirt. "I really need to get out of here," I whispered for our ears only.

They questioned me first. I tried to tell the officer everything, but keeping the strain from my voice made it hard, especially since he kept asking me to repeat the same thing because he couldn't believe someone had abducted me because he thought I shifted into an animal. Ethan held me close to him, his heartbeat steady, which eased mine but not enough. My nails dug into his back, and he tensed and pulled me closer. I needed to change.

"Do you need to go to the hospital?" the officer asked. I shook my head, but he continued his assessment, then directed his attention to Ethan. I knew I looked ill and panicked; perspiration glistened on my brow. I leaned into Ethan more as he hugged me to him.

"She should get medical attention," the officer said with rigid concern, not a suggestion but a command. A growled reverberated in Ethan's chest, and I held him tighter.

"She hasn't eaten anything. She was locked in a cage. Sky's not hurt—she's tired and ready to go. Let me take her home." Ethan reached into his pocket, pulled out a business card, and handed it to the officer. "If you have any more questions for us, feel free to give us a call. But I'm taking her home now."

As soon as I was settled in his car, Ethan sped away, driving faster than most people would with the police in view. I let the seat back and closed my eyes, blocking out the streetlights. Everything about my body felt sensitive, and pain drummed through me.

"We should be at the house in twenty minutes," he informed me.

I was panting, my teeth clenched together, my fingers balled into tight fists.

He looked around the surrounding area. "Do you want to change in here?"

He turned down a two-lane street, taking a back road to his house. The car's tinted windows and the limited streetlights would make it easy for us to change unnoticed. However, the car was too small. I looked at what should've been a backseat, but it was too tight even for a small child. "I can't change in this Matchbox car!" I snapped.

"Sky," he said gently, resting his hand on my thigh, "I know you're upset and are having a hard time, but you don't need to insult my car."

I laughed and then punched the side of the door. He growled; I growled back louder. He gave my thigh a gentle squeeze. When we got to the house, I removed my ring and placed it in the console, spilled out of the car, and relaxed into my animal form the moment he pulled into the garage. My nails scratched against concrete. Ethan opened the door to the house, and I jogged into his living room and splayed out in the middle of the floor. I'd been in throbbing, uncontrollable pain and relaxing into my animal half was a relief. Ethan's fingers sank into my fur and rubbed my back and legs. "Are you okay?"

I nodded. Moments later, he shifted, laying his body over mine. I would have loved to go into the woods to run, hear the crunch of the grass underneath my feet, feel the night breeze, and truly appreciate being a wolf with Ethan. But I was so exhausted that it wasn't an option. Instead, I lay there, reliving the events of the night. The sheer look of disappointment and horror on Andrew's face when I hadn't changed and the betrayal when he'd looked at Dexter. Dexter's blank face washed of his smugness. That moment of fear when the bullet had entered his body. The realization this act wouldn't go unpunished.

A shiver ran through me. Ethan moved closer, nuzzling his face into the curve of my neck. It didn't relieve me of the memories. It didn't stop the sound of gunshots from playing a violent soundtrack in my head.

Would this end things? They'd tried and failed to show the world the existence of something that went bump in the night. Would they continue to hunt were-animals, driven by suspicion, by a cause, by the inexplicable need to prove supernaturals existed despite all evidence against it?

After several hours of lying together, we both melted into our human shells. We stretched out, becoming acclimated to the bodies that housed our other halves. Ethan rolled on top of me and softly kissed along my jawline and cheek, allowing his hands to languidly glide over my body, and then he tasted me at the pulse in my neck.

"You delayed a change?" he mused, as his warm breath brushed against my skin.

I nodded.

Pulling back, he smiled, and it held pride and deference. He kissed me again, hungrier. His tongue explored my mouth, tangling with mine. Warmth sparked against my skin as his nails grazed along it. He pressed his supple lips against my body, laving the delicate parts of it, teasing. It was slow, sensual, and gentle. He teased me, making me yearn for more. For him. I tugged at him, urging him. He grinned and settled between my legs. I wrapped them around him as he slid into me and moved in a slow, gentle rhythm. He quickened his pace, and his kisses became harder, fervid and commanding. I gave in to him on a level that was more than just physical.

I tangled my fingers in his hair, pulling him closer to me, breathing in his scent. I inhaled again and ran my tongue along the corded muscles of his neck. The beat of his pulse hummed at my lips. I moved my face deeper into the curve of his neck.

I couldn't fight a growing desire to nibble at his neck. He tensed before relaxing into my touch. I tightened my arms around him and dug my nails into his skin, thrusting my body closer to him. With him still sheathed in me, I nudged him onto his back.

I hovered over him, panting against his lips. I kissed him again, harder, insatiably. I inhaled his oaky spice, and my body ached with a need that couldn't be quenched with feeling, touching, or kissing him. I wanted more. Needed more. I turned his head, exposing the veins in the side of his neck, and buried my face there. Licking at the pulse of his neck, I grazed my teeth against the skin. He whispered my name. The hunger intensified. Need, so strong it overtook my very existence. His fingers curled into my back as he bared more of his neck to me. I inhaled his scent again. My gums ached as if they were waiting for fangs to descend. I bit into Ethan; he hissed. I pressed harder. The uncontrollable craving rushed through me. I sucked in, allowing blood to fill my mouth. Drawing in the warm berry and metallic liquid, I sated the lust that had overtaken me.

Ethan continued running his hands along my body as we pounded into each other. His pants became a calming white noise as his blood spilled into my mouth. Our movements became more frenetic and erratic, trying to find the same pleasure. My fingers entwined in his hair. We thrashed against each other, uncontrolled and wild, until we both shuddered into our climaxes. I collapsed on his chest. He ran his fingers through my hair, kissed me on the head, and then lifted my chin until my eyes met his. Cradling my face in his hands, he said, "That was different. You want to explain?"

I shook my head. Not because I didn't want to, but because my suspicions scared me.

"Okay."

I rested my head on his chest. I knew it wasn't the end of the conversation, but for now, he let it go.

The next morning, I awoke on the floor alone. Ethan's scent commanded the room. I was used to it and didn't wake up until the smell of food permeated the air. I inhaled again: fruit and pastries. I went to the car to retrieve my ring, slipped it on my finger, ran upstairs to his—our bedroom, and took a shower. Rummaging through one of my drawers, I found the necklace I was looking for. Removing the stone from it, I took the ring off my finger and slipped the chain through it. The day before, I'd nearly forgotten to remove my ring before changing; it probably would have been destroyed if I hadn't taken it off. I wouldn't have to worry about it when I changed.

Worst-case scenario, the ring would fall off, and I could find it later. I hoped the length of the chain was enough to accommodate a change without breaking. I didn't mind being the odd wolf running around the city with a ring dangling from a necklace. Still exhausted from holding off my transition to wolf, I couldn't do another so soon. I'd have to test how it held up during a change later.

Ethan was drinking a cup of coffee and held out a red velvet cake as soon as I walked in. I wasn't sure where he'd found one this early in the morning, but I was happy he had. He *always* found a place. My sympathies went to whoever he'd bothered in the middle of the night, inquiring about a cake. Some unsuspecting baker or restaurateur had been inconvenienced. I didn't bother cutting a slice when I knew I would probably eat the whole thing. I grabbed a fork and started on the cake.

After several large forkfuls, I looked up, and Ethan's attention fell to the necklace. He moved close enough to trace his fingers along the tiny links until he reached the ring. Several beats of silence passed before he raised a brow in inquiry.

"I'm afraid I'll forget to take it off and destroy the band during a change or, worse, lose the ring."

Slipping his hand behind my neck in one graceful sweeping move, he unclasped the necklace and let the ring drop into his hand. He placed the ring back on my finger. "I'll get another band or replace the ring," he said quietly.

Holding my hand in his, he looked at the ring on my finger, his tone firm as he said, "I want you to wear the ring."

Nodding, I knew it wasn't something he wanted to discuss further. Smiling, he clasped the necklace, took several steps back, and picked up his coffee cup. "Last night was different," he observed and took a drink. My attention was devoted to the cake because I didn't want to see the concern on his face that I'd heard in his voice.

"Yeah." Warmth inched up my cheeks. I really hoped we

wouldn't discuss it. That intense desire and lust were hard to explain. I found my gaze shifting and lingering on his neck.

"It wasn't just a want; it was a craving, wasn't it?" With renewed interest in my abnormalities, his gaze lingered on me.

I nodded. "It was as if I had to have it. Had to have you," I said, finally looking up and putting the fork down. I'd lost my appetite.

"I called Dr. Jeremy this morning. He's going to have blood delivered every two weeks for you. If you do it that way, you shouldn't have cravings."

I frowned. "I'm not a vampire. I don't need blood."

"No, you're not one. You don't need blood to survive, but obviously, the cravings are getting stronger. And you'll need a way to quench them." He looked at the bare wall as he considered the situation. He sighed. "Your terait is showing more often, too." Ethan was always sensitive to that little orange ring around my eyes. Mine was often just flecks that most people missed, but not Ethan. I wondered if it was concerning or irritating because it was a constant reminder that the person he was with was connected to vampires on a physiological level. Ethan hated vampires, as did most of the pack members.

"I don't want to drink a stranger's blood as if I'm a vampire," I rebuked. It was more than just drinking from a stranger; I was devolving into something I didn't want to be. I wasn't remotely like any vampire. I didn't have light sensitivity, as they'd had before we'd changed that. A stake through my heart would hurt, but I wouldn't go through reversion as vampires did. Both were-animals and vampires possessed preternatural strength, speed, and healing. I didn't know which traits I could attribute to the vampire and which to the were-animal in me. I didn't possess an aversion to silver, either. I didn't know what I could attribute to Maya. Could I be some odd hybrid?

"Then what do you want, Sky? I felt your need last night. It was lust. You might not want to accept it, but you were in the throes of bloodlust. It was strong."

"Then it can be you. I'll use you," I asserted. His jaw clenched as he looked down at the floor. I knew he didn't want to be a willing donor. I felt selfish for requesting it. "Unless you don't want to do it?

He ran his fingers through his hair, mussing it. "No, I don't want to do it. I don't like the idea of being anyone's meal, but if this is what you need, then I'll do it."

"Wow, be still my heart. Your sexy sonnet is making me swoon."

He chuckled. "Would you prefer me to lie and tell you how much I enjoyed it and would love to be your daily meal?"

"Exactly. Now if you can do that with a little more enthusiasm, we can move on from here," I teased.

He made a face and came closer. He grabbed my fork, scooped up a piece of cake, and held it. I opened my mouth, expecting him to give it to me; instead, he turned the fork around and shoved it in his mouth. He laid the fork down on the table and headed for the bedroom.

"You can be a pain in the ass sometimes."

"I know. And you know I'm okay with that, right?" He turned and flashed me a smile, but it lacked enthusiasm. My need for more blood wasn't the only thing going through his mind. He stopped midstep. "That was your first time staving off the change at a full moon." He moved closer to me, intrigue filling his eyes.

I nodded. "I've never had to. I've wanted to many times but couldn't."

"But you did it yesterday."

"It was a matter of life and death. Do you think they would have allowed us to leave if I'd changed? I did what was necessary."

"Sky, it's not that easy. It took months before I could control my change, and it took Sebastian just as long. Most of the unranked were-animals can't do it at all." A smile danced over his lips, and his face brightened. The smile I didn't mind, but the look he gave me seemed dubious.

"We need to give you more responsibilities in the pack. Maybe you can teach others how to hold off the change."

I took a strawberry off the plate of fruit he'd laid out and nibbled on it. "No, thank you. I'm content with my role as Gavin's 'kitty wrangler.' If I could give that job away, I would."

"It really wasn't a request, Sky. As Beta—" He stopped abruptly. He brushed his lips lightly against my cheek before retreating into the bedroom. Before he disappeared into the room, he said, "You can start in a couple of days. I'll set it up. Start with the strongest of the pack—it should be easier."

I didn't argue because it was a skill most were-animals should learn. In my case, it had saved our lives; others might need to do the same. Teaching other were-animals to delay change when called wasn't nearly as troubling as trying to figure out what was going on with my body. I was having a hard time making light of the situation. Ethan was right. What I'd experienced last night hadn't just been a craving but full-blown lust. Ethan had smelled so good I'd *wanted* him, and not just sexually. Part of me had wanted to devour him.

CHAPTER 14

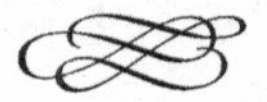

Dexter, Andrew, and the Red Blood wouldn't be tied up in a neat little bow no matter how hard we wished. Ethan seemed just as irritated about being asked to come down to the police station as I was. I was doing a better job at hiding it, though, as the officer questioned us about who shot and killed Andrew.

"I just have a few questions since you left so quickly." The cop looked me over. "How are you doing, Ms. Brooks?"

"Better than yesterday."

Taking my quiet response as anxiety, he gave me a sympathetic smile. "Did you know them?"

I decided to take the same approach I'd taken with my abductors and give him a variation of the truth. "I met Dexter at a bar. He was quite obnoxious and behaved the same way when I saw him later in court." Which was partially true. I'd first met Dexter in his bar when we'd questioned him about Kelly's disappearance, and he had been insufferable.

The cop's brow rose. He shifted to look at Ethan, and I could see the recognition in his eyes. Ethan wasn't just an attorney—he was *that* attorney. The one representing the case that had escalated to a media circus. Or it had initially. It would dwindle to nothing more than "you remember that case with that guy."

"And Andrew?"

"He approached me at a different bar. He'd been watching me at my friend's trial." It wasn't as if the officer wouldn't have figured out my connection to Steven, Ethan, and the trial.

"Did he say anything odd, make you uncomfortable?"

"Yes, he kept going on about supernaturals and how he believed they existed."

"Then later he suspected you were one?" He was having a difficult time hiding his emotions. Disgust and frustration peeked through several times.

I nodded. His frown deepened as if he couldn't understand how someone could believe something as bizarre as that so wholeheartedly that they would resort to kidnapping and eventually murder.

That line of questioning continued for nearly half an hour. Based on the tight, withdrawn look on the cop's face, he wasn't any clearer about their motives or how they'd pulled me into it. He'd probably seen many strange things in his career but not someone going to such extremes to prove the existence of werewolves.

"There are people who look for the Loch Ness Monster and Bigfoot, and I can't tell you how many people believe in sirens," Ethan said at the completion of the interview. "People want to believe in the supernatural because what-ifs are oddly comforting. You might not understand it, but it doesn't make that desire any less necessary for many people. For some, it's just an unhealthy distraction." The policeman seemed to find some relief in that. He nodded.

I kept my focus on anything but Ethan because it was hard not to show an overwhelming look of awe as he pretended that supernaturals didn't exist when he was one of them.

Ethan held my arm and guided me out of the office. His hold was too tight for it to be remotely comfortable.

"You realize no one is going to try to snatch me in broad daylight just feet from the police station, right?" I pointed out as we headed to the car.

He made a sound and loosened his hold.

"Mr. Charleston," a low-pitched, hesitant voice called from behind us.

Ethan was steel and ire when he turned, his lips fighting the snarl threatening to emerge. "Price."

The DA didn't look as refined as he had in court. His hair was disheveled, and his eyes were red and droopy as if he hadn't slept in days. His tie was askew, and he was tugging at it.

"I … I'd like for us to talk. I heard about what happened to your friend, and in light of everything, I think we can come to an agreement about the case."

Ethan released my hand and moved closer to the weary attorney. "She's not my friend, she's my fiancée," he growled. "You can't even imagine how pissed off I am about what happened to her." Ethan was just inches from him. Price looked uneasy and was having a difficult time holding his feral gaze. "What exactly do you want to talk about? How you are an active member of the organization that abducted her, held her in a cage, and put a fucking gun in her face?"

"I didn't have anything to do with that," he blurted.

"Yeah, you did. You may not have committed the act, but you are by no means innocent. The multiple motions to revoke Steven's bail—why? Because in your head he turns into a wolf when the moon is full—the same thing that was thought of my fiancée and that I've been accused of, Mr. Price? What the hell shall we talk about? How I will make it my mission to let your affiliation with this organization be known? Or your staunch belief that there are animals running around wearing human shells? Or your association with the person who modified the video, released it, and has been verified to have altered it to implicate my client?"

He was being awfully indignant about something that was absolutely true. We *were* wearing human shells. It *was* a video of Steven, albeit altered to cut out a man changing to a wolf. He was really committing to his role in getting people to believe the reality in which he wanted them to and giving an Oscar-worthy performance.

Ethan continued, his voice still cold and incensed, full of restrained rage, "I don't have time for you until you're planning to drop your case. The man who gave you the video was murdered by one of your associates. This doesn't bode well for you."

Backing away from Price, he finished, "You think long and hard about what this conversation will entail and whether it will be worth me giving you the time because I am thoroughly prepared to go nuclear on this and ruin your reputation and career."

Ethan turned, his hand on my back as he guided me toward the car.

Once we were inside, I asked, "Can we make a stop?"

"What do you need?"

"To get you a trophy for that performance." He cut his gunmetal eyes in my direction. *Easy, wolfie.* I hadn't considered how well he'd been holding things together after last night. Going into more detail about the events of the previous night and seeing Price were almost more than Ethan could handle without incident.

"I'm fine, Ethan."

Taking several long breathes, he coaxed himself into a smile. It was rigid and barely curled the corners of his lips. His mood solemn. "Are you?" It was more than the abduction; it was what had happened after: the bloodlust. Something was changing.

~

"Be nice?" I cautioned Ethan several hours after we'd returned home from our meeting with the investigator. I straightened his tie as he got dressed to meet with Price again. I was surprised he wanted to meet with Ethan after their interaction outside the police station. But it seemed as if the DA was in a hurry to end everything and sever all ties with Dexter. I winced thinking about the newly departed pain in the ass mage. It wasn't that he hadn't deserved his ending—he had. I just wanted it to have been more climactic, for someone to have listed his misdeeds before taking his life. I wasn't ashamed to admit I wanted it to have been far more violent. He'd deserved it.

"Nice?"

"Yes, it's what the rest of us call *common courtesy*. You should try it sometime. Don't tell him you want to ruin his career, go nuclear, expose him, or beat him to a bloody pulp."

After a low growl, he muttered, "I didn't tell him I wanted to beat him to a bloody pulp."

"Your eyes did," I said pointedly. "As did your hostile posturing."

"He was going to allow people to perjure themselves in court and use an altered video to convict Steven. Let's not forget that, on some level, he knew what they were going to do to you. Asking me to be kind is a stretch."

"Steven isn't innocent."

"Based on the evidence he is," Ethan was quick to point out. And to Ethan that was all that mattered.

He headed for the door but stopped. "You'll be here when I get back?"

"Of course. I don't have a car." Mine was in the shop getting new tires. "And I have research to do." The key to his office was calling to me.

"Have fun."

I might not have fun, but Ethan had a wealth of information that he didn't like to share. He'd been the first person to introduce me to the history of the Faeries and accounts of their existence. It had been a rude awakening to what was actually inside me —inside us.

Coffee in hand, I headed for his office. I put the key in the door, but it wouldn't turn. I tried the other two keys he'd given me despite knowing they were for the front door and the storage shed in the backyard that looked like a miniature version of the house.

"The key doesn't work," I fumed as soon as Ethan picked up the phone.

"Really? I can't believe I gave you the wrong key. I'll have to check."

"You can't possibly think I believe that," I snapped back, unable to hide my irritation, which seemed to amuse him because I could hear a smile in his words as he spoke.

"Sky, I'm allowed to make mistakes. I guess you'll have to wait until I return to snoop."

I snatched the front door open when I heard a light knock, expecting it to be Ethan since he couldn't have been that far away. At the speed he customarily drove, it was plausible for him to return at the house so fast. Instead, it was Josh, hair disheveled, black shirt with a Rubik's Cube on it, frayed jeans, a backpack slung over his shoulder, and a mischievous grin on his lips.

"Do you want to help me with research?" he asked, stepping into his brother's home without an invitation. I suspected he wasn't used to waiting for one. He probably just let himself in when he visited.

"Is that my brother?" he mouthed.

I nodded.

He asked for the phone. His smile didn't falter. "Ethan, I did as you told me. I came over here and asked her to help me research. It's going as planned. I don't think she suspects I'm here to guard her."

Clenching my teeth together didn't help with suppressing my

laughter. Ethan growled and barked a few choice words, which only entertained Josh more. "I'm not sure why you're getting angry with me—I did what you asked. Our ploy is working. She's none the wiser about your covert plan to have your brother come over to do research, something he *never* does. She'll never suspect you don't want her to leave the house unescorted. You're a stealthy ... a very stealthy one," Josh continued, and I could feel Ethan's anger as if he were in the room.

I took the phone from Josh and ordered, "Stop it." I felt like I was reprimanding a child, and when it came to Ethan and Josh and their sibling squabbles, I wasn't far off.

"Ethan, I want the office door opened when you get home," I asserted.

"Of course." Which was Ethan-speak for putting any and every obstacle in place to prevent it. The walls of secrecy weren't likely to come down without constant urging. It was who he was, and I had to work with it—or rather around it.

"He gave you the wrong key, too?" Josh asked, dropping the backpack near the coffee table and walking to the office with me close behind. He studied the door and frowned. "It's warded, too, which is why I can't open it, either. The last time I tried, I had weakened the ward enough to break it when Ethan came home."

He touched the door, whispered a couple of words, and sparks of lavender and orange swirled across it. A halo of illumination and then a shrill sound came from the door before we were pushed back several feet. Josh gave an exhilarated smile. A challenge. He loved a challenge. His ocean blue eyes turned cloudy gray as he called on stronger magic. His lips moved rapidly. Magic pulsed off him and coils of color and power pushed into the door. The door groaned, and the ward wailed in protest as it struggled to stay in place.

Josh stopped, his mouth parted for a few seconds before a flash of magic shot out of him. He expelled more words quickly. He collapsed to the floor, still. His magic was squelched. Nothing. I checked his pulse; it was fine, but when I peeled back his eyelids, his eyes were looking straight ahead. Just as I grabbed my phone, Ethan called.

"Sky, what's the matter?" I'd deal with the weirdness of him calling just in time later.

"Josh—he's hurt. I need to call Dr. Jeremy. Meet us at the pack's house."

CHAPTER 15

Dr. Jeremy was exceedingly patient with us as we hovered around, watching him and Kelly examine Josh. Ethan was pushing his tolerance by positioning himself so close that Dr. Jeremy moved him back several times. Ethan gave him the space he needed only after Sebastian had threatened to force him out of the room. They were looking for the *Tod Schlaf,* or sleeper. That was the most logical explanation for Josh's condition. Josh's breathing was slow and steady, and so was his heart rate. Both were slower but within normal limits. Dr. Jeremy went over every inch of his tattoo-covered body, looking for that odd leech-type creature that had once infected Kelly with a venom that had paralyzed her.

After several minutes, it wasn't Dr. Jeremy who found what was wrong—it was Ethan. When they finally rolled Josh onto his stomach, Ethan gasped at the mark on top of his thigh. Everyone thought it was a birthmark, but it was actually the mark of a spell that had been done to Josh to keep him alive. He'd been cursed to punish their mother for performing a *rever tempore,* a dangerous and forbidden spell that reversed time. It had been the catalyst for Ethan hosting a spirit shade. I'd read books and documents about the Faeries' vicious and cruel treatment of others. Their power was second to none. Why would they have wanted someone who'd surpassed them in brutality to live on? What did he possess? More importantly, what did Ethan now possess that they'd wanted to preserve?

Ethan took several steps back as he looked at his brother's mark, which was starting to fade. It was shades lighter than what I remembered. If it was removed, it would be the end of Josh. Ethan's eyes glistened as his mouth moved slowly in an incantation. Magic roiled from him in an aggressive, fierce wave. It felt like Maya's magic—dark, strong, ominous. Josh's magic was a cool ocean breeze, gentle and calming; Ethan's was the opposite. It was turbulent, stygian, the blasting wind of a hurricane, and it quickly overtook the room. Like everyone else, I gasped as though someone had punched me in the chest, forcing out any air I had. Taking the smallest breath was painful and difficult.

Ethan continued the incantation, and the room darkened sporadically as the lights flickered. The ground shook, and another explosion of magic knocked us to the ground. Everything came to a standstill. Ethan approached Josh and looked at the mark. There was no change. He'd failed. He lumbered back like a wounded animal. Although he was silent, I could almost hear the wolf's howl of sorrow as he stood there frozen, unable to help his brother.

Ethan took a deep breath and held it for a long time before exhaling. His lips started to move again, foreign words floating through the air. I recognized the same ancient language that I'd used before—Faerie. The incantation predated anything we knew of. The room cooled until it felt like we were inside a freezer. Ethan's breath was visible as words flowed from him. Sebastian was the first to gasp in a ragged breath, the thick cords of muscle in his neck bulging as he desperately tried to breathe. Dr. Jeremy wrapped his hands around his throat indicating he was choking. I could hear his panic-stricken heart beating wildly. Kelly's legs buckled under her, and she dropped to her knees, face pale, eyes wide, mouth gaping.

"Ethan, stop!" I yelled. His eyes were vacant and glassy. He didn't respond, engrossed in a single-target mission—saving his brother. I feared he was willing to do it at any cost, including our lives.

"Ethan!" I cried again. His eyes snapped to me; he didn't stop. His eyes were strained and uncertain. I suspected he was performing a dark and powerful spell to siphon a little life from everyone in the room to give to Josh. The profound struggle between his obligation to the pack and his dedication to his brother was displayed on his face. Indecision and fear were making him reckless.

Sebastian growled Ethan's name. When he didn't respond, Sebastian lunged through the air, plowed into him, and drove him into the wall. His hands were fixed around Ethan's throat, cutting off his air. His movements were aggressive and primal, but when he spoke, his voice was soft and compassionate. "Ethan, we will save him. You can't go into destruction mode. You can't."

Until that moment, I'd always questioned whether Sebastian and Ethan were friends. Most of the time, I didn't feel confident saying yes. They were honor bound to protect the pack and adhere to any rules that maintained its integrity. They protected each other as well, and it seemed to have more to do with mutual respect and like for each other than pack obligation. Sebastian was sympathetic to Ethan's affection for his brother and their closeness, despite the fights, that made them as one. Josh lying on that bed was paramount to Ethan being there—his Beta.

Ethan relaxed his head back against the wall and struggled to calm himself. The room warmed, and the erratic heartbeats shifted back to normal. Part of me expected anger from those who'd been affected, but there was only sympathy.

"They will fix it, Ethan," Kelly reassured him. Gavin rushed into the room, his eyes sweeping over everything before landing on Kelly. He looked at Ethan and snarled.

"My intention wasn't to hurt her," Ethan offered in a weak and reedy voice. Sebastian stepped away from him. Ethan pushed off the wall and walked to Josh's side. He cupped his hand over Josh's shoulder and bowed his head as if making a silent agreement, or maybe a plea to anyone he thought could help.

"I don't know what else to do," he whispered. He blinked back tears several times. I knew Ethan—if he let them fall he would give in to hopelessness and accept defeat.

I moved closer to him until we were face-to-face. I pressed my palms against his cheeks and tried to get him to focus on me and not his brother lying in the pack's hospital bed lingering between life and death. I couldn't pull his eyes from Josh. I said his name several times before he looked at me. I didn't want to give him the platitude that everything would be okay because he knew better than I did that it probably wouldn't. If he couldn't save him with Faerie magic, what could anyone else do? We were going up against things we didn't know how to counter.

Comforting him was my first impulse. I hated that I couldn't offer consolation with the promise that things would be handled and Josh would be saved. That certainty wasn't there. We were in unchartered territory, dealing with magic that we didn't understand, and our expert on all unique magic was now a victim of it. Ethan was nothing more than magic and frustration.

Sebastian stared at his Beta, who for the first time was showing vulnerability, indecisiveness, and fear. Sebastian's concern reached his eyes. He pulled his phone out and made a call.

"Ariel, I need you to come to the pack's house. Now. You should bring your best."

I rolled my eyes and swore. I hoped Sebastian's terseness and lack of social niceties wouldn't keep her from coming. The muscles in his neck pulled taut, and amber rolled across his eyes, drowning out the brown. It appeared Ariel was giving him a refresher on social skills. Most people ignored his rudeness because of his position in the otherworld.

He took in a breath, held it, then slowly released it, finding the calm he needed to deal with her. Sebastian's voice was level, polite; but still held an edge to it. He expected his request to be followed. "Ariel, please understand I wouldn't be asking for your assistance if it wasn't an emergency. I respect your power and your time and wouldn't request your presence on a whim. I need your help *now*. If you're serious about us forming an alliance, then you will be here within half an hour. If you're not, you're no friend of this pack and will be treated as such." He ended the conversation.

Ethan hadn't taken his eyes off his brother. He looked shattered, and I hoped he wasn't beyond repair. He stared at the mark on his brother that was fading as the minutes passed. That little circle that meant the difference between life and death was being erased from Josh's body.

We waited for Ariel and the others in a room next to the infirmary; Ethan was reluctant to go any farther from Josh. Anxiety heightened when the thirty minutes had passed and there was no sign of them. Cole, watching the entire scene unfold, wasn't helping. When we were inching toward the forty-five minute mark, I was prepared to call them myself and barter a favor. Before I could take my phone out to call London, Winter poked her head in the door, a glint in her hazel eyes as she caught Sebastian's. A warning. She opened the door wider and escorted in the Creed with Ariel in front. They were dressed as they had been the first time we'd met them after the group was restructured. They were in all black—except Ariel. She wore a white fitted shirt and slacks. Gray boots were the only nonwhite part of her ensemble. They clicked and clacked loudly as she made her way to Sebastian with determination. Her lips were pressed firmly together, and her brown eyes held a crystal shimmer of anger and virulence. Sebastian had several inches on her, even though her boots had three-inch heels; she stood taller, bringing her shoulders back, her indignation and anger adding inches to her.

"You *summoned* me?" she said sarcastically, obviously affronted that he had and trying to shame him for it. It wouldn't work, and anyone who'd spent any time with him would have gathered that. Sebastian expected compliance and often forgot it didn't extend any further than the pack. Or maybe he didn't forget and expected it from everyone else anyway.

His gaze roved over her casually as she stood in front of him, eyes fiery with unspoken rage. "I do not appreciate your subtle threat," she said sternly.

His smile lacked mirth and just bared his teeth. Ariel was new to this. For all her confidence and bravado, she was out of her league and it was obvious. She undoubtedly held her own against others—a force that most didn't want to deal with. But Sebastian wasn't just a force; he was an indomitable, brazen power. He didn't care that she was affronted by his summons because it was what he did.

"There was nothing subtle about what I said, and I assure you it wasn't a threat. Your little game of arriving late"—his eyes narrowed on her—"I don't like it and we won't play it again. We've had this discussion, and there isn't a need for us to discuss it every time we meet. It's a mutual alliance. When I call, you all come. I will extend the same courtesy to you. No questions asked. Are we clear? If not, you can leave—but I guarantee there will be a time when you will need us. Believe me, you will want me there."

Ariel bit down on her lip, and I knew she was searching for a comeback, something profound and menacing, but the rosiness that streaked along the bridge of her nose and cheeks made it clear she had nothing. She found herself at a loss for words. Sebastian had that effect on people.

She turned her back on him and addressed Ethan. "What happened?" It was a subtle insult against Sebastian, who seemed amused by it; a smile tugged at the corners of his lips.

In silence, Ethan led her into the infirmary. Before he could say anything more, London broke from the formation and ran up to Josh.

"What happened?" She rested her palms against his face, her lips moving ever so slightly. "He's performing magic," she informed us softly.

I inched closer, trying to feel it. I could often tell when he was performing magic, feel the subtle undercurrent of it. I didn't feel that and found it disconcerting that London could. Something was wrong. I didn't have the same connection with Josh and his magic as I once had.

"What the hell is he fighting?" Despite her rainbow-colored hair, gentle russet eyes, and delicate round features, she looked intimidating.

Several beats passed before Ethan attempted to answer her. And when he did, his tone was emotionless and dry. "It's complicated."

"Is it truly complicated, or are you just having a hard time editing the situation? It's not the time for the latter. We need to know everything," she snapped.

"This information stays in this room. My telling you this is an implied expectation that you will adhere to it. A bond of secrecy," Ethan said reticently.

Ariel looked at Sebastian before focusing on Ethan. Then she looked at London, who nodded her consent, and to each member of the Creed for their agreement.

Ethan exhaled a ragged breath but hesitated and looked at Sebastian. Sebastian was suffering the same feelings of discomfort. Secrets were their fortress. They gave them comfort and provided security to the pack, and now they were revealing them to the witches, our former enemies.

When Ethan finally spoke, it was as if he were giving a confession, afraid others would hear it. "You all are familiar with the *rever tempore*, and you know the penalty for performing it is quite steep. My mother performed it, and the penalty was Josh's life."

There were various looks of curiosity and suspicion as they waited for him to continue. They were really interested in finding out how Ethan had circumvented the curse.

Ethan continued, "We used the Vitae to prevent the spell by melting a piece of it down and using it on Josh."

Ariel's face blanched. She swallowed. Hard. She stammered out her question, losing her usual cool confidence. "H-how did you get a Faerie object?" She shook her head. "I guess the better question is how the hell did you *use* a Faerie object?" Her hard look landed on Sebastian and then Ethan as though they had pulled her into a cataclysm, leaving her floundering to get out. Her eyes widened as she struggled to control her breathing. Obviously, Faeries were as bad as the stories painted them.

"We had access to their magic," was all Ethan offered.

"That's BS. Faerie magic isn't something that's easily accessible. You don't just get *access* to extinct magic."

"It's not extinct magic," Sebastian offered in a low voice. He sounded almost apologetic, as if he were taking responsibility for lifting a veil that he otherwise would've kept over her eyes, exposing her to something most people wished they didn't know. I had the same feeling every time I had to tell David more about the otherworld. Ariel lived in it, and yet there were things she had no knowledge of. Was allowing blissful ignorance really an act of mercy? Was it better to live not knowing such vile magical creatures existed? Ethan and I hosted those vile creatures. Those horrific, powerful beings. Little did the Creed know that when they'd restricted my magic, they were going up against a being they believed was extinct.

Ariel took several steps back and looked at the door, probably contemplating getting the hell out of there. She looked as though she was ready to instruct her people to do just that, when London pulled herself away from Josh and went to an empty space a few feet away. She started to whisper spells. Vibrant colors swirled around the room; numbers, words, and symbols went through almost every color of the rainbow as they danced around. London was using the air instead of a whiteboard to come up with a spell. Watching her do magic was almost like watching Quinn at his computer. They were composers, artists giving beautiful and imaginative presentations. She presented as such; moving to music with an eclectic rhythm. Eloquent words, lithe and evocative motions. She appeared proficient with her magic, although I knew it wasn't innate. Her talents were the result of going to magic school and intense training, unlike Josh's natural gifts. She took a more methodological approach to magic.

She moved around the different spells, invocations, words, and symbols, searching for the right combination. Ariel joined her, examining and moving things around. The others joined, too, working in harmony as a team. I was intrigued by movements so coordinated they looked choreographed. Anticipating one another's next steps, they kept adding to the existing structure, reinforcing it until it was something masterful, powerful, conquering.

Ariel scanned each and every line, a maestro directing the composition as it came together. The Creed stood in a straight line in front of the tapestry of spells and magic. Ariel pulled out a small knife, sliced her hand, and handed the blade to the next witch to do the same; after cutting her hand, that witch passed the knife to the next, and so on. Ariel began a quiet invocation, and the others joined in a lulling melody, so gentle and somnolent that it was hard to imagine it being powerful enough to stop what was going on. When they stopped, they sagged into themselves before gathering the strength to stand taller.

London approached Josh. "Where's the mark?" she asked.

Ethan came over and rolled Josh to his side, revealing the mark. It now had a light orange glow over it. London smiled, satisfied, and then joined the rest of the Creed near the infirmary door.

Ariel addressed Sebastian. "It will not stop the spell they are using to remove the mark, but it has enough roadblocks to make removing it harder. We don't have the strength or resources to stop whatever is going on. If you guys are dealing with Faeries, I hope *you* do. And all I have to say is good luck." She started out the door but stopped and turned to Sebastian, who looked cautiously impressed. Her eyes were cold and full of ire. A scowl remained fixed on her face as her eyes snapped to Ethan, then to the mark on Josh's upper thigh, and back to Sebastian, her curiosity apparent but not strong enough to override her instinct for self-preservation. "I'm not sure what you're involved in. I assure you, had I known this, striking an alliance with you would've been the last thing on my list. I entered that agreement foolishly and have no one else to blame but myself. It won't happen again."

"Don't ever think that because we're the ones dealing with Faeries you won't eventually have to," Sebastian warned.

"Perhaps we will. But if we do, believe me, the fight will come to our door—we won't go looking for it." She left, the others falling in line behind her.

London lingered to say, "There's nothing you can do to reverse it without getting to the source. Stop the source, and you will stop the spell. They aren't trying to kill him; they're trying to retrieve the magic from the mark. Do you know where the Vitae is?"

Ethan nodded.

"Are you sure? Because I'm willing to bet whoever is doing that spell to retrieve the magic has it and not the original owner."

London swiftly left to catch up with the others.

CHAPTER 16

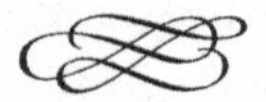

Ethan ran out of the house, and I had to push myself to keep up with him. Distracted, he didn't bother to tell Cole where to go or how to get there when he started out the door behind us. I tried to stop him with a quelling look.

"You're going to risk your safety and his over your feelings for me? His brother is already lying in a hospital bed. Do you want him in one as well? Let me be there to help if needed."

As much as I hated to admit it, he was right.

Cole and I barely had time to get into the car before Ethan sped off. His knuckles were white as he gripped the steering wheel and focused on the road.

I said his name gently. He was gone, far gone, and I could hear the erratic pace of his heart and the ragged sounds of his breath. His turbulent emotions were so strong I found myself gasping for air as waves pulled me under. I always knew what he was feeling from his expressions and the emotions that came off him. I could withstand a tolerable storm when necessary. This wasn't the same. I felt his feelings as if they were my own, and they were violent and uncontrolled. Flashes of anger blinded me, and my heart was beating so hard I thought it would explode. I understood Ethan on a visceral level and couldn't control it.

"Ethan!" I yelled. He jerked back, and I slipped my hand over his and gave it a squeeze. "It's going to be okay." I hated lying to him because it wouldn't be okay on so many levels. He calmed down noticeably, even slowed the car down, which was good because he was going to get us arrested for reckless driving or in an accident we wouldn't likely survive.

"Sorry," he finally said. "That's how I knew something was wrong with you and Josh. Everything was racing out of control. But I was glad I kept feeling it because I knew you were okay. It's when you don't feel it that you should worry. That's why it bothered me when I didn't feel anything else after they abducted you. The feeling was hard and palpable, barely able to be contained; it calmed, and then nothing."

That little smidge of information should have come with the mating pamphlet. I wouldn't have changed my mind if I'd known, but it would have prepared me for dealing with my mate when emotions were so extreme.

"If I hadn't stayed calm, I couldn't have staved off my change."

He nodded as I told him something he knew.

I couldn't panic because I needed to be there for him, but I kept thinking about London's final words. Claudia was the Moura who protected the Vitae, but I had a feeling that was no longer the case.

Ethan pulled into the driveway of her pristine white Colonial style home, which had intricate pillars surrounding the porch and supporting a crescent-shaped balcony on the second floor. Rows of pastel-colored flowers led up the walkway. Claudia's refined elegance was on full display in the sculptures on her lawn, the unique carvings on the pillars, and the hint of lavender and honeysuckle that wafted through the air. An unnatural mixture of unique scents and magic claimed the area.

When we got to the door, we discovered it was unlocked.

There weren't any signs of forced entry, but we felt strong, unfiltered, unique magic. Something I wasn't exposed to on a daily basis. Something so new that I couldn't detect its nuances to link it to a single individual. My mouth dried out at the taste of the magic—ominous and dark. A raven's song of death filled the room. I took a step back and turned my head, taking a deep breath before entering—it wasn't enough. The layers of magic in the front room suffocated me. Claudia was sprawled on the sofa, her breathing slow and labored. Ethan rushed to her side and was about to touch her.

"Don't." Her voice had lost its gentle lilt and was darker and harsher, different from any way she'd ever spoken to Ethan or Josh before. With them, she always had a maternal yet regal way of speaking.

"Step back some more," she rasped as she sat up. When she opened her eyes, they weren't their normal color. They were smoldering black, pulling me into a dark abyss. She rose slowly, and Ethan stepped back—far. The warmth I'd become familiar with from Claudia was gone. She felt cold and deadly. I wanted to hear her kind, dulcet-South African accented voice, something familiar that would indicate she was Claudia, our Claudia. The person in front of us wasn't the elegant seller of expensive, unique art. The person I knew as Claudia was the shell the Messor used daily.

She slipped by us and lumbered to a row of large, leafy plants that lined the room's back wall. She extended her fingers to touch one leaf; the plant withered slowly at first until it was nothing but a dead, lifeless vine. Her breathing eased a little but was still measured and rough. She went to the next plant and ran her fingers languidly over its leaves. It dried and crumbled into shriveled particles that floated away. She continued touching plants, and I stared in fascination. Ethan watched as if he'd seen it a thousand times. When she finished, seven of the ten plants were dead. She turned to face us. Her eyes had returned to normal and so had her breathing. A polite, welcoming smile feathered across her lips.

Unintentionally, I had distanced myself from her and was just inches from the front door. Cole studied her and the shriveled plants with astute interest. In need of a distraction, I looked around the house. Bland white walls surrounded us. There were a few paintings, but they were nothing like the lively and vibrantly colored works that covered the walls of her gallery. Nothing like the recherché sculptures I adored there were displayed here. She'd gone through great effort to make her home a place of comfort and calm. It all had a purpose. She returned to the dead plants, observing them as if paying them tribute for their offering. Her face bore a pained look of remorse and the embarrassment of losing control. Seemingly resigned to the situation, she returned her attention to us. Her gentle and familiar face that used to comfort me seemed counterfeit, a mask.

"Hello, Ethan and Sky," she greeted warmly before noticing Cole. She appraised him for several long moments. Her fingers moved in a circular pattern as if she were testing the air. "Cole," she said, a terse greeting that lacked any warmth or cordiality.

I was still several feet away from her, close to the front door, fighting the urge to back away even more and get away from death and its wielder. Her gaze dropped to the ground as a smile emerged. Sensing my discomfort, she kept her distance. I didn't want her to feel uncomfortable, so I moved my legs, which seemed rooted to the ground, and eventually decreased the distance between us.

I waited until her eyes met mine. "How are you?"

"I'm fine, but Josh isn't well, is he?" she said in a strained voice.

Ethan shook his head. Her gaze shifted to the door. "His wards are all down."

I hadn't even thought of that. He'd put blood wards around the pack's home. My house had one, and Ethan's most likely did as well.

"What happened?" Ethan asked.

Her gaze traveled around the room. She shook her head. Everything was meticulously in place.

"I have no idea. I felt Josh's wards go down, but I didn't think anything of it. But then I felt the magic, and it reminded me of—" She stopped abruptly and looked at me.

"Go ahead. Sky knows everything." Ethan made a face as he looked at Cole. "He knows as well."

I might have been mistaken, but she looked relieved by the information. "It felt like the magic you used to evoke the spell for Josh. Then I blacked out. I didn't pass out. I was forced into it—with magic." Eyes widening, she moved quickly to her purse, took out a key ring, and went to a small room adjacent to the one we were in. She checked a lock; it was open just like the front door had been. Her face paled, and she frowned. We followed her into the small room. She walked to a closet; the safe inside was open and contained only papers.

"The Vitae is missing." She didn't seem surprised. Even if I hadn't heard her heart racing, I heard the panic in her voice and saw it on her face. "Where are the rest of the protected objects?" she asked.

"Sky still has the Aufero, and the Gem of Levage is with us. The witches have two of the three Clostra, and we have no idea where the Fatifer is."

"I wouldn't worry about it. I'm sure they have it by now." She took in a breath, released it slowly, and frowned. "I know it was never your intention, but you have all mishandled the objects. You've awakened the beast."

I had so many questions. Had we unwittingly literally awakened some unstoppable creature? Were *beast* and *awaken* metaphors? Or had we stirred up something that shouldn't have been disturbed?

"You need to get all the other objects. Now."

Ethan didn't move, and his impassive facade broke. "You think they're trying to retrieve them all."

She shook her head. "I *know* they are. They want to restore the strength of the Vitae by taking it from Josh. The Clostra will have any spell they need to do it. The Aufero will allow them to change the magic, to manipulate it to do whatever they please."

"Who are they?" I asked.

"The Faeries," Claudia and Ethan said in unison.

I was getting frustrated. I was having a hard time putting the pieces together. "Did we somehow wake them from a magical sleep?" I asked, exasperated.

Claudia offered a small smile. "They've existed among us for a long time. Like Ethos, they prefer to remain hidden until they have a chance to return the world to the way they once knew it. They tried it ..." She stopped to think. "A hundred and eighty years ago. It failed." Her voice held a level of familiarity, as if she'd been there. She moved closer to Ethan and spoke quietly, but not low enough for us not to hear. "I think they want to mimic your magic, Amizial's magic."

The king of badass Faeries, whom they'd reduced to a shade because his magic had been stronger and crueler than theirs. Now they wanted it. Things were getting worse by the minute.

My head started to hurt. I tried to prioritize things, but they were all important. We had to save Josh, prevent the Faeries—the badasses of the otherworld—from getting the protected objects, and stop whatever they were planning. It was hard to focus when I found myself fixated on the fact they were trying to be like Amizial.

Claudia was drifting, her personality cooling, her eyes darkening. Turning away from us, she walked over to the three remaining plants. The tips of her fingers traced the edge of a leaf, turning it brown. "Ethan, don't let your brother die."

He nodded. I was infuriated. He would never do that. I'd just talked him out of a downward spiral, and I didn't want her to cause another.

Let it go, Sky. I wanted to, but I couldn't. "Ethan's never failed Josh. He doesn't need to be reminded of his obligations; they are the most important things to him." I somehow managed to keep the anger out of my voice.

She nodded once and kept her back to us. "Of course, Sky. You are right. Please accept my apology."

It was more of a dismissal than an apology. We took it as our cue to leave.

As soon as we were in the car, Cole sank into the backseat, his mouth resting in a small *O* as he grappled with everything that had transpired.

When he finally spoke, his voice held a mixture of fascination, fear, and disbelief that he attempted to mask with a blank face. "The Midwest Pack has had knowledge of and access to the five protected objects that most people thought were myths. And you are hosting a Faerie?" He directed his rhetorical question at Ethan. "A powerful one. And I guess it's safe to assume Sky's peculiar magic is the result of hosting one as well." He cursed under his breath. "And your godmother is a Messor." A mirthless laugh filled the small space of the car as he shook his head. He said "a Messor" over and over. "They're thought to be a clear work of fiction, yet the godmother of the Midwest Beta and the pack's witch is the unholy combination of vampire and Faerie. I thought they were killed off."

Ethan nodded once. "Most of them were, but those who learned to control their powers were left undiscovered."

Cole made a choking sound.

I'm right there with you, buddy. Knowing that a Messor was a vampire/Faerie mix explained why Demetrius treated Claudia with such reverence and the fae allowed her to represent them.

She was old and probably stronger than the fae we currently knew of. And to Josh and Ethan, she was just the godmother who sold expensive art and made them drink tea.

Weighted silence reigned as Ethan barreled down the road. After several familiar turns, I realized we were on our way to my home.

"You're going to get the Aufero?" I asked.

He nodded. "We need the objects in safer places. I don't know what they're planning, but we need to make sure it can't happen."

At my front door, I felt flicks of fractured magic, strong energy coming from the ward being broken by stronger magic. And the strong smell of blood filled the air. I opened the door, fully aware that the Aufero was probably gone. But I hadn't expected to see David lying on the floor in a puddle of blood, a cut running across his stomach and another along his shoulder. Purple bruises covered half his face, and his head rolled back and forth as he tried to hold on to consciousness. The sword Winter had given him lay discarded a few feet away. Trent was there, also injured, but he seemed to have fared better. Facedown, he struggled to push himself up. His arm was definitely broken and possibly his ankle. There was a shotgun on the other side of the room, and the heated metal smell of a discharged weapon lingered in the air. One wall had three bullet holes. Ethan went to Trent and eased him onto his back. My friend cried out in pain. He wasn't better off than David. Crimson covered his chest where a sharp object had stabbed him.

Ethan's voice was low and calm as he spoke to Trent. "I'm going to position you so you don't cause yourself further damage."

Trent nodded. His eyes glistened with tears. I knelt next to David, who'd fallen unconscious. I looked at his wounds. They were deep—really deep. Blood from the wounds on his arm and stomach had soaked through his shirt. I pressed my finger to his neck to feel for a pulse. It was light, reedy, barely there. David was clinging to life. I couldn't let him die.

"Trent, what happened?"

He whispered, "We saw someone breaking in. Thought they were there to hurt you." A pang of guilt hit me hard. David was going to die because he'd been trying to help me. I looked over at Ethan, blinking back tears. One escaped, and I wiped it away, smudging David's blood across my cheek. Trent closed his eyes.

"You call Quell, I'll call Dr. Jeremy," he instructed me.

My brows inched together. "Quell?"

He nodded. "He can travel, which means he'll get here before Dr. Jeremy. Vampire blood will help them heal faster and increase their chances of survival."

I pulled out my phone and quickly called Quell. The phone rang and went to voicemail. I got an automated recording. I debated whether to leave a message. He wouldn't call me back. He'd severed all ties with me. I was okay with that if it helped him. It wasn't fair to either Ethan or Quell if the vampire was indeed in love with me. We could never have anything more than a friendship. If my absence in his life gave him peace and happiness, I'd reluctantly sacrifice our friendship. But I wasn't willing to sacrifice David's life. "Quell, when you get this message, will you please come to my house. I need your help," I said urgently to the recorder.

Ethan's back was to me as he continued his conversation with Dr. Jeremy.

When he hung up, he looked at me, silently concerned.

My heart was heavy, and my voice cracked as I said, "I don't think he's going to call back or come."

Ethan sighed and picked up his phone again. "Demetrius, I need you to come to Sky's home. I will owe you a debt."

Whether he did it intentionally, Demetrius spoke too softly for me to hear. "She is *not* obligated to do that nor will she," Ethan said firmly. "David is injured, and if I'm not mistaken, you injured him first and also bit Sky. You almost killed her, and I didn't retaliate when I should have. This is not a threat—it's a promise. If her friend dies, I'm not likely to be so civil again."

Then I heard Demetrius and the fiery anger in his voice. "I will not be threatened by the likes of you!" he bellowed. If he were in front of us, he'd be pulling back his lips and exposing his fangs, ready to use them.

Their battle of wills was going to devolve into threats and posturing, and that wasn't what we needed. "I'll give you whatever you want," I said, raising my voice just slightly while keeping my position next to David. I knew Demetrius had heard me and had to be salivating over the offer. I would be indebted to him. Without even asking, I knew what he wanted. I bowed my head in shame. I might have been willing to trade my friendship with Quell, but now I'd agreed to trade someone else as well: Chris.

Demetrius cut out the middleman and ignored anything Ethan had to say. I heard him as clearly as if he were in the room. "Sky, I will not take this lightly. If you're willing to sign a blood oath, I will be there."

A blood oath. A promise or a debt could be reneged on. The only thing you'd lose was your credibility. But the blood oath had more severe repercussions, including death. Of course Demetrius would go for something extreme to ensure he got what he wanted most—Chris.

I barely moved my head into the nod. Ethan's lips pulled into a frown. Steel gray washed over his eyes, and he looked like a feral animal peering out into the night, ready to attack. He grappled with that emotion for several moments before he forced himself to say, "She agreed." He hung up and spoke in a mild voice, "Sky."

"Don't you even think about talking me out of this!" I spat through clenched teeth. It didn't deter him.

He came close to me, and his voice dropped to a low rumble: "Sky, I understand you want to do everything you can to help your friend, but—"

"*But* nothing. Ethan, don't ask and don't even suggest it."

Except for things that involved his brother, Ethan was pragmatic, often ignoring his humanity, which he considered a vulnerability. I hadn't reached that point. I loved the pack and accepted that the things they did to protect us were rarely extended to others who weren't considered friends of the pack. I didn't know David's position. Was he considered a friend of the pack or just my friend, which didn't hold the same vow of protection? I didn't care. He was *my* friend and *my* responsibility.

It didn't take long before there was a knock on the door. Demetrius. I quickly walked to it, pulled it open, and was shocked to see Quell standing there.

"You need me?"

I nodded.

He walked past me and did a quick survey of the room, taking in the scene. Trent was lying on his back, cradling his arm, his neck muscles tightened to cords as he dealt with the pain. David had come to, but he was only conscious for a few seconds before he was out again. He'd been drifting in and out since the phone call.

"They need vampire blood to heal." Were-animals could change someone, and that could help the person heal, but if their injuries were too severe, it could kill them.

Quell sank his fangs into his arm and slid them down, creating a large opening. Blood welled, and he knelt, pressing his hands to David's cheeks and tilting his head up to feed him.

"Quell," Demetrius said firmly from the door. "It is not your place to do this."

Quell tensed. "She needs my help."

"I have an agreement with Sky, and you are aware of it." Demetrius moved aside to reveal another person behind him. Probably a witch or elf to establish the blood oath. He had a scrolled paper in his hand. Quell didn't move, maintaining his place close to David. Demetrius's black opal eyes sharpened on him as he tilted his head, studying Quell with contempt. "Quell, we've had this discussion before. This is not about Sky but your loyalty to the Seethe and me. This is the defining moment. The choice you make is important, Quell."

I was so sick of the Seethe using my friendship with Quell as a rejection of his allegiance to them. It was cruel. But Sebastian and Ethan had given me a similar ultimatum. It had started with them saying that if he became a problem they would make sure he was no longer one.

"I won't let them die," Quell said.

"And they won't. That is the reason I'm here."

"I give it freely without obligation. That is best for them and her."

"But it will not be the best for me or our Seethe. *Your* Seethe. You must learn loyalty. Your betrayal of and wavering dedication to it is the reason Michaela, your creator, is dead. Skylar is the one who killed her. Will you allow that to go without some form of retribution after all I've done for you?" Demetrius's accent, usually masked, had eased into his words, indicating he was losing control.

Who knew what he'd done for Quell, but Quell's eyes were vacant, his body still as he stood in deliberation. Ruby stained his arm and the cut closed. My eyes darted in David's direction, taking in his paling complexion.

"One of you do something!" I snarled, my hand clenched angrily at my side.

Unaffected by my outburst, Demetrius kept his eyes locked on Quell. His voice was soft, somnolent, and mesmerizing, as if he was trying to usher Quell into a pliant state. He eased farther into the room with a graceful assurance, his magical companion close behind.

"Remember our bonding. You are to treat me as your creator now. I expect the same deference and respect. The same loyalty and love." I didn't know what type of bonding ceremony vampires had. Switching creators, allowing another to act as a surrogate, had to differ from mating. Demetrius had invoked that odd link and blind loyalty vampires had to their creators, but the way Quell looked at the Master of the Seethe wasn't the same way he'd regarded Michaela. He'd had an almost hypnotized adoration and veneration for her that she hadn't deserved—it couldn't be broken.

"Quell," Demetrius said, firmer, more commanding.

Looking at David's colorless face, his bloodstained shirt and gaping wound, and then looking at Trent, Quell twisted his face into a grimace.

He held my eyes, sighed, bit into his arm, opened David's mouth, and let blood seep into it. He fed David until he had the strength to raise his arm and pull Quell's wrist in closer, drawing in more blood. Quell stopped him and gently removed his arm from his lips. He moved to his feet, went over to Trent, and again offered his arm.

I kept a steady eye on Demetrius, who seemed unmoved by Quell's disobedience. He wore a rueful smile as if he were resigned to the fact that Quell would not follow him blindly or grant him the same power Michaela had held. He dealt with the defeat in silence. When Quell finished, he moved away from Trent. Trent's eyes widened; he had to be feeling some of the benefits of vampirism. Small meshes of scar tissue formed around David's wounds. They weren't totally healed, but they looked a hell of a lot better. Slight color was coming to his face, and pain didn't seem to overtake him. As I watched them heal, I took comfort in Demetrius's immobility. Then there was a barely visible flash. Before I could comprehend his motive, Demetrius had grabbed the sword at David's feet and struck. In one clean, sweeping arc, he'd beheaded Quell. The body and head didn't have time to drop to the ground; they exploded into ash that lingered in the air.

Demetrius stepped back with malicious confidence as he took hold of his magical companion and disappeared. I looked at the bloodstained, ash-filled spot that Quell had left behind. That quick moment replayed in my mind a hundred times over in the minutes I stood frozen, paralyzed by sorrow and anger. Tears coursed down my face—streams of them like a river—and I couldn't stop them. He had killed Quell. It felt like he'd punched through my chest and twisted my heart. Bile rose in the back of my throat and my vision blurred with my tears.

He killed Quell. My head pounded and my heart ached. I needed to make it stop.

I grabbed the sword and headed for the door, ignoring Ethan and Cole, who called my name. Fueled by vengeance, anger, and sorrow, my body ran on autopilot. All I wanted to do was kill. I wanted to kill Demetrius and make it the most painful thing he'd ever endured. I nearly ran into Sebastian on my way out the door. He grabbed my arm.

"Sky," he said, concerned.

I yanked my arm from him and kept going.

He grabbed it again and whipped me around to face him. "What's the matter?" he demanded.

My throat was too tight, sawdust coated my tongue, and I couldn't get the words out. I'd reverted to something so primal and bloodthirsty that communication wasn't something I could manage. It was too much of a higher-level activity. I was driven by bestial, ravenous rage. I could taste it, feel it, smell it. It dwelled deep in a place where darkness lived, and I couldn't drag myself out. I pained at the thought of doing so.

His grip on my arm tightened as I tried to move away. He repeated my name, a hard command for me to respond. And I did. I snarled. A growl reverberated in my chest as I bared my teeth and tried again to snatch my arm away.

His eyes locked on mine and narrowed; they were overtaken by molten amber. His growl was deeper and more aggressive than any sound I could ever make. An undeniable ripple of power emanated from me as he exerted his dominance. I didn't cower. I met his challenge, so fueled by fury that I didn't understand dominance, rank, or pack rules. At that moment, I didn't give a damn about them. I couldn't grasp consequences. Only revenge. Only death. I held a hunger that would only be sated by killing Demetrius, which I had every intention of doing. My emotions had reached the darkest recesses of my being, where feelings I'd attributed to Maya lay, but she'd been subdued into silence. This was solely, undeniably me.

Sebastian pulled his eyes away from mine to assess the scene in my living room. His grip remained tight as he gently pulled me closer to him. He nodded at Dr. Jeremy, urging him to go in while we stood just outside my front door. When he spoke, his voice was soft and warm. "Sky, you have to stay here. This is a command. Don't make me force you."

I kept blinking, trying to push tears of virulent anger back. My thirst for blood ravaged my body beyond logic. I didn't have a plan. I just wanted to get to Demetrius and cut, strike, and punch.

Sebastian's thumb lightly stroked my cheek, wiping away tears. "Whatever you're planning will fail. Right now, you're not driven by anything other than rage. You're unfocused and more of a danger to yourself than anyone else." He reached for the sword and waited for me to release it to him.

I didn't.

"Hand it to me." There was a gentleness to his command, even a hint of sympathy. "Now, Sky. I won't ask you again."

I gave it to him, and he placed the palm of his hand against my back and urged me back inside. I stayed in the kitchen, unable to look in the living room as Dr. Jeremy worked on Trent and David. I tried to keep my mind blank and block out images of Quell's death and the haughty look of contemptuous entitlement Demetrius had worn as he'd taken my friend's life so freely.

CHAPTER 17

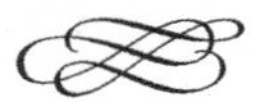

David and Trent were taken into the pack's infirmary, and Dr. Jeremy treated whatever the vampire blood hadn't fixed, which wasn't much. Their wounds looked dramatically improved from when I'd first seen them. I couldn't look at Trent and David without remembering Quell's death and feeling unbearable anguish. It wasn't a death—it was a murder. I slipped away to the room I always went to whenever I was in the pack's home and needed an escape. The room where I'd first been introduced to them after vampires had attacked me. After *Demetrius* had attacked me.

Forcing myself to focus on something else, I directed my attention to the view outside. It didn't help. The ambient golden glow of the setting sun was a reminder that it wouldn't have been possible for Demetrius to destroy Quell if the pack hadn't done the spell that had lifted the vampires' restrictions. As dusk draped over the area, I looked out to the woods and focused on the trees, longing to go for a run and find comfort in my animal. I really needed an escape—a reprieve.

"I can feel the thirst for blood and violence radiating off you," Gavin said. His voice sounded closer than I thought he was, but I didn't bother to turn away from the window to see. "Sky, are you okay?" He sounded concerned, really concerned, and I wondered how I appeared to everyone else. Did I look as vengeful and out of control as I felt? Did I seem blindly driven to violence?

Gavin's presence overwhelmed the space we shared. He eased past me and relaxed into the corner next to the window, and I shifted my eyes to look at him. His usually foreboding, cool, and distant eyes were warm and sympathetic. "When you feel anger and hate this deep, it's never good to act on it."

Really? I was about to get a "stay calm" lecture from Gavin. *What, am I encroaching on your trademark behavior?*

"Did Sebastian send you up here to talk me into being a good little wolf?" I snapped and immediately regretted it. Sebastian probably couldn't care less about me not seeking revenge. We had more important issues to deal with. We had to fix Josh, find the Faeries, and recover the magical objects. The last thing we needed to deal with was the Northern Seethe and, depending on the potential backlash from Demetrius's death at my hands, perhaps the Southern Seethe as well. The reality of it didn't make my ire any less fiery.

"Even if he had, I wouldn't," he admitted sourly. "Personally, I think you should seek revenge. I think you should make him hurt. But fighting him—and I'm sure you wouldn't win—won't be as satisfying as actually fucking destroying him. Instead of standing here and grieving, put that anger and those emotions to better use. Figure out how to destroy Demetrius. Death is easy and killing isn't nearly as satisfying as watching someone try to live through a devastating storm of your creation."

He pushed up from the wall, stepped closer to me, and hesitated a moment before resting his hand on my shoulder. I knew he was probably uncomfortable doing it. I decided to intensify his discomfort. I attempted to hug him. With a startled noise, he stumbled back, nearly crashing into the wall. He hissed. Gavin hissed like a startled, angry cat. I expected him to arch his back and raise his hackles. I shouldn't have garnered so much pleasure from his reaction, but I did.

"What's with you? Stop trying to feel me up," he said as he slipped past me, his ordinarily tawny face red and twisted into a ruddy scowl. He was at the door by the time he looked back over his shoulder to snarl at me.

I simply smiled. "I thought it was a hug it out moment!" I yelled after him.

No less than five minutes later, Kelly knocked softly on the door. She greeted me with the consoling smile she was known for. Her cheery personality wasn't contagious now.

"I'm fine," I said before she could ask.

"I figured you would be. But I caught Gavin in the hallway mumbling about you needing a hug and how you'd accosted him. And then he nearly ordered me to come up here and hug you. I think his exact words were, 'Someone needs to fix her. She's accosting anything within ten feet of her.'"

I laughed, louder and more hysterically than intended. But navigating through the darkness had consumed me for more than two hours, and I needed that veil lifted, if only temporarily.

"Mr. Dark and Broody doesn't like to be touched, does he?"

She grinned and gave me a sly look. "Oh, he likes to be touched."

Sky, you walked right into that one. I had a feeling if I didn't change the subject fast, it would devolve into us talking about how "delicious" Gavin smelled. I'd learned my lesson from our last conversation about him. I didn't say anything, and her taunting grin mirrored the one I'd had after I'd attempted to hug Gavin.

"David and Trent are doing very well, except for the side effects of consuming vampire blood. Trent is downstairs trying to arm wrestle anyone who neared him. His ankle wasn't broken, but sprained. He's bouncing up and down on it like he's getting ready to enter the boxing ring. He challenged Winter to a fight. It didn't end well for him." She chuckled. "I see why you like him and David."

"They're very brave and great friends." That pain and heaviness returned. This time I refused to give in to it. I just couldn't. I was in a weird place. Anger had numbed me, and the thirst for revenge left me distracted. Neither was something I needed at the moment. David and Trent were safe. Now I needed Josh to be safe as well.

For fifteen minutes, Kelly remained with me. I was at one end of the room, and she was at the other, lingering in case I needed to talk. "Being human in this world is hard, and no matter how strong you are, something will happen that makes you feel utterly vulnerable," she confessed earnestly. Her eyes glistened with unshed tears, and I knew she was remembering the time she'd felt the most vulnerable—when she'd been a victim of Dexter's machinations. A long, pregnant silence followed. "When confronted with defenselessness, your instinct is to do whatever it takes to never feel it again."

She chewed on her lip for several more moments, withdrawing into her thoughts as if she'd forgotten I was in the room. "David and Trent have vampire blood in them. They don't feel weak anymore. I have a feeling they will do whatever it takes to continue feeling that way." She didn't elaborate, but I understood what she was saying. They would probably seek out this feeling again and try to find a way to obtain vampire blood again. I couldn't let that happen.

I nodded in understanding, and eventually, she started out of the room. I was just a few feet behind her. I needed to see them. Ethan was ascending the stairs as I descended them, and we met halfway.

"I'm okay," I said, not giving him the chance to ask.

"I know you are."

"Do I sound that unbelievable when I lie?" I teased.

He laughed and nodded. Warm lips pressed against my forehead. *"Eu gostaria de poder melhorar isto por ti." I wish I could make this better for you.*

He didn't wish he could bring Quell back, but I truly believed he wished I didn't have to go through the pain.

"May I ask a question?"

I nodded.

"What did you do to Gavin? Whatever it was, don't do it again." He grinned. "He's ranting about you attacking him and how the pack has changed. Apparently, I need to help you control your urges. We are a pack of puppies and kittens, and before we know it, people will be scratching us behind our ears. He's not happy at all."

I snickered.

"Sky, stop messing with Gavin," he playfully scolded me, as he backed down the stairs and followed me to the infirmary. Josh lay in a bed on his side so Dr. Jeremy could monitor the ward over his mark. It seemed to be in the same condition as when the witches had first put it on.

David and Trent were sitting up in beds on the other side of the room and didn't look like they'd been near death just hours ago. Despite being physically better, David looked wary and overwhelmed. He worked up a smile as I approached.

"Hey, pumpkin," he offered weakly. I pushed the guilt down, but not far enough to keep it from resurfacing.

I smiled. "How are you?"

"Fine. But if I have to deal with that for much longer, I'm not sure what I'll do." He rolled his eyes and jerked his head in Trent's direction.

Suppressing a laugh, I looked at Trent. He was bouncing around on his once injured leg, in awe of his recovery, movements, and enhanced abilities. His coltish body moved more gracefully than ever.

Winter stood in front of him, a cordial smile on her face, but it was fading as her patience thinned. "You'll be stronger and faster than you can imagine for a couple of days, maybe even weeks. Don't get used to it."

"I won't. Is this how you feel all the time? It has to be amazing to move this fast and see everything so clearly all the time."

Kelly was right. They were being seduced by the benefits of vampire blood. Well, Trent was. David was pensive. Winter might not have meant to be intimidating, but it was hard not to see her that way when her eyes were vertical slits that bored into Trent. Her voice dropped, low and grave. "Vampire blood is good for a quick fix, and you needed it to survive. It's not a long-term solution and never should be." She looked over at David, giving him the same stern look. She'd go to her grave denying it and would probably threaten bodily harm to anyone who mentioned it, but she was concerned for them. "It can quickly become an addiction, and you'll sacrifice more than what you will get in return. Do you understand me?"

Trent nodded.

"I need to hear it."

"I understand."

She moved closer, and her tone lost its rough edges. "I will show you how to protect yourself, and you have the pack here if you need us. Don't ever use vampire blood again."

Winter shot David a look. He nodded and made the same promise as Trent.

With great effort, her scowl lifted into a smile. "Now sit down," she ordered Trent. "You're hopping around like a bunny and it's annoying me."

"Of course, cupcake." He hopped back on the bed.

Shooting him a dagger stare that was full-on snake, she said firmly, "No." Trent retreated, but I could see the challenge in the wayward smile he gave her. It wasn't the last time he would try it, and if his persistence was anything like David's, he'd win the battle.

I turned my attention back to David. "Do you remember what the people who came into my house looked like?"

Sebastian, Ethan, and Cole appeared next to me before I'd completely gotten the question out. David remained focused on me, most likely repelled by their intensity.

After several moments of concentration, he finally said, "I don't know." Full awareness of the situation overtook him. "It's like the memory was taken away. I don't even remember how we were injured. All I remember is going into your house and the fight, but I can't picture the people we were fighting." Staring past me, he struggled to grasp memories he couldn't retrieve. Frustration contorted his face into a rigid scowl.

"It's fine. Why don't you lie down for a little bit and we'll bring something for you all to eat after you've rested. Both of you," Winter said, glaring at Trent, who was again springing around the room. In a dramatic movement, his body twisting and wavering, he dropped back onto the bed, allowing his hand to fall over his head he closed his eyes. He opened one to peek at her. She mouthed, "I hate you," which no one, including Trent, believed.

Sebastian looked at her, his head inclined. She gave him a small apologetic smile; he responded with a nod. If a human was considered a friend to the pack, our protective urges were strong. Resisting them was difficult, and at the moment, Winter's were heightened by David and Trent consuming vampire blood and the possible repercussions.

CHAPTER 18

Gavin still hadn't forgiven me for trying to hug him and was seething in the corner, glaring at me as Steven, Winter, Ethan, and Cole surrounded Sebastian's desk. Sebastian rested back in his chair, his hand washing over his face several times before he spoke.

"You're sure it's the Faeries?" he asked in exasperation.

"No one is strong enough to use magic against Claudia except them," Ethan said.

"Why now? What do they want?" Sebastian asked, voicing the question that had plagued us all, and there wasn't an answer. "They'll be going after the Clostra soon," he said, coming to his feet. "The witches … they'll be next and—"

"Then us," I finished. We had one of the books in the set of three and the book that held the Gem of Levage. Everything was a blur as my mind tried to put the pieces of the puzzle together. The Gem of Levage could transfer power and lift curses; the Aufero could take magic from a source, weakening it; the Vitae restored life; the Fatifer brought death; and the Clostra had spells so dangerous that the three volumes were kept apart so no one could use them. *What the hell do they want to do with them?*

Sebastian was out of the door, directing Steven, Cole, Winter, and Gavin to follow. He turned to Ethan and me. "You should stay here in case they come. Worst case—" He looked at Ethan, and I knew what he was implying: we could protect the third Clostra with magic or in wolf form. Ethan nodded, giving Cole a cool, hard stare as a satisfied smile eased over Cole's face. Cole seemed to like where he was—at Sebastian's side. It made sense, and I'd rather Ethan be here with me than Cole.

An unknown enemy was the hardest to combat. We didn't know how many there were, and based on what I'd read about the Faeries, their only weakness was us. It wasn't really their inability to kill us that made us a threat, but the fact they couldn't use magic against us. We were the only thing that had stopped them before, but back then, we hadn't been the creatures we were now. I shuddered at the memory of the lifelike visions of our past I'd been treated to—how we'd behaved and our savagery. Even on our worse days we were nothing like our ancestors.

"They dropped the case against Steven," Ethan said, breaking the silence as he looked up from one of the many books stacked in front of us in the library where we'd been since the others left. There wasn't much time to discuss what had transpired, but I'd figured that would happen after our run-in with DA Price.

"Is there a way for him to relitigate it?"

"Not with the charges filed. They don't have a case for anything else." Ethan seemed so sure it put a lot of my worries to rest.

"And what about the Red Blood? Do you think that's the end of them?"

"No. They're zealots. Quinn has been monitoring things, and they're still active but afraid to pursue their agenda more aggressively. They'll wait until everything has died down, see whether your abductors are convicted, and then I'm sure they'll go from there."

"Have you told Joan about Steven?"

He nodded. "She was the first person I told. She's doing her best to deal with it, but I don't know if she will change her mind about him returning to the South." He frowned at the thought.

"Maybe. The situation ended quickly enough. He didn't have to go to trial. Eventually people will lose interest in him and the story and things will go back to normal. It will look bad if he leaves." I made a note to point that out to her if Joan persisted in trying to get Steven to move.

There wasn't any doubt Joan was still holding on to maternal guilt over returning to her pack. She couldn't fix things for Steven and I knew that bothered her. Not just as a mother but as an Alpha, as well. Alphas fixed things—that's what they do. The situation was resolved.

I stood looking over the titles in the library, feeling Josh's absence in what I considered his office. We wouldn't find anything of use here; the books we needed were at Ethan's home, as were his dossiers on me and on the Faeries. I grabbed another book and aimlessly perused it. "Do you think it would be better if we came out?" I asked Ethan as I looked over at David. He'd been standing at the door for several minutes. The knowing look on his face showed he knew he wouldn't go unnoticed.

He sat in one of the chairs. A wave of relief came over me as I watched him ease back, calm and confident, more like himself.

"How do you become an Alpha?" he asked Ethan.

"I'm not. I'm the Beta."

David nodded but scrutinized Ethan. "But it's kind of like the Alpha. I see how people respond to you, like you're in charge."

"In any other pack, he probably would be the Alpha," I explained.

David continued, "I guess the better question is, who did you have to kill to get that position?"

Ethan's jaw clenched, and his eyes sharpened on David. "Excuse me?"

"You guys are animals, right? In the animal kingdom, the strongest is the one who can beat everyone else. Sometimes, animals kill their own. I'm assuming the same pattern exists here. How many people did you have to kill to get your position?" This David wasn't the kind, soft-spoken person who'd given me monthly pre-full moon baskets. This person was assertive and acerbic—and tap-dancing his way into asshole territory.

"In some packs, people do challenges to the death and in others to submission."

"But I didn't ask that. I asked how many people you've killed to either get your position or maintain it. Please answer the question, Ethan."

"That's none of your goddamn business," Ethan snapped.

David conceded with a pleasant smile and then shifted his head to look at me. "I think I've answered your question as to whether it would be better if you all came out. It wouldn't. Once you open that door, expose what you guys do, how you operate, those are the very questions they will ask you. And your answers, whether you do it honestly, get frustrated, or choose not to, will be the way humans perceive you."

He widened his smile at Ethan, who was still bristling over the questioning. "Yes, you all have the dark, sexy, and broody thing down, and if this were a supernatural TV show, it'd be great. Top ratings. But this is real life, and people will be curious about you. They'll want to know your structure, hierarchy, and most of all, how you became the way you are. That question is just a basic one. Imagine what you'll be confronted with if you went before Congress. Believe me, the moment you guys come out, people won't be like, 'Oh, look, how cute. They change into wolves.' It'll be more like, 'Shit, they turn into wolves, and panthers, and dingoes,' and whatever else you have."

Ethan's scowl relaxed; he now understood the point to David's questions. He understood it, but he still wasn't happy about it.

David had withdrawn into his thoughts, and his brows inched together. He stared at the walls as if seeing things for the first time without the filtered lens most humans had. He closed his eyes. Sound—that was another intriguing thing about his dalliance with vampirism. A result of his new enhanced hearing David heard the front door swing open the moment we had. He came to his feet and followed us out of the library as we responded to a commotion at the front of the house. Sebastian pushed his way through the front door with a person in his arms. I felt the wave of magic; it couldn't be ignored as six angry witches came in behind him. Cole carried another. The two injured witches didn't look too bad. David and Trent had been worse off, but they also didn't have access to magic.

"The moment you thought you were under attack, you should have called," Sebastian grumbled as he headed to the infirmary.

It didn't take him long to hand over his witch to Dr. Jeremy and return to the hallway where Ariel was standing, her face flushed, her lips drawn back to expose her clenched teeth.

"I had everything under control," she shot back defiantly.

Waves of undiluted and unrestrained frustration came off him, directed solely at Ariel. She stood taller, jutting her chin and chest and meeting his gaze. "As I said before, I had it under control before you came barging in."

The tendril of his patience snapped. "What part did you have under control? Them whipping you around the room with magic like a ragdoll? You seemed particularly in command when you crashed into the ground. You hit the ground with pure grace. Go ahead, Ariel, tell me about this control you speak of, because from what I saw, you were getting your magical ass handed to you!"

"You only helped because you wanted to make sure the books were okay."

Sebastian started to speak, but based on the amber bleeding

into his brown eyes, his words wouldn't be kind. He snapped his mouth closed and took several long breaths. He forced a smile on his face, but it was so strained it looked like a grimace. With a couple of steps, he swallowed up the few feet between them. "You are new to your position, and I know you want to make a statement that you are in control and competent. I'm not challenging that. I think you are both. But when dealing with magical beings, *we* have an advantage you don't have. Sometimes help is needed. Today, it was. You have two options: continue to behave like a petulant child and an ingrate and lose the respect of those you lead and mine, or accept there is a time when help is needed and asking for it doesn't make you less of a leader. A leader understands the many facets of being in charge."

Insolence appeared to be one of Ariel's core behaviors, and I could see she was grappling with the decision. It didn't take long to realize it wasn't any authority she was railing against—it was *Sebastian's* she had a problem with, and the arrogant smirk that tugged at his lips wasn't helping.

"Thank you for the assist," she finally acknowledged, her voice emotionless and flat.

He leaned into her. "You're welcome."

"Why don't you pull her pigtail?" I mumbled under my breath.

Sebastian's head snapped toward me. "What was that, Sky?"

I nearly displayed all my teeth with my fake, sweet smile. "I was just inquiring about the books," I responded in an overly saccharine voice.

He pinned me with a warning look. I made a silly face, which shocked him. He looked away. It would take me years to understand the pack, and I'd probably never get used to their overpowering presence, were-animal dominance, and predaceous aura that sometimes prompted the flight-or-fight response in people, but I'd discovered that countering it with an atypical response was calming and freaked them out. It was a win-win situation.

Sebastian was still giving me an odd look when Cole handed

me the books. His hand lingered on mine longer than necessary. I wasn't the only one who noticed it. Ethan had come closer, and before he could advance any farther, I shoved the books into his chest. "Please put these away," I requested.

Distracted by Cole, who was swathed in smugness, Ethan was difficult to redirect.

"Ethan!" I said sharply to get his attention. It didn't help, and Cole was enjoying it too much.

"Cole, see if Dr. Jeremy needs help," Sebastian ordered. "Now," he added when Cole didn't move.

Without Cole as a provocation, Ethan took the books to the library to put them in the secured cabinet we kept the other protected objects in.

CHAPTER 19

The next morning, Ethan and Dr. Jeremy looked anxious as they examined the orange illumination on Josh's thigh, which was fading. The Faeries had finally removed two of the rings surrounding Josh's mark.

"It took them twenty-four hours to remove two," Ethan said solemnly. At that rate, we had three days to figure something out.

"I'm not sure why he won't wake, at least while the wards are there," Dr. Jeremy speculated as he walked around Josh's bed. Josh was alone in the infirmary, Trent and David having been released with sentinels guarding them until we were sure they were safe. They couldn't get away from us and the situation fast enough. I understood. Tension stifled the house, and no matter how much Ethan and Sebastian seemed to appear like things were under control, they weren't.

The Creed didn't have to announce their arrival, but if by some chance someone missed the sudden tide of magic rushing through the house, they couldn't miss the clicking of Ariel's heels on the floor. I left Ethan in the infirmary and went to greet them alongside Sebastian. The two witches who'd been severely injured weren't with them. For people who'd left the pack's home earlier that morning after being up most of the night with the injured witches, they looked more rested than I expected.

"Where's the library?" Ariel asked.

I waved her to follow and led her into Josh's sanctuary.

They all looked around the vast room, taking in the bookshelves' contents. It wasn't the first time London had seen it, but she had the same look of awe the rest of them wore. Josh had gotten so used to the collection that he didn't share the same appreciation. It had been reduced to a place that allowed him to perform stronger magic.

Ariel walked along the bookshelf-lined walls that held books in various languages. Lying between their bindings were pages of spells that had been long forgotten. Most of the tomes were originals and some languages had fallen into disuse, which had proven to be a problem on occasion. But between the various members of the pack, we usually found someone to translate. Worst-case scenario, we had Google Translate. Ariel's fingers brushed against the spines of the books as she circled the large room.

"I was told you were quite resourceful; I had no idea to what extent." I couldn't determine if she was comforted or disturbed by that. I wasn't going to ask, figuring it would come off wrong.

Sebastian, standing in the doorway, didn't have such restraints. "Does that bother you?" he asked, his arms crossed, waiting for an answer.

She held the same intense look as he did. They were always assessing each other. Friend or foe? Was the other to be trusted or feared or both?

"I haven't decided yet," she responded in a dulcet voice, which didn't give Sebastian the information he needed. She had to answer the question so he could determine if her reply was a lie or the truth. I leaned in to listen to her voice, to the intonation and cadence. I heard her heartbeat and respiration. They were steady. She turned away from Sebastian and continued to peruse the titles.

"That's a very interesting talent were-animals have, using a person's vital signs and changes in their voice to determine if they're lying. I'm sure it comes in handy often, especially with those who don't have the skills to mask it with magic. Although I never condoned or understood the animosity and contempt Marcia had for you because you are immune to our magic in animal form, I can understand her concern. I don't think you're cruel at all, but your dedication to your pack and the boundaries you blur to protect it and achieve its goals often puts you in ethically compromising positions. Don't you think?"

"Perhaps, but I have a feeling you do the same for your witches."

"And I'd say you were right. However, we are still bound by the rules of magic. The consequences of not doing so include becoming a person like Marcia. I have no intention of anyone becoming like her under my watch."

"Quite admirable of you. It's easy to think that way when you haven't been confronted with something that could decimate your people. You come back to me when you have so I can see if you have that same haughty look of contempt for those who do." He moistened his lips; his eyes traveled the length of her body before meeting her eyes with a hint of amusement and challenge. They were flirting wrong. Maybe that was the way people like them did it.

Ariel returned her attention to the bookshelf and removed several books from it. "We either find them and stop them or find a spell that can undo Josh's curse. Without any of their blood, it will be hard to locate them." She'd said it aloud, but it appeared as though she was talking to herself. It didn't seem like she was ready to be confronted by the Faeries again.

"There wasn't any blood from the altercation?" I asked.

She sorted the books she'd taken off the shelves into two piles, but I had no idea what criteria she was using. At first, I thought it was based on language, but within seconds I was proven wrong. I quickly realized this was *her* nervous tell—reordering things. This was Ariel fidgeting. "There was plenty of blood. They retrieved it. All of it. It was a unique thing to see." I'd heard the fear in her words. It wasn't unique—it was scary. She was failing at putting forth a brave facade.

"Is there a way for you to reverse the magic and look it up, the way you would an IP address? Pinpoint where the magic is coming from?" asked Quinn. He hadn't bothered to introduce himself after slipping past Sebastian.

Ariel's head tilted as she assessed him. "I'm Ariel, and you are?"

"Quinn, but my friends call me Casper."

"Casper," she said softly to herself and scrutinized him for a long time. "Well, Quinn"—ice covered every letter in his name—"is it safe to assume that's your cute way of letting people know you can go ghost?" I felt silly for not catching on to his moniker as quickly as she had.

Ariel was clearly amused by what she saw. "Let me guess. You're the person who makes situations or things disappear, or you're just a computer person."

He bit his lip to hold back a response. She waited for him to answer. He didn't. "So, can you look up the magic that way?" he repeated.

"It can't be done. Unlike blood, which is a direct link to the person, magic is just magical energy. You can feel it, but you can't trace it that way. That is why Josh has put himself in an induced coma. He's diverting all his energy and strength to fighting the magic and preventing it from doing any further damage. It would be useless for him to try to trace the magic's source."

She grabbed a piece of paper and a pen from the desk and scribbled things down. London came to her side and looked over her shoulder. She then grabbed her own paper and pen to take notes. They paged through more books, most in English and Latin. Ariel pointed to a book on a bottom shelf. "Arabic?"

I nodded. She grabbed that off the shelf and pulled out her

phone. "The thing that makes breaking curses so cumbersome and nearly impossible is the variation. It's like finding a key to match each person involved. It's damn near impossible to do." She made a face.

~

Four hours later, another orange ring over Josh's mark had been removed. The attackers were going through the wards faster, and Ethan was barely holding on. He'd left his position next to Josh to check on the Creed's progress in the library. He watched them work in nervous anticipation.

"Can't we transfer a spirit shade to him?" Ethan suggested.

"Spirit shades?" Ariel asked. She was obviously probing to determine how much we knew about darker magic and spells.

We needed their help and didn't have time to cull through information to decide what we should withhold. Josh's life was at stake. "We both host spirit shades. Faeries," Ethan admitted without hesitation.

Ariel's gaze bounced between Ethan and me. She studied us with a twisted look of abhorrence and curiosity. "You two are very *different*. Werewolves that are the offspring of witches, who both host powerful and dangerous spirit shades. One connected to the elves, the other to the vampires. It's like a match made in Frankenstein's lab." Ariel mused over the information she'd discovered about us, which I was sure was a combination of her extensive research and the information Sebastian and Ethan had shared with her.

Ethan asked the spirit shade question again.

"A spirit shade cannot force itself into someone's body; it's one rule of their existence."

"But I didn't accept mine," I rebutted.

"What were the circumstances of your becoming a host?" she asked, her interest piqued. She took a seat at the table and gave me her undivided attention. Revealing our secrets felt weird. We'd protected them for so long it was disconcerting baring it all. I even wondered if it was necessary, but the situation dictated the full truth because we weren't sure which secret could be the very thing that helped.

I told her everything I knew.

There were several minutes of silence before she spoke. "Your mother did it while you were in the womb. You were an extension of who she was. She was able to do it on your behalf."

"If Josh can't give consent, can Ethan do it on his behalf?" I asked hopefully.

Ariel, London, and the other witches looked at one another, considering my suggestion. I could see by the intense looks on their faces they were thinking of every spell they'd ever encountered, trying to figure out how they could make it work. Josh was able to mix spells to create new ones and was pretty good at it. The six of them had to be able to come up with something.

After moments of deliberation, London spoke up. "It might be possible. But we'll need some time to come up with something."

It was possible. I held on to that more than anything. "Give us time," Ariel said, dismissing us. Ethan and I continued to stand in the library until all their eyes were trained on us waiting for us to leave.

They came up with something, and it was awful. I was standing between Sebastian and Ethan, trying to reconcile the many emotions running through me. The strongest were fear and sorrow. They wanted to transfer the curse from Josh to someone else, but they weren't confident it would save him.

Josh was going to die. Tears welled in my eyes—I couldn't lose another person I cared about—but I blinked them back. I needed to be stronger because Ethan was barely keeping it together.

"Sky," he comforted as he brushed his hand against mine. Our emotions were in tune and he felt my grief and anxiety, as if they were his own, in the same manner I'd felt his on our way to Claudia's home.

Ariel didn't look as put together as she normally did. Her hair was mussed from more than just running her fingers through it. All the witches looked disheveled and tired. They'd been at it for three hours and looked like they hadn't even taken a break.

"You still have the Gem of Levage, right?" London asked.

"Yes." Ethan moved to a safe, pulled out the book that contained it, and handed it to them.

"Isn't it an actual stone?" London asked.

"It was before Josh placed it in the book for safekeeping," I said, opening it to the page the gem had bled into.

Ariel glanced in Sebastian's direction. "Nothing is ever simple with you, is it?"

"Keeps us sharp." He tried to smile but couldn't commit and waited for them to explain their plan.

Choosing her words thoughtfully and carefully, London slowly gained our trust in them and the process. I trusted her. I knew she cared for Josh deeply. "For us to make him a host, he will have to drop his wards and we will have to drop ours to allow it to happen. During that time, if they can remove the mark, he will die, so trying to get him to host a spirit shade isn't a plausible option." Her gaze traveled to each of us. "If we do a transfer, the curse will become active and the person it's transferred to will die. We think we can transfer it to a vampire. Reversion we can fix but we can't undo human death."

Cole lurked in the shadows in silence. I still didn't trust him; he was just there to gather information about the Midwest Pack and use it to his advantage. We were that pack who'd *had* all the secrets. We were exposed, floundering, and trying to save Josh and defeat the Faeries.

"Are you sure that the curse is still active?" I rushed out. I went on to tell them how we'd used the Clostra to remove my death curse.

"And so many other curses," Cole provided once I was finished.

Great, that's what we need—a historian.

Several witches closed their eyes. A couple took deep breaths. The looks on their faces indicated they really hadn't wanted to hear what I'd told them. Every time we revealed a secret, we exposed them to even more disturbing aspects of our pack's history or another way we'd abused and misused magic. Perhaps they were impressed, but nothing on any of their faces showed that. They probably considered us reckless and in possession of far too much power that we used without any thought of the consequences. There was some truth to that. We hadn't thought about the consequences—just the goals, which was why the Tre'ase were no longer restricted and vampires walked in the daylight. And those were just the things we knew about. It was a big world out there, and things we knew little about had happened because of our reckless handling of magic.

"If the cursed one wasn't a magic wielder, it might be easier because we could detect the presence of magic. In Josh's case, we don't know," London responded, her finger tracing the imprint the Gem of Levage had left in the book. "Besides, are you willing to risk his life?"

We were risking his life anyway, but I kept my observation to myself.

"Unless you can guarantee Josh will survive it, we can't do it," Ethan said.

"Ethan, I can't guarantee success with any of this," London entreated softly. "We're doing exactly what you told me the vampires tried to do to Sky using the Gem of Levage. The vampire will absorb the curse." She ran her fingers over the book in small circles exhibiting a nervous condition. All the witches had one.

"Ethan, it's worth a try. He'll die if we don't do something. At least this will give him a fighting chance," London implored.

Sebastian's face remained expressionless.

Ariel studied Sebastian, but he gave nothing away. "It would be best to use an old vampire. The older, the better. If they have recently fed, they go through reversion much slower than a young vampire, which will give them a better chance at survival. Do you think you could get Demetrius to agree to this?"

He nodded once. "I can."

Really? If Sebastian could convince Demetrius to not only show up but participate in the spell, I would give Sebastian the new title of not just Elite were-animal but also Elite wizard. He slipped out of the room. His confidence intrigued Ariel but left me baffled. Sebastian remained poised in the face of danger and when dealing with situations where hell freezing over was more likely than success.

Cole's gaze lingered on Ethan. "I know Chris is a new vampire, but she's proven to be quite resilient, hasn't she, Ethan? Your history with her"—he let his eyes drift my way then over to London—"and what she's had with your brother surely would persuade her to help. Perhaps she would be a good backup," he suggested.

Cole had planted his seed and seemed to gather great pleasure in watching London's response. I remained emotionless, fully aware of Ethan's history with Chris. I'd let go of any jealousy and doubt I had. But London seemed shaken by the news that Josh had been involved with Chris, although she worked to hide it. Her movements became stiff, and she seemed determined to find something to focus on. Eventually, she settled on the book and studied it as we had just minutes before.

Although I knew Cole's suggestion had a nefarious intent, there was some truth in it. Ignoring the delight that made him smile and brightened his eyes, I left the room and went straight to the infirmary.

"What are you looking for?" Dr. Jeremy asked.

"Josh's phone."

His brow furrowed in curiosity, but he handed it to me.

I felt an ache when I thought about Josh's odd interaction with Chris. I didn't think it was salacious. Well, he'd often denied it, but I wasn't convinced he wasn't more than a food source for her. I'd fed Quell numerous times and knew it could be done without being sexual, but I wasn't sure it was possible for Josh to feed Chris without it going that way. I grabbed his phone and cursed under my breath; he had it locked. Staring at the phone, I tried to think of possible passwords. The two I tried were unsuccessful.

"Let me," Ethan said, taking the phone. He punched in a couple of numbers and handed it back. I scrolled through the call log; there were no calls labeled "Chris," but there was a number without a name. I called it.

"What do you need, Josh?" Chris asked on the other line.

"It's not Josh," I said.

"Bambi?" she asked, surprised. "What's wrong with Josh?"

Before I continued, I eased out of the room and walked down the hall to get some privacy. I was surprised Ethan didn't follow. Apparently, if he thought Chris could do anything to help his brother, he'd give me space. No one quite understood the unusual relationship I had with Chris. I couldn't say I understood the nuances of it. Maybe we were bound by a mutual disdain that had somehow mutated into an odd form of respect. Or maybe our history was so warped we were connected in a manner that neither one of us understood.

"I need your help," I said, unable to keep the desperation out of my voice.

CHAPTER 20

We were in a state of panic. The witches were preparing to add more wards to Josh because there were only two rings around his mark. The troubled looks on their faces belied the confident front they put forth. The Faeries were removing the wards fast, any replacements would be removed just as fast.

No one expected Demetrius to show—except Sebastian—but an hour and a half after Sebastian had first left the room, someone pounded on the front door. Sebastian opened the door, letting Demetrius in. *All hail the wizard king. Elite wizard. Or whatever title Sebastian will take.*

Demetrius looked bored as he entered the house, flanked by vampires—Chase on his right, Gabriella on his left, and their protégé Sable behind him. He made a production out of tugging on his crisp gray shirt and smoothing out his pants as he neared us. He slipped a steely look my way, which I returned.

"Unfortunately, I have been delayed since I am in need of guards now whenever I visit. I can no longer be in your presence alone for fear that your pup will attack me." He gave me a contemptuous, cold look. It was doubtful that Demetrius feared me enough to require guards. The other vampires were a less than subtle threat.

I started to roll my eyes but cut it short as Chase and Gabriella directed a look of virulence and fury at me. I'd killed Michaela; they wanted to avenge her. It was written on their faces, in the way they stood, and in the sly way they bared their teeth like weapons, daring me to make a move or do anything that would incite a response. They were walking on a knife's edge, ready to dole out retribution.

I stood taller, rolled my shoulders back, and took a defensive stance. I felt less confident that this was going to end civilly.

"You are safe here," Sebastian said.

Demetrius scoffed. "I'd love to believe that, but you don't seem to have control over Skylar. She's rabid. They used to put those things down, didn't they?" The look he gave me showed he was ready to euthanize me. Ethan's growl reverberated throughout the room, and Sebastian strategically placed himself between them.

"We didn't call you here for violence. We need your help."

"Well of course you do. Why else would you call me? But I'm sure you understand that if it does not benefit me, I have no interest in helping you."

Ariel spoke first. "We need you to help us save Josh."

Demetrius shrugged and gave a mocking grin. As he gave her a slow and lingering once-over, he ran his tongue over his teeth. His voice was low and velvety, as though he was speaking to a lover, when he said, "Ariel." She didn't let his inappropriate familiarity unnerve her. It was one of Demetrius's classic moves. He kept his eyes narrowed on her, watching her, and she approached but left several feet between them.

"Why love, I really hope you have a backup plan. Surely you know I care even less about the brother's life than I do Ethan's," he purred.

"You should care. Josh is the only person preventing the Faeries from taking over. We need him." I wasn't sure how much creative license she was taking with the truth, but if we were going to figure out what the Faeries had planned, we'd need him. There was no denying it.

"And what pray tell do you plan to have me do?" he asked, his tone dry and disinterested.

Ariel described how they wanted to use the Gem of Levage to pull the curse from Josh and transfer it to him.

Demetrius gave a small smile of disbelief. "And this is your plan? You actually thought I would agree to this? I applaud your gumption in even thinking I would agree to such a thing. Good luck finding any vampire to agree to this foolishness." His mocking laughter rang throughout the house.

The moment Chris came through the door, Demetrius's attention fixed on her, exhibiting the same longing he'd had each time I'd seen them together. I stared at her, too, and made a poor attempt not to pass judgment. She was doing me a favor, and possibly helping Josh. I couldn't risk any condescending remarks about her vampy outfit, which included leather pants that stretched seamlessly over her body and left nothing to the imagination. Or the bright red tank top that she must have gotten from the kids' section. I kept a keen eye on her as her three-inch heels hit lightly against the floor moving with the ease of a person wearing a pair of casual flats. Not one snarky word would be said about her lipstick that was as red as her shirt and the heavy mascara that framed her eyes. She was a walking cliché, and the sly smile she gave me made it clear that she knew and didn't care.

"Chris," Demetrius whispered. She didn't look at him, keeping her focus on me.

Okay, Sky, you can do this. No snide comments about her clothes. I knew she could sense my dilemma.

Winter couldn't exercise the same level of restraint. Twisting her lips in derision, she said, "Really?" as Chris walked past.

She dismissed Winter's insult as inconsequential and asked, "What happens to Josh if we don't do this?"

"We don't have many options," Ariel admitted.

"If you were to give me a survival rate, what would it be?"

"I wouldn't. I don't want you to go into this blindly. By all standards of magic, it should work, but as you know, magic can be unpredictable. It's not science." Ariel looked over at the Creed then gave a solemn and heartfelt pledge. "But if you do this, we will do everything in our knowledge and power to ensure you live."

Chris didn't need to breathe, but she exhaled her answer. "Okay. Tell me what I need to do." She glided toward the infirmary.

"You will do no such thing," Demetrius ordered, taking hold of her arm. Anger sparked in his dark eyes. He closed them briefly, and when he reopened them, they looked gentler, softer.

Is this his first time meeting her? If someone forbade Chris from doing something, she'd do it three times just to make a point.

She looked down at his hand on her arm and pulled her lips back, exposing her fangs in defiance.

Demetrius kept his hands in place and moved closer. "No matter how you have behaved, you are still part of this Seethe. You exist because of me. I saved you, and you do not have the right to be frivolous with your life. I won't allow it."

She snatched her arm out of his grasp and looked at him through narrowed eyes. Several moments passed as they each asserted their dominance. He was the leader of the Northern Seethe and used to getting his way, and she was a person who prided herself on possessing unwavering obstinacy and will.

Her voice was pure ice. "You may be able to stand around and let them handle this and do nothing but reap the rewards, but I won't." She relaxed and stepped closer to him, dropping her voice so low I had to strain to hear. "Demetrius, do something. Don't be a useless observer in this, because it might not end well for any of us. If you don't know the history of the Faeries' reign, you should learn it."

He listened intently and kept a steady gaze on her as he leaned in, placing his hand on her waist. He pressed his cheek against hers and inhaled. His lips brushed against her ear as he whispered something I couldn't make out. She pulled away enough to look him in the eyes. They stood in silence as if they were the only people in the room, and in Demetrius's mind, they were. His narcissism made his desires and needs the only things visible to him. Everything else was inconsequential. We were no more important than the furniture.

"We have to do something to help. They can't keep shouldering the responsibility of protecting us. They've done everything, and all you've done is benefit from it," she said.

"I've done enough." It was loud enough for us to hear—his only acknowledgment of our existence.

"Then do *more* than enough," she urged, leaning in to let her lips brush delicately against his. It started off innocently enough and quickly escalated into something intense and heated.

He gently purred, "Chris, don't be fooled. Nothing they do is out of pure selflessness; the agenda is always to help themselves. Don't be naïve and think otherwise."

"Whether selfless or not, we have benefitted," she countered.

His jaw clenched, and he allowed his gaze to drift to the other people in the room. Eventually, he brought it back to her. Once again forgetting our presence, he slipped his hand under her shirt to caress her bare skin. He whispered something, but it was for her ears only. He kissed her, and it was definitely a prelude to something far more lascivious. I wasn't totally confident they'd give us the courtesy of going somewhere else before they took things to another level. I could feel the heat of their interaction and smell the lust and hormones that wafted through the air.

I cleared my throat—loudly. They ignored me.

When they finally pulled apart, Chris asked, "Will you do it? If you don't, I will. You have a better chance of surviving than I do. It will be easier for you."

He nodded slowly. "Will you come back?"

Not even giving the question a moment of consideration, she shook her head. He sucked in a ragged breath and looked down at the floor. After a long pause, he looked at me and asked, "What is needed of me?"

Everyone knew his decision had nothing to do with goodwill. He hoped that pseudo acts of kindness would curry favor with her and sway her decision, and there was something in the way she looked at him that made me believe it might work.

Ariel waved him toward the infirmary where Josh was lying on his side. Dr. Jeremy stood nearby, frowning at the single orange circle that covered Josh's mark. With the book that held the Gem of Levage in hand, London went to Josh and tenderly stroked his hair before leaning in to say something in his ear. No one was sure whether he could hear. She pressed her lips to his forehead.

London was faltering under the pressure; it showed on her face and the way she shrank into herself. She pulled out a knife. "Demetrius, you'll need to make a blood sacrifice, and so will Josh."

He nodded, moving closer to Josh and taking the knife from London. Demetrius offered the knife to Chris. She inched forward enough to take it from him.

London had laid everything out: the books, candles, and a bowl with several herbs and salts. The other witches gathered close to her, although they weren't needed to do the spell. I figured it was for support. She instructed Demetrius on what he needed to say to initiate the spell and told him she would take over after that.

Ethan's heartbeat at an unnatural rhythm, and his breathing came so irregularly I feared he would pass out from the lack of oxygen. I interlocked my fingers with his, but he was so distracted by what was unfolding that his fingers stayed straight.

Josh's hand was cut first. He jerked. He'd felt it.

Chris, knife in hand, took Demetrius's hand in hers. There was an unintentional intimacy to their interaction. They held each other's eyes as the knife slid across his arm and blood welled. He winced but kept his eyes on Chris with an undeniable longing that demanded empathy I fought not to give in to. I hated him. I wanted him miserable. Actually, I wanted him dead, but I'd find comfort in his misery, too.

"Do the spell," Demetrius instructed. He whispered the same things he had in my dreams when I'd seen visions of what would have occurred if they'd used me during the sacrifice with the Gem of Levage. Despite failing that time, the vampires had ended up with what they wanted: an unrestricted life.

As the spell was initiated, magic flowed through the room, twining around me and everyone else. It came to life. It mellowed to the comfortable breeze that was solely Josh's resting magic. It wasn't as aggressive and defensive as it had been before.

Demetrius fell to the ground. Gabriella, Chase, and Sable came to his side, ripping away his shirt and exposing graying skin that was showing signs of reversion. The witches didn't move.

"He needs blood."

"Not yet," Ariel told them. "We need the spell to run its course." All eyes went to Josh—the last ring around the mark disappeared. Slowly, the mark faded. Ethan squeezed my hand. His heart beat so hard that Sebastian looked up from across the room. With the orange ring of wards and the mark that had sustained his life removed, Josh lay there, unmoving.

"Josh, wake up," London commanded, her soft voice as hard as it could be. Nothing.

Ethan released my hand and started toward his brother, his eyes glistening with unshed tears. My heart broke for him. There wasn't a heartbeat or respiration, nothing to indicate life coming from Josh. I clung to the fact that Demetrius was going through reversion at an advanced rate—something a well-fed vampire of his age shouldn't do.

"He's going to die. Feed him. *Now,*" Chase demanded, rising to his feet and baring fangs. He was only going to give the witches a few seconds to do it willingly.

Ariel was the first to kneel, but she kept a careful eye on Josh. Still nothing. Reversion had crept up to Demetrius's chin. Ariel hesitated, waiting for Josh to respond. Again, nothing.

Ethan held back his tears; London couldn't, and they streamed down her face.

"Josh, please," Ethan whispered.

Nothing.

Ariel and the other witches conceded failure and began to feed Demetrius. The stench of grief and sorrow filled the room. The only thing that could be heard over the overwhelming silence was Demetrius feeding on the witches.

It took five witches to make Demetrius whole again. He sat up, his charcoal eyes alight, and he was breathing—real breaths. Not the ones vampires took to not seem off-putting. He looked fearful when he heard a heartbeat coming from himself. He cursed under his breath, enraged. No one cared that he was breathing and had a heartbeat. I knew it was selfish and cruel, but I didn't have room in my heavy heart to care about anything other than Josh's life and the fact it was ending. Just as the beating of Demetrius's heart stopped and his breathing became nonexistent, Josh's started.

He was slow to move, rolling to sitting but slumped, too fatigued to stay fully erect. Ethan moved quickly to his brother and pulled him close enough so that he could rest his forehead against Josh's. Both closed their eyes, and they remained in that position as seconds became minutes. Ethan moved back. "You scared the hell out of me."

Josh grinned. "Well, I'm always good for an adventure." He looked pale and weak. His eyes traveled around the room, taking everyone in. He didn't seem surprised by the crowd of people. When he saw London, he attempted to stand but decided against it and opened his arms to her. Neither one seemed concerned about their public display of affection. IV nutrition hadn't been enough to maintain his strength, and he leaned too much into the hug.

"We're glad you're okay," Ariel offered, keeping her distance from Demetrius and running her fingers along the red mark where he'd fed. He'd laved it to close the wound, but it didn't take away the pain caused by someone puncturing the skin and drawing blood from a vein.

"Thank you for all your help," Josh offered sincerely, nodding his gratitude to every member of the Creed. "I'm indebted to you."

Ariel shook her head. "No, you are our brother in magic. No debts. I expect you would do the same if the situation were reversed." Her words seemed earnest and sincere, and for Josh's sake, I hoped they were. I couldn't hear any deception or changes in her vitals and looked to Sebastian for his thoughts. He was unreadable.

I hoped she didn't plan to exploit Josh, his resources, or the pack, but the witches had helped; they wanted to be allies and had proven invaluable when we'd needed them.

Gabriella, Chase, and Sable concentrated on Demetrius, who lay on the ground, unmoving. The beating of his defunct heart and his need to breathe appeared to have stunned him. I wondered if he missed them or hated the reminder that he had once been human.

Dr. Jeremy politely tried to usher everyone away from Josh to examine him; he became more assertive and less gentle with his request as time ticked by and people didn't respond.

Chris started to ease out of the room, but she stopped in front of Ethan. She pulled out her phone and punched a few things into it. Both Ethan's and Sebastian's phones buzzed. In unison, they looked at them and then her.

"You'll have money later today," Ethan informed her softly.

She nodded.

"Thank you so much," he added.

She shrugged indifferently, a direct contrast to her dark, blistering stare. "I helped save his life. That's what you do when you see someone about to die and you can help him. You don't let them die." Her attempt to keep her emotions out of her voice failed—and her voice cracked.

"I'm sorry." It was an earnest, heartfelt apology that put cracks in Chris's composure. Clearly unable to rebound from his apology, she stood frozen in front of Ethan. They'd had an antagonistic relationship, even when together. This piece didn't fit. They'd never shown remorse for anything they'd done to each other, and they'd done plenty they should not only have regretted but been ashamed of. Never before had they been capable of either.

Moments passed before Chris was able to find her words and still she struggled. Fumbling her acceptance, her voice low and raw, she rasped, "I accept." Then she was gone.

CHAPTER 21

Josh didn't like the twenty-four-hour observation he was put under after the curse was transferred to Demetrius; he liked being *released* to his brother even less. He stood by the door, arms folded across his chest, glaring at his brother as Ethan brought his things into the house.

"Are you kidding me! I'm not staying here. As you can see, I'm fine."

Ethan didn't dignify that statement with a response. "You can stay in the first guest room to the left. It's larger."

Josh's face reddened as his lips tightened and his eyes hardened in a glare. It definitely wasn't the time to point out that he was behaving the same way his brother was treating him—like a child.

Ethan's defiant demeanor and indignant scowl indicated he wasn't in the mood to be reasoned with. He'd thrown reason to the wind. He was riding high on overprotective-big-brother crazy. It had started when Dr. Jeremy had given Josh the okay to leave the infirmary. It only escalated when Ethan had taken Josh home only to get more clothes. They'd had a short battle of obstinacy and posturing, and since Josh was now in Ethan's home, it was apparent who'd won.

"I'll stay tonight, but that's it. Tomorrow I'm going home to sleep in my own bed." I was sure he wanted to add "with London."

Once again, Ethan ignored him. "I'll take your bags to your room," Ethan said in a stolid, controlled voice as if he were handling a business transaction and not dealing with his brother. He'd expended so much emotion over the past two days he didn't have much left. He was on autopilot protection mode.

Ethan shrugged the large overnight bag over his shoulder and turned to take it upstairs. Josh glared at his back, letting the small illumination of magic twirling in his hand expand each time he rolled it between his fingers. It started off like a small snowball, and grew bigger until it was the size of a kickball. He'd been about to hurl it at his brother's back when I caught his hand.

After a few moments, he squelched it, but fragments of it lingered in the air, powerful enough for Ethan to notice. He turned and saw me holding Josh's wrist, with him backed up against the wall. He gave Josh a warning glare, which just agitated his younger brother. Most of the pack found their antics amusing, and at times, I did as well. I found them exhausting now.

"Let me talk to him. You'll go home tomorrow. Okay?"

He shrugged. "You can talk to him if you want, but it's not up to him. I'm giving him today and that's it."

I sighed, exasperated. *It's like you just met Ethan today.* I smiled, placating him, and went about my day.

Observing them throughout the day, it appeared Ethan and Josh spent most of the day in conflicting states of appreciation that the ordeal was over and quiet frustration with the way the other was handling it. A little past ten, after they'd settled on a truce, Josh retreated to his room. They were similar, not only in their good looks, but also in their tenacity and dogmatic ways when they felt they were right. And they both thought they were right. After negotiating the two-day stay with them, I felt like I was thoroughly prepared to do a world peace talk.

It had taken a lot of coaxing, but Ethan had found some semblance of rationality. Staying upset with him was hard because he occasionally looked past Josh, and the fear and heartache at the idea of losing his brother crept over his features. We'd come too close, and those brief moments when the memories were too raw and deep for him to maintain the facade revealed a vulnerable Ethan. A side he wasn't used to or able to deal with.

I was ready for a drink, a whole cake, and a nap, and I was trying to figure out how to do all three simultaneously when someone knocked on the door.

I pressed my eye to the peephole and stared incredulously.

"Sky, I can hear you breathing," Chris pointed out.

I opened it.

"Will you have a drink with me?" she asked. That would've been pretty far down on the list of all the things I expected her to say or ask. Matter of fact, I wouldn't have put it on my list at all.

"O-okay," I stammered, apprehensively.

I opened the door wider. She shook her head. "No, let's go out to a bar." Answering my furrowed brow of curiosity, she said, "I want to talk."

"To me?"

"No, to the surly werewolf you're mated to," she replied sarcastically. I was never quite sure if her sarcasm was actually mocking. Chris always had odd bedfellows and didn't discriminate against who she dealt with. The person who was her enemy on Monday could easily be her ally on Wednesday.

"Sooo ..." I drawled. "Do you *really* want to talk to me?"

"Yes, Bambi, I *really* want to talk to you."

"About what?"

"Now Bambi, if I wanted to discuss it here, I would've accepted your invitation to come in. Instead, I invited you to a bar. I'm pretty sure that indicates I want to discuss it there."

"You know, you can catch more flies with honey than vinegar."

Blowing out a breath of irritation, she softened her voice. "Bambi, I would like us to go out and have a drink or two and talk. Would you join me?"

That did not feel good, did it? She wore it poorly on her face. If she rolled her eyes any harder, they were going to slam into the back of her head.

I gave her a saccharine smile and responded in a similar voice. "I would *love* to join you for a drink, Chris. Thank you *so* much for your kind gesture and for asking me so *nicely*."

She turned on her heel and left without making the acerbic comment she had to have chambered, ready to release. She seemed to practice a lot more restraint than most vampires and more than she had as a human. Well, as much restraint as Chris could manage. After all, she'd held a knife to Demetrius's throat and had been prepared to use it if I hadn't stopped her.

Ethan was leaning against the wall on the opposite side of the room, a disbelieving half-smirk on his lips as he looked over at the door.

"I'm having drinks with Chris," I informed him.

With a wolfish grin firmly fixed on his face, he stalked toward me. Once, I would've felt like prey under a predator's watch. I didn't feel that way anymore.

"Are you?" he asked, amused. "I don't want you to go."

"Now I *really* want to go," I taunted.

He kissed me lightly on the lips and trailed more kisses down my jawline and my neck. "I'm sure we can find more interesting things to do."

I moved out of reach. "Seriously, are you trying to seduce me? Now? Did you really think that would work? If you can figure out how I can sleep, eat cake, and have a drink all at the same time, you might have something I can work with."

He frowned.

I grabbed my purse and backed out the door. He growled, baring his teeth.

I growled back. Mine were never as aggressive as his. Mine were cautious. His were roaring sounds of displeasure. He growled again, louder.

Giving him an exaggerated shiver, I said, "Oh, the big bad wolf is angry. Whatever will I do? Don't wait up. Instead of worrying about me, you can check on your brother. I think he's a flight risk."

He frowned. "What does she want?" he asked.

I shrugged. "I won't know until we talk." That answer wouldn't relieve any of his apprehension—or mine. "If it weren't for her, Demetrius wouldn't have agreed to help us. I ... we owe her this much."

"We paid her," he rebutted.

"And I'm sure it wasn't nearly enough for Josh's life."

I started to exit and stopped midstep, backing up until I was near Ethan again. I leaned in, hardening my voice as I said, "Don't cuff your brother." The deviant glint that sparked in his eyes told me that placing his brother in iridium manacles was a clear option if he thought Josh might be a true flight risk.

Smiling, he offered half-heartedly, "I wouldn't think of doing such a thing."

Yeah, right.

After dealing with one ill-tempered supernatural, I was in no mood to deal with another but I also wasn't ready to see another vampire die which was about to happen. That appeared to be what was about to happen. Chris had the dark-haired vamp pushed against the car and was about to stake them. I ran and grabbed Chris's arm just before she could jam a stake in a young vamp's chest.

"Chris, put it down," I commanded. After a few moments of glaring at me while seething through clenched teeth, she relaxed. I didn't trust her to be compliant for long, so I kept my grasp on her arm.

Her gaze drifted to my hand. "I'm fine. I need them to stop following me."

I lowered my voice to reason with her, but she was so enraged I wasn't sure it was possible. "They're not doing it because they want to. It's Demetrius. You know it's always Demetrius." I sighed. It was. His obsession with her consumed so much of his time and resources. She hadn't come back as he'd expected. He wanted to be rewarded for his single act of kindness.

I nodded in the vampire's direction, and he moved quickly. I wondered if Demetrius had scouts throughout the city, waiting for her. This one had the fortune, or rather misfortune, of finding her.

Once the vampire was gone, she went to my car. "You're driving," she informed me. I didn't mind because I'd seen her drive. Even before she'd become immortal, she'd driven like she was.

Chris was adamant about us talking once we were at the bar, with just music on the radio to entertain us, it made the drive to the bar in an industrial area right outside Chicago seem longer than the twenty minutes it took. I hadn't expected her to take me anywhere extremely posh, and she didn't. We walked into an old brick building that reminded me of a warehouse. The inside was so dark my eyes had to adjust.

The thrum of music filled the room, low enough that you could just listen to it and enjoy your drink or ignore it and enjoy the company of the person you were with. This was definitely a place where people came to have a drink and talk. It wasn't a fancy bar, but it was cozy. There were a few tables scattered about, nothing trendy, just round, dark wood tables and chairs. Some chairs matched, and a few were just leather barstools. The black lacquer bar was in the center of the room. Behind the counter were three modestly dressed bartenders. They didn't have the typical uniform I'd seen at other bars or even at the pack's bar. The two men weren't dressed swankily in black button-down shirts. Or trendy t-shirts. Nor did the woman wear a barely there tank and a fake smile plastered on her face. This wasn't the type of bar where you were likely to see men with muscles straining the seams of their shirts as they made a show out of mixing drinks for people seated at the bar. The bartenders looked like they came to work to serve drinks—nothing more, nothing less.

I followed Chris to the back, where the lighting was even worse, and we sat at one of the few tables that had fabric-covered chairs. The others had worn leather seats. The florid scent of air freshener mixed with the odors of the various alcohols that had been spilled on them. We hadn't even settled in when a tall, dark-haired woman wearing jeans and an oversized shirt came to take our orders.

Chris ordered a whiskey straight, and I requested the same and tried not to take offense at the condescending grins they gave me.

We sat in silence, and I watched her wrestle with her thoughts, which she wasn't doing a great job of hiding. She'd gulped down her first drink and requested another before she finally asked, "Should I go back?"

I had an idea what she was talking about, but I couldn't believe she was asking my advice. I froze under the intensity of her dark gaze. Part of me wanted to tell her no and that she should run like a serial killer was after her, which wasn't far off. But I didn't. I remained silent, sipping from my glass and regretting copying her drink order.

Chewing on my bottom lip, I gave it a few more minutes of consideration. "Do you love him?"

"No," she said decisively right after I'd finished my last word.

"Do you like him?"

This time, she took longer, her fingers circling the rim of her glass as she withdrew into her thoughts. I took that time to study her; her life was more complicated than I could imagine. It was about survival. As a human, she'd learned to navigate the otherworld on her own terms. I hadn't agreed with her ethics—most of the time they'd been as convoluted and obscure as the pack's—but they'd been about surviving, the same as ours.

"I don't hate him," she finally said. There were so many other emotions between love and hate I wasn't sure why those were the only two choices. The gradations were complex, but she'd reduced them to something simplistic. She didn't hate him. Her perception of emotions was real, unencumbered, and direct. Was it indifference? That didn't evoke any emotions, and clearly, she had some emotional connection to him.

Chris took another long draw from her glass. "He's saved my life more times than I can count. His blood allowed me to continue to work and do it well. And when Ethan and your pack thought I should die, it was Demetrius who thought I should live."

I wondered if she could hear my heartbeat increase. Chris's conversion to a vampire was a topic of contention between Ethan and me. He'd been prepared to allow her to die because she was dangerous. And there wasn't any question about it—Chris was definitely dangerous. I hadn't forgotten that as I sat across from her; dark marble eyes that used to be light brown held a predatory alertness, as if every moment she was with a person, she was deciding whether they were a predator to challenge or prey. No one was born that way. A lot of things had happened to make her the person she was today, but she seldom discussed her past.

"Okay, you don't hate him, but you don't love him. Let's go with *lukewarm*. You lukewarm him. Now what?"

I'd dealt with her long enough to know every decision she made had an ultimate goal. She was a strategic player, manipulating situations to her advantage. She reminded me of Sebastian in many ways. "What's your endgame here?"

Her brows rose as she gave me a bemused grin. "I'm sorry?"

I watched her with the same intensity in which she studied me. "I'm not under any illusions that this is a friendly meeting. I'm not sure why you're asking me, but I know you have ulterior motives. I'm just asking what they are."

"What in the world has the Midwest Pack done to the brunette with the shocked-by-the-headlights doe eyes to make her so cynical?" She grinned appreciatively. "It's a good look. I like it."

Of course you do. Hey, I have a were-snake I'd like to introduce you to. After you two try to kill each other, I'm sure you'll hit it off quite nicely.

"I'm glad I've met your approval, but you didn't answer my question," I pointed out.

"I'm asking you because of all the people I've encountered, despite your interest in any situation, you give an honest answer without any concern of how it will affect your pack or even you. You're honest to a fault and oblivious to political maneuvering. You wouldn't see my return to the Seethe as an advantage for your pack. The first question you asked was whether I love him."

I nodded slowly. "You still haven't answered my question. What is your endgame? What do you hope to gain by going back to him? Because as you pointed out, I might not care about political maneuvering, and sometimes I don't necessarily play the long game, but you do."

"You're right," she acknowledged softly. "And whether you want to believe it, we are all playing a game. Ultimately, we want to make sure we're not the pawn but the queen." Her sharpened gaze settled heavily on me, intently appraising me.

"You don't necessarily want Demetrius, but you want something, right?"

She barely moved her head in a nod, and she took several moments of consideration before she spoke. "I want the South." She relaxed a little and looked down into her drink, studying the golden-brown liquid. "And possibly the North," she slipped in quietly.

It was that pursuit that had provoked Demetrius's wrath. A failed assassination attempt on the Master of the South. He was Demetrius's favorite and had been gifted the South by him. Based on rumors, he'd taken a once strong organization and weakened it because of his narcissism and arrogance. He penalized and even killed those he felt were too strong and anyone he felt was positioning themselves to take over. Often choosing pleasure over pragmatism, he'd started wars and broken alliances Demetrius had established. Steven had mentioned on several occasions that he was concerned the South's Master would start a fight with the Southern Pack just to make a point—as an effort to subjugate them and make his presence known. He hadn't acted on it, but there'd been whispers and warnings that he would. He was impulsive and erratic and had reduced the Seethe to nothing more than a gang of undisciplined vampires that were slaves to their own needs. That wasn't a huge difference to the way Demetrius reacted to most things. He was arrogant, narcissistic, self-indulgent, and often cruel; he'd be dangerous if he was capable of any rational strategizing. Chris was a good strategist; she had to be to survive. It would be better for the pack if she did rule both the South and the North.

I remembered Gavin's advice. "Okay, since we're playing nice and being honest, let me say this: I don't care if you go back to him. But I am interested in how you can help me get back at him. I want him a broken vampire. I want his Seethe to turn against him, for him to feel the pain of their betrayal, and in the end, I want to look him in the eye and tell him how much I loathe him before I kill him." The cruelty and anger with which I'd spoken shocked me and left Chris wide-eyed, her lips parted in a state of horrified awe.

"I wasn't expecting that from you." Then she grew silent for a moment. "I heard about Quell. I'm sorry, but—"

"If you try to explain his actions or make excuses for Demetrius, I'm leaving," I informed her with a huff.

"I don't plan to. It was cruel and unnecessary."

"Even if you go back, given his obsession with you, I doubt he'll let you take the South."

The coy smile she offered was a flagrant attempt to soften her words. "You might be right, but that's doubtful. Demetrius wants me *now*. His affections are fleeting. Another will eventually capture his interest. The same thing that happened to Michaela will happen to me. I have no interest in filling my time with beautiful boy toys. He'll probably offer me the South to clear his conscience as he moves on."

I wasn't aware that he had a conscience, and he'd never had a problem with participating in polyamorous relationships. Michaela had been very aware of his affections for Chris, and Demetrius had been aware of Michaela sleeping with half the members of their Seethe. I never understood their complicated relationship or how they claimed to love each other with such intensity. He hadn't grieved for her very long. Maybe he'd been silently grieving, or as their relationship had progressed, maybe he'd already grieved that he had nothing more to offer.

"Well, you already have this figured out. What do you need me for? I doubt you cared what my answer would be."

She leaned back in her chair and clasped her hands together on the table, examining her nails, painted a purplish black color. "Of course I care about your answer. If you were too appalled by the idea of me going back, you would be of no use to me. You and your profound wisdom have convinced me to go back to Demetrius because that is the best thing for me and for the Seethe. Enough of the Seethe, as well as this pack and others, have seen us together to know we're not enemies."

She smiled with a predator's allure. "I'll go back to Demetrius and make it known you convinced me. One, I won't have to worry about him trying to convince me to come back if I ever leave again because he'll know he doesn't have that kind of influence. He'll think *you* do, and that will be advantageous to you."

I snapped my gaping mouth shut. She wasn't like Sebastian—she might be better. The one thing she never wanted Demetrius to think was that he had control over her in any way, shape, or form. If he was convinced she'd come back on her own, he'd assume she had feelings for him that he could manipulate. Instead, she'd handed the reins over to me to make it seem like I'd orchestrated the whole thing. It worked out for me, but it would work out even better for her.

"Do you ever do anything just because you want to?" I asked.

"I wanted to have drinks with you, so yes."

"No. You wanted to make me a player in your game. Make no mistake—this wasn't acquaintances having drinks; this was a business deal."

She shook her head. "I could have spoken to you any place, anywhere. I wanted to have a drink with you, so we did. We aren't friends, and I doubt we ever will be, but we understand each other and I'm fine with that." She placed a few bills on the table and rose to her feet. "I guess you should get me to Demetrius and then get back to Ethan. I'm sure he's been thinking about this all night."

She was right: we weren't going to be friends. But she was also wrong. I didn't understand her. She worked on a level beyond my comprehension. And no matter how many years I lived, I doubted I'd gain the necessary understanding of her mind to anticipate her actions.

But if I was going to be a player in her game, I needed to go all in. "I don't want you to *possibly* take the North; I want you to do it," I said firmly.

An odd combination of surprise, respect, worry, and fear shone in her eyes. Once again, I figured she was wondering what had changed in me. A lot. Her lips kinked into a hesitant half-smile. "Very well. I guess I'll take the North, too."

Before she could walk away from the table, I couldn't resist asking, "Have you ever been in love? The kind that makes you forget about strategies, manipulations, and what benefits you? Have you ever cared for someone so deeply that you would put that aside and only worry about being with them?"

I really thought she would scoff, laugh at me for being ridiculous and emotional and having a fairy-tale view of love and romance. Instead, she looked at me for a long time, her dark eyes glassy. She cast them to the ground, a veil of thick lashes covering them. "No." Then she headed for the door.

She was lying. I didn't need to hear a heartbeat or a change in the cadence of her voice or respiration to know. Her denial had been the sorrowful cry of a wounded animal—a wounded person. Her lie was probably easier to deal with than the truth.

I hesitated at the edge of Demetrius's driveway, remembering his words about finding pleasure in breaking people. It was a cruel thing to think and an even crueler thing to do. My hands tightened on the steering wheel and I was plagued by the same numb feeling I'd had when I'd almost delivered her to the Tre'ase Logan, another monster. I could feel her eyes on me. She was okay with this; I needed to be.

"Bambi, I can assure you I've never needed a guardian. I'm fine. If I didn't think I could handle this, or if I thought it wouldn't benefit me, I wouldn't be doing it."

I nodded. As soon as I turned in and stopped, she got out of the car and went to the door without so much as a good-bye.

Demetrius answered her knock. Initially, his arrogance failed, and he stood before her with wide eyes and lips slightly parted in shock. Words were exchanged, but they were too far away for me to hear. I didn't bother trying to read their lips; I didn't really care what they had to say. Probably went something like this: "I'm sorry I'm a sadistic narcissist." "That's okay, I knew you were one. That's my thing, anyway. I don't know how to be in a functional relationship. So, I'll just take our big bowl of crazy and deal with it." "Great, because I'm terrible—just awful." "That's fine, I know you are, and I plan to destroy you." "Sounds good, come in."

After several more moments of talking, he leaned down and kissed her gently on the lips. She was stiff, unresponsive. And I didn't have to be right there to see the hurt Demetrius felt at Chris's response. He dropped his head, saying what I suspected was an apology or a plea for forgiveness.

She said something else to him, and he stepped out of the house to look at me in the car. He inclined his head and looked at me for several long moments before bowing his head in thanks. I nodded and backed out of the driveway. I needed several showers, and even then, I wouldn't feel clean.

CHAPTER 22

I was surprised to see all the members of the Creed had returned to the pack's house the next day to help Josh. I kept trying to douse my skepticism, especially since Josh didn't have any. They stood before a whiteboard with the names of all the protected objects written on it.

London stepped back and studied them.

Periodically, I caught Ariel eyeing me with a mélange of curiosity, aversion, and derision. She couldn't dismiss the look fast enough to keep me from noticing. When she finally yanked her gaze from me, she looked at the board, too.

"Their magic is different and stronger than ours combined." Ariel shuddered and made a face. I'd seen that same face on many people when they'd encountered some of the pack members and realized they weren't just "beautiful monsters." Were-animals were fettered violence, holding on to humanity to allow them to function in both worlds. But the Faeries were more than fettered violence and didn't have an encumbered relationship with humanity. They didn't want simple power. They wanted to dominate and return the world to the one they'd once ruled, before technology and advancement.

Ariel drummed her fingers on the desk. "We think we know what they're after, but based on Ethos's behavior, are we sure?" she asked. "Something is missing from this picture. What do they plan to do with the objects?" She went over to the board and wrote: "Clostra: Key. Vitae: Life. Fatifer: Bringer of Death. Aufero: Remove. Gem of Levage: Wild Card."

"Why do you have the Gem of Levage as the wild card?" I asked.

"It's the only object that can be used by people who don't have magical abilities. That's why the vampires were able to use it." She glanced over her shoulder from the whiteboard. "The Aufero can be used by strong magic, our magic, which is the only magic that can rival theirs."

Based on Sebastian's account of the Faeries' battle against the witches, it hadn't been much of a rivalry. It was like comparing a lion to a kitten. Same feline family, except one could rip a person's throat out with their teeth.

Suddenly, strong magic poured into the house, undeniable, and familiar. The witches folded over, feeling the blood wards they'd placed around the house shatter. They were connected to their wards and felt it when they were destroyed. It was supposed to be a way of alerting them of a breach. Most people couldn't destroy witches' wards because they were so strong, but Faerie magic demolished them as if they were inconsequential.

The house shook with such strong vibrations I thought it would collapse. Plaster broke from the walls. I rushed out of the library to the front of the house to find the windows in the front room shattered and shards of glass covering the floor. The seams of the house strained, and overpowering magic shoved me back several feet as the Faeries used magic to push their way through the front door. It flowed unimpeded over those positioned in the front room, waiting for an attack: Gavin, six from Worgen, Cole, Steven, and Sebastian. All had shifted. We waited for them. Nothing. For several long moments, the house underwent an aggressive assault that would have reduced a less sturdy building to rubble. I moved to the front, were-animals flanking me.

The same distinctive magic brushed against me as Ethan took up a position next to me, in human form. I decided to stay in human form as well.

A force like a tornado swept through the room, destroying everything in it. Six Faeries entered, but the power that inundated the air and thrashed our bodies made it seem as if we were facing an army. There were thrums of unearthly magic. Like Ethos, they had luminous amethyst-colored eyes. These weren't the faces of evil, the things depicted in the book Ethan had given me. Their ethereal appearance, gentle and delicate, belied their infamous depravity. Although their skin ranged from ivory to deep mocha, their features seemed quite similar, as if they'd been formed from the same mold.

I saw their beauty for what it was: a deception. Ethos had changed his appearance so he hadn't looked like the grotesque monster he was, and that was exactly what they'd done. They'd used glamour to give themselves the faces of gods and goddesses, but they didn't need to fake the strength to match. I gagged from the putrid smell of unfathomable magic. Its heaviness dragged me down. Just like I had when I'd gone up against Ethos's magic, I wondered if I could control it—truly control it. Or would I become a servant to its whims the way I had with Maya? Anxiety rose in me as I remembered the time I'd attempted to master and control Ethos's magic. I hadn't mastered it; it had mastered me.

When they saw the pack of animals nearing them, they backed away. I thought it was the animals that had caused their retreat—it wasn't. Their focus turned to me as they began chanting. I felt a pull, then a yank, as a woman emerged from their ranks. She possessed magic, weak magic, but magic nonetheless. The new host. Maya's new host. A powerful force shot into me, slamming me into a wall. I crumbled to the ground and rolled, preparing to change. That was my best chance. Sebastian soared through the air and sank his teeth into one of the Faerie's arm, ripping at flesh. A sword materialized in the Faerie's other hand. Sebastian disengaged in time to avoid the blade.

The trails of blood left on the floor lifted. Red misshapen forms floated in the air before disappearing into nothing. Blood was absent from Sebastian's teeth when he exposed them. They knew we could track them with their blood. There was a rush of footsteps behind me, then wisps of familiar magic brushed against my back. Relief flooded through me; we had magical backup. Ariel lobbed the first blast of magic at them. It met a field that sent it rebounding with twice the original force, and it hit her in the chest, sending her flying back. Another witch turned, using magic to soften the fall as Ariel struggled to breathe. Josh joined the four witches, but their combined magic hit the field with no effect. I kept my eye on the two Faeries who stayed away from the field. The woman followed them as they continued to work in tandem. One distracted me with magic, preventing me from changing, and the other worked to remove Maya.

The protective field shattered. Ethan advanced and grabbed a Faerie by the throat. The Faerie stopped moving and went through a strange twin of the vampire reversion: skin darkened and became scaly, drying and shriveling before collapsing to dust. The other Faeries disappeared with the woman, leaving behind hints of their magic and a battered house.

I got to my feet, feeling each bruise and cut on my body as I moved. Ethan stood in the middle of the wreckage, trying his hardest to ignore everyone staring at him. If they'd forgotten or missed Ethan's battle with Ethos, they'd just witnessed a replay of his profound power. Sebastian shifted, and as he inched toward Ethan, clothes knitted around him. He nodded in appreciation to the witch a few feet away who had dressed him. Ethan's eyes shifted to Sebastian, their stolid masks firmly in place as they addressed the situation like it was a typical occurrence.

"We should find out as much as we can about them. If we find their weakness and their motives, we can stop them," Sebastian said unnecessarily.

Or we can just send Ethan in to exterminate them.

Ethan stood at the door of his home office with the same pained look as when he'd opened it to give the witches access to all the information he had on the Faeries. Watching them examine his collection of books, notebooks, and dossiers of information, he looked as if he were experiencing slow torture. In some ways, it was. His secrets were his armor. They gave him comfort. Provided security. His office, his sanctuary, the very place where most of his secrets were hidden, was being invaded. He'd lived his life in secrecy to protect himself, his brother, and his pack. He'd hidden parts of himself that were the very essence of his being. He'd only ever shared everything with Sebastian, not me. At times, I even questioned how much Sebastian knew and if Ethan had kept some things to himself.

Josh went to a chestnut armoire with a built-in lock placed in the corner and looked back at his brother, raising his brow—a nonverbal request to open it. Ethan's jaw clenched, and his irritation flared; he was obviously grappling with the instinct to keep his information secret.

"Ethan, we have to find out everything we can about them and their motives, or we can't stop them," Josh said, urging his brother.

"I know," he said quietly. "I heard the debate the first time. I realize that."

I pressed my hands against his back, guiding him into the room.

Even for a house the size of this one, the room was huge. One wall was lined with shelves filled with an impressive collection of books. There were two desks, one in a corner and a large executive desk in the center with binders stacked on top, one with my name on it.

After a few minutes of deliberation, he walked across the office, opened the armoire, and returned to his position next to me, watching them sort through his stash of information.

While he watched them, my eyes took in the room again and were immediately drawn to a saber with a gilded, intricately marked handle on the wall to Ethan's left. I lifted it up, unsheathed it, and looked at the razor-sharp blade, light gleaming along the edges.

He gave me a weak smile and leaned in. "It was a gift."

"From whom?"

I thought he was trying to avoid the question, but he might have simply been distracted. Everyone was going through his things. Fingers brushed over the weathered bindings of his books. One witch sat on the floor, flipping through papers and what looked like journals that he'd had on a bottom shelf. Ariel tugged on a small cabinet next to the armoire.

"It's locked," Ethan said with a hint of irritation.

"Will it continue to be?" she inquired with the same level of annoyance.

"Yes," he answered; coolly.

"Ethan, we promised we'd maintain your pack's confidences, and we will. If it's related to the Faeries, you need to share."

"It's not." It was a terse, sharp response.

Ariel ended the uncomfortable exchange by smiling and returning her attention to the books. Ethan continued to watch them as they went through the books. *His books.*

"The sword was a gift from Chris," he said, moving his attention from the witches' activity long enough to address me. "Would you like me to get rid of it?"

"Does it work?" I asked, confused by the question.

"It's an excellent sword."

"Keep it."

"You're an odd woman, Sky," he acknowledged softly.

I'm odd! You're having a man tantrum about people touching your things.

I shrugged. "You knew what you were getting." I grinned, leaned in, and whispered, "Don't think you aren't going to show me what's in that cabinet. No secrets between us, Ethan."

His smile slowly unfolded. "Of course, Sky." He was placating me, but I had every intention of making him keep his promise.

Apparently, Ethan was going to spend the day glaring at everyone as they perused his books. I grabbed several journals and sat at the larger desk. Half an hour later, I quickly regretted my choice. Beautiful script filled the pages with the horrors of the Faeries' reign in graphic detail. Initially, I read each word, going over the accounts of unnecessarily cruel torment at the hands of Faeries. Entry after entry, including one about a witch helpless at the hands of people who saw her as nothing more than a source of entertainment, something to be used for whatever they deemed would satisfy their needs. A group so powerful even the strongest witch's magic paled in comparison. The elves' magic was even less effective against them. Ethan and I served as hosts for two of these monsters. After reading over a hundred pages of the travesties people had endured and died of, I started skimming for information that would help us.

I glanced up from the book to find Ethan watching me. "Are you okay?"

"No, these people were vile. I hope their deaths were painful and cruel, which is exactly what they deserve," I spat. "I want to kill the ones who still exist."

I knew my spirit shade thirsted for power—perhaps it was so innate that they didn't know anything else—but I couldn't help but think of Ethan's, so powerful and reviled that his own people had turned against him to contain him. Ethan had so much magic coursing through his body.

Josh looked disturbed. I caught a glimpse of disgust as he stared at Ethan and me.

"If you're hosting a Faerie, why can't you read the Clostra?" Josh asked his brother. He'd said it softly, as if posing the question to himself.

"They warded it against Ethan's shade, Amizial, just like it was against anyone who wasn't a Faerie. They saw you as the enemy and rightfully so." It was Nia, the soft-spoken witch whose voice matched her appearance. She was tall and wiry, with asphalt-colored shoulder-length hair tucked behind her ears. Her wide moss-green eyes and full-bowed lips overpowered her narrow face. Usually, her coloring had a peachy glow, but now it was pale. Her eyes widened in antipathy as she looked at me and Ethan. She tossed the journal she was reading on the table and shook her head. "This is happening because of you." She swallowed hard and looked at Ariel. "Have you read the stories? They want it the way it used to be. Whether there's ten or a hundred of them, they are stronger than us—because of them," she said through tightly clenched teeth.

She took several breaths, but the color didn't return to her face. "The stories. What they did to people. To those who denied them." She stopped and shrugged as if trying to shake off the images. "Their goal was to procreate, often with witches. Some of them chose willing partners, some didn't. They didn't always use glamour. They don't look like what we saw yesterday."

She leaned forward, flipped through pages, and left the book open for us to read if we wanted to know how others described the Faeries. I didn't need to read it; I'd seen Ethos's true form. Nia looked at the book, but I doubted she could read anything through her glassy eyes.

"I know, Nia," Ariel said, her tone gentle and soothing as she attempted to coax her witch out of her spiral.

Nia frowned and her lips quivered. "You all aren't much better," she accused the only two were-animals in the room. Ethan's face had relaxed, and he looked at her with sympathy. I felt it for her as well. I vividly remembered the accounts of violence, savagery, inhumane treatment, and the abuse of magic I'd read.

Nia flipped through the open book again and pointed. "Look at what the *animals* used to look like. What *they* were like."

"I know their history, Nia." Ariel maintained her somnolent voice. Curiosity had the other witches looking at the book. Even Josh took a peek. I didn't bother to look; I'd seen what we had been. Beastly animals that did not remotely resemble humans. Strange bipedal creatures that walked around on two legs, with elongated snouts and fur covering the upper half of their bodies. They spoke, but it had looked grotesque coming from the mouths of feral animals.

I kept my tone light and kind as I responded, "Yes, were-animals were monsters. But it was those monsters, those primitive beings that disgust you, that enabled your ancestors and the elves' ancestors to defeat the Faeries. We'll do it again. We just need your help."

"You are the reason they resurfaced. You made it easier for them to find the objects," London added matter-of-factly, but she seemed surprised by it as well. "You and especially Ethan."

Nia didn't look any calmer but appeared to be just as curious. London took the journal she'd been reading, walked over to Ethan, and pointed to a word. "Can you confirm this word means *beast*? You speak Faerie, correct?"

Shocked by her assertion, he nodded. "A little. I learned it to do some spells."

"That's what you spoke yesterday, when you killed the Faerie." She didn't wait for him to confirm it. "Then we know why they have resurfaced. The desire to reign over us as they once did is still there. And because of you, they can." London looked at Josh, smiling weakly as if she hated relaying the news to him. "Your shade was the only Faerie whose magic could control beasts. Control you all."

London flipped through other books she'd gone through. She gave Ethan a pointed look. "He didn't play well with others." She kept on opening books to pages she'd bookmarked, offering evidence of her findings. "But he tolerated his brother, Ethos."

Josh's eyes widened, and he grabbed the three books he'd been going through. "Then this makes sense: Ethos helped the elves and witches hide the protective objects that were obtained during the war."

"Let me guess, he agreed to this so he would be the last Faerie standing. And he planned to betray the witches and elves at an opportune time," Ethan said with a sigh.

Josh nodded. "And his brother. The Clostra was warded against Amizial; it was also warded against Ethos. The witches and elves may have accepted his help in hiding the protected objects, but they obviously didn't trust him. As the last Faerie, he could have read the Clostra, so it had to be warded against him. I suspect his brother was made into a shade so Ethos could have access to his magic later, when he had all the protective objects. He'd be the most powerful Faerie and have the ability to control the beasts. Unstoppable." He looked at me. "That's where you came in, Sky. Ethos went after you because he would have been able to use you to do the spells in the Clostra."

I turned to Ariel. "How did you know I started to perform a rever tempore?"

"It's very powerful magic, and you can feel it. Never underestimate magic. It can be felt, especially strong magic."

It was possible that we were more responsible than we could imagine. I looked at Ethan, and if my expression mirrored his, the others had to know what I was thinking.

Nia spoke in the same accusatory tone as earlier. Her stunned appearance lingered as well, a result of reading countless records of the otherworld under Faerie rule. "It's your pack's fault. You all don't respect magic. There's a reason you shouldn't have access to it." She shook her head. "You don't care about consequences, just as long as the results lean in your favor. Everything and everyone else be damned." I wanted to be upset with her, but there was truth to her allegations.

The emotions in the room were so strong that the breath I took heightened my frustration and anxiety. "You're right, Nia. We have fucked up. A lot." I turned to her. "We didn't think enough about the consequences or take enough precautions, and perhaps we were selfish. The pack is the closest thing I have to a family. We screwed up, and the only thing I can offer is an apology, not for what I did, but for the consequences that are affecting you. I will not apologize for saving my life or protecting my pack."

Nia's frown relaxed but not her intense gaze. "What happens now?"

"We fix it."

~

We fix it. That's all I had, but I'd said it with enough faux confidence that it had seemed like I had a plan, and when I left, no one objected.

I needed a moment. I stood at the edge of Ethan's backyard, looking at the surrounding heavily treed area that had trails and space between them to allow for a good run—something I desperately needed. I was almost open to hunting something to expend the excess energy from my heightened anxiety and frustration.

"Are you considering going for a run?" Cole asked from behind me. I'd heard the car when it had driven up, but I'd cared more about the serenity of the woodland than another arrival.

"No. Just wondering if I can part the trees with my mind," I shot back sarcastically.

His rich laughter filled the air. "Your sense of humor is refreshing. In fact, Skylar Brooks, you are invigorating."

"If you came to help, the others are in the house."

"I'm aware." He moved closer but directed his attention to the woods. His gray eyes shone with longing as he peered into them. He inhaled, appreciating the hints of oak and the sweet redolence of wildflowers that mingled with those of the trees and grass. We'd been around so long that the air reeked of magic as well, and although it wasn't unpleasant, it was potent, at times uncomfortable and overpowering.

It was peaceful and breezy, and I managed to enjoy the quiet with Cole just inches from me. "I'm glad Chris convinced Demetrius to help Josh."

I didn't answer. I knew this was a prelude to something more. And it was. "Chris and Ethan have always had a peculiar dynamic. But I guess that's to be expected. He's had *a lot* of unique interactions with so many people. But now he's mated to you. Most of your pack didn't see that coming. I wonder why?" he said quietly.

I met his speculation with silence. I'd let him get it out, because one way or another, he would. I kept my attention on the trees, feeling his gaze on me. Glancing at him, I noted the glint of satisfaction in his silvery-gray eyes.

Moistening his lips, he continued, "At least there aren't secrets between you two or the pack. That has to be comforting. I wonder if he shares that comfort? He operates in secrecy. I guess it's safe to say no one will never truly know Ethan."

This time, I was the one who moved closer; I held his gaze, giving him my full attention. It was cool and assessing. Holding an Alpha's eyes was hard, and my eyes inevitably dropped past him. "You can stand here and list all of Ethan's flaws and you probably won't miss any I'm not already aware of. I fell in love with him because the positives outweigh the flaws. I'm not as naïve as you seem to believe I am because I see right through your little act.

You once said Ethan considers me a prize; I believe you do, too. I'm a prize you'll never have."

He didn't seem very convinced of it as his lips curled into a smug smile. "Ethan is Ethan. Without any uncertainty, I know he will screw this up. It's in his nature. No one person ever holds his attention for long. People have seen it time after time."

"Hmm. Then instead of working so hard to plant your obvious seeds of doubt, why don't you just stand back and watch the relationship implode? After all, it's inevitable, right?" I countered. "If you're so confident it will, just grab a bag of popcorn and watch the show. But you're not so confident that it will, are you?"

"Duly noted." His arrogance annoyed me, and I doubted anything I said would sidetrack his agenda.

"You're awfully smug for someone who should be in a grave." That didn't wipe the look off permanently, but I gained a great deal of satisfaction in watching it falter. "I guess Ethan isn't always a servant to his nature. If he were, you wouldn't be standing here."

Maintaining his composure was getting harder each moment. "If you are going to go on a run…" his fingers trailed along the buttons of his shirt. He opened one. "I think I'll join you."

"There's absolutely no way in hell that's happening," Ethan growled. He stalked in our direction with powerful and aggressive strides. A frown strained his face, and I knew this would end badly. We didn't need them ripping each other apart. It infuriated me that Cole derived so much pleasure from this.

"Ethan." I said. His head snapped in my direction, but he was unfocused.

Blinded by his emotions, Cole added fuel to a fire that would set the place ablaze in a matter of minutes. "She didn't decline," he offered. I could hear the amusement in his voice.

"What Ethan said: there is no way in hell that's happening. If you want to be of any use, they need help inside."

"I am here to help," Cole said smoothly as he made his way to the house, smart enough to keep a respectable distance from Ethan.

"I hate that guy," Ethan said, his voice still hard and rough, growling his resentment.

Running my fingers deftly over the buttons of his shirt, I quickly undid them. "Really, I never would have guessed. You hide it so well," I teased as he shrugged off the shirt and let it fall to the ground.

I helped him out of his pants, and he kicked them aside. He'd shifted to his animal before I could fully undress. He waited until I'd changed, and then we both ran full speed into the woods. Ethan gave me my space as I ran. The crisp air brushing against my muzzle was invigorating, and my paws struck the ground, kicking up dirt into the air. Minutes of high-speed running was enough, and I relaxed, becoming one with my wolf and processing all the information I'd acquired. Amizial and Ethos were brothers, and we assumed Ethos was responsible for turning his brother into a spirit shade in order to grab power and control the otherworld. The Clostra was warded against Ethos. His brother was the only person whose magic could be used against were-animals. The protected objects were Faerie creations and could be used to their advantage. The biggest advantage they wanted was magic they could use against us. They had the Aufero, which could neutralize the witches and elves; now they just needed Amizial to take us out. I didn't know what they needed from the Clostra or if it was of any use to them. They likely just wanted to reacquire all the protected objects.

The feeling that I was missing something niggled at me. Was it really Ethan's use of magic that had drawn them out of a quiescent state? Or had it been Ethos's death? I couldn't figure out the link or even if there was one. Ethos and Amizial had been the most powerful Faeries, and Ethos had wanted ultimate power. He hadn't been willing to share. Was that the reason they'd waited?

Or were all the pieces in place? They had another Faerie—me.

They knew a way to get magic that could be used against were-animals because of Ethan. I assumed they could read the Clostra, the same way my cousin Senna and I could. Upon meeting her, I'd felt that she was too cynical and intemperate for her perceived age. I'd seen a lot over the years, and that had opened my mind to the impossible. Sebastian had once pointed out that Senna didn't seem related to me. He suspected she was adopted. She knew about the Clostra and its use. She knew what the symbols in the book meant.

I shifted back to human form and sat in the middle of the wooded area, naked, sorting through all the information. When Ethan approached me in his human form, his brows inched together as he scrutinized me. I had to be a peculiar sight, seated in the middle of the weald, legs pulled to my chest, staring blankly ahead as I dealt with my new findings.

"Sky?" Ethan said quietly as he knelt in front of me, obscuring my view.

"Senna is a Faerie, and she might be able to help us."

CHAPTER 23

Sebastian didn't waste any time scheduling a flight to Virginia for us to go see Senna. Sebastian entertained Ariel's suggestion that she come along, and the ensuing debate lasted longer than most of us had expected. The Faeries were a problem for all supernaturals, but for some reason, Sebastian only wanted the pack to deal with Senna. The only people with me on the plane were Sebastian, Ethan, and Josh. The same three who'd come to get me at my family's home the first time I'd visited them.

"I can hear you," Sebastian said to the closed door after knocking several times without anyone answering.

Senna snatched open the door in the false image of a dark-haired young woman with delicate round features and keen green eyes very similar to mine. I'd wondered at our similarities in the past, but now I wanted to be very different from her. I didn't see the face she presented to us but the monstrous visage of Ethos. I thought about how much magic they'd expended to present the faces they'd had when they'd attacked the pack's house and why they'd bothered. They were monsters and should look like them. I didn't want to see halation that made them look ethereal. Nor did I want to see attractive, striking features. Those were masks. I wanted to see horns, leathery skins, and tails that forked at the end.

"Is that glamour?" I asked softly.

Her gaze traveled over each of our faces. She swallowed. "You know what I am?" Despite the situation, I got the impression she was relieved.

Opening the door wider, she invited us in. "No one is here."

"They don't know, do they?" Sebastian inquired, following her into the living room, where she invited us to have a seat.

She didn't answer until she was seated in a chair across from us. "I would like it to stay that way. They're my family."

My family. But they weren't mine. Even after meeting me and no longer seeing me as a threat, they hadn't made any efforts to make me a part of it. I didn't have time to deal with the hurt that came from that.

How had she infiltrated my family and started living as a witch without anyone being the wiser?

After watching me in silence and seeing I was coming up with the right questions along with everyone else, Senna spoke. "I am what you think I am, and so were my parents." Her contempt for them was the same as ours. "There are so few of us that I thought people would continue to believe we'd died long ago. Most of us did, but the majority of those who didn't were the ones who had the greatest desire to see the world they once knew rise again: to see you all in your old form; the witches and elves subjugated; the vampires horrible, vicious creatures of the night; and the Tre'ase cruel demons given full rein to do as they pleased. That's the world they want, and you will make it possible for them to get it."

How she'd become part of my family should have been the least of my worries—stopping the Faeries should have been my priority—but I couldn't let it go. "How … when … how did you become a part of my family?" I stammered out.

"*My* family," she corrected, her voice harder than before. I could see her fear that it might slip away. Her family, the life she knew. Everything.

"As I said before, what's happening isn't new. It's just more organized because they have access to the protected objects. But they've been building their army for years, and either you join them or face the consequences. My parents suffered the consequences, but they made sure I found a home with witches—people who were equipped to keep me safe. I think they'd have preferred were-animals, but that wasn't an option." She shrugged. "How many do they have now?"

"We don't know. There were six when they attacked the pack's home," I said.

"What did they take?" Senna asked.

"Nothing. But I think they were trying to get the Clostra and Sky," Sebastian responded.

"For Maya, right?" she asked, her gaze slipping my way. She frowned and fixed me with a hard stare. "We should have removed her."

"I would have died."

"You're probably still going to die," she responded, her voice low, rough, and emotionless. She stood and paced around the room. Every so often, her focus moved to us. "Why are you here?"

"We need to be proactive and find them before they attack again," Sebastian answered.

"And how am I supposed to help you with this?"

"If you are a Faerie, we can use your blood to locate them. To call them to us like we did with Ethos." It was Josh who spoke up this time. Usually calm and composed, he seemed anxious.

Senna sighed, exasperated. "You can't use a sourcing spell with my blood—it will just locate me. If you do an *ad beatam* spell, my blood will call all Faeries." She gave Josh a chastising look for suggesting it. "You want the ones who attacked you. Leave the rest of us out of it."

"But we don't have the blood of the ones who attacked.

They've retrieved it every time we've encountered them."

She made another irritated sound and then turned to Josh. "I'll give it to you, but use it as a last resort. You won't have to find them; I assure you, they'll find you." She gathered everything to give us a sample of her blood: knife, vial, and bandages. She beckoned Josh to follow her to the kitchen. We followed, too.

Senna didn't flinch as she slid the knife over her hand, allowing the blood to well before letting some drop into the vial. "Why now?" she asked, looking at the blood drip into the clear container.

I knew what she meant. They'd been silent for so long. What had emboldened them? That heaviness I'd felt when I'd had to admit to Nia that all this was happening because of us returned. Because we'd been careless with magic and these were the consequences. They'd found another Faerie who thirsted for power the same way they did: Maya, who'd tried to help them destroy the were-animals with a curse. In the process, Ethan had exposed Amizial, the only one who could wield magic against were-animals. We were at the root of all this.

Sebastian answered before I could. "A series of things we've done to protect ourselves." He rarely showed remorse because he prioritized our safety above everything else. This was one of those rare moments when it seemed like he was reevaluating all the things we'd done—manipulation of magic and crimes against magic we'd involved ourselves in, rules we'd ignored—and concluded that we may not have protected the pack but ensured its demise.

Senna's face softened as she looked at him. She stood from the chair, and instead of giving Josh the vial, she handed it to Sebastian. As he reached for it, she rested her hand on his. "The pack is like a family to some extent, and we will do anything to protect them, right?"

He nodded. "I don't take that obligation lightly."

"I've lived many years denying my magic. I use glamour to

maintain my form and never use magic stronger than what a witch would possess. I've been cautious never to be discovered. I ask you to respect that."

Sebastian looked down at the vial and nodded as if he were promising not to be as careless as we'd been in the past.

Senna stayed in place. "I've lost my other family. I don't want to lose this one." It took her longer to continue. When she did, her voice had lost its melodious lilt, becoming dark and so cold it seemed as if the room had chilled. Her green eyes were drowned out by an inhuman burnt orange, light supple skin was replaced by thick, leathery, coal-colored skin, and her petite form heightened by several inches. The true face of the Faeries. Nothing beautiful or human. They were powerful, magic-wielding monsters with the appearance to match.

Senna, or the being posing as Senna, spoke, and the deep, powerful voice echoed with the promise of a wrath we would not likely endure. "I will do whatever it takes to protect this one." A slight shift of her head and we were again seeing my dark-haired cousin with the roundish face and sparkling green eyes. Her hair was lighter, however, with odd streaks of red and a few highlights of silver and pale blonde. Sebastian moved a little closer and took a strand of her oddly colored hair in his fingers to study it.

"Is that why you color it?" he asked, bemused.

She flushed. It was hard to even imagine that she had been a monstrous creature just seconds ago. How easily she settled into her human role, taking on the traits as if they were her own. It was both comforting and disturbing. She wasn't a menace. She wasn't one of the vile creatures we'd read about. "I can't seem to get the color right."

Sebastian bagged the vial of blood and nodded. "Well, your secret is safe with us."

Before we could leave, she said. "Remember, it's a last resort."

It had to be. If there were Faeries actually trying to live a normal life, it would be cruel to bring them into this.

CHAPTER 24

We heard the crackle of thunder when we turned down the single-lane road leading to the pack's home, then hard rain obscured our vision before suddenly stopping. Josh narrowed his eyes and looked around the area.

"It's just here," he said.

We stopped abruptly when a figure crashed into the car and fell to the ground. The rain stopped. Sebastian parked the car, and we jumped out. Gideon was crumbled against it, his arm turned in an odd position, possibly broken. Claw marks ran along his face, and blood stained his hand. Whether it was adrenaline, pride, or commitment to his position as the leader of the elves, he tried to stand, wincing at the attempt.

"Stay down," I ordered him, gently taking his arm. I leaned in to look at his shoulder. "I don't think it's broken, just dislocated." I touched it gently, feeling the shoulder joint where it had slipped. I wasn't sure if he had fast healing like we did, but it would feel a hell of a lot better repositioned. I'd seen a doctor do it during one of my assignments, and thanks to my mother, I was very knowledgeable about the body.

"Do it," he said through clenched teeth.

There was a crash behind us; while he was distracted, I pushed it back in the joint. He groaned and started panting. After several moments, his breathing returned to normal, but his face was strained and red. "The animals have been released from the dark forest. We're trying to catch them all."

"You don't know how they got out, do you?"

He shook his head.

We did. Senna was right. We didn't have to find them; they'd continue to attack until they'd achieved their goal.

I stayed in human form, although I questioned my choice. Sebastian quickly changed and ran toward the house. I waited for Ethan to change, but he didn't. Gideon stood behind us, guarding his left arm; his other hand glowed, and I quickly felt the emergence of magic.

The Faeries were spread around the house, their magic so strong it mirrored the blast of wind Abigail was producing on the other side of the grassland. Doing a quick sweep of the area, I saw more than the six Faeries who had attacked us the first time. A lot more. This was a war they had come prepared to win. I would have to use magic and contend with Maya, who would try her best to use it for her own benefit. I quickly assessed our allies: between the elves, witches, and animals, the area was crowded. There was too much magic thrumming through the air to figure out who was doing what.

Ethan and I ran closer to the house, doing a swift count of the Faeries. "I see twelve," I said.

"There are some around the back." He didn't see them, but Cole, Gavin, and Steven were running toward the back of the house, following a trail of blood. Behind two of the Faeries were mutated monsters that had at one time populated the dark forest. They moved in unison with the Faeries, seemingly under their control.

Something that looked like a cross between a rhinoceros and a bear came up on its hind legs, and with a swipe of its disfigured paw, it sent Sebastian back several feet. He careened into a tree so hard bark broke off.

Another dark forest creation padded toward me, a horrid combination of a tiger with wings that were too small to be functional. They couldn't be used as anything but a distraction, which worked; while I was focused on the wings, it had cleared the several feet between us and lunged at me, teeth bared, ready to take a chunk out of me. A shot rang out, a bullet tore through the animal, and it fell to the ground with a thud. I got a glance of Chris holding a shotgun.

I didn't have time to thank her before another inhabitant of the forest charged me. I forced magic outward, feeling resistance. Maya, who'd freely enjoyed magic, was fighting against me using it. It pushed the creature back. I looked around for a discarded weapon I could use. Nothing. The animal regrouped and came at me again, but it was stopped by a flash of movement. A human—or humanlike—body crashed into it, wrapped around it, and gave its head a quick jerk. When the creature stopped moving, Chase rolled it off him.

Blinking several times, I tried to make sense of things. The elves I understood being here; the vampires I didn't. Out of my peripheral vision, I saw Demetrius approaching a Faerie. Before he could get close, he was dropped to his knees; then he keeled over, face forward. A cruel, dark smile covered the Faerie's glamoured lips. The faerie struck his fingers through the air, driving in the magic. Demetrius stilled and wailed in pain. Distracted by his torture session, the Faerie was shocked when Chris shot him in the chest. He stumbled back. Gabriella was quick to strike, beheading him. I used to think nothing could live without a head, but when we'd killed Ethos, removing his head hadn't stopped him. I waited for the Faerie to move. He didn't.

Six witches, powerful ones, were having problems with two Faeries. Nia was high enough in the air that the fall would surely kill her. The Faerie holding Nia mid-air curled its lips sadistically, bringing a shiver to my spine. From his position behind the Faerie, Gavin started toward him. He didn't see Nia suspended in the air. If his target died, she'd crash to the ground. He lunged at the Faerie, clawing at his back. He slashed and clawed at the monstrosity until it dropped to the ground, mangled and bloody.

Nia was free-falling, her hands moving frantically to cast spells, but nothing slowed her descent. A powerful wind spooled under her. I assumed Gideon intended it to be gentle and didn't correctly estimate the necessary force, but it was enough to slow her fall.

Cole was a few yards from me, taking down another resident of the dark forest. Crossbow arrows flew through the air. In the few minutes it took me to find Winter among the chaos, she'd taken down five of the dark forest creatures.

The havoc was overwhelming and trying to make sense of the players involved was difficult. I focused on the two Faeries advancing toward the house. I knew their targets: the Clostra and the Gem of Levage. I shoved strong magic at them hard, and with waves of their hands, they formed a bastion that blocked it and sent it back into me. I hit the ground hard but continued shoving magic at them, throwing up fields to protect myself from their return fire. But it was two against one. Two extremely strong Faeries against me, a person who hadn't mastered magic the way they had. The one thing I had in my arsenal that they didn't was my immunity to magic, so I dropped the field and took a running leap toward them while shifting into my wolf. I opened my jaws and clamped down on an arm. The Faerie growled, shaking her arm to detach me while the other beat against my side. I held strong, and when I finally released, I took a chunk of her muscle with me. She stumbled back, grabbing her arm, and leaned against the side of the house, her breath labored. Her glamour dropped. I attacked again, clawing and mauling. I thought the other Faerie approaching me would attack, but he was distracted. His gaze sharpened on something with interest. He changed course. I whipped around to see what it was. Ethan.

Focused on the Faeries' activity around him and the two elven creations he was fighting, Ethan didn't see the Faerie approaching him from behind. But Cole did. He looked directly at Ethan. I howled to make sure he saw it. Cole's gaze fixed on the Faerie, and he charged, but in another direction, lunging at another creature that was approaching Steven. I howled again to get Cole's attention and redirect him. Steven had seen the attack and was prepared for it. He didn't need Cole's help.

I turned back to Ethan, but I heard Steven's aggressive growl, rips, and crashes. I started running toward the Faerie attacking my mate. I lunged at him to find only air. He'd disappeared and reappeared just inches from Ethan. He jammed a sword into Ethan's back, twisted it, pulled it out, and plunged it in again. He disappeared. Ethan fell, facedown. A dark forest creature was about to take advantage of the situation and take a chunk out of him, but I plowed into it. I ripped open its belly. My claws and teeth finished the job.

I didn't want to use claws and teeth anymore. I needed a sword—nothing but Ethos could live without a head. As if he'd read my mind, Sebastian appeared in human form, wielding his sword. I looked around to see if others had followed suit. Cole was in human form. Demetrius looked wrathful as he started toward a Faerie. I shifted to human form and glanced back at Ethan, who hadn't moved. I had two Faeries in my sight and concentrated, forming a ball of magic. I had to work harder because Maya was fighting me every inch of the way. I tossed one in the back of the first Faerie. When she turned to retaliate, Sebastian beheaded her.

Between the efforts of the elves, vampires, witches, and were-animals, the animals from the dark forest were either dead or contained. It was hard figuring out which parts went with what animal since they'd been abominable mixtures of things that shouldn't have been together. We hadn't accounted for all the

Faeries I'd seen. Even Sebastian was doing another check. "I count four," he said.

"There are six more over there," Gavin added from a few feet away. Good, that was ten of the twelve I'd seen.

"There are four in the back," Cole offered, coming to Sebastian's side. Then he turned to Chris, who'd just come out of the woods.

I started toward Ethan, my heart lifting when he moved, trying to roll onto his side. I felt magic wrap around me—Josh clothing me. An invocation floated in the air, and I followed it to two Faeries who'd dropped glamour. They had the Aufero in hand and were quickly making their way toward Ethan. Josh was the first to react. A withering firestorm of strong magic moved toward them. They weathered it behind an egg-shaped barrier they'd thrown up. Josh's onslaught rammed into it. Ariel added hers; the shield bulged, and as it had done with me, it returned her magic with the same force. We ducked, but it grazed our backs. It burned, and excruciating pain seared through me. "Get the Aufero from them!" I didn't want them to remove Ethan's magic, which was stronger and deadlier than anything they possessed.

Chris shot at the egg-shaped barrier, and her bullet came back at her, penetrating her shoulder. She cursed and grabbed it, letting the shotgun drop to the ground. Blood soaked her hand, and her string of curses was louder than the invocations the witches were doing behind the Faeries trying to bring down their barrier.

Pain marred Chris's face as she bent down to retrieve the dropped gun, but before she could, Demetrius wrapped his arms around her waist firmly. "We've helped, and we're done." And with that, they disappeared. The other vampires took his departure as their cue to leave, too. Most of the elves had already left, taking the creatures that had survived back to the forest.

Ethan groaned loudly as he stood. He'd lost that primal grace that dictated his movements. He lumbered heavily, the back of his shirt soaked with blood. A light silver glow came from the cuts the Faerie had given him. With much effort, he made it to their barrier and leaned into it. The field wavered. Nothing happened. A ripple formed along it again. Ethan's magic was stronger and suffocating; it felt necrotic and wrong. As the field came down, the Faeries screeched, a high reedy sound that couldn't be drowned out despite covering my ears. I expected to feel blood coming from them; I didn't. But I couldn't remove my hands. I wasn't sure how Ethan was bearing it. But he was. He grabbed a Faerie, his fingers curling into its leathery, coarse skin. Then moments later, the wailing stopped as the Faerie went through a strange version of the vampire's reversion like the other he'd killed in the first attack on the house. The dark scaly skin dried and shriveled before collapsing to dust. Ethan grabbed the other Faerie holding the Aufero. Before he could deliver the same lethal treatment to this one, the thing stabbed him in the stomach with a knife.

"Ethan, let go!" I yelled, running toward him, my ears still ringing. He didn't. The Faerie pulled out the knife and shoved it into Ethan's chest, leaving the blade embedded. Ethan destroyed his attacker. I could see why they so desperately wanted the magic Ethan hosted—it was powerful and deadly.

When I yanked out the knife, it crumbled to pieces that floated away, following the same fate as its creator. I lifted Ethan's blood-soaked shirt, exposing the wound. The silvery glow illuminated his stomach before whisking to nothing as the skin pulled together and formed a mesh, leaving behind a small scar of newly formed tissue. Sebastian helped me ease him to his side so I could look at the wounds on his back. They looked exactly like the scars on his chest and stomach.

Ethan struggled to keep his eyes open. Finally, he held them open long enough to look at me. His eyes were clear blue, not a hint of his wolf present. Even the distinct wisp of magic that the were-animal possessed was gone. I felt its loss, and I wondered if the others did as well. The aura that signified the presence of the animal was gone. That predaceous counterpart that lay in waiting to be unleashed was gone. Was I the only one who sensed it?

"Change," Sebastian instructed him. It was a gentle command, meant to trigger that deep preternatural connection that existed between the Alpha and his pack members. Ethan closed his eyes in concentration. His face became flushed. He worked to call forth his wolf. His heart pounded from the exertion, his breath became ragged, and sweat glistened on his brow. It was in vain. He stayed in human form. He was human now. I felt magic, but not that of the enigmatic were-animal. Hints of Faerie and witch magic wafted off him, but that was all. Before, his wolf had overpowered his other magic

Sebastian dropped his head in concentration, slipped his hand over Ethan's, and instructed him to change. Several minutes passed, and both Ethan and Sebastian were on the floor, drenched in sweat. Sebastian had changed to his wolf and back to his human form, trying to force a change in Ethan.

Cole said it before the rest of us were willing to. "He can't change."

Ethan tried again, which took everything he had because he passed out. At least I hoped he'd passed out. We all waited for his chest to rise because his heartbeat was so faint; it was as if his heart had given up as well.

CHAPTER 25

Ethan was barely breathing, and calling what his heart was doing an actual beat was generous. Dr. Jeremy got him on the exam table. Kelly tried to usher everyone out. When she tried to direct me out, I held my ground, refusing to go anywhere.

"Everyone out. Sebastian and Gavin, I need you to stay," Dr. Jeremy instructed in a rush. I knew everyone was moving quickly, but it still seemed too slow.

Dr. Jeremy must have felt the same way because he yelled, "Everyone out *now*! I won't ask again!" People moved past me, but I didn't budge. Dr. Jeremy gathered medicine and brought a crash cart next to Ethan, and Kelly tore the clothes from Ethan's body.

"Get her out of here," Dr. Jeremy commanded anyone who would listen. Gavin approached me, and I glared at him, daring him to touch me.

"Sky, you have to leave."

"I'm not leaving," I informed him with the same command in my voice as he'd delivered his request with.

"You will have to, and I really don't want to force you out." He stepped closer, his voice becoming low, a whisper. "Please, don't make me force you." His eyes were gentle, pleading for compliance.

Reluctantly, I backed out. The door closed and locked behind me, and the curtains were drawn, something rarely done. *What does that mean? Good or bad prognosis?* I tried to remember a time when the curtains had been drawn or Dr. Jeremy had looked that panicked or he'd yelled. When had he dealt with a shifter who couldn't shift?

Josh was sitting against the wall, his head resting against it. A vibrant colorful string of magic twirled along his fingers. He appeared to be using it as a distraction.

"Is it true, he can't change?" he asked softly, concentrating fully on the magic as he made it respond to his command. I understood what he was doing. He felt out of control and needed something he *could* control.

I took too long to answer because I didn't know what to say. It was the animal part that allowed us to heal, and now his brother had lost that and had four stab wounds. It also appeared that whatever magic had been on the Faerie's blade was sealed inside him, preventing him from changing and healing.

Through the haze of my grief, sorrow, and unease about Ethan's prognosis, I looked for the right words to comfort Josh.

"No, he can't change. Even Sebastian couldn't force him into a change. The Elite." I glared at Cole, who had come through the double doors to give his two cents' worth, something I could have done without.

Josh nodded slowly and wore the same look of defeat I'd seen in Ethan when Josh had been in the hospital bed. The magic disappeared, and he stood and walked away through the doors Cole had entered. He needed time alone, but I knew he needed someone—London. Most of the witches had left, and the only two I'd seen as we'd rushed Ethan into the house were Ariel and London. I hoped London had stuck around.

"What the hell is wrong with you?" I snapped.

Cole inclined his head, and his brows pinched close together as if he didn't understand my anger. "Did I do something wrong?" His inquiry and bewilderment seemed so sincere.

"You did a lot of things wrong," I asserted. "You didn't have to tell Josh that."

"I didn't have to tell him the truth?" he asked, incredulous. When he moved closer, I smelled blood on him. He'd changed his shirt, but the stench of spilled blood, magic, and death lingered. "This pack has held so firmly to their secrets and lies of omission that you don't think twice about concealing the truth." He reached to touch me, but after I gave him a look, he thought better of it. "Sky, don't let that be who you become."

"I wasn't going to lie to him, but you doused any hope he might have had. You pretty much told him his brother is going to die."

"But he probably is. It's wrong to give him false hope."

"He's not going to die!"

I moved back toward the door to the infirmary, hoping they'd opened the curtain. They hadn't. Pressing my ear against the door, I strained to listen, but all I heard were muffled voices and sounds of machines. After several minutes, I gave up.

"You didn't help when you should have," I squeezed through clenched teeth as Cole took a position next to me.

I relaxed against the door, ignoring him. He was probably trying to come up with a good lie.

"I helped, just the wrong person. And for that I apologize. I made a split-second decision of who was in the greatest need of help. I truly thought Ethan had it. Based on what I've seen of his skills and what I know of him, he is exceptional. You must believe me. I won't benefit from his death. I won't get his position; it would go to Winter."

"Until you challenge her," I said.

He peered into the window as if he could see behind the

curtains. "From the looks of things earlier, she'll get his position. Sky, it will hurt worse if you don't consider that an option."

I closed my eyes, unable to bear the thought of it. Cole was right. I didn't see how Ethan was going to survive the injuries if he couldn't change. Changing helped us heal; the magic in him would be ineffective. Dr. Jeremy was talented, but he was used to working with us, people with an exceptional ability to recover. I couldn't shake the images of Ethan's injury, his ragged and clipped breathing, and his failing heart.

"Whatever I feel about Ethan, I put it aside when it comes to pack obligations. That's what an Alpha does. If the pack is strong, we are all strong. The strength of all our packs rests in that of the Midwest Pack. You fall, then so do we."

I swallowed and tried to brush the tears away as quickly as they spilled. He placed his hand on my shoulder, and I felt guilty that I didn't shrug it off. I welcomed the warmth and the comfort it provided.

He continued, "I'm asking for your forgiveness, even though I did nothing wrong. I tried to do what was best. I wouldn't do that to you." Cole looked sad, and it was hard to keep painting him as such a cold, calculating person. Had it been it a mistake? Had he acted in good faith? I kept thinking about Steven's contempt for Cole. Could he be wrong about Cole, or was I naïve in thinking Cole was genuine?

I nodded.

"For what it's worth, I really hope I'm wrong," he offered in a low voice. After giving my shoulder a gentle squeeze, he left.

I swallowed hard, looking at Ethan hooked to machines, unconscious. He looked so different, so human. So broken. I attempted to swallow again, but my mouth had dried so much that it was impossible.

"I've tried ten times over the past five days to initiate a change, and he can't," Sebastian said; soft and sympathetic. "Josh, London, and Ariel have tried everything, and nothing has worked."

Sorrow had seeped into his last words, and he was staring at Ethan with the same look of grief and pain as I had to have.

"I should try to use the Aufero again," I suggested.

"What has changed since you tried four days ago? Three days ago? And yesterday?" It was like the damn thing was dead. I'd felt the magic coursing through me, but when the Aufero had tried to mimic it, nothing had happened. It had brightened to a vibrant orange, darkened like it had been eclipsed, and then turned a pale yellow. And it hadn't done a goddam thing.

"Sky, you're not eating. You've been here every day, all day."

"So has Josh," I pointed out.

"He left once, and he's at home now."

"He'll be back soon," I said.

"True. But he's getting a break. Let's go to dinner." Although he'd attempted to keep his voice devoid of emotions, I'd heard something in it. Regret? Frustration? Sadness?

"Claudia will be here in a few, and I'd like to give her time alone with him."

I spun around to face him. "What do you want to talk about at dinner? Let's talk about it now."

"Let's discuss it at dinner."

"No, I'm not having dinner with you. Spit it out. What do you want to discuss?"

"He's not getting better. We've tried everything. Everything. It's been five days and—"

"And what? You're going to let him die?"

"No, of course not. But no were-animal has ever been down this long and come out the same. Ethan is exceptional in a lot of ways, but we're asking a lot to assume he'll come out of this. Faerie magic and—"

"Call Senna. She can fix it."

"We have. She doesn't know of anything that can help. She didn't even know it was possible. And you've been through the Clostra, what? Five or six times?"

Sebastian was right. Everything that could be done, had been done. And it had all failed.

I didn't have dinner with Sebastian. He didn't seem to object because he made only a half-hearted effort to convince me to go. Instead, while Claudia visited with Ethan, I roamed the grounds, looking for my ring. I hadn't remembered to take it off when I'd changed. My clothes had been destroyed during the change; something similar had to have happened to it. I'd changed so fast I'd given little thought to my ring, and I felt awful about it now. There wasn't any blood on the grounds thanks to the witches and the rain. Instead of thinking about Ethan, I diverted all my attention to looking for the ring.

I scoured every inch of the former battleground on my knees, running my hands through the grass and sifting through the dirt.

"Are you looking for this?" Cole asked, holding something between his fingers as he approached me.

He took my hand and placed the thing in it. My ring—the stone was intact, but the band was broken and would have to be replaced.

"It's a beautiful stone," he acknowledged, looking down at it.

I nodded. I didn't have much energy. I hadn't slept in days and was eating just enough to keep Sebastian and Dr. Jeremy off my case. I didn't want to expend any energy talking to Cole. He stayed close, watching me. He opened his mouth to speak, closed it, and took several more moments before he spoke. His eyes were sincere and had a clarity that made it hard not to hold them as long as I could.

"You will hurt for a long time, and that is to be expected," he said with earnest kindness. "Being mated to someone is nice, but it's not nicer or more special than a marriage. Partners die and people grieve, and then they must move on. You'll get there."

"Stop talking like he's dead."

His next words were poignant and sympathetic. I didn't want any of it. "You've probably liked Ethan for months and loved him for weeks. You should remember those feelings, but remember you lack experience. You will find someone more suitable for you. Maybe then you'll realize how incompatible you two were."

I blinked back tears, pretending his words didn't affect me. I hated feeling the way I did because I doubted myself. Not my feelings for Ethan, but Cole's motives. Was he truly being kind and helping me to accept the inevitable? Was he just awkwardly trying to show me I'd eventually heal? Or was he being cruel and masking it as good intentions? His speaking so dismissively about my lack of experience before my relationship with Ethan made it seem trivial. It wasn't, and my feelings were real—too real. I hated not being able to control them to keep the tears from coursing down my face.

"I'm sorry. I wish I could make this better." He pressed the palms of his hands against my face and brushed the tears away. I felt vulnerable, but I remembered Steven's words of caution about Cole and didn't want to feel weak around him. Whatever his motives were, I didn't want to have anything to do with him.

I stepped back, paused, and then moved several more feet away. Maybe I was mistaken, fatigue making me irrational and paranoid, but I thought he'd been about to kiss me. When he moistened his lips, it made me more suspicious.

"Why are you still here? Don't you have your pack to worry about?"

He smiled. "Like this pack, or rather the way it was, my pack is more than capable of operating in my short absence." He inched toward me, and I moved back accordingly. "I'm sure this isn't the first time someone's admitted it, but you bring out my protective urges. I want to make sure you're okay. It's rare for anyone to evoke them so strongly. But you do. I'm not sure what it is about you. So, when I feel you're okay, I'll leave."

I backed away toward the house. "You're welcome to leave—I'm fine. Even if I weren't, you're the last person I want having any urges toward me. I'm sure there are plenty of other people you can extend that offer to. People who actually want it."

CHAPTER 26

Day six wasn't any better, and I was easing into the idea that Ethan wouldn't make it. I hated that Josh was entering the stages of grief as if he'd accepted Ethan was dead. Watching him made my heart ache even more.

"Ethan." I leaned into him, pressing my cheek against his as I spoke, blinking back tears. They were the last thing I needed. "No one knows how to fix this, but I think you do. So, you will do it. Help me, help you." It was my last-ditch effort, a moment of irrational hope, one I had to force myself to believe. It didn't help. False optimism wasn't helpful. It was acting. As much as I wanted to believe it, I couldn't.

I just couldn't stand idly by and do nothing. I lifted my head and pressed my hand against the wound in his chest. It was the closest to his heart, and I was drawn to it. I closed my eyes and listened, waiting for instructions. A sign. Something. There wasn't anything. Instead, I heard music. Not quite music—notes. It reminded me of when I was learning to play the flute. How I'd positioned my fingers on the keys, pursed my lips, and blown just right to make the same sound as my instructor. Magical notes played. I duplicated the magic that coursed through him, hitting all the same magical chords and reciting the invocations as they came to me. We were as one, performing the magic. It crossed my mind that it could be Maya casting another spell. I was desperate and felt Ethan's death was inevitable if I didn't do anything.

I opened my eyes after making the last note. The scars hadn't healed—they were open. The same silver glow pulsed over them. The scars on his chest and stomach puffed out a glittering silver and blue substance. Magic. But it wasn't Faerie magic, or at least nothing I had felt before.

"Okay, Ethan. That worked." I had no idea if it had worked. I was going on pure speculation and hope, the worst combination of magic. But it was all I had. The wound wouldn't close.

"You need to change. Now."

He didn't move. His eyes were still closed. His heart rate and respiration were too low.

"That's okay. I'll help you change. You haven't done it in a while," I said soothingly. I pressed my hand to his and relaxed into my wolf. I lay half of my body over him, anticipating a change. It never came. I wasn't sure how long I stayed in that position, but eventually, I slid to the floor, buried my muzzle under my leg, and howled—a grief-stricken, melancholy sound. Several other wolves returned the mournful cry, and it rang throughout the room and outside the house.

Bereavement made it difficult to move. I'd been on the floor long enough to see the sun rise and set again. I had to get up—but I couldn't. I was weighed down by another body lying over mine.

Ethan. I whimpered his name while in wolf form. It sounded like a smothered howl.

He made a weak sound and licked my face. It didn't bother me as much as it would have under any other condition. I didn't move.

Twenty-four hours later, Dr. Jeremy couldn't stop looking at

Ethan in disbelief. Several times, I caught his curious, furtive glances. Ethan was weaker, and he required assistance the three times he changed into his wolf and was markedly more tired after it. But each time was an improvement. "The wounds are healed."

Ethan nodded. "I feel slower, not the same."

"I'm confident that will come back. Give it a few days. We thought you were dead."

"Me, too," he admitted.

I thought they would have me go over what had happened again. I'd told the story more times than I'd cared to, and no one could figure it out.

When Sebastian walked into the recovery room, he didn't have the countenance of someone whose Beta had come back from the brink of death. He worked too hard at the smile and eventually gave up on what was a fruitless endeavor. "How long do you think it will take for him to be back to normal?" He directed his question to Dr. Jeremy, but he wanted Ethan's input as well. I'd heard the urgency and strain in Sebastian's voice, and if I had, I knew Ethan had as well. The last couple of days hadn't been kind to Sebastian, either, and hiding it was getting more difficult every day.

He looked grim and amber flecks of restrained anger and frustration overtook his eyes.

Ethan scrutinized Sebastian for a mere second. "Someone has issued a challenge?"

Sebastian moved enough into the nod for it to be discernable. He sighed. "I can consult Council, but they're not likely to rule in your favor."

"Council won't agree with you, Sebastian," Cole asserted coolly, standing in the threshold of the door. "And it would not look favorable for you to go to them on something so explicitly defined in our rules. I've waited thirty days since the last challenge. Tomorrow will be Ethan's seventh day from injury. I am an Alpha, challenging for a lesser rank in another pack. Which part of this doesn't adhere to the rules? What do you need counsel on?"

Sebastian's hard gaze homed in on him. Ethan wouldn't give him the satisfaction.

Alphas had audacity to spare. I'd gotten used to it from Ethan; with others, it was off-putting, and from Cole, it was just infuriating. He sauntered even farther into the room, arrogance lying heavily over the sharp lines of his face. He seemed taller and more powerful, a force that overtook the room.

"You aren't capable of being Beta. No one knows whether you will heal to one hundred percent. This pack needs a Beta at full potential. Having a weakened Beta might work in other packs, but I've seen firsthand what you all have to deal with. You need someone up to the challenge. If you were attacked tomorrow, Ethan would need protection, not be the one protecting. Which means he is unable to fulfill his job."

"You challenged before and lost. Do you really want that humiliation again?" I asked.

He gave me an easy smile. "If I lose, then you have what you need: a Beta who can do his job. I will hold no ill will." Then he moved his attention to Sebastian. "It's easy to make me the bad person for wanting to enforce rules you are ready to ignore. Your friendship and compassion for Ethan are quite admirable—but they can't come at the cost of the safety of the pack. As the Alpha, the pack's protection is your responsibility and should be your top priority, no exceptions. As the Elite, it's important you follow the rules and remain unbiased. Your reputation and position depend on it."

Cole seemed admirable, or at least that was what his words indicated. It was easy to forget he always had an ulterior motive that was to his advantage. He hadn't helped Steven because it had been the right thing to do; he'd done it in hopes that Ethan would get injured so badly he couldn't defend his position. The rage that roiled in me was getting harder to control.

I studied Ethan as he considered the situation. The days had worn on him—he'd nearly lost his brother and his own life. I wondered if being Beta was still a priority and worth keeping. Which would he choose: stepping down and giving Cole the position, or the challenge? He'd promised me he would only do submission fights, but anytime there were two powerful, ferocious people fighting, there was no guarantee a life wouldn't be lost. Cole certainly wouldn't be careful with Ethan's life.

"There's no shame in stepping down, Ethan. There is honor in it. You have your mate." I didn't like the lingering look he slid in my direction. It was deviously hopeful. Cole's interest in me was a result of my relationship with Ethan; I was something he desired for no other reason than Ethan had me.

Hands shoved deep in his pockets, Cole gave Sebastian a respectful bow. Sebastian remained stoic, his face unreadable, but if the turbulent energy that rose off him was an indicator of what he was feeling, he didn't have to express it on his face. I wondered if Sebastian was grappling with the things that Cole had pointed out. Social norms, federal and state laws, and societal expectations meant little to him. He adhered to them only when they benefitted the pack. The pack laws, rules, and obligations were the foundation of the pack. It was who he was, and who they were. How much would things change if he helped his Beta by not following them?

When Cole made his way out of the room, he looked over his shoulder, giving me another look that neither Ethan nor Sebastian missed. Ethan tensed. I followed Cole out and caught him when he was just a few feet away.

"What's wrong with you?" I asked. "Why are you doing this?"

Taking easy, graceful steps as he strode in my direction and moistening his lips, he was more predator than man. He spoke so low I had to strain to hear him, something I knew was intentional. A conversation for our ears only. "What happened between us and the Faeries is in part because of Ethan. He is culpable. You have a love and commitment to him that I believe have left you blind to his actions." He considered me for a long time. Reaching out, his finger brushed lightly against my hand. I jerked my hand away as if I'd been singed.

Cole sighed. "He's not the man he was before. He's injured and weaker—not a true Alpha anymore." As he moved closer, his eyes sought mine. "Your feelings can't be the same for him. It's okay. Let him accept the challenge. He only falters because of you. If you want him to fight for the position, he will." I knew exactly what he was saying. It was what I was thinking earlier: even in a submission fight, not everyone survived.

Anger moved through me like a rampaging animal. My hands balled at my sides; the pain of my nails embedding in my skin, piercing flesh, gave me something more to think about than doing as much damage to Cole as possible.

"I didn't fall for Ethan's position. I fell for Ethan."

"That's unfortunate, because the way I see it, either way, he is undeserving of you."

"If he is, then you definitely are," I said flatly. If I let anger into my voice, it would spiral into something I wasn't likely to control because part of me didn't want to. I raised my voice loud enough for Sebastian to hear. "Sebastian." I kept my eyes on Cole, watching the haughtiness that was just as tailored to him as his clothing. I heard and felt Sebastian step toward me. He hadn't lost his anger or frustration. "As Ethan's mate, can I accept a challenge on his behalf if he can't do it?" I asked.

The smile fell from Cole's lips. His eyes narrowed on me.

"Technically, you can," Sebastian said, amusement hitting every word.

Cole diverted his attention to Sebastian and back to me. "I don't think it's a good idea. You don't know what you're getting yourself into," he warned.

"No, I do. I *really* want to kick your ass."

"I don't want to fight you, Sky," he said.

"You're not fighting me. You're challenging me for a position I have every intention of defending. You can wait until Ethan is fight-ready and let him kick your ass to defend his position, or you can call your Beta, let him come down—since that's the rule—and let me kick your ass when he arrives."

"He's on his way. He'll be here tomorrow." That just added insult to injury, how calculated it was. He would have challenged Winter, who would have moved up to the Beta position if Ethan hadn't survived.

"Sky, this is a bad decision on your part," he started mildly. "I don't want to hurt you."

I so want to hurt you.

He struggled to maintain his warm, soothing tone—camouflage to mask his true intent. "Sky, don't make me hurt you." I was surprised by the concern and apprehension in his voice, including the sadness and conflict of emotions. In some twisted way, it seemed that Cole had claimed me, and the only person in his way was Ethan. I didn't understand it.

"I don't come with the position," I reminded him softly. It felt odd I had to keep reminding him of this, as if I were some consolation prize. I wasn't flattered by such debauched thinking, and I was tired of defending my relationship with Ethan to him. I was getting even more frustrated with people seeing me either as a naïve woman who couldn't navigate the world or a peculiar anomaly that whetted their interest. Perhaps he saw Ethan and me as a power couple, but I thought we were nothing more than the mess that could have been developed in Frankenstein's lab, as Ariel had described us.

"I am very aware of that, Skylar," he said.

"Then what exactly do you want?" I asked sincerely. His attention was solely on me, as if he'd forgotten Sebastian was present. After several moments of silence, I said, "I love Ethan. And I love this pack, and I will do anything to defend both—especially from the likes of you."

I knew I wouldn't get the total truth from him with Sebastian just feet away. He addressed the question diplomatically, as the politician he had proven to be. He spoke eloquently, sincerely, and with heart, convincing his audience of the sincerity in his words. "Most of the votes to come out to the humans were in favor because of me. Because I convinced them it was a good idea and we could weather the storms that came from it. I did that. I gave you the idea of using Chris to help Josh. Do you think Demetrius would have agreed without her there? I did that! I had to assemble the allies to help us in the fight while you all were visiting Senna. I did that! I took command when the Alpha wasn't present. I did exactly what a Beta should do. Contrary to what you believe, I would be an asset to this pack. I have no secrets that would ever put this pack in peril. My loyalty is only to the pack." That was a lie. His loyalty was to himself. As I looked at him, I made sure he could see how I felt. He swallowed hard but kept his eyes on me and continued, "The witches trust me. Abigail trusts me. And believe me, that's a lot more than what can be said about Ethan. He is a conditional asset, and you two have led with your emotions to the detriment of this pack."

He stood taller and directed his next statement to Sebastian. "My challenge still stands." And with that, he turned and left the house.

Dr. Jeremy released Ethan because he didn't need observation anymore. That might have been part of the reason, but my facing a challenge against Cole was most of it. As soon as we made it to Ethan's house, Ethan sat on the sofa and waved me over. When I attempted to sit, he pulled me over and nudged me until I was straddling him. His arms wrapped around me, and I buried my face into his neck. In a slow, steady rhythm, he rubbed his hands over my back. I listened to his strong heartbeat, which just days ago had been weak and barely audible. It had a soothing effect.

"Sky," he finally said.

"You won't talk me out of it," I said before he could continue. I pulled back and looked at him. Refusing to be dissuaded, I steeled, my voice. "I'm doing this."

He gave me a faint smile. "Thank you for what you did." It was heartbreaking—the look he'd had when Josh was dying. "I can't let you do this."

"Ethan—"

"Sky, no. There is nothing you can do to win. My position will still be lost, and you'll be injured. How are we winning?" he asked. "I met his other challenge, and it wasn't an easy win."

I looked away from him, feeling betrayed. "If Winter were sitting here in my place, would you be giving this speech?"

"Well"—he looked at my position on his lap, his hands under my shirt, caressing my back, and his bare chest—"if Winter were sitting here, I do believe there'd be more discussion taking place than just about a challenge, because *so* many things would be wrong with the situation. But yes, I'd give her the same speech, Gavin and Steven as well. They wouldn't win. It's nothing more than a symbolic but hollow gesture—one that will not benefit any of us. Let him have the position, and in a month, I will take it back."

"Will he still be part of this pack?"

"Unfortunately, yes. He can request a transfer, but I doubt he'd want to return to his pack." Ethan looked away, irritation and anger eclipsing his face. "He won't because what he wants is here." I wasn't sure if he was referring to me or the position as Beta.

I frowned at the idea of both. Trusting Cole was difficult. It was like playing a game, deciphering the intentions behind everything he did.

"I should at least—"

"Sky, please," he whispered. "Don't do this."

It was a struggle to concede, and it took me several moments. I rested against Ethan again, looked at him, and nodded.

Seeing his fear and concern made it an easier decision. "Okay. If you concede, you won't have a position in the pack. You'll become unranked."

"I know."

Ethan would have to offer a formal capitulation to Sebastian. I tried to be strong about it, mirroring Ethan's behavior. We were both full of crap. Five hours had passed, and it was close to ten at night when Ethan picked up the phone to call.

"I was just about to call you," Sebastian said in a rush. "Don't worry about the challenge—we need to find Cole. He and his Beta are missing."

If we were honest with ourselves, no one cared that Cole was missing, but we had to find his Beta.

Sebastian continued, "So are Joan and her Beta ..."

"Who else?" Ethan asked.

"Demetrius."

Ethan rubbed his hands over his face. "Have you heard from the West Coast Alpha?"

"I'm waiting to hear from them. I'll let you know when I do," Sebastian informed him, worry and agitation coursing through his words. Ethan disconnected with a sigh. Clasping his hands behind his head, he slumped back into the sofa.

"You think it has anything to do with the Red Blood?" I asked.

He shook his head, and I knew he had an idea what or who was behind it. "It's worse."

MESSAGE TO THE READER

~

Thank you for choosing *Darkness Unleashed* from the many titles available to you. My goal is to create an engaging world, compelling characters, and an interesting experience for you. I hope I've accomplished that. Reviews are very important to authors and help other readers discover our books. Please take a moment to leave a review. I'd love to know your thoughts about the book.

For notifications about new releases, *exclusive* contests and giveaways, and cover reveals, please sign up for my newsletter at www.mckenziehunter.com

www.McKenzieHunter.com
McKenzieHunter@McKenzieHunter.com

Made in the USA
Coppell, TX
01 July 2020

29900033R00187